DENISE BARI
unpacking
countries an
she cares t

events include selling lipstick in a Denver department store to top English model of the day, Jean Shrimpton; typing on a French keyboard for the UN Narcotics Director in Geneva; chauffeuring a lonely Swiss multi-millionaire lawyer in Zurich; being the first fashion model in Atlanta to dance to pop music; working as a PA to a film producer and delivering a film script to Richard Harris in Rome and not recognizing him (he was not amused); and cooking in a vegetarian sanatorium in Bavaria, which gave rise to her first hilarious memoir.

Back home in England, Denise reluctantly trained as an estate agent – and loved it! Juggling the running of her chain of eight offices in Kent with taking an Honours Degree with Open University, Denise had difficulty finding the time to pursue her life-long passion for writing.

To give herself the freedom to write she sold her business after 17 years, but unfortunately to the wrong buyers, namely a couple of tricksters, which resulted in a second, more serious, memoir. Buying back the business and after six years selling it once again, she is now able to resume her love of fiction writing, under the pen-name, Fenella Forster.

Find Denise on her blog: www.denisebarneswriter.com and follow her on Twitter: @denisebarnesuk.

Praise for *Juliet's Story*

'The Voyagers series takes a leap forward in time to Juliet, Annie's grand-daughter, and once again, Fenella Forster has penned a totally compelling and enchanting novel that will keep you turning the pages to the very end. Juliet is a refreshing heroine who takes a once-in-a-lifetime opportunity, and it's a joy to share her adventure as she finds love, healing and the answers to some long-held family secrets.'
– Joanne Walsh, Romance Author

'Fenella Forster is a natural story-teller and has created a wonderfully woven tale in The Voyagers Trilogy, that will take the reader across the world and through generations of a family. In *Juliet's Story* we're in the present day and the vivid, brilliantly-coloured adventures of Juliet. This is a seductive novel, that moves at a fast pace even though some of it takes place on a slow boat to Australia. The subtle plotting and descriptive powers wonderfully balance the characters that strut across the pages. I couldn't put it down and can't wait for book three in the series.'
– Nina Milton, Author

THE VOYAGERS

Juliet's Story

FENELLA FORSTER

SilverWood

Published in 2016 by SilverWood Books

SilverWood Books Ltd
14 Small Street, Bristol, BS1 1DE
www.silverwoodbooks.co.uk

ISBN 978-1-78132-428-8 (paperback)
ISBN 978-1-78132-429-5 (ebook)

British Library Cataloguing in Publication Data
A CIP catalogue record for this book is available from
the British Library

Set in Sabon by SilverWood Books
Printed on responsibly sourced paper

For Rosie. I miss you.

Also by the Author

Prologue

King's Lynn, Norfolk

September 1976

The girl is prostrate, her features dull, her hair dark stripes against the crisp pillows.

The elderly woman scrapes her metal chair closer to the bed and takes the girl's hand.

'It's all over, darling. Now we have to build up your strength.'

The girl's eyes remain closed. She doesn't answer. Only the flicker of her lashes gives any sign of life.

The matron swishes back the skimpy curtains. She's carrying a bundle.

'Are you awake?' she asks.

The girl opens her eyes. She struggles to sit up; stretches out her childish arms. The bundle passes from the woman in the starched apron to the girl.

'Just half an hour.' Matron glances at her watch.

The girl's eyes widen. Still she doesn't speak.

'I'm afraid they're the rules.' Matron's voice is firm but her eyes are misted with sympathy.

The girl nods. She looks down at the little mite. She says nothing. There's nothing she can say. A tear, and then another, fall silently onto the baby's forehead.

The matron disappears, leaving the three of them – three generations of a family – together for the first...and final time.

PART I

The Decision

1

Kingston-upon-Thames, Surrey

July 2005

Jay always quickened her pace as she passed the Golden Turmeric, avoiding even a glance. But she couldn't this evening. Why hadn't she told Lydia the truth, that she was dog-tired, particularly given Lydia's choice of restaurant? All she'd wanted to do was go home and flop in front of some soap with a ready meal and a glass of wine. But it had been difficult to refuse when Lydia had promised to bring the final cheque. And Lydia always insisted on paying Reece & Co's invoices in person. Jay looked at her watch and grimaced. Oh, well, she may as well get it over with. She stepped inside the restaurant.

It was dark. Spicy aromas filled her head, reminding her... she closed her eyes for a brief moment. Indian music vied with the din of voices. She looked round at groups of young people pressed together, standing and sitting, wine bottles and beer mugs scattered on the nearby tables. A bearded man was tossing nuts in the air and catching them in his open mouth to the amusement of the females in the party, and young men waved glowing cigarettes like fireflies, using them to dominate the conversation. They all seemed to belong to one another, to be part of some unnamed club. She watched them for a few moments, envying their easy familiarity, before a receptionist in a tight-fitting dress and a fall of thick dark hair came to ask if she had reserved a table.

Jay followed her down a flight of steps scattered with rose

petals and couldn't help being impressed by the way the girl stayed upright on her four-inch heels. When was the last time *she'd* worn shoes that elegant? Five years ago? More likely ten. The receptionist steered her through another candlelit room filled with diners, and there was Lydia, seated in a corner, half-hidden by a decorated wooden screen and jungle-sized fern.

'Sorry if I'm a few minutes late,' Jay said as she approached the table. 'I had a last-minute phone call. One I'd been waiting for all day. You know how it is.'

'Don't I just.' Lydia rose, smiling, as she blew two air kisses somewhere in the region of Jay's cheeks. 'Hope you don't mind but I've ordered a bottle of red. I thought you might need to get stuck in straight away after a day at the office.'

'Perfect.' Jay tried to conjure some enthusiasm.

Lydia looked serene and cool in a cream skirt and matching blouse, the collar trimmed with some kind of animal print. Her blonde hair was shiny and short-cropped, showing off her long neck, and Jay had the sudden image of a very clean camel. Feeling a little mean, and conscious of her own dark suit creased from being buckled in the car all morning and seated at her computer for an interminable afternoon, she tried to smooth her skirt as she sat down, but caught her tights on the underside of the chair. She cursed under her breath as she felt the ladder begin to creep down her calf. They were her new Wolfords.

A waiter appeared with a bottle and Lydia nodded to him to pour.

'Cheers.' She clinked her glass with Jay's. 'I've been meaning to treat you to a dinner before now as a big thank you, but my time's been eaten up. When you're no longer working, all sorts of people ask for help. "Now you're retired, Lydia..."' She mimicked a wheedling voice. 'Still, I suppose it's nice to be wanted.'

'You look well on it. Terrific, in fact,' Jay said.

'How about you?' Lydia asked. 'I don't like to say it, but you're looking awfully stressed, darling.'

'It was non-stop today and unfortunately the hair appointment had to go.' Jay sighed as she scrunched her chestnut hair, making it look even more unruly. 'And you're looking so relaxed.'

'It's only since you sold my business for me.' Lydia swirled the ruby liquid in her glass, sniffed deeply, raised it to her lips, rolled it in her mouth and swallowed. 'Mmm, not bad.' She looked serious. 'People think if you've got your own business you're a free agent just because there's no boss to kowtow to. Huh. They don't know the half of it.'

Pretending to listen to Lydia, Jay wondered how much longer she would have to keep building up Reece & Co before she felt financially secure. Or burnt out. She eased her neck from one side to the other, recalling the excitement of those early years. The thrill when she read the letter saying she'd won first prize for Businesswoman of the Year. She could see the headline in the business section of the local paper right this minute. And the photograph beneath which showed a striking dark-haired woman beaming as she accepted the silver cup.

When had this jaded character taken her place?

She'd willingly put all her physical and mental effort into the business and she'd had some fun and fame along the way, but now she had to admit the buzz was no longer...well, quite so buzzy.

I put my career before everything, including Gerrard...and having a family.

Her heart began to beat hard against her ribs. If only she could light up, but of course Lydia had chosen the no-smoking area.

'And you don't miss it?' Jay said after a few moments.

'Actually, it *was* a shock suddenly not having to go into work. As you know, we'd agreed I'd stay on as a consultant and be invited to meetings and such, but the new chaps have made it clear they want to run it themselves. Seems they know best, even without any experience.'

There was a slight curl to her lip, as though Lydia wasn't happy with the arrangement. God knows why, Jay thought. When *she* finally sold she had no intention of remaining involved.

She looked at the menu and noticed a chipped nail on her left hand she'd meant to re-varnish last night. She'd fallen asleep over her magazine instead. Glancing up, she saw Lydia waiting for a response.

'You don't know how lucky you are, Lydia, to be free of responsibilities. Mine's not just the business...there's Dad. Oh, God, I sound like a rotten daughter...'

But the truth was, since 'that time' she'd never been able to think of him with genuine affection.

'Where is he?'

'We've had to put him in a nursing home.'

'Well, he's safe enough there, but *you* need to take care of yourself. If you don't you'll be no good to anyone.'

Jay was silent. Will and Antonia had made the decision for their father to go into a home. They'd reminded their younger sister they didn't live near enough to help out with their father on a regular basis, and that Jay had a business to run. It was for the best. But when her father looked at her with reproach and suppressed anger in his eyes, she knew he hated it.

'You've got a good team, haven't you?' Lydia's challenging remark jarred her thoughts. 'Just take off. They'll cope. I sometimes used to go away for a few weeks and the staff were fine. They like to let you know they can manage without you.'

A young Indian waiter appeared at their table. Jay looked up and the muscles in her throat tightened.

Oh, Mani.

'Maybe you just need a man to pep things up.' Lydia chuckled, glancing from Jay to the waiter and back to Jay. He shifted a little and gave a nervous smile.

'Don't embarrass the poor boy,' Jay said, trying to keep the annoyance out of her tone. Oh, God, this evening was going to be even worse than she'd imagined.

'Hasn't there been anyone since the divorce?' Lydia persisted after the waiter had taken their order and vanished.

'Not really. The odd date.' She shrugged. 'More often a meal with Gerrard.'

'Your *ex*?' Lydia wrinkled her nose in disbelief. Jay nodded. 'You need to move on. An attractive woman like you with those eyes – I'd have thought you'd be inundated.'

'I wish.'

'So what would you do if you *had* the time? You know, the six-months-to-live scenario.' Lydia leaned her elbows on the table, steepling her hands.

Jay's eyes sparked as she replayed images in her mind of parched open spaces, iconic cities, crashing surf…and somewhere out there, under a broiling sun, one dear man she wouldn't even recognise – but thought of every single day.

Without warning her eyes filled with tears and her head felt like candyfloss in the airless warmth of the room. She knew she shouldn't have come. And now, because Lydia couldn't put a cheque in the post like normal people, she was being forced somewhere she'd sworn never to be. Panic rose in her chest. She swallowed hard, momentarily closing her eyes, and held on to the edge of the table. *Keep calm.* Lydia would think she was having some sort of breakdown. Maybe she was. She couldn't think straight. Her heart was beating too rapidly, making her feel dizzy, and she could feel a trickle of perspiration running down her back. *Must get out. Get some air.* She scooped up her bag and jerked to her feet.

'Darling, are you—?'

'Sorry, Lydia…need the loo.' Jay struggled to keep her voice even.

She stumbled between the packed tables and a waiter gestured for her to go back upstairs. A few heads turned from their conversations but she ignored them in her rush. Once in the cloakroom she slumped on a dressing-table stool and put her head in her hands, the tears squeezing through her fingers as she fought for control.

Please don't let anyone come in and see me like this.

It was the first time in years she'd broken down in a public place after she'd been so careful for so long. She choked back the sobs, all the while telling herself not to act like a bloody fool instead of a woman of forty-five. As she grabbed some tissues from the box by the sinks she caught sight of herself in the wall of mirror. The dark-blue eyes were wet and blotchy and she dabbed away the streaks where her mascara had run. *So much for waterproof.* If only she had time to smoke a cigarette, but Lydia would wonder where on earth she'd got to and come looking for her. Instead, she searched her bag for the bottle of Rescue Remedy, unscrewed the stopper and tipped her head back, letting a few drops of the brandy-tasting liquid run down the back of her throat. She breathed deeply, like Nannie had taught her, and after a few minutes began to feel the worst moments had passed.

Composing herself, she blew her nose, then opened the door and slammed into another woman.

'I'm so sorry,' the woman said.

'My fault,' Jay mumbled, not looking at her.

'Are you okay?'

'Yes, thanks. It's just hot in the restaurant.'

'I was beginning to get worried,' Lydia said, glancing at her watch.

'There was a queue.' Jay was grateful for the dim lighting.

Lydia threw her a sharp look but for once made no comment.

Their small table brimmed with curry and rice, okra, hummus and a large bowl of creamy raita. A basket of warm nan bread was jammed next to a dish of potato and spinach. It smelt delicious, but anxiety had taken away the edge of her appetite. She sipped some wine, hoping it would relax her.

She watched Lydia help herself first, then push each dish across after she'd exactly halved everything. Jay took a little from the remaining food.

'You've mentioned Australia before,' Lydia suddenly said, 'and how your grandparents went out there. Why don't you go and see the place for yourself?'

How had Lydia guessed it was her dearest dream to go there and investigate what really happened to her grandparents? And of course— Jay could feel her heart beating fast again. *No. Stop thinking like that. Go back to what Lydia's saying.* The trouble was, she only knew Lydia Mayfield through selling her estate agency business. Yes, they'd had a few pleasant evenings but the conversation had usually kept to Lydia's sale.

'I'll definitely go one day...when I've sold up...like you,' Jay managed.

Lydia took a mouthful of wine. 'I do sometimes regret – just a teeny-weeny bit – selling the business.'

'Really?' Jay raised her head in surprise. 'I thought you were dead keen to get rid of it.'

Lydia gave her a green-eyed stare. 'Jay, I've been thinking...why don't you take off for two or three months? Have a proper break.'

'There's nothing I'd like better...but I can't just leave it—'

'That's where you're wrong. I'll run the business for you.'

Jay's eyes widened. 'You're not serious?'

'I'm perfectly serious. But first, let's eat. Then we can talk.' Her tone was light.

'Selling businesses is a whole different ball game,' Jay blurted.

'You sound rather patronising, darling, if I may say so. Selling houses, selling businesses...they're both the service industry.' Lydia picked up her fork, examined it, and wiped it on her napkin, then raised her eyes to Jay. 'Anyway, you have a sales team for that. I'd just make sure everything ran smoothly...the day-to-day stuff. Plus a bit of networking, of course, to bring in fresh business.'

It was too preposterous for words. To fill in the silence while Lydia waited for her to answer, Jay said, 'What on earth would your husband say?'

'Robert? Even if he tried to talk me out of it he knows I wouldn't take any notice.'

Jay drained the rest of her glass, barely tasting it, wondering how to answer without offending Lydia again.

'Sure it's not the wine talking, Lydia?' she tried to joke.

'What, one glass?' Lydia chuckled, topping up both glasses. 'To be honest, this isn't something I just now thought of.' She looked directly at Jay. 'It was some weeks ago when you first mentioned you'd like to go to Australia but couldn't take the time off to do it justice. That gave me the space to do some serious thinking about standing in for you. And the more I thought about the idea the more I liked it. Besides, you'd be doing *me* a favour.'

Jay put down her knife and fork. 'How come?'

'If I'm honest, all this free time makes me feel old. I'm like you – I like being the boss and getting results.'

'I thought you'd do some more theatre stuff with your am dram group.'

'Too old, darling, for any decent parts. At my age all you get offered are mad women or grandmothers. I'd love a last challenge before I call it quits.' Lydia's face was alight with the possibility.

'It's a fantastic offer, Lydia, but for me to leave the company in someone else's hands...' she trailed off, biting her lip. *To be free. Just for a few weeks.* 'It's impossible,' she finished flatly.

Lydia leaned forward. 'Is anything wrong, darling? Is it *just* the business? Or something else?' She touched Jay's hand.

'I...er...no, nothing else. The business is fine. I'm shattered, that's all. It's been quite a week, and it's only Wednesday.'

It was just a fantasy to leave Reece & Co in Lydia's hands and charge off to Australia. A bit of fun pretending she could really go. But she *would* go, one day.

'So what do you think?'

It seemed as though Lydia wasn't going to let the idea go. It hammered in Jay's brain like a rhythm. To be in the same country.

Same city. No, it was crazy. Reece & Co was her livelihood. Her proof to her parents that she was a success. She wasn't about to be pressurised by Lydia because the woman was bored.

'I'd never forgive myself if something went wrong because I wasn't there.'

'So who'd be in charge of the accounts if you were ill?' Lydia demanded.

'Luckily, that doesn't happen. You can't be ill when you run the show, can you?' Jay gave a nervous laugh. 'But if I was off for any reason it'd be Neil. He's the deal manager...though obviously it's down to me in the end.'

'You're not very good at delegating, are you?' Lydia smiled, fixing Jay with another of her green stares.

Jay rubbed the back of her aching neck. How could she tactfully tell Lydia there was no way she would accept? She'd just have to say it gradually. 'Let me sleep on it. But it's not half tempting.' She gave Lydia the kind of smile she hoped would satisfy her for the time being.

'It's a big decision,' Lydia said, 'but sometimes you have to let go. Even something precious to you.'

I've already let something precious go.

Both women were silent for a few moments until Lydia leaned forward, her voice a stage whisper.

'Jay, I do have a real reason for offering to do this. I didn't want to have to explain, but since I stopped work Robert doesn't treat me in the same way. He treats me like a...a *hausfrau*. As though I had nothing better to do than clean house and put his dinner on the table.' She raised her eyes heavenwards. 'Taking over Reece & Co will make him sit up and notice me again.'

'But—'

'Don't think it's me doing a good deed,' Lydia interrupted. 'I'd want to be paid, but it would benefit both of us. An absolute win-win.' She reached for her bag and brought out an envelope with

'Reece & Co' scrawled across it. 'Talking of being paid,' she handed it over, smiling, 'here's the final one.'

'Thanks.' Jay tucked the envelope inside her bag, wondering how she was going to get out of this crazy suggestion. She knew Lydia was waiting for her to say something. 'It'd be a huge responsibility.' She realised she was sounding patronising again, when Lydia raised an eyebrow. 'Sorry, Lydia, but I honestly can't see it.'

'Maybe it's time for you to do something impulsive for once in your life.'

Jay laughed. 'Is that a challenge?'

'You might say it is. Tell me, where did your grandparents live when they were in Oz?'

'Melbourne.' Jay tried to keep her voice matter of fact. 'They worked in a country house. I never got tired of hearing about it. Dad was born there.'

'Well, you'd love Melbourne,' Lydia said. 'And Sydney.'

Jay's stomach turned over.

'You were very fond of your grandmother, weren't you?'

'More than my own mother,' Jay said without hesitation. 'I adored her.' She got out her wallet and extracted a black-and-white photograph, then passed it to Lydia. 'I had this made smaller so I could keep it in my bag. It's one of my grandmother as a girl, taken with her sisters before she went to Melbourne. She's in the middle. Ethel, her youngest sister is on the left, and Ruby's on the right.'

'They're all pretty girls,' Lydia said, scrutinising it. 'Particularly Ruby. She's gorgeous. That sexy mouth.' She held it closer. 'But your grandmother's beautiful.' She looked across at Jay. 'You take after her, you know.'

'Do I?' Jay said, secretly pleased. 'That's a nice compliment.'

'I mean it.' Lydia handed back the photograph. 'What was your grandmother's name?'

'I called her Nannie. But her real name was Annie.'

'What made them come back?'

'Nannie said she was homesick but I always had a feeling there was something more she wasn't saying. Something to do with the family. And Pop would never talk about Australia – he used to clam up and change the subject. It's always been a mystery to me. Wouldn't I love to find out?'

'Well, now's your chance,' Lydia purred.

Jay automatically returned the smile. She'd never tell Lydia the real reason why she was so desperate to go to Australia.

2

It was late when Jay drove up to the modern apartment block on the edge of town. She glanced at the time. Already quarter to twelve. And she'd got another big day ahead.

Two hours later she was still wide awake and could feel the beginning of a migraine. She was getting too many of these lately. Except for the move six months ago, after the divorce, life wasn't any more stressful than usual, she didn't think. All right, she wasn't always eating healthily or regularly, and she really must try to stop smoking. Drink more water. But it wasn't that. If she was truthful, the business was getting on her nerves. Lately she found herself getting irritable with the staff for no reason. But that wasn't a good enough excuse to leave it in someone else's hands…someone who was little more than a stranger.

What should she do? The question spun like a carousel, making it impossible to think logically. Lydia had confessed tonight she'd almost regretted selling her estate agency. And that she'd been thinking of this bizarre idea before this evening. Jay frowned. It was obvious now why Lydia had wanted to meet for dinner.

She thumped her pillow and turned it over so it felt cooler to her throbbing head. If only she hadn't had that last glass of wine. She stretched her legs apart, luxuriating in the whole space of the double bed, and the action made her think of Gerrard. Should she discuss it with him? He was a lawyer, after all, but that didn't make him qualified to judge. He was so damned conservative – never taking risks. Probably because he could see how risks got you into trouble and it would take a lawyer to sort you out. No, she should leave Gerrard out of this decision.

No point either in talking to her father. He would think her mad. If her mother were alive she would have thought the same. But she'd died on the operating table in what should have been a straightforward hysterectomy. Except for the shock, she couldn't honestly say she'd grieved that much for her mother. They'd never been close, her mother always disapproving of her…especially at that time…

Jay squeezed her eyes tight.

But the thought refused to leave her. Australia wasn't just where Nannie and Pop had gone. It was—

No. Leave it alone.

Exhaustion finally overcame her.

An insistent shrill pierced through Jay's head and she jerked up to turn off her alarm. It persisted a few seconds more until she realised it was the phone.

'Jay, it's Lydia. Hope I'm not calling too early.' Lydia's impatient tone implied she'd been up since dawn. 'Darling, are you there?'

'Yes, I…hold on a minute.' Jay staggered out of bed, carrying the phone with her, the polished floorboards feeling cool and slippery under her bare feet. She glimpsed herself in the hall mirror, and pulled a face. How could that haggard woman possibly be her? And the *hair*. She could pass for Rochester's mad wife. Concentrate. What was Lydia saying?

'Just to tell you my offer last night still stands.'

Jay gave a sharp intake of breath. 'Lydia, I'm grateful, but I can't think straight at the moment. I didn't get a lot of sleep last night.'

'Surely you've got some idea.'

'Yes…well, no…I thought you were ringing to say it was a joke.'

'I never joke about important things.' Lydia sounded indignant.

'Look, I wouldn't dream of influencing you in any way. You looked so worn out, that's all.' Jay tried to think how to answer. A sickly fuzzy sensation had taken over her head and all she wanted was to get in the shower, and then drink two mugs of coffee straight off. A smoke if there was time. She trudged into the kitchen, tucking the receiver under her chin, and filled the kettle, keeping an eye on the wall clock.

'When we spoke last night,' Lydia continued, 'you were so animated telling me about following your grandparents, you looked like a different person…and I don't want to pry, darling…but I felt there was some unfinished business in Australia. Am I right?'

Jay swallowed hard.

'Are you still there?'

'Yes. I'm here.'

'Darling, if you've got a problem and you need a friend, I'm a good listener. It wouldn't go any further.'

Lydia's voice was beguiling but Jay had been conditioned over the years. *Never breathe a word to anyone, not even to Will and Antonia*, Jay heard her mother's firm voice once again. There was an expectant silence from the receiver. Jay stammered, 'I…yes, one day…maybe…not now…I'm sorry to sound so negative, but I've got to get to work.'

'Of course, darling,' Lydia said soothingly. 'Well, you know where I am. Call me as soon as you've made a decision.'

Jay hesitated, biting the inside of her mouth. Wasn't it Mark Twain who said it's not the things you *do* that you'll regret, but the things you *don't*? Shouldn't she be grabbing such an opportunity? Lydia was more than capable of running the business. She'd had half a dozen branches, for heaven's sake, while Jay only had the one. And she'd be free…for several weeks…to go to Australia. To find—

She caught sight of the clock. Oh, God. She'd got to face Mr Baldwin this morning. Rachel would have to give him a cup of

24

coffee and tell him she'd been held up. He'd be put out but this was important. Keeping her voice neutral she asked: 'It's only hypothetical, but how do you see it working?'

'We'd start whenever you like. You could give me...what... three or four weeks' induction? And away you go.'

'My grandparents went in September,' Jay said slowly, her scalp prickling.

'Just the right weather for your introduction to Oz.' Lydia's voice was enthusiastic. 'They'll be coming into spring. Why don't you make a few flight enquiries?'

Jay could almost hear Lydia holding her breath in suspense. What had Lydia said last night in the restaurant? That she'd be doing *her* a favour. It wasn't just a charitable offer. Lydia was worried about Robert. It'd be a business deal. Just like Lydia said. And she would be on her way to Australia.

You'd be a fool to even consider *letting Lydia take over. Someone you barely know. You'd be risking everything. Forget it.*

Ignoring the warning voice in her head she put a teaspoon of instant in one of the mugs, and heard herself say, 'Maybe we should meet up again – discuss it further.'

'That's my girl,' Lydia laughed, and then her tone changed. 'We should pencil in a date when you'd want me to start training.'

A bubble of irritation rose in Jay's throat. She hadn't given Lydia a definite answer but already Lydia seemed to be taking it as a foregone conclusion. Typical estate agent. Jay gave a tight smile. Lydia may have run a successful company but if she was *too* forceful she'd get everyone's backs up. There were some strong characters at Reece & Co but so far they all got on well. They'd likely resent a new person in charge, even on a temporary basis. Jay sighed. They'd have to get used to her, that's all. *If* she said yes. Which of course she wasn't going to.

The kettle whistled but when she checked the time again she realised breakfast was no longer an option. She'd hit all the traffic if she didn't get a move on. She switched the kettle off and took the phone into the shower room.

'Lydia, I really am late…'

'Yes, you go, darling. Why don't we meet up tomorrow?'

Jay braced herself to take back some of the control. 'Let's have a meeting on Monday at the office – after the others have gone home.'

That way, she still had the weekend to come up with some kind of answer.

3

Jay's eyes alighted on her father's old desk in the sitting room where her computer was set up, and hesitated. Surely there'd be no harm in surfing the net for flights to Melbourne. She sat down and switched on, ignoring her brain sending seductive messages for her to relax with a chilled glass of Chardonnay after a difficult day at work. It would only be a cursory look, she told herself. See what was on offer while her frozen dinner-for-one was heating.

For a few seconds she closed her eyes, visualising the voyage her grandparents had taken. She'd always dreamed of following in their footsteps and going by ship, but somehow the image of a luxury liner carrying a couple of thousand passengers continuously rushing for mountains of food and puerile entertainment didn't appeal. No, that kind of voyage would have nothing in common with what she remembered of Nannie's stories.

She looked up BA and Qantas, which gave her their latest dates and fares, then surfing a little deeper, she spotted a website called Travelflight. She opened it and was puzzled with the advertising slogan 'the alternative way to see the world'. What were they talking about? Peering at the screen she realised it was Travel*freight,* and nothing to do with planes. Intrigued, she scrolled some photographs of a handful of smiling passengers on the deck of a cargo ship, drinks in their hands, looking out to a calm blue sea. It looked idyllic and would certainly be an unconventional way to travel. Her heart began to beat faster as she skimmed through the terms and conditions. Facilities were provided for up to twelve passengers. Only twelve? Maybe not so idyllic, she thought, pulling a face. They'd really have to get along together, and if any of them were bores there'd be no escape. Then she read the reason why only such a small number was allowed – there was no doctor on board. How did they work that one out? Fewer than thirteen and no one got sick? Wouldn't it be risky – a voyage with no doctor? And what would several weeks at sea with a bunch of strangers really be like?

She opened some images of sample cabins which looked comfortable and modern, all with en-suite bathrooms. Everything appeared so normal. Could she – should she – really make this trip? Trust Lydia? Take such a gamble? Leave everything familiar behind? She bit her lip. Really, she was being ridiculous even contemplating such a move.

Jay swung her office chair round to gaze at the twin paintings of the *Orsova* which hung in the dining area. It was the ship her grandparents had sailed on. Though it was a liner, she knew by Nannie's description there hadn't been much comfort in third class. One of the paintings portrayed the ship in calm seas, the other stormy, and Jay knew the details of both by heart. Whenever she'd gone to visit Nannie as a child, Antonia and Will used to rush on ahead to greet their grandparents, and she would always lag behind in the front parlour where they hung, and just stand and stare at them, wondering what it would be like to sail away on such a huge ship. How the ladies would be dressed and what jewellery they would have worn. Her grandparents wouldn't have been able to mix with the first- and second-class passengers – they were in another world – but she could dream...that was, until her brother and sister shouted for her to buck up and come and give Nannie a kiss.

'One day, Nannie,' she'd said when she was eleven, 'can I have the two ship pictures which you and Pop went on to Australia? Oh, not for years and years and years yet,' she added hurriedly, realising her request hadn't sounded very tactful.

But Nannie had smiled. 'Of course you can, dear. I'm glad you like them so much.'

'I *love* them,' she'd assured her grandmother. 'And I love hearing all the stories about what happened on the ship and when you got there.'

Her grandmother hadn't been a good traveller in rough weather, Jay now recalled, as her eyes fixed on the painting of the ship in the rolling sea, but she was a plucky young woman considering she'd never been further than King's Lynn, as far as she knew. Nannie must have really been in love with Pop.

Jay's thoughts flew. If she really decided to go to Australia at least it would galvanise her into action. She might even carry out some of the instructions in the health book she'd bought on impulse a few weeks ago and barely skimmed the pages. On the back cover the author was a slim attractive woman, bursting with vitality, and promised that she, too, could feel and look the same.

That would take some doing.

Jay's lips became an unflattering grim line. All it needed was discipline. She'd visit the local health shop and stock up on vitamins. And she just might replay the exercise disc which had been stuck on to the health book and do a few minutes work-out before breakfast every morning. There was a lot of improving to do in such a short time…that is, if she could get a ticket for a September sailing. That is…if she went.

The smell of the lasagne wafted into the room and Jay suddenly realised she was hungry. Hoping the oven timer would soon ping, she got up and poured herself a glass of wine, then wandered over to the patio doors. And there was her view. The reason she'd bought the apartment. Paying way over the going rate she'd known it was still a good investment, simply because it overlooked the river. She slid open one of the doors and stepped out onto her balcony. Lighting a cigarette she stood for a few minutes watching the boats, thinking about Australia.

With Travelfreight, the voyage as far as Melbourne would take thirty-three days. She could stay in Melbourne a couple of weeks and then fly to Sydney. Her pulse quickened. Could she really do this? Surely there were too many years to bridge, yet the pain was still there, as strong as it ever was. She should leave well alone. But wasn't it too late? Lydia had already provided her with a fantastic opportunity. A thrill of excitement shot down her spine. *Do I dare? Do I have the guts?*

She drew on her cigarette but for once neither the action nor the taste had the usual appeal, and after one more drag she came back into the room and crushed it into the ashtray.

The long journey would eat into the time but she'd fly home. Going by cargo ship simply felt right. It would make the journey into more of an adventure. Be a complete contrast to what she'd been used to with her short luxury breaks. She shrugged off any last vestige of apprehension and went back to her computer, put her now empty glass down on the desk, and filled out the registration form. She was only gathering information. She still wasn't committed. She pressed Send.

'You're going to do *what*?' Gerrard's head jerked back, accentuating his double chin. His rimless glasses slipped down his nose.

Jay sipped her wine while studying her ex. She tried to keep her voice even.

'Gerrard, I know you heard me so don't pretend you didn't. I'm taking some time off and going to Australia to see where my grandparents lived. You know it's what I've always wanted to do.'

'No, not that bit. That's bad enough, but letting a *stranger* take over the business for *how* long? *Three months?*' The group on the neighbouring table swivelled round. 'You must be mad, that's all I can say.'

'You don't need to tell the whole wine bar,' Jay hissed. 'First, Lydia's not a stranger and second, she's perfectly experienced to run my kind of business. It's not that dissimilar to hers—'

'Jay—'

'No, let me finish. I wanted to say that I totally trust her.'

She wasn't going to tell him he was reacting in a similar way to how she'd felt when Lydia had first made the offer.

Gerrard frowned. 'Why don't you appoint Neil? He could do it standing on his head.'

'I need him in sales. Besides, he hasn't any experience of running a business. Lydia has.'

'You must be mad,' Gerrard repeated, his face getting red. 'It's like *you* trying to run her estate agency. What would *you* know about selling houses? It would be a disaster.'

'Thanks for your unswerving faith in me.' Jay glared at him. Why on earth had she married him? But she knew the answer. Gerrard, ten years older than herself, was a successful lawyer. She'd never found him exciting but he was reliable and had seemed to genuinely care for her. What she hadn't bargained for, after the wedding, was his self-righteous attitude – *never* admitting he might occasionally be wrong. Worse, he had a knack of making her feel inadequate, particularly where her business was concerned.

The most important reason for marrying him, she'd finally admitted to herself, was that her parents had been delighted. They'd never failed to remind her that she was the difficult one out of their three children, so it was probably the only thing she'd done they'd ever approved of.

She stored these memories away and focused on the man she'd shared her life with for the past decade, noticing how slack Gerrard's face had become. His disbelieving expression made him look older than his fifty-five years.

'I didn't mean it like that, but you are an idiot sometimes.'

'You're right.' Jay drained the rest of her glass. 'I've been an idiot many times in my life,' she looked at him meaningfully though she knew it was wasted, 'but I hoped you might be pleased for me to have a break from the rat race…a chance to do something for *me*, for a change. Obviously, I was wrong.'

'You always do things for *you*.' Gerrard emphasised the last word. 'That's your trouble.' He paused, and took a deep swallow of wine. 'We should have had children. It would have settled you down.' He stared at her as though she were a child he'd done his best for and she'd turned out to be a disappointment. 'To this day I don't know why you refused.'

And you never will. I've never told you because you wouldn't understand.

'Don't start all that again, Gerrard.' Jay's eyes darkened. 'It's far too late.' Why had she bothered to have a farewell drink with him? She got out her wallet to pay for the drinks, wondering what Gerrard would say if she told him the answer to his question was tucked behind one of her credit cards, dog-eared and creased no matter how carefully she always fingered it. A simple black-and-white photograph.

'Don't leave in a huff.' He jumped up to help with her jacket. 'If you're really intent on doing this crazy thing you'll need a contract for Lydia so it's a proper businesslike arrangement. I can do that for you.'

'Of course I wouldn't dream of going without putting a legal document in place.' Jay's voice was cool. 'I'm not such an idiot as you think I am.' She stuffed her arms down the sleeves in an unladylike fashion.

Gerrard flushed. 'You're a clever woman, Jay. I didn't marry you just for your body.' She threw him a withering look. 'Just joking. But let me help you. Don't be too proud to ask.'

'All right, Gerrard, but just back me for once in your life.'

Jay dreaded calling her sister. There was such a big gap in their ages that Antonia often seemed more like a distant aunt.

'It sounds foolhardy.' Antonia's voice was clear and confident, as though she were down the road instead of in Toronto. 'Who cares why they went and why they came back? Just get on with your own life, Jay. And if you must go, go on a proper liner, not some rusty old freighter.'

Jay lifted her eyes heavenwards.

'How's Dad?' Antonia sounded worried.

'Not any worse.'

'I wish I lived nearer. You've had a lot to put up with and I doubt you'll get much help from Will in the state he's in. What's he say about this trip?'

'I haven't spoken to him yet.'

Will was equally negative.

'They were only servants so they're going to be difficult to trace. And this Lydia person...you don't know that much about her except you sold her business. Suppose she buggers it all up. I should just go for a three-week holiday and let the others cover for you until you get back.' He'd gone on a bit longer but by then Jay had tuned him out.

They'd been full of advice but none of it suited her. Of course they knew nothing about Charlie.

Jay entered the meeting room, perfectly composed to all outside appearances. She'd tried to picture each individual and pre-empt their response, rehearsing the answers and hoping she'd be able to persuade them it would be A Good Thing to have some fresh blood in the company for a few weeks. She pulled her shoulders back, physically bracing herself for the barrage of questions.

'Hi, everyone. Thanks for coming in early. I've got something special to tell you.' She looked round at the five faces, all trying to look merely interested but aware something important was about to be sprung on them. 'First, I want to thank each one of you for the incredibly hard work you put into Reece & Co.'

'You're not selling, are you?' blurted Jamie Hall, the newcomer and trainee.

'No, no, nothing like that,' Jay said quickly. 'The company's doing well, thanks to everyone's efforts. But I've decided to take some time off.'

She noticed Neil's frowning expression had relaxed into a slight smirk.

'There's nothing wrong, is there?' Rachel looked alarmed.

'I'm not ill or anything,' Jay assured her, 'but I need to recharge, and this is as good a time as any.'

'I think it will do you the world of good.' Neil tweaked his perfectly straight tie. 'Are you taking off somewhere? Or is it a big secret?'

Jay looked sharply at him. 'I'm going to Australia. There's some family history I want to look into, and it will take more than a fortnight's holiday to do it.'

'Sounds wonderful,' said Rachel. 'We'll miss you…but I'm sure we'll cope.'

'You needn't worry about us.' Neil's voice was smooth. 'Things will carry on exactly the same, and we can keep in touch by email.'

'Things won't be *exactly* the same, Neil.'

'Well, no, what I meant was – I'll be pleased to take care of things for a while

There were some raised eyebrows. This was awkward.

'Thanks for the offer, Neil, but you're much too valuable on the sales floor. Plus looking after my particular clients will give you plenty of extra work. No, I need someone who has experience in the day-to-day running to take over.' She kept her gaze on him. 'I'm appointing Lydia Mayfield.'

There was a stunned silence.

'Lydia Mayfield?' Bob finally spoke. 'The woman whose estate agency we sold?'

'That's the one.'

The atmosphere became tense. Neil flushed and Jay noticed a look pass between Bob and Kirsty that told her they were not entirely convinced either. Rachel chewed her nail though she gave Jay a weak smile. Jamie was the only one who seemed unconcerned. Probably relieved he still had a job.

'She's got masses of experience in running a company,' Jay continued, 'and her business was similar to ours, just houses instead of companies. And she's a nice person. You'll like her.' She knew she was trying too hard.

'Jay, I am perfectly able to run—'

She held up the flat of her hand. 'Neil, I've made up my mind. I plan to go in September and be back the first of December. Lydia will come in to meet you next week, and then in August she'll work closely with me until I leave, so you all feel confident that Reece & Co will carry on, not *exactly* the same...' her gaze lingered on Neil, 'but still a good, tight team who will continue to work together without having to worry about everyday stuff. In the meantime I shall be calling my own clients to let them know I'm transferring their files to Neil and assure them they'll be in perfectly safe hands.' She threw a confident smile at Neil. 'Now...are there any questions? Kirsty?'

'What do we do if something goes wrong?'

'You'll discuss it with Lydia. She's used to sorting out problems.'

'But what if it's to *do* with Lydia?'

'As Neil reminded me, I'm only an email away.' She ignored Neil's dark expression. 'And if there's a real emergency you've got my mobile.' She paused. 'Bob, you haven't said anything.'

'I think it'll work,' Bob said cautiously. 'We'll miss you, of course, but we should look upon it as a challenge. To work even better than if you were here.'

She saw Neil glance at him with a scornful expression. *Toadying up*, she could imagine him thinking. He'd once told her how he loved the adrenalin rush every time he sold himself and the company, and Jay had to admit he brought in the lion's share of new business. But Neil was apt to do his own thing. Still, Lydia would be able to handle him.

4

There was a rhythmic tap to Beethoven's Fifth on Jay's office door, and without waiting for an answer Lydia strode in.

'Reporting for duty, ma'am,' she announced with a salute.

Jay smiled, though inwardly she felt apprehensive – not so much where she herself was concerned but for the staff. It hadn't gone too badly when she'd introduced Lydia to the team a month ago. Only Neil had been less than warm. Well, he'd have to come round. She paid him enough.

'I thought we'd do some basics first,' she said, taking her chair. Lydia had already sat down. 'Rachel will show you the filing system and go through all the suppliers we use. The others will explain their roles – they have their own accounts to work on, but everyone has to have a general knowledge of *all* the business in hand in case someone's on holiday or sick. Jamie, of course, is still training and I'll talk to you later in the week with my development plan for him.'

Lydia nodded. 'Sounds good. Maybe when I've learned the admin side and got to know the team better, I should shadow you for the last week so I understand exactly how you fit in.' She wrinkled her nose. 'What's that smell? It reminds me of old ladies.'

'Just some lavender spray.' Jay felt like a schoolgirl being caught out. 'I was trying to get rid of the smoke.'

'Why don't you give up?'

Jay sighed. 'It's easier said than done.'

'If I can do it, so can anyone. One day I smoked, next day I gave up.'

You would, Jay thought, a little unkindly. She took a calming breath to quell her irritation.

'Where were we? Oh, yes. Shadowing me. Good idea. But today I'll leave you in the capable hands of Rachel. I've planned the next few days without too many appointments so we can catch up at lunch.'

'Perfect, darling. Don't worry at all about me. I'll see you at one, then.' She disappeared.

Jay sighed with relief at having a few hours to herself. She knew Lydia would have got on her nerves long term, but it was kind of nice having her around. It was what she'd missed most of all when she'd started the business. There'd been no senior person behind her, or anyone on her level who she could discuss problems with or ask for advice. She could hear the hum of voices downstairs, Lydia's clipped accent mingling with the others, and couldn't resist a smile. It wouldn't hurt them to have a change – shake them up a bit. She had the weird sensation of a weight lifting from her shoulders, and for the first time since Lydia had made such an incredible offer she felt more relaxed. After all, it was only for three months. Which was only a few weeks if you broke it down.

At lunch at the nearest bistro a week later, Lydia said, 'By the way, do I detect you've given up the ciggies?'

'Thought you'd never notice,' Jay laughed. 'It's the hardest thing I've ever done. And that includes running a business. But I do have a little help from my friends.'

'Oh?'

'Nicotine patches. I just started using them a few days ago. I'm not there yet but they've helped me cut right down. I'm also trying to lose weight. And I've even been to the gym twice this week, which is a record.'

'Well done, you. By the way, is it still the 10th?' Lydia asked.

'Yes, supposed to be – but they say they can't be held to it. Apparently, it's not unusual to be delayed for a few days. Sometimes much longer.'

'I still can't believe you're going on a banana boat. You're mad when you could be on a luxury liner...all those rich widowers.'

'No thanks. I don't want their baggage. I've got enough of my own.'

5

'Neil, can I see you in my office for a few minutes?' Jay caught him as he was trying to slide into his.

'Can't it wait?'

'No, it's important.' He'd appeared busy every time she tried to have a word with him on how Lydia would fit in, but now she was determined to confront him.

'Great hairstyle, by the way,' he said, as she ushered him in.

'Thanks.' She nodded in acknowledgement but was determined not to be side-tracked. 'Take a seat. I need to talk to you about your role when I'm away. Obviously, I want you to carry on bringing in new business and looking after your own clients. And as I mentioned at the meeting, I'd like you to take over my clients. There are only half a dozen and I leave it to you if you want to hand any of them to Bob or Kirsty.'

'And Lydia?' His tone was offhand as he crossed one leg.

'Lydia has her brief. She'll do the things I do.' Jay looked directly at him. 'I'm relying on you to support her.'

'I'll help all I can, but I still wish you'd let me take over.' He watched her. 'She's never run this kind of business and I don't think she'll find it easy.'

'What are you saying, Neil?'

'I know the business as well as you.' He looked across the desk at her, his eyes hard. 'I'm surprised, that's all, that you haven't put me in charge.' He paused. 'It's not too late to change your mind, you know. Woman's prerogative, and all that.'

'There's no question of changing my mind.'

'If Lydia cocks it up, your reputation will be shot long before three months. Remember what happened to old Bignall when his son took over the newsagent...and *he* was family.'

'Philip was a *slightly* different character to Lydia,' Jay flashed. 'She's got too much pride to let anything slip. She'll want to prove to me how well she's managed.'

'You never know what people do when they get a bit of power.' His eyes never wavered from Jay's. 'Well, don't tell me I didn't warn you.' He got up to leave.

Jay frowned. Was she being irresponsible? Was Neil right? It wasn't too late to cancel. Yes, she'd lose the full fare but that was nothing compared to the risk. Not one person had thought it a good idea except Lydia. She was debating what to say next when the phone rang, making her jump.

'Call for you, Jay.'

'Tell them I'll call straight back.'

She signalled for Neil to remain but he left the room, not quite slamming the door behind him. Jay gave an exasperated sigh. She sat at her computer trying to write more notes, but her hand was shaking so badly she threw down her pen.

She'd noticed before that the staff never went much on change and it was probably a male thing with Neil. He'd been usurped. She smiled grimly and opened the desk drawer for her cigarettes. *Damn!* She was supposed to have given up. She banged the drawer shut. Well, she'd be leaving in just over a week. They'd all have to get on with it.

'Who was the caller, Rach?'

'He just said Paul. And that it was urgent.'

Jay furrowed her brow. 'I don't know a Paul. Can you get him back and put him through?'

A minute later her phone rang.

'Is that Ms Reece?'

'It is.'

'It's Paul from Travelfreight.'

What was so urgent? Had *they* cancelled? Maybe her decision would be made for her. And yet, suddenly, after all the planning, she wanted to be on that ship more than anything in the world.

'The ship's still going, I take it?'

'Yes, of course,' Paul sounded surprised, 'but the date's changed.'

Jay breathed out. 'That's okay. I can do with a few extra days.'

'No, it's not delayed. It's been brought forward.'

'That's impossible.' Jay clenched the handset. 'I'm geared up for next week.'

'Well, sorry about that.' Paul's tone was brisk. 'I'm afraid as a passenger you come second.'

Jay frowned. 'So what date will it be?'

'This Friday.'

'What!' She glanced at the calendar. 'That only gives me three days. I'll never be ready in time.' Jay bit her lip as she tried to work out everything she still had to organise. 'I'll never do it.'

'Well, that's when we'll be sailing. So, I'd better let you go.' Paul's voice was sympathetic but firm. 'I'll email you today to confirm the arrangements and attach a map of Tilbury docks. Once you get there you'll need a taxi to take you to the right zone. Ring me if something's not clear.'

She swore softly to herself, then picked up her intercom and asked Lydia to come up.

Jay's routine was to see her father every other evening after work, but she hadn't been to the nursing home since Paul had informed her of the earlier sailing date. She'd intended to sow the seed weeks ago, but just when she was about to open her mouth she always changed her mind. What a coward. But telling him at the last minute was better. It would be way too late for him to try to dissuade her.

She knocked on his door. No answer.

'He's having tea with the others,' one of the nurses told Jay as she hurried by.

This was a change. Her father always refused to mix with the other residents; he had nothing in common with them, he said, and preferred to have all his meals in his room. Jay cursed under her breath. She wanted to see him privately, then go home and finish her packing. Dear God, what sort of a daughter was she? Poor old boy had suffered a heart attack. Who knew how much longer he had?

She was about to ask if she could have a cup of tea and wait when she saw him tottering towards her, a walking stick in each hand.

'Hello, Juliet.' He gave her a thin smile.

'Hello, Dad.' For once she managed to squash the irritation at his use of her full name.

'They told me you were here. Go in.'

She held the door open and he tumbled into a chair. She picked a cushionless seat, her thoughts flying, wondering how she should broach the subject. It was no good analysing. You just had to say the words.

'Dad, I've got the chance to leave the business for a few weeks and I've decided to go to Australia for a holiday.'

'On some mission, I presume?' His tone was flat.

Don't rise to it.

'Not exactly,' she tried to steer him in another direction, 'but I'd like to see where Nannie and Pop lived, even if it's only being in the same city.'

Her father cleared his throat as though he were about to say something. Jay counted time by listening to the thud of her heart. He looked at her, an unfathomable expression in his eyes. His silence began to unnerve her.

'What do you think, Dad?' Here she was again, needing his approval.

'I wouldn't do it if I were you.' He scrutinised her with his piercing blue eyes. 'Think about it carefully. Any digging can only cause pain.'

He was definitely not referring to Nannie and Pop. She swallowed. She'd have to pretend it was only her grandparents she was anxious to follow.

'Dad, you know how I feel about Nannie. How close we were. I want to know what happened...why she came home. They'd planned to emigrate. Why did they change their minds?'

'Your Nannie pined for her father and...' he stopped.

'Ruby and Ethel,' Jay finished.

'Not Ruby,' her father said, with a curl of his lips.

What was her father holding back?

'Dad, I'm forty-five. I have a right to know about my own family.'

Her father shifted in the chair and coughed. He reached in his pocket for his handkerchief and blew his nose. Finally he said, 'They had money problems.'

This was unexpected.

'What kind of money problems?'

'Debts. I don't know the details.' He dropped his eyes.

'Nannie never said anything about that to me.'

He looked at her. 'It was never discussed. You didn't, in those days.'

'So they must have thought they'd be better off going home?' Jay persisted.

'Something like that, I expect,' her father muttered.

'Did her sisters know the real reason why they came back?'

'Ruby knew, of course.' Her father's tone became bitter. 'She stayed behind.'

'Oh, yes. I'd forgotten. Why didn't she come back with them?

Nannie always changed the subject when I asked her.'

He shook his head.

'Did Great-Aunt Ethel know about their money problems?'

Her father glanced at her. 'Your Nannie always protected her baby sister. And she was loyal. More than you could say for Ruby.'

If Nannie was loyal it must mean that Pop was the one at fault. That he was the one who had got them into debt. But why that bitter tone her father used whenever Ruby's name was mentioned? Jay was determined to get to the bottom of it.

'Nannie must have written to her family, so who would have her letters?'

'I don't remember any letters.' Her father glanced round the room as though he were searching for such evidence. Then his brow cleared but still he hesitated. Finally his eyes met Jay's. 'There was something…a diary she used to keep. So your Aunt Frankie once said, anyway.'

Jay almost stopped breathing. A diary. Even better. Where you wrote your innermost thoughts.

'Do you have any idea where it is?'

'I expect she got rid of it before they came back. It would be the last thing Mum would want Dad to stumble across if she'd poured her heart out.'

Why should Nannie worry about Pop seeing it? It didn't make sense.

His next question made her jump.

'So when are you planning this trip?'

'Tomorrow.'

'*Tomorrow*? And you only thought of letting me know today? God Almighty.'

'I'm sorry, Dad.' Jay felt the warmth creep up her neck to her face. Just as it used to when she was a teenager, she thought crossly. 'But if I'd told you sooner you'd have tried to talk me out of it.'

'And now it's too late, I suppose,' he said peevishly. 'Who, may I ask, is going to look after the company?'

By the time Jay explained about Lydia her father's expression had changed from surprise to incredulity.

'You must be out of your mind,' he said, his voice growing strong as he drummed his fingers on the arm of the chair. 'This woman…what does she know about your business?' He didn't wait for an answer. 'What does Gerrard say about it?'

'It has nothing to do with Gerrard,' Jay snapped. 'You might remember we're divorced now. I'm my own person, making my own decisions.'

'Let's hope they don't get you into trouble,' her father said, 'like they've done before.'

He cleared his throat again, and the hawking sound made her feel queasy. She glared at him but he kept his head down. His next words were so quiet she only just made them out.

'Wherever you plan to visit I should keep away from Sydney, if I were you.'

She felt the bile rise in her throat and stick there. It was as though she was choking. That she would never be able to take an easy breath while she was in the presence of her father. Her heart began to beat hard and fast. Her hair felt damp on her neck, and her stomach went into a spasm. Against her will she closed her eyes and the past hurtled to meet her.

She opens her eyes. She's lying on her back looking up at the ceiling of her bedroom. There's a brown stain in one corner where the roof once leaked when she was a child. It looks like stale blood. She wishes her father would dab some white paint over it but he's always stuck in his office writing one of his dull books about people she's never heard of. For a few seconds everything's normal; then with a sickening heart at the enormity of what's happened she slithers further down, pulling the covers over her head.

The sheet smells stale from her restless night and she throws the covers back, knowing there's no point in putting off the dreaded moment. She's starting to show. Any second her mother, or bloody hell, her teacher, will confront her and that will be even more dreadful. Best get it over with at breakfast – then with a bit of luck she can escape.

'Good, you're early,' her mother remarks as Jay appears at the kitchen door, already dressed in her school uniform. 'You'll have to help yourself to cereal this morning. I've got to go in earlier with the manageress away this week.'

What's new, Jay thinks, as she watches her mother pour some milk in the saucepan for the coffee. She hears her father's footsteps going into the dining room, and her heart feels it will jump out of her chest.

'Go on, Juliet, don't just stand there.'

'I'm not Juliet, I'm Jay. *Jay.* How many times do I have to tell you?' She stamps her foot, then remembers she must act like a grown-up, today of all days.

'Don't be rude. Jay is *not* your name. I don't know why you don't like Juliet. It's lovely.'

Jay can't believe they're having an argument about her name at such a time, but of course her mother has no idea she's about to drop a bombshell. *Get it over right now. Just between me and Mother.*

'Mummy, don't be—'

'Don't what?' her mother interrupts, looking round at her, vague as usual, as she pushes down the knob on the toaster.

'N-nothing.' Jay can't go on. She thinks she will choke with fear, but her mother doesn't appear to notice anything amiss as she clatters the cups and saucers onto a tray to take through to the dining room.

'Well, if it's nothing, then you'd better get a move on.'

Jay opens the cupboard door and takes out the box of cornflakes.

She shakes some out, pours on the milk, puts the bottle back in the fridge, and takes the bowl into the dining room. By the time she sits in her place to the left of her father she's already slopped some of the milk onto the carpet. She glances at him. Why can't he look up for once? No, he goes right on reading his paper, his horrid ginger head bent forward, oblivious to her, his daughter.

I don't think I can do this. She puts her hands beneath her thighs as if it might stop them shaking and watches her mother glide into the room in her red satin dressing gown, carrying the tray of coffee. Her mother takes her seat at the opposite end of the oak dining table facing her husband.

'Can you bring the other tray in, Juliet?' she says. '*Juliet*, did you hear me?'

'Um...'

'Never mind, I'll get it myself.' Her mother sighs.

'Toast, Harry.' Her mother is back, setting down the toast rack near her husband.

Jay puts her spoon into her cereal bowl, hardly aware of what she's doing.

'Thank you, dear.' Her father puts down his paper and reaches out for the butter. He glances at Jay and frowns. 'Your tie's crooked.'

Jay flushes with the criticism, then blurts, 'I'm going to have a baby.'

Two pairs of astonished eyes swivel round. Well, at least she's got their attention.

'*What* did you say?' her father asks, enunciating each syllable, his eyes cold with disbelief.

'I'm pregnant.' It feels as though she's talking through sandpaper.

'What do you mean – *pregnant*?' Her father half rises in his chair as though to see his daughter more clearly. 'You don't have a boyfriend. Your mother and I made that perfectly clear. Not until you finish school.'

'I've had a boyfriend for ages.' Jay's voice is firmer now she's given them the worst. 'His name's Mani.'

'*Mani*!' Her father's lips quiver with anger as he sinks back onto his chair. 'Why don't we know about him?'

'You do. I told you about him.'

'Not the *coloured* boy? I thought he was just one of your friends. You didn't tell us he was your *boyfriend*.' He makes the word sound dirty. 'How old is he?'

'He's not coloured, he's Indian. And he's eighteen.' Jay crosses her fingers under the table.

'If he's eighteen he should know better,' splutters her father. 'I'm sorry, Juliet, I won't allow it. *We* won't allow it.'

She turns to her mother whose face is ghostly white, in terrible contrast to her scarlet robe.

'How could you, Juliet?' she says in that controlled tone that Jay hates, her cup of coffee frozen in mid-air. 'How could you bring shame on the family after the way we've brought you up to be a good Catholic girl?'

This is worse than she feared. Tears burn in her eyes as she realises the full impact her announcement has on her parents. They're never going to forgive her and neither will the church. She watches them looking at one another, shaking their heads in denial. She counts under her breath like she used to when she was small, forcing herself not to cry. Six…seven…eight…

'What are we going to do, Harry?'

Her father shakes his head. 'I'd like to wring his friggin' neck.'

It takes Jay a few moments to realise her parents have got it all wrong. They think Mani is abandoning her. Trembling with relief she says:

'It's all right. We love each other. Mani wants to marry me.'

'*Love*!' Spittle flies from her father's lips as he flings his newspaper on the table. 'You don't know what love is. And *marriage*. You're far too young. There you'd be, tied down with a squalling brat, no money, and no husband in a matter of time, more likely.'

I hate you. How can you call yourself my father? You're just a horrible old man.

'Besides, he's not one of us,' her father goes on. 'That makes it even more impossible. Not that I've got anything against coloureds,' he adds hastily, as Jay's face contorts with rage, 'but you'd have serious problems with a coloured husband and a half-caste child. Believe me.'

'He's *Indian*, I keep telling you,' Jay shouts, adrenalin forcing her to jump to her feet. 'You sound like a racist. You're against everything we're taught in school.' She draws in a ragged breath. 'Mummy...' she begs as she did when a little girl, tears now streaming down her cheeks. 'Mummy, please—'

'Sit down, Juliet,' her mother warns. 'Shouting won't help. We need to make a plan. Have you been to the doctor?'

'No.' Jay's voice is a whisper.

'How do you know you're pregnant?'

'Mother, can we go somewhere in private? I can't talk about this anymore in front of Daddy.'

'You can say anything in front of your father. Don't you think he knows by now where babies come from?'

Jay flushes and bends her head so it almost touches her bowl. 'I haven't had the curse.'

'How many have you missed?' She feels her mother's eyes boring into her, but it's as though a lump of concrete is tied to the back of her neck, making it impossible to look up.

'Four or five...I'm not sure.' Her voice is barely audible.

'Four or *five*!' Her mother spills coffee into her saucer. 'You're not *sure*? Dear God.'

Jay bursts into fresh tears.

'It's a bit late for tears, young lady,' her father says, his fingers tapping the table, one at a time, over and over until Jay thinks she will go crazy. 'Your mother and I will discuss this in private. Now, get on with your breakfast. You'll be late for school.'

'You're talking about *my life*!' Jay explodes. 'And my baby's life. I'm not going to give it up for adoption if that's what you're thinking. Me and Mani are getting married.'

'Mani and *I*,' corrects her father.

'Me and Mani, Mani and I – what does it matter?' Jay's voice rises. 'All that matters is we love each other.'

'Stop shouting, Juliet,' her mother intervenes. 'Just listen for once.'

It's no use. They're too old. They'll never understand.

'And where were you and Mani and the baby thinking of living?' her father asks, his question threaded with sarcasm, though it barely registers with Jay, so intent is she on putting Mani in the best possible light.

'Mani says we can live with his parents. Just to start with.' Her voice calms as she relays her plans. At least her parents will realise she and Mani are treating it seriously. 'They're so excited they're going to be grandparents. They're longing to meet you and—'

'We don't even know this Mani, let alone his parents,' her mother cuts in. 'Or what kind of house they live in. Or where. What does Mani's father do, for instance? What does Mani do, come to that?'

Jay takes a breath. 'He's just finishing school. He'll get a job right away, I know he will.'

'A schoolboy. That's all he is. A schoolboy,' her father spits the words out. Jay shrivels under his glare. 'You still haven't told us what this Mani's father does.'

'He's a…a…' Jay struggles. 'I'm not sure.' She knows Mani has told her, but try as she might, she can't remember.

'Well, unless I'm wrong and he comes from a wealthy family, they won't have much say in it. The baby would grow up neither one thing nor the other. A half-caste, and you're too inexperienced to deal with people's hostility. It's an unfortunate mistake that you're going to have to live through and then forget about. You'll have

50

babies soon enough when you're older and properly married. Now's the time to continue your studies. You'll thank us one day.'

Jay twists round to her father, her eyes black with anger. 'I *won't* thank you. I'll never forgive you...because what you're saying is, *you* won't accept a grandchild with coloured blood, as you call it.'

'That's enough, Juliet. I won't tolerate rudeness.'

Have they forgotten what it's like to be in love? Surely her mother won't let this happen to her. 'Mummy,' she sobs now, 'Mummy, please, *please* talk to Daddy. At least meet Mani. Then you'll understand.'

'There's nothing more to say,' her father says, his lips drawn into a tight line. 'We know what's best for you. We'll continue to know until you're twenty-one and can make your own decisions. As for now—'

'I WISH I WAS DEAD!' Jay screams as she rushes from the room.

'Juliet, are you all right?'

Jay came to with a start. Her father was tapping his fingers on the arm of his chair, just as he had that awful morning. Her instinct told her he knew she'd been reliving the scene just now. How much better it would be if she could only bring it out in the open, challenge him as an adult instead of a teenager – but what was the use? He was a sick old man.

'Yes,' she said shortly. 'I'm all right.'

He opened his mouth to say something, then appeared to change his mind. Jay watched him for a few seconds, not trusting herself. Why couldn't he simply wish her luck and to enjoy Australia like any normal person would? He closed his eyes as though it were the end of the conversation. Jay waited a couple of minutes and then got up to leave.

She was quietly opening the door when he called out, 'Aren't you going to give your old dad a kiss goodbye then?'

'I thought you'd nodded off.' Jay awkwardly put her arms round him as he sat there, neither of them used to such a gesture. She touched her lips to his yellowed cheek and he took her hand in a surprising grip.

'Go to Australia if you must,' he told her, 'but I just hope you're not doing this with some ulterior motive.'

Part II

The Crossing

6

Tilbury, England

September 2005

'Ms Reece?'

A cheerful young man wearing a bright yellow hard hat broke into her thoughts as he caught up with her at the dock gate.

'I'm Simon, the port agent for the *Alexandria*. Here, put these on.' He handed her a yellow waistcoat and matching hard hat. 'This is a dangerous area so keep a sharp lookout. You've got to have your wits about you. Though if a container drops on you, you'll be a goner, hard hat or not.'

Jay gave a weak smile.

'The ship's not far away.' He took the handle of her suitcase.

She strapped on the hat and waistcoat, picked up her hand luggage, checked her handbag was on her shoulder, and feeling more like a road-digger than a voyager she followed him, cursing each time her new high heels caught in the steel lines embedded in the tarmac. Hundreds of figures and trolleys darted in front and behind her, and men's shouts and the drone and clanging and whine of machinery deafened her as she and Simon wound their way over to the ships.

'That's it,' Simon gestured.

Her first close-up of the *Alexandria*, sporting a Russian flag, was not at all what she'd expected. She'd schooled her mind not to think 'cruise ship' in any way, but in her head, the image of *her* ship was modern and freshly painted with neatly packed containers in one designated area that hardly showed, and didn't impair any view from her cabin window. This ship in front of her was probably once a rich shade of blue but now looked in dire need of a paint job to cover the smears of rust and generally to smarten it up. She frowned. The containers were the only bright spots of colour.

She strained her neck even higher. A crane was dumping a container on top of several others, and the deck was beginning to resemble an IKEA warehouse. At this rate it was extremely likely any view from her cabin would be blocked. But this was a working ship, she reminded herself; cargo took precedence over the passengers, and passengers on these ships weren't entitled to unimpeded sea views or any other niceties.

Her thoughts were interrupted by a wiry young man leaping down the gangway.

'Hi, you must be Juliet Reece. I'm Dan, one of the stewards.'

'Please call me Jay.' She shook his hand.

'I'll take back your safety gear,' Simon told her. He looked at his watch. 'I'd better go. There's a few more to meet.' He glanced curiously at Jay as she handed over the hat and waistcoat. 'Well, have a good trip.' He nodded to Dan and his yellow head disappeared.

'The crew's mostly Russian,' Dan explained. 'They're a decent bunch, though not wildly jolly unless they get some vodka inside them, but we get on fine. There's a couple of Russian stews who also help in the bar and the captain's Russian, of course.' Dan looked up at the sky. 'Looks as though we're in for some heavy rain any minute. I'll take you straight to your cabin and you can dump your stuff.' He picked up her cases.

From below, the gangway looked as tall as a Shanghai hotel.

'Mind those steps,' Dan warned. 'It's been raining so they're slippery. And they're steep when you're not used to them.' He paused and looked down at her feet. 'Didn't anyone tell you to wear sensible shoes?'

'I meant to change them, but I forgot.'

Damn. Not quite the impression she wanted to give.

'High heels are dangerous on ships. But never mind. You go first, and I'll follow in case you slip. And if you don't like heights, I suggest you don't look down.'

Determined not to appear like a pathetic female, Jay made her way up the longest flight of steps, the heels making an annoying click on each one. She silently thanked God when she reached the deck without mishap.

Once inside Dan took her through a door marked Chief Officer. It was crammed. A worktop supported several computers and piles of books and papers beneath a half-glazed wall. Maps were pinned onto the walls alongside various graphs and timetables. Half a dozen men were gathered; two staring at one of the computers, and four, all wearing dungarees, sat round a small table in the corner drinking coffee. They gave her a welcoming smile and a heavily accented 'Good afternoon'. One of the two men looking at the computer screen kept his back to her and continued talking to the second man in English about the freight. The room was small enough for Jay to steal a glance over his shoulder where she saw a computerised outline of the *Alexandria* showing the cargo. Unless her cabin was half a mile up, it wasn't good news.

'I've brought Ms Reece in to sign the paperwork,' Dan ventured, but the officer ignored him. Jay began to feel uncomfortable.

'Take no notice,' Dan said as he steered her out of the office and into the lift. He pressed a button. 'That's Alexei, the Chief Officer. He's always a bit het-up when we're about to sail, but he's fine when we're on our way.' He gave a grin. 'I'll bring the forms to your cabin. Here's your deck. It's F.'

The door of the lift slid open and she followed him along the narrow corridor, feeling the gentle sway of the water beneath her. Several pairs of men's shoes, obviously soiled, were neatly placed outside some of the cabins, as though the ship were a hotel and a porter would come along and whisk them away to clean them.

'In case you're wondering,' Dan said, nodding to one pair, 'it's filthy on deck, so when you go inside your cabin please remove your outdoor shoes and wear slippers.'

She wondered if there'd be lots of rules on the *Alexandria* but this one made sense. She'd had plenty of training from her mother to remove her shoes before coming into the house. They walked to the far end.

'You're at the left of the ship, known as portside. The right-hand side is starboard. In about an hour,' Dan unlocked a door at the far end and handed her a key, 'I'll be giving everyone a tour of the ship. The other passengers should have embarked by then. We're expecting to sail at 20.00 hours. Dinner's usually 17.30 for the passengers, but because it's the first day and a later start, it's 18.30.'

'How many passengers are there?'

'We're expecting six.' Jay raised her eyebrows. 'A married couple,' he responded to her unasked question, 'a young woman, two chaps, and yourself.' He disappeared.

It was hard to gauge whether six was good or bad. Was it better to have the full complement so it was less likely she'd be stuck with someone she didn't want to be, or would so many others have been too much? At least she wouldn't have to make so much effort with only five. Quite honestly she was exhausted, and this was going to be a perfect time to crash out. And keep a little distance.

The blurb in the brochure Travelfreight had sent her had praised the cabins for their generous sizes, but Jay had assumed they'd exaggerated. Now she stared at the size of the sitting room. Sparsely furnished, it was far bigger than her room at home, though in a seventies time warp. A cherry-red sofa and matching easy chair were paired with a glass-topped coffee table. Worktops ran along two walls incorporating a small sink and fridge with cupboards below. And not one, but five portholes: three on portside, as she must now learn to call it, and two forward. She slipped off the ridiculous high heels and climbed on one of the chairs to see outside, but immediately her view was blocked by a crane which swung by, clawing a container. To her dismay the operator set it squarely on top of the increasing pile.

She dropped back down to the floor and removed her tights, mentally flinching as her bare feet came into contact with the cheap pile of the carpet, the pattern resembling thousands of twisting and dancing razor blades. The razor blades continued into the bedroom where there was an inviting double bed pushed against the wall, a double wardrobe, cupboards and drawers, and another porthole. Even the en-suite shower room was well fitted, and to her relief, and contrary to the outside of the ship, all was as clean as any decent hotel.

She hurriedly unpacked, shoving the ship's tattered copy of the Bible to the back of one of the drawers, and propped her travel clock and one of her books on the bedside table next to the lamp. Her desk diary she placed on the worktop opposite which acted as a dressing table, and next to it the precious photograph of her grandmother as a young girl with her two sisters – the same picture she'd shown Lydia in the restaurant, but this was the original framed one. Strange how neither Antonia nor Will had been particularly interested in the picture of their grandmother and great-aunts when they were young. She picked it up again and studied it as though for the first time, then feeling a little silly she kissed it and set it down again.

Back in the sitting room she laid her box of blank cards, yet to be transformed into greetings cards, along with the various paints and glitter and glue at one end of the long worktop. On the oversized coffee table she set a jigsaw puzzle of Hatherleigh Hall, the stately home in Norfolk where her grandfather, Ferguson Bishop, had worked as a footman. It could come in handy to wile away some of those hours at sea as a change from making cards and reading.

The company had provided an electric kettle, a thermos of ice-cold water, canisters of tea, coffee and sugar, and glasses of various sizes slotted into their own holes in a special tray. Ready for bad weather, Jay presumed. She knelt to open the fridge and discovered in the door next to the milk a half bottle of Krug. *Mmm.* Nice touch, though it didn't look as though whoever had filled the fridge expected her to have any company. She smiled as she stretched up and glanced towards the front of the ship again.

The portholes streamed with the latest bout of rain, smearing the dirt that had collected from the previous crossing. Typically English autumn weather. Exactly what she was escaping from. Melbourne was sure to be drenched, but in spring sunshine instead.

All at once she flung her arms wide with sheer joy, a big grin plastered over her face. She was free. She'd done it.

She flexed her legs, aching from sitting too long in the train and taxi, found her loafers and looked at the time. Quarter to five. She'd just have time for a quick look outside for a view of the sea before Dan came back to show her around and to introduce her to the other passengers.

A tall figure was standing by the ship's rail, her wavy blonde hair blowing out at all angles with the stiff breeze. At the sound of Jay's footsteps, she turned.

'Hi, I'm Petra.' She stuck out her hand. It felt smooth and young. 'Petra Sandys. Are you a stew or a passenger?' She didn't wait for an answer. 'What fun to meet another single woman. Oh,' she tried to look contrite, '*are* you single? That's me all over – making presumptions.'

'You're forgiven,' Jay laughed. 'I'm a passenger. And yes, I *am* single…again. But I can't believe *you're* on your own.'

'Not sure if I'll have company or not,' the girl grinned, her eyes dancing.

'Sounds mysterious,' Jay smiled.

'Depends on what time the boat leaves.' The girl glanced at a huge plastic watch on her delicate wrist.

'Ship,' corrected Dan, appearing behind her.

'Boat, ship, whatever.' Petra wrinkled her nose. 'I *do* have a fiancé, though. Back home in Sydney. An adorable one.'

'I'd love to hear about him later,' Jay said, noticing Dan was tapping his foot impatiently.

'Some of the others are here so we'll start the tour,' Dan said. 'I'll leave your papers in your cabin for you to sign. You can give them to me after supper.'

Jay nodded and the two women followed him back down the corridor to the lift.

'We're meeting in the officers' lounge,' he told them. 'Deck C.'

The lounge looked big enough to hold a party. There was a bar halfway along one wall, with a few tables scattered nearby. Cream emulsioned walls were covered in shelves of books, games, videos and DVDs, and a jumbo television protruded from one corner. A couple, probably somewhere in their sixties, were seated at a card table. The woman had impossible pink-coloured hair, and wore a floaty dress as varied as an artist's palette, with several strings of crystal beads. She'd tied an orange bandeau around her forehead which made the top part of her look like a wilted tennis player. She smiled, showing a smear of cherry-red lipstick on protruding teeth.

Maybe she's a vampire. Jay suppressed a giggle.

'I'm Jay. Jay Reece.' She held out her hand.

'Seraphina Smith,' the woman announced, remaining seated. Her hand was covered in rings. The voice was forceful and croaky. '*Was* Davenport until I got married.' She threw an accusing look at her husband who pretended not to notice. 'This is my husband, Ronald.'

Ronald stood up and gave her a loose handshake. He was several inches shorter than his wife, with bulging eyes that reminded Jay of a lizard, and one section of his hair was long enough for him to do an amazing comb-over. Who was he kidding? She smiled hello, hoping she'd be around to see what happened to his hairstyle on a windy deck.

All five turned as a heavily-built older man ambled in.

'Evening...well, I s'pose it's evening,' he said, looking at his watch. 'Won't be long before the G and Ts turn up, no doubt.'

'I hope you're joking.' Dan looked at him meaningfully. 'And by the way, no one's allowed in this room unless invited by one of the officers. Nor are you allowed to mix with the crew or officers in the dining room. They each have their own table.' The older man rolled his eyes, but Dan didn't appear to notice.

'Trevor Manning.' He held out his hand to each individual, and Jay could tell he wasn't taking in anyone else's name as he slid from one person to the next, repeating his own. As he grasped her hand, she looked straight at him, taking in the receding grey hair, the curls thinning out well below his ears. The pale-blue eyes, darted with red money spiders, were topped by bushy grey eyebrows, and a matching moustache twitched over petulant lips. His stomach, which had taken the brunt of good living, hung low. This was one man she'd definitely avoid, though with so few passengers it wouldn't be easy. He squeezed her hand, cutting into her grandmother's garnet ring, and winked.

She gave him a frosty smile. 'Jay Reece. Nice to meet you.' She pulled her hand away. So this was the group. There was only one more passenger to meet, so Dan had said. She wondered idly if he was the same one Petra had hinted at.

By the time Dan had given the party a quick tour round the ship, Jay was completely disorientated. Two flights below they'd seen the officers' restaurant where the passengers also ate, and the fitness room, again shared with the crew. Then back into the lift and down to the bowels of the ship they saw the laundry room and a cloudy swimming pool surrounded by cracked yellow tiles. It was no bigger than a child's paddling pool, Jay thought, disappointed. From there, they took the lift all the way to the top. Dan pointed out a door to the bridge ('strictly prohibited to passengers unless invited,' he told them), and above that the monkey deck, the highest point you could go.

'Don't forget,' Dan said, 'dinner's at 18.30, and just to remind everyone, the latest we sail is 20.00 hours…but don't set your watch by it as they're still loading.'

'What's our cargo?' Trevor Manning demanded, raking stubby fingers through his scant curls.

'You name it, we're carrying it,' Dan replied. 'Right now you've just got time to freshen up.'

'How about a G and T first?' persisted Trevor Manning. Another rake through.

'The Captain will invite you to the bar on some days, but there's too much going on at the moment. We're serving wine with this evening's meal, so I'm sure you can hold off until then.'

Trevor Manning's face reddened. 'It's the least we could have on the first day – a pre-dinner drink. I think I'll go and check the lie of the land.' He snorted at his little joke and tottered off.

Dan gazed after him, and Jay saw he was frowning.

Dinner at half-past six in the officers' dining room was a sombre affair considering it was the beginning of the trip, and Jay wondered if it was because Russians weren't really noted for their humour – not that she knew any personally. Even Trevor Manning, Jay was amused to see, was quiet, though that was probably because he had somehow managed to secure himself a tumbler of gin and tonic.

Three of the officers were already sitting at a separate table by the time Jay and Petra walked in, and although they all stood up and solemnly shook hands, Jay was acutely aware of her own isolation. Why hadn't she opted to fly? Why had she been so determined to go on a banana boat, as Lydia called it? Was it just to be different from everyone else? Well, if she felt lonely after only a few hours, how was she going to feel for the next month? It had been a stupid mistake. At that moment Petra, who had taken a seat at the far end of the table, sent her a beaming smile which immediately warmed her. Of course she'd get to know her fellow passengers. Of course she wouldn't be left on her own. Jay picked up her glass of water for something to do while she waited for her meal.

The chef had produced a more than satisfactory first-night dinner of Russian salad, steak, sautéed potatoes and courgettes, followed by fresh fruit salad. Jay watched Trevor Manning, who sat opposite, taking full advantage of the complimentary wine, not appearing to worry if one of the two attractive Russian stewardesses offered him red or white, but simply nodding at either bottle.

Jay's eyes strayed to Seraphina and Ronald as they faced each other across the table. Seraphina was dominating the conversation, sounding perfectly at ease, but Ronald's expression was weary as though he'd heard it all before. He carried on eating, putting his knife and fork down after every mouthful, offering his wife only monosyllabic replies.

Jay smothered a yawn. It had been a long day. She caught Ronald's eye. She had a bet with herself that if she spoke to him, Seraphina would answer.

'Have you and your wife been on a cargo ship before, Ronald?'

Ronald jumped as though surprised at being addressed, but to Jay's astonishment he answered.

'No. This was our daughter's madcap idea. She thought her mother should do something different. Seph's been all over the world, haven't you, dear? But never on one of these.'

'Do you think you'll like it?' Jay asked him.

'I don't hold too much store by holidays,' Ronald continued, appearing to enjoy some unexpected attention. 'Pottering around in the garden's more my idea of a holiday. But Seph's in her act. She adores it.' He beamed at his wife. Seph rolled her eyes and gave an exaggerated shake of her pink head.

Jay looked at her watch. Twenty-five-past seven. They were supposed to leave at eight. So where was the missing passenger?

7

Jack

Jack looked at his watch for what must have been the twentieth time in as many minutes and swore. If the traffic didn't move soon they'd leave without him. He'd cut the timing fine before he'd even started out this morning because of Isobella's unexpected and bloody annoying phone call, and made little allowance for anything unforeseen. Like this traffic accident.

They were just about to come off the motorway when it happened. Some crazy woman had been yakking on her mobile instead of concentrating on the road, must have realised she was in the wrong lane and swung over to the left with no signal, causing three cars behind her to pile up. Bloody woman had carried right on driving. Well, if the helicopters were doing their job there was a chance she'd be nicked. He rolled down the car window and poked his head out, craning his neck up at the sky, half hoping to see one already hovering.

Using his common sense the taxi driver had been travelling several cars behind. He'd been keeping a safe distance the whole journey so they'd avoided ploughing into the car in front, and no one had bumped them from behind.

'I'm pulling over, mate, just to see if there's anything I can do, or if I can phone anyone,' the driver said as he guided the taxi onto the shoulder. It was dangerous so near the junction, Jack thought, but realised it couldn't be helped.

'I'll take a look, too.' Jack opened the rear door.

The road was slick from rain which had started in the morning and showed little sign of abating, but few drivers were slowing down. Half of them hadn't even got their lights on. He looked carefully to make sure he had plenty of space to step into the road, and sprinted to where a small group had gathered.

'We've already called an ambulance,' a short stocky man told him. 'Dippy woman. Typical. Always doing their lipstick and on their mobiles.' His lip curled. 'I hope she gets done for this.'

'Is anyone seriously hurt?'

'No telling, but these two probably got it worst…they were directly behind her.' He glanced at Jack. 'D'ya want a dekko?' Without waiting for an answer the man stepped to one side.

'I have first-aid training,' Jack said.

He rushed back to the taxi and yanked out his briefcase where he kept a first-aid kit. Running back to the group he knelt down by two injured people who had been covered by raincoats. Just as well. He glanced up at the sky. Thank God the rain was letting up. He hoped the worst would keep off until the ambulance arrived.

The two women were bleeding; one woman from the head. She was whimpering with fright.

'Don't worry,' Jack told her as he pressed a piece of gauze firmly on the spot. 'It's just a nasty graze. I doubt you'll even need stitches.'

He peered under the blanket of the younger woman and saw that her leg was sticking out at the wrong angle. She was unconscious and was going to need attention.

'Better leave her until the ambulance arrives,' he said to the rest of the group, who only had superficial cuts and bruises. 'I don't want to do any further damage.'

By the time the ambulance arrived and had got the two women safely inside they'd lost nearly an hour. Jack groaned inwardly. If the ship sailed on time he wasn't going to make it.

He glanced at the spot where the accident had happened. Blood on the grey tarmac road had mixed with the rain, making scarlet rivulets. If it wasn't so horrible the effect was quite artistic.

8

On board the Alexandria

The dining room door opened and a man paused in the doorway. Jay looked up.

He reminded her of a detective about to make his dénouement. He panned the room, caught Jay's eye for more than a split second, then made his way over to Petra. She noticed he had a slight limp. So this must be Petra's 'company', she thought.

'Hi, sweetie,' he said, as Petra scrambled up. 'Sorry I'm late.' He kissed her on both cheeks.

Sweetie? Didn't Petra have a fiancé?

'Jack!' Petra let out a peal of laughter. 'I wondered if you'd make it.'

'I nearly didn't. There was a last-minute problem.'

Jack, whoever he was, had a light Australian accent. He was tall, dark and…well, not handsome, but when he turned she could see he was definitely arresting. There was a shadow along his jaw. In his late thirties, Jay guessed. The bright-blue shirt enhanced the breadth of his shoulders. Especially chosen to bring out the colour of his eyes, no doubt. Jay pulled her gaze away, trying to quell the flash of irritation. She concentrated on her fruit salad but she couldn't help sneaking another glance. Faded jeans ended in enormous, thick rubber-soled shoes.

The evening had suddenly become more interesting. Who was he to Petra? Friend? Lover? If a lover, what about the fiancé? The newcomer introduced himself to the others, leaving her till last.

'G'd evening. Jack Delaney's the name.'

She looked up at him. His eyes weren't blue after all. They were hazel under dark quizzical eyebrows. He had a strong nose and well-defined lips. Then he grinned, showing even teeth. She was aware of the warmth of his fingers as they shook hands, the warmth spreading up her wrists and arms. She hadn't met such an attractive man in years.

'Juliet Reece.'

'Ju-li-et.' He rolled his tongue around her name as though tasting a fine wine and gazed down at her, still holding her hand. She wondered what on earth he was thinking. Just as she was about to speak he let go of her hand, then suddenly threw back his head and roared with laughter.

'What's so funny?'

'Some other time,' he said, and sauntered over to the officers' table, still chuckling.

Jay was furious, mainly with herself. Why had she told him her real name? She hated the name Juliet. Never used it except for business. But why had he found it so funny? Flustered, she ignored Trevor Manning who bent towards her, opening his mouth, and instead pretended to look round the room for one of the stewards. Out of the corner of her eye she noticed the three officers get up and shake hands with the newcomer, and one clapped him on the shoulder. She forced herself to look indifferent as she flicked her eyes over to where he stood, his back now towards her. *He has a nicely shaped head, though his ears stick out just a tiny bit.* She was glad to find fault with him. How dare he laugh at her name? But in spite of herself she couldn't help noticing the way his jeans stretched across a most enticing...

Stop it!

She was grateful when Seraphina, sitting on her right, asked where she was headed. At least she didn't have to watch this Jack Delaney walk back to the end of their table and take a seat beside

Petra. Immediately, Tatyana, one of the stewardesses, fluttered over, bringing him a bowl of soup without asking what he preferred. Jay tried hard to listen to their conversation.

'Now, my dear,' Trevor raised his eyes as he shovelled a forkful of Russian salad in the direction of his mouth, 'why are you here? Travelled on one of these things before?'

Jay was reluctant to give him any background as to her reasons for making this journey but politeness won. 'My grandparents emigrated to Australia. I'd just like to see where they were.'

'Fascinating,' Trevor murmured. A dribble of mayonnaise escaped down his chin.

'And you?' She tried to tell herself it was the mayonnaise on Trevor's chin which made her want to avert her eyes and stare at Jack Delaney.

'That's a good one.' Trevor put his fork down, swallowed, and leaned back. To Jay's relief he wiped his mouth with his paper napkin, inspected the result, then crumpled it up and threw it on the table. 'No ties now...wife died...she wasn't keen on flying...been on some cruises...well, my wife and I...they were our holidays... but now she's gone, I thought...must watch the weight,' he patted his paunch lovingly, 'and it's too tempting on the cruise ships. Fed every couple of hours, y' know. Just like a newborn baby, ha ha.' He snorted.

'Where are you going?' Jay asked, praying he was on a short hop.

'New Zealand, to see friends, but stopping off at Melbourne. My mother's in a nursing home there.'

So that prayer won't be coming true, Jay thought grimly.

'Excuse me, am I interrupting?'

Jay turned and found Jack Delaney's amused hazel eyes looking down at her.

'Trevor and I were discussing our destinations.'

'Then may I join you?'

'If you wish.' She kept her voice cool, still smarting.

He grinned.

'You'll have to pull up another chair,' she told him.

But she was glad all the same that she'd changed for supper and worn her best pearl earrings. She shifted her chair to make a space for him which made her jog the glass of wine she was holding. Half the contents spilt over his shirt.

'Oh, I'm so sorry.' God, he'd think her some gauche teenager. She grabbed a napkin and handed it to him. 'At least it's only white.' There was a smear of blood on his sleeve which she didn't think he'd spotted. If he had, she was sure he was the type of man who would have changed his shirt. Idly, she wondered how it had got there. It was such a bright colour it looked recent.

'No worries,' Jack Delaney grinned, not attempting to use the napkin. His eyes crinkled at the corners. 'There'll be plenty more accidents before the trip is over. Just wait till this baby starts rocking.' He laughed at her expression. 'Is this your first time?' he drawled, making the question sound as though she were a virgin and they were about to embark on her first sexual experience.

He's doing it on purpose.

She felt Trevor Manning's eyes on her. She kept her tone even.

'Yes, it is. Normally I'd have flown but I've been given a reprieve at home so I've got plenty of time to get to Australia.'

'Sydney?'

'I hope to.' She couldn't stop the faint tremor in her voice. 'But Melbourne first.'

'D'ya have a particular reason?' Jack turned his body towards hers, casually sliding one arm along the back of her chair. His other arm rested on the table.

'I want to look up some family history.'

'Seems to be the fashion these days. What period?'

'My grandparents went to Australia in 1913. My dad was born in Melbourne. They'd intended to emigrate but were only out there for a few years. Pop loved it but my grandmother pined for home and her family, so they returned to England.'

'Tough,' remarked Jack. 'Tough on your grandfather if he wanted to stay in Australia.'

She'd never thought of it from Pop's side. She'd always felt sorry for Nannie being forced to live her husband's dream. Irrationally her annoyance flared.

'Trust a man to stick up for another – even one he's never met.'

'Seems we need to where you sheilas are concerned,' Jack grinned. He had a crooked lower tooth.

'Your steak, Jack…just as you like it.'

He glanced up. 'You're looking very lovely this evening, Tatyana.'

Jay watched Tatyana closely. The girl took her time to arrange his napkin. There was something going on between them, Jay was certain.

'Do you know the name of the ship?'

She came to with a jolt. What was he saying?

'The ship they went out on,' Jack prompted. 'It'd make it easier if you knew her name.'

'Oh, it was the *Orsova*.'

Letter dated 4th September 1913, on board the *Orsova*

My dear Dad, Ruby and Ethel,

This will be the first letter you receive from me and I hope it reaches you safely. Everything happened so quickly at the end. I was in a daze by the time Ferguson said it was time for us to board the ship. I watched and waved until you were all little specks and then we were called to put our baggage into the cabin which I share with four other girls and a large middle-aged lady. It's very small. No space to hang anything, but everyone seems pleasant. Ferguson was separated from me right from the start, even though we're married, but we will have the opportunity to see one another during the day, I'm told.

The food is not as good as Mrs Jenner's or mine, but I mustn't grumble. We don't go hungry. So far the sea is calm but I'm not sure I will be a good sailor if it gets rough. You will be surprised to know I've already made a friend. Her name is Adele. She doesn't share our cabin but I've sat near her at mealtimes. She's a few years older than me but I like her. So would you, Ruby. She's a bit unusual.

This is all for now. I'll write more whenever I get a chance.

I'm thinking of you all the time and wish you were here with me, going to a new life.

Your loving daughter and sister,

Annie

'You could make a start at the Maritime Museum in Melbourne,' Jack continued. 'It's a good one, though I haven't been for years.' He cut off a piece of meat and gave her a sideways glance. 'I'd be glad to take you...that is, if you'd like.'

Before Jay could reply, Trevor cut in. '*I'm* interested in history and ships...love 'em. Mind if I join you? We could set a date right now.'

Over my dead body.

'I imagine Juliet—'

'Please call me Jay.'

'Jay?' Jack frowned. 'Why would I call you Jay?'

'That's what I've always been known as. And anyway, the name Juliet seems to be a big joke with you.'

Jack looked puzzled, then laughed and said, 'Oh, that. I told you I'd tell you later. And I will. I always keep my promises.' His eyes danced. 'But you're definitely Juliet...it's a beautiful name. You don't really mind, do you?' he added softly, letting his hand fall to her bare arm which immediately crawled with goosebumps. She

73

prayed he wasn't aware of them. If he was he'd laugh at her even more. He obviously loved flirting. 'I was saying,' he said, raising his voice a little as he turned to face Trevor, 'Juliet will need to settle in for a few days before she makes any plans.'

'Understood. I'll write my mobile number down for you both after dinner. Jay and I are going to get on well together, aren't we, m'dear?' Trevor beamed as though they already had an understanding.

'I don't have much time for socialising, Trevor,' Jay replied in the tone she used when dealing with difficult clients. 'I'm not here for a holiday. In fact, I'm writing a book.'

It was the first thing that popped into her mind as an excuse to avoid any shipboard time-wasting with Trevor Manning. Out of the corner of her eye she saw Jack's disbelieving smile.

'My dear, how thrilling. Calls for a toast.' Trevor waggled his stubby fingers in the air to grab the attention of the other stewardess. 'Champagne, I think. And none of your cheap Russian rubbish either.'

'Oh, please don't,' Jay said, embarrassed enough that he was going to make a toast to her outright lie, but more so because of his derogatory remark about Russian champagne in front of the Russian girl.

Thankfully Lena looked unperturbed. 'Will Brut suit you, sir?'

'Brut it will be.' Trevor glanced round the table. 'Better make it two bottles, m'dear.'

Lena made a ritual of opening the champagne, then carefully poured the same amount into each glass and placed them round the table.

Jay was able to block Trevor's ruddy face out of sight by tipping her glass, but the bubbles caught in her throat and she spluttered as some of the liquid frothed down her new white top.

Jack Delaney looked highly amused. 'That's the second time you've spilt your drink tonight, Juliet.'

'Thanks for pointing it out to me.'

'No worries.'

'I'm not drunk or anything.' She wiped furiously at herself with her napkin, annoyed that she'd risen to his teasing.

'Course you're not...well, not totally,' he smirked, as he took the napkin from her. 'Here...let me.'

She gave a sudden intake of breath as he began to dab her chest. What an infuriating man.

'So what's the book called?' Jack's face was close to hers as he raised one dark eyebrow, the linen cloth still in his hand. She noticed his nose was slightly hooked, rather like an idealised Roman emperor. And his eyes weren't just hazel – they were flecked with gold.

'Oh, I haven't got a title for it yet,' she stuttered, willing him not to pursue the subject.

'What sort of book is it?'

'It's a novel.' She looked at him, certain he knew she wasn't really writing a book.

He winked. Oh yes, he knew all right.

9

Jay was in bed just after ten o'clock. She'd tried to keep awake so she was there for 'take-off', but exhaustion finally overcame her. Everything felt strange: her head on an unfamiliar pillow, the heavy metal covers over the portholes creating near blackout, and the relentless hum of the air-conditioning. She guessed she would get used to the noise but at the moment it was intrusive. Earlier, she'd turned it down, but twenty minutes later she was uncomfortably hot and was forced to switch it back up.

They still hadn't set sail. Dan said these delays were normal but she was impatient to begin her journey. Once again she thought how lucky she was to have time away from the business. If this was what they meant by being out of your comfort zone she was all for it. She refused to think Jack Delaney was partly responsible for her excitement and turned over to block him out. Safer to think about her grandparents.

She remembered Nannie saying that even though you were married, women were segregated from the men. What must Nannie have felt as she lay there on a narrow bunk, sharing the cabin with women she'd never set eyes on before? Jay imagined them all talking at once; some laughing, innocent of what lay before them, others crying with homesickness. But Nannie would never have let her emotions show with strangers. Jay smiled in the dark. She could almost see her calm, neat grandmother, young and newly married, wishing she could be near her husband instead of a bunch of other unknown women.

There'd been a smallpox outbreak, Jay remembered, and hadn't Nannie said she'd helped in the hospital because the nurses hadn't been vaccinated or something? All the time she'd had to cope with seasickness, because there were probably no stabilisers in those days, Jay thought. Not that cargo ships had any, but at least the weight of the cargo was supposed to keep them steady, or so Travelfreight Paul had assured her.

Jay wondered what *she'd* be like if there was a bad storm. Her travelling until now had mostly been by air.

She pictured her room where she'd hung her grandparents' two paintings of the *Orsova*. It was easy enough to visualise the pictures themselves but Kingston-upon-Thames felt light years away, even though she'd left her apartment only hours ago and they were still on the English coast.

Her ears pricked up. The ship's engines had been running for two hours. Naively, she'd thought at first they would be away within minutes and had set up a chair ready to watch the action from one of the portholes. Half an hour later still nothing had happened. But now, the engines began to roar and she felt the vibration surge through her body. Heart racing she slid out of bed, reached for her dressing gown and climbed on the sofa to see what was happening. The *Alexandria* was finally on the move. Peering through the grubby porthole she saw they were crawling out of the dock, slipping past a row of container ships, draped in a string of lights. The scene satisfied the romantic streak in her and she couldn't stop smiling.

A shame, though, she was on her own. Then a thought struck her. There was a bottle of Krug in the fridge. If this wasn't the time to celebrate…

She switched on the radio, tuning it to some light classical music, and popped the cork. She had just drained a small glass – pity whoever had stocked her larder hadn't thought of flutes – when there was a soft tap at the door.

'Who is it?'

But she knew.

'It's Jack. Are you up?'

She unlocked the door, her heart beating harder than it should have, to find him leaning against the doorframe with a bottle of champagne – only his bottle was full-sized.

'Thought you might like a bit of company on your first trip,' Jack grinned. 'I've brought some bubbly to celebrate we're on the move at last.'

'Where's Petra?' Jay asked to hide her confusion.

'Petra?' He shrugged. 'She said she was exhausted and going to bed. Didn't care about seeing the ship pull out. But I had a feeling you might be waiting up for the big moment.'

He was right, damn him.

She held up her empty glass.

'I see you have a head start.' His smile was wicked, his teeth gleaming. 'Shall I come in and catch you up?'

'I don't know about catching me up – I've only had one.' She desperately tried to act nonchalant though she could feel her face begin to flush. 'Well, don't just stand there or my reputation will be ruined.'

'On the consumption of alcohol or because there's a man lurking outside your cabin?' Jack raised a dark eyebrow.

'Both.'

He stepped inside. She walked in front, aware of the swish of her cream silk dressing gown skimming over her figure, and was half glad, half sorry she was wearing pyjamas underneath. God, he really was too attractive for words. Trying to hide her confusion she busied herself setting the two bottles, her glass, and another for Jack, on a tray.

'Here, let me take that.' Jack took the tray from her hands, his warm breath falling lightly on her neck, and placed it on the coffee table, then parked himself on the sofa.

'How come I was only given half a bottle?' Jay pretended to

grumble, acutely aware of the heat of his breath spreading up to her face.

'Probably because they knew it was going to be occupied by a woman,' Jack grinned.

'That's a typical remark...' She stopped. 'No, I'm not going to fall for a wind-up.'

'Shame.' He grinned more broadly and began to unwrap the seal of the new bottle. Fascinated, she watched his narrow strong fingers, almost like a pianist's, the fine dark hairs showing between his wrist and the cuff of his shirt.

'No, don't open it,' she managed to say. 'Have the rest of mine. I can't drink any more, I'm so worn out.'

Oh, God...how old did that sound?

And where was she supposed to sit? No way was she going to rush to join him like some infatuated teenager. She needed to take control of the situation. Act blasé, as though sipping champagne with a gorgeous man on board a ship was something she did every day.

'Come and sit with me.' Jack seemed to have read her thoughts as he patted the cushion. 'I promise I won't bite...unless of course you want me to.'

What she wanted to do was to knock the smug look from his face. Tomorrow morning she would think of a pithy reply.

'Juliet?'

She stood, hesitating, then blurted, 'I've told you, it's not Juliet. I'm always known as Jay. But I want to know what you found so funny when I told you my real name.' She threw him a furious look which only made him laugh. 'You promised to tell me later. Well, later is *now*.'

'Okay. First of all you introduced yourself to me as Juliet and that's what I shall continue to call you.' He beckoned again. 'Come on, Juliet, don't be mad. I'm sorry I laughed when you first told me your name but I suddenly remembered "Juliet" is one of the maritime signals. It means: "I'm on fire and have dangerous cargo;

keep clear."' He chuckled. '*Are* you dangerous? *Should* I keep clear?'

He really was maddening but his laugh was infectious and she couldn't help smiling. She decided to play his game.

'I'm not on fire...yet,' she emphasised the last word as she ran her fingers along the side of her neck, flicking out her hair in a provocative manner, 'but when I am...' she lowered her voice and put on an even stronger accent than Marlene Dietrich ever knew, 'I'm *verrry* dangerous.'

'Mmm, I like it.' Jack's lips curved into a grin. 'So are you going to offer me that drink you promised?' He nodded towards the coffee table.

Swaying a little she walked towards him. Was she already tipsy or was it the motion of the ship? Jack stretched his arms out to steady her, and all at once her irritation vanished and a huge grin spread across her face as she half fell onto the sofa beside him.

'I don't seem to have my sea legs yet,' she said, as he tipped the remains of her half bottle in her glass. His lightest of movements made her conscious of thigh brushing thigh.

'I'll get my bottle.' He rose up and she watched him as he eased off the cork, making a loud pop. He filled his glass and came back to sit beside her.

'Cheers.' Jack clinked his glass with hers as he turned to face her, still smiling. 'Or what do you Poms say? Bottoms up? Always sounds a bit rude to me.'

She flushed. 'Cheers will do.'

'So tell me more about this mission of yours.'

'There's not much to tell. I want to find out about my grandparents – what happened after they landed in Melbourne. They were servants at two of the grandest houses in Norfolk but Pop wanted to travel. They worked in the same house in Melbourne.' She paused for breath. 'Trouble is, I can't remember the name... but I'd love to find it. It'll come to me in the middle of the night, I expect.'

He grinned and she flushed again. She needed to choose her words more carefully.

'Go on.'

'My grandmother used to tell me stories about Melbourne, but I was only a teenager when she died...' Jay felt her eyes begin to sting, 'so I've forgotten a lot of it.'

Jack caught hold of her hand and gently squeezed it. 'What's the matter, Juliet?'

'Nothing...'

Why did he think something was wrong?

'Has someone given you a hard time?' His eyes scanned her face. She didn't answer. 'Do you want to talk about it?' he said quietly.

She swallowed hard. 'No. It's just something I need to find out.'

'In Oz?'

She nodded, strangely comforted by the touch of his hand.

'Sometimes it's dangerous to uncover the past,' he muttered, his eyes staring at the floor.

How had he guessed it was anything to do with her past? Or was he still teasing her? No, he sounded dead serious. What was he on about? She looked at the way his hair waved slightly at the nape of his neck. It was just a little too long but it suited him.

'I shouldn't think they had anything to hide. My grandmother was very straight-laced.' She knew she sounded defensive for no reason.

'That's only how you saw her when she was an old lady.' Jack's tone was cheerful again as he regarded her. 'She might have been a little goer for all you know. The Sydney Stripper.' His mouth quirked.

'I hardly think so.' Jay's voice became as cool as the iced champagne. She glanced at Jack. 'They didn't go to Sydney for one thing.'

How thick his hair is. The darkest chestnut. Beautiful hair. She had a mad urge to run her hands through it.

'Now I've annoyed you.' Jack touched her arm, making her jump. 'I'm sorry.'

'That's the second time you've said that this evening and I don't think you're sorry in the least.'

'Yes, I am. I don't want to spoil your first evening.'

'You're not,' she said, suddenly slumping. 'It's me. I seem to have lost my sense of humour today. It's been a long one and when we finally moved it was an anticlimax.'

Jack smirked. 'That's not what they usually say.'

'I fell into that, didn't I?' She couldn't stop the heat rising to the roots of her hair.

'Yep. But I'm prepared to take a rain check.' He laughed. 'Relax.' He touched her arm again and her skin tingled underneath the thin silk. 'Tell me what you do when you're at home.'

'I run my own business.'

Jack raised an eyebrow. 'Doing what?'

'Selling other people's businesses when they want to retire or change career or, too often, when they're going down the pan.'

'Sounds like hard work. And bucketloads of stress.'

'That's why I took a chance to have a few months away.'

'Who's looking after it?'

'A woman whose business I sold. She wanted to retire but found she was having withdrawal symptoms. She offered to take over so I could go to Australia.'

'Good God. That's quite something.' He raised his glass to his lips and swallowed. 'You must really trust her.'

'I do.' Jay bit the inside of her mouth. 'Implicitly.'

'That's great.'

He glanced down at her hands. She followed his gaze. She had long since removed her wedding ring and exchanged it for her grandmother's engagement ring. A silence hung between them. After a few moments Jack took her left hand in his and studied the ring. The garnets glowed softly in their flowerlike setting.

'What about the man in your life?' he pressed. 'Why isn't he with you on this trip?'

'I'm recently divorced. But Gerrard wouldn't have come anyway. He's got no interest in Australia and definitely wouldn't have gone on a rusty freighter.'

'Well, you'll certainly have enough free time here to finish that novel of yours.'

'You know perfectly well I'm not writing a novel.' Jay couldn't help laughing. 'I just had to say something to Trevor to shut him up.' She glanced at Jack. 'I just don't want to encourage him, that's all.'

'He's harmless enough. But we don't want him with us when we go walkabout in Melbourne – that is, if you insist on unearthing dark family secrets.'

'He can certainly put the booze away,' Jay said, trying to ignore a frisson of excitement at the thought of sightseeing with Jack. 'No, I definitely don't want him hanging around.'

'I'm sure we can give him the slip.'

Was she reading too much into his remarks? She realised she knew nothing at all about Jack Delaney. Where did Petra fit in, for example? He was the one asking all the questions. She hadn't had a chance to ask any of her own. He was undoubtedly a smooth operator, but although they'd met only a few hours ago it seemed as though she'd known him much longer. With a trembling hand she swallowed the last mouthful of champagne and set the empty glass on the coffee table. Immediately he began to fill it but she waved her hand at the halfway point.

'No more,' she smiled. 'But don't let me stop *you*.'

'One more and that's it. I don't want to drink alone. Might be tempted to go through the rest of the bottle. Now, where were we?'

'It's my turn to ask questions. So what do *you* do?'

'Me? I'm a training captain for Qantas.'

'Not a *real* pilot then,' Jay teased.

Jack narrowed his eyes and looked away.

Oh, God, what have I said?

Instinctively she added, 'Don't you get free flights everywhere?'

'Mmm.' Jack's eyes returned to her and travelled down to her cleavage.

What did that mean? Yes, he did get free flights or was he letching after her body? She should be so lucky. She hid a smile.

'Then why do you take the long route?' She must keep matter of fact.

'Bit of a busman's holiday if I fly. I'd accrued some leave so thought I'd travel this way. It's not the first time by any means – I've been all over the world on freighters and cargo ships and know half the crews and most of the captains.'

'And Tatyana.'

'Oh, yes, Tatyana and I are old friends.'

'You know she fancies you rotten?'

Oh, why did she blurt that? He'd think she was jealous.

Jack chuckled. 'She always falls for someone. Usually, it's the captain, even if he looks like the back end of one of his freighters. No, Tatyana and I are just good friends.' He made the cliché sound fresh and natural.

'That's nice.' Her tone belied the words. Jack looked at her and raised a mocking eyebrow. 'Petra's a lovely girl, isn't she?' Jay persisted, without being able to help herself.

'Yes, she's adorable.'

She tried again. 'Have you met her fiancé?'

A shadow passed across Jack's face. There was a silence and Jay began to feel uneasy for the second time. What had she said now?

Finally Jack answered, but he didn't look at her. 'No. But they say he's a nice guy. He's a dentist.' He paused again as though trying to work something out and she felt the atmosphere imperceptibly change between them. The cosy teasing had disappeared. Without warning he rose to his feet. 'Look, Juliet, do you mind if we call it a day? It's been a long one and you're tired. I am too.'

Excuse me. I wasn't the one who came knocking at your door.

Suddenly he didn't appeal quite so much. She pretended to yawn and stood up. 'You're right. I *am* tired, and the champagne's made me even more sleepy.'

'Right. See you tomorrow then. Hey...steady...'

The ship tilted. Jay lost her balance and only just managed to grab the back of the sofa with one hand while Jack caught her other arm. Being flung against his body would have looked so embarrassingly obvious, but when she looked at him he was grinning like a cat.

'I believe you, though thousands wouldn't,' he said, irritatingly, holding on to her arm. He looked straight at her, his eyes gleaming. 'Or did you by any chance throw yourself at me on purpose?'

'In your dreams.' She managed to keep her face neutral.

For one glorious second he looked disconcerted. Then he laughed and let go of her arm. 'Night, Juliet. Thanks for the company.'

With a swift peck on her cheek he was gone, and the room returned to normal.

10

Jay hadn't been entirely truthful when she'd told Jack she was sleepy. Tired, yes, but she was too wound up to drift off, although the ship had settled to a steady vibrating rhythm. But even the drone of the engine failed to lull her. She blamed the mattress which wasn't as yielding as her one at home. In the end she gave up and decided to read. She switched on the bedside light and pulled a face at her travel clock. Two-twenty. She twisted over the side and groped around for her book and read until her eyelids drooped.

She awoke to the telephone ringing. It was Dan. 'Good morning, Ms Reece. It's gone eight, and breakfast is cleared away at eight-thirty.'

'Oh, no.' Jay automatically checked the time. 'I forgot to put my clock on. I'll be down in five minutes. Thanks for calling me.'

She splashed her face, ran her fingers through her hair, which she hoped looked tousled rather than having just climbed out of bed, and pulled on jeans and a sweater. A slick of lipstick and she'd have to do. By the time she arrived the chairs had already been pushed back under the tables with military precision. Jack was seated at the remaining empty table and had finished his breakfast.

'G'day, Juliet.' He saluted her with his coffee cup and grinned. 'Sleep well?'

'Like a top.' She wasn't going to let him know any different. 'Have the others been down?'

'No one yet.' Jack gestured for her to sit beside him.

'Morning, all.' Trevor Manning blustered into the room.

'Spoke too soon,' Jack murmured. 'G'day, Trevor.'

'Don't know if it's a good one or not. Where is everyone?'

'You'll have to make do with us, I'm afraid,' Jack smiled. 'Lena will be here in a moment. She's gone to get some more coffee, but the breakfast buffet's over there.' He pointed. 'Just help yourself.'

Trevor glanced across at the various packets of cereal, tubs of yoghurt, and bowl of fresh fruit, somewhat haphazardly displayed on a white tablecloth.

'I can't be doing with all that muck,' he said, pulling a face.

He looked as though he'd dressed in the dark, having dragged on a saggy fawn-and-green striped jumper, which only served to enhance the size of his paunch, over the top of a red and black checked shirt. The blotch of dried-up food looked like a permanent fixture. He ran his hand through his curls which didn't quite spring back to their original position. Jay guessed he'd also been woken up by Dan and it showed, whereas Jack looked fresh and...well...sexy was the only way to describe him.

'Bacon and eggs is what I'm after. If they do them, that is.' Trevor sounded doubtful, but cheered up as Lena came back.

'Ms Reece, what can I get you?'

'Just toast, please.'

'You need more than that.' Trevor scrutinised her. 'No wonder you're skin and bones if that's how you eat.'

'Why, Mr Manning,' Jay did a mock Southern drawl, 'that's the sweetest compliment I've had in a long time.' She was gratified to see Jack's lazy smile, but it was lost on Trevor.

'Trevor, *please*. Can't be doing with formalities when we're all thrown together like this, what?'

Petra breezed in, looking delightful in a swishy pale-blue skirt and matching T-shirt, just as Dan set a fresh pot of coffee on the table.

'Morning, everyone. Jack, darling, where were you last night?

I knocked on your door and there was no answer.' She plopped down next to Trevor who beamed, then lifted her delicate features to the steward. 'Dan, don't clear my plate away, there's a love. I'm ravenous.'

'Yes, you sit by me, m'dear,' Trevor said, handing her a paper napkin.

'Mealtimes are to be strictly adhered to,' Dan warned, 'but I'll forgive you as it's your first day. Do you want cooked?'

Petra nodded. 'Wicked. But no bacon or sausages, and no—'

'What about a poached egg on toast.' Dan's voice was a touch impatient. 'Will that do?'

'Cool.'

'And for you, Mr Manning?'

'I'm trying to order bacon and eggs. With fried bread.' Trevor looked even more doubtful.

'Sorry, not possible. You need to be down much earlier for the full cooked. I'll get Chef to make you a couple of poached eggs – same as Petra.'

Trevor rolled his eyes but Dan took no notice and disappeared.

'So,' Petra said, looking at Jack, 'where were you?'

Jay held her breath.

'I took a turn round the ship.'

'You should've asked me to go with you,' Petra pouted.

'I thought you'd be knocked out. You said you were taking a pill.'

'It didn't work…it was so loud in my room. I couldn't work out all the sounds…plus the bed was shaking.' She laughed. 'I guess I'll get used to it.'

'You will,' Jack assured her. 'And you'll find when you get home you won't be able to sleep in a normal bed.'

'Whether you slept or not, you look lovely,' Jay said. 'Just like a model.'

'Maybe 'cos I *am* one.' Petra's smile broadened. 'That's why it's important I get my beauty sleep.' She whipped out a mirror, grimaced into it, and shoved it back in her bag.

'A model, you say.' Trevor patted his curls as he studied her. 'Well, I never.'

'Have you just been on an assignment in England?' Jay asked.

Petra nodded. 'I had a booking in London but I dreaded all those hours flying home. So because I had time I decided to go home by boat. Jack said he was going home on a cargo ship.' She smiled flirtatiously at Jack. 'It sounded cool. But it takes a while to get used to the motion.'

'You'll soon find your sea legs, sweetie,' Jack said. 'And you know where I am if you need me.'

Jay tried to ignore the flicker of jealousy.

'Anyone seen Mr and Mrs Smith?' Dan asked, as he brought some toast over.

'No,' Petra said. 'I haven't seen them, and their room's right next to mine. P'r'aps they're having an extra kip...or making mad passionate love.'

'Somehow Ronald doesn't seem the passionate type,' Jay broke in. 'Anyway, if you'll excuse me...' she got up and looked pointedly at Jack, 'I had an interesting dream last night which should fit perfectly in my next chapter.'

Three long days at sea before they reached Hamburg, the first stop. Jay had never spent so much time doing so little. She'd finished one of her books, she'd completed the jigsaw puzzle of Hatherleigh Hall, she'd made half a dozen greetings cards, she'd jotted down some notes in her diary, and she'd been called to the ship's office to be photographed for her ID. In desperation she decided to do some laundry. She took the lift and bumped into Ronald who was coming out of the gym.

'I keep meaning to have a go but I'm not familiar with the machines,' she told him. 'They're a bit scary.'

'I'll be glad to show you...anytime.' Beads of sweat had gathered on his forehead and above his lips. 'Seph refuses to come anywhere near. Not that she needs to lose weight or anything.' He looked at her and blushed furiously. 'Not that you do either.'

This was one of his longer speeches, and she smiled encouragingly. He pulled himself a little taller. 'Come and join us on our deck tonight. Deck D.' His lizard eyes were alight with enthusiasm. 'We should be arriving in Hamburg about ten tonight, according to the captain.'

'That would be lovely,' Jay said, but even though she felt mean, she knew she would leave her options open.

Jay had watched with the others as they sailed up the Elbe, marvelling how incongruous it seemed for green banks to border both sides of the ship when all they'd been used to was sea and more sea. Jack and Petra had been chatting and laughing together and she noticed at one point he put his arm lightly around her shoulders. She shrugged and moved away before they saw her.

Tonight, she stood on one of the lower decks, breathing in the mild air and taking in the view. She could make out the houses on the edge of the river, their gardens inevitably ending with their own boat moored. Another row or two of houses were perched on the slope behind, giving the lucky owners a view of the busy river. She stood contented for half an hour, until it began to feel cold and a feeling of aloneness cut through her. She realised she was so used to talking to her team, planning her business day, dealing with clients, and all the other jobs; it was strange to have the luxury of having time on her own when she wasn't dog-tired. This was what she'd craved, but now she longed to share the moment.

She decided to go up on the bridge for a better view. Alexei, the Chief Officer, had mellowed since that first time she'd set eyes on him when she'd boarded the *Alexandria,* and had invited her, in his heavily accented English, to come up anytime during his very early morning or late evening shifts, to watch what he called 'action-packed sunrises and sunsets'. When she'd mentioned it to Jack he'd told her she was privileged. Jack had explained the engine was the 'gearbox' of the ship, but the bridge was the brain. Visitors were not usually welcome, he'd added.

She climbed the stairs and was faced with a notice fixed to the door. NO UNAUTHORISED PERSONS ALLOWED. She hesitated. Alexei had definitely invited her. She pushed open the door and at the same instant all the lights pinged out behind her and she was plunged into darkness.

Oh, God, I've fused the whole bloody ship!

Heart thumping madly she stood rooted, waiting for an explosion. Nothing happened. She narrowed her eyes and could just make out from the pinpricks of light on the bank of computer screens five seated silhouettes, their backs to her, faintly murmuring but oblivious of any disturbance. She dared herself to creep towards them.

In the silence, except for the hum of the instruments, Jay knew they must have been aware of her presence as she peered over their shoulders, trying not to breathe, but still no one turned and spoke to her. She drank in the unimpeded view of the smooth dark sheet of water which reflected the profusion of multi-coloured harbour lights. She'd never watched at the front of the ship, or rather the bow, as Dan had corrected her. It would have been pointless with the tower block of cargo, but now she could clearly see over the top of the highest containers as the *Alexandria* slipped into Hamburg harbour. It was like gliding into fairyland.

After a few minutes she backed out as quietly as she'd entered, but before she could turn to navigate the stairs in the blackness, she heard footsteps from behind. A pair of arms slipped round her waist, making her jump.

'G'd evening, Juliet.'

She spun round to face him. Was too close to him in such a small space. Her heartbeat throbbed in her ears. She willed her voice to sound nonchalant.

'Good evening, yourself.'

'You should have waited for me. *I'd* have taken you up on the bridge. Outside, though, where it's more romantic.'

She wished she could see his expression, but she imagined an amused glint in his eyes, knowing he intended to irritate her.

'I don't need romance, thanks very much,' she said cuttingly. She could picture Jack's grin. Blast him. He'd won that round if she didn't change her tone. 'Anyway, I'm happy I've seen it from inside. It's fabulous.' Her eyes shone now with her enthusiasm. 'I never dreamt Hamburg docks could look so beautiful.'

She could feel exactly where his hands had touched her. Smell the V of his bare skin where he'd left two buttons of his shirt undone.

'Come up to the monkey deck with me. It's the highest we can go so we'll get a good view. We should just be in time to see the pilot.'

'Pilot?'

'Every ship has to have a pilot who knows the waters around the port better than the captain,' Jack explained as they climbed the last flight of stairs and he led her over to starboard. He pointed. 'Do you see the little red boat coming towards us?'

Jay squinted in the near dark as she leaned over the rail. 'Oh, yes.' She was aware of his shoulder against hers.

'Look! He's bringing it alongside us.'

Jay watched, fascinated.

'Does he actually steer the ship?'

'Not usually. He mainly acts in an advisory capacity. Except for the Panama Canal. That's tricky, so he has to take complete charge on that one.'

'I wish I had my binoculars.'

'Use these,' Jack said, and handed her a pocket-sized pair, but by the time she had adjusted the lens the pilot had swarmed up the ladder and hauled himself on board.

'Do they ever have female pilots?' she asked, giving him back the binoculars.

'Never heard of a sheila doing it,' Jack said. 'Why? You thinking of changing careers?' He chuckled.

'I can't imagine anything more ghastly.'

'Well, it's a man's job anyway.'

She didn't have to look at him to see him smirk.

'I didn't mean that,' Jay snapped. 'If a woman wants to do it – good for *her*.'

Jack threw back his head and laughed. 'You're so easy to rile.'

Damn him. But didn't they say someone liked you if they teased you?

'I've got to stop it, haven't I?' She looked steadily at him. 'Lighten up, I mean.'

'When you smile, Juliet, you're stunning. But I think you've gone through something that's crushed you. Am I right?' His eyes never left her face.

She gave an involuntary start. For one mad moment she visualised telling him about Charlie. Instinctively, she felt he'd understand. But the moment was gone.

'Juliet?' He was standing close to her; so close she could smell the musky scent of him.

She struggled to keep her voice even. 'I'm not in the mood to offload right now.'

'When you are, I'll be happy to listen.' He glanced at his watch. 'D'ya fancy a drink?' He smiled at her.

'Love one.'

The officers' bar was almost full. Most of the crew, it seemed, and all the passengers were already chatting and drinking by the time they sauntered in, Jay trying desperately to look as though it was a complete accident she happened to be with Jack. Ronald looked hurt. Petra raised her eyebrows but said nothing.

'Let me buy you a drink, Juliet.' Trevor wheezed over.

And that was the end of any further conversation with Jack.

11

The safety drill would have been over sooner if they hadn't been waiting for one particular passenger. The alarm signal to abandon vessel screamed out at precisely 10.07, and by 10.10 all the officers, crew and passengers had grouped on the muster station on Deck 2 wearing bulky life jackets, and carrying hard hats. Everyone, that is, except Trevor. The second officer, a stern-looking Russian called Ivan, who stood with a clipboard checking off names, looked at his watch every few seconds. Finally, at fifteen minutes past, he sent Dan to look for him.

'He won't be taking part in any safety drill,' Dan snapped, when he returned to the waiting group. 'He's flat out on his bed and there's an empty bottle of gin by the side of him.'

'He is liability,' Ivan said, his expression thunderous. 'We teach him what happens when rules are broken. We go without him.'

To look at Ivan's face, Jay had the feeling he would leave Trevor behind on a real emergency; she couldn't help a twinge of sympathy for the old boy.

'Hard hats on,' barked Ivan, 'and remember,' his dark eyes scanned the passengers, 'this is no game. Is dangerous procedure. And there is wind today.'

Jay shivered but she was determined not to let anyone, particularly Jack, see she was nervous. Luckily, she thought grimly, I can swim. At least I *can* in a swimming pool. She didn't dare think further. She jammed her hat on and pulled the strap firmly under her chin.

'Follow me. And no talk unless absolute necessary.'

'I hate this,' Petra's horrified whisper came from behind Jay. 'I'm terrified of water. I'm going to be sick.'

'You'll be fine,' Jay murmured, even though she could feel goosebumps prickling her arms. 'Stay close to Dan.'

'I'll see she's all right,' came Jack's smooth tones.

He would.

Everyone moved swiftly towards the emergency door. Ivan clanked it open and two officers disappeared through it on to the deck. One by one they stepped through the gap, then Ivan motioned Jay to go next. The cold air hit her face. She could taste the salt on her lips as she glanced at the sky. Solid cloud. No chance of any sun today. She tried to gauge how many feet above the sea the lifeboat was, as two of the crew shinned down a rope ladder which didn't look all that substantial.

'You!' Ivan jerked his head towards her. 'Go down ladder *now*!'

Really, he didn't need to be so rude.

Jay stepped onto the first rung. It swayed from her weight. She knew she shouldn't but she looked down at the waves crashing beneath her. *Dear God.* One of her feet dangled in space.

'Move!' Ivan roared above her head.

Desperate not to panic she managed to bring her foot back onto a rung. She counted the steps...seven, eight, nine... Dear God, how many more were there? She didn't think she could keep this up much longer. Her other foot slipped on the rung and went straight through the gap in between. Grasping the sides of the ladder even harder, she burnt her skin. If only she'd worn gloves. This was horrible. Another step. Then another. She must be near the end but she didn't dare look down again. She bit the inside of her mouth so hard she tasted blood. Something felt different. More solid. The lifeboat. She'd reached it. Oh, the relief as she placed her second foot down on the deck. She squeezed her eyes shut, aware of her forehead dripping with rain or sweat. She didn't know which. Didn't care.

'You sit here,' Alexei indicated towards the stern.

Jay sat on the wooden bench, cursing the fact that she hadn't thought to wear thicker trousers. The air swirled in cold gusts, and the boat smelt musty. She adjusted the strap of her hard hat which was biting into her neck, trying to think of the drill as an adventure, but her nerves jangled. All around her the crew were shouting orders.

One of the men showed Seraphina and Ronald some seats near Jay. Ronald gave Jay a nervous smile as he made for the seat next to his wife, who seemed perfectly composed. Watching everyone descend the ladder, Jay finally saw Jack with Petra close behind. He turned and put out his hand to help the girl in. Alexei waved them towards the bow but not before Jack caught her eye. He winked, and suddenly she felt calmer. Before she could smile back a crew member bellowed, 'Let's go!' as he undid the cable.

The lifeboat swung out from the side of the ship and began its descent, swaying to one side, then the other. It was like being in a lift that had come loose of its cables and was dangling in mid-air. Her stomach turned. Some of the crew were talking quietly but the passengers were still under orders not to speak. She remembered Ivan's words, that this was the most dangerous part. The back of her neck prickled beneath the hard hat, and she noticed Ronald take Seraphina's hand. There was a thump as the boat landed on a windswept sea. Jay gripped the edge of the bench as the boat immediately began to roll. She thought of Nannie, who would have been quietly terrified and probably seasick. Ronald had his head in a bag and was making awful choking noises. She caught Seraphina's eye but the woman shook her head and pursed her lips. Poor Ronald. He obviously wasn't going to get much sympathy from his wife.

After what seemed like hours but was only a matter of minutes, it was over and the lifeboat was back on the ship. Jay pulled herself up the ladder and onto the deck. Just as she was congratulating herself that she'd come through the exercise without causing any embarrassment, she tripped on one of the plinths holding a coil of rope. She struck the planks, and with one hand grabbed the rope. A curse escaped her lips as a burning pain shot through her palm. *Ahhh! That hurt.* She turned the palm towards her. Blood was dripping from an angry graze.

Trevor Manning avoided everyone's eyes when he appeared just before noon, as Tatyana was serving the main course.

'Naughty boy,' Petra told him, wagging her finger. Jay was pleased to see her sounding more confident now she had come safely through the drill.

'Bit too much of the giggle juice, I'm afraid,' Trevor blustered. 'Couldn't make it.' He raked his hair.

'This is not going to happen again,' Dan said with some force, planting himself in front of Trevor. 'Not on this ship.'

'All right, my boy, I've had my lecture.' Trevor squinted at the menu. 'Nothing takes my eye. Think I'll just go back to my quarters...have a lie down.' He shuffled out of the room.

Lunch was a quiet affair with only four of them. Jay could barely hold her fork, her hand was so sore, and the plaster she'd hurriedly stuck on wasn't helping.

'I'm perfectly happy not to make small talk with the lovely Trevor,' Petra said, 'but I don't know why Jack's not turned up.' She took a mouthful of crab salad. 'Mmm, this is delish. He's missing a super lunch, not to mention our scintillating company.'

'That's the trouble with a small group like ours.' Seraphina's voice was a rough emery board. 'You notice when someone's not there.' She had changed out of her boating shoes into her usual high-heeled mules. Today's were a pink feathered affair which matched her tie-dyed caftan.

Usually Jay was intrigued with Seraphina and her outfits but today she had other things on her mind. She was determined to find, or make, an opportunity to talk to Petra about Jack…to drop her a hint, if nothing else.

Are you really so concerned about a girl you've barely met? Isn't there another reason, which you won't admit?

'Shall we take our coffee into the lounge?' Jay stood up and smiled down at Petra. 'It'd be nice to have a chat on our own.'

'Sure,' Petra said, a quizzical look on her face. 'Sounds like you've got something on your mind.'

Sitting at one of the card tables, Jay tapped the surface with her fingernails. Petra smiled, a little perfunctorily, and waited. Jay plunged in.

'Actually, there is something, Petra. Look, I'm a bit worried. Are you being entirely sensible about Jack?'

Petra's eyebrows shot up. 'What on earth are you talking about?'

'Well, he's an attractive man. I know you're friends but from what I see, he's Jack by name and Jack by nature.'

'What's that supposed to mean?' Petra gave her a flinty stare. 'Oh, I get it. Jack the Lad.'

Juliet flinched. 'I wouldn't want you to get hurt, that's all. Or hurt your fiancé.'

'Why would you worry about me?' Petra screwed her eyes up at Jay. 'You've only known me three days. And never even met Louis.'

Damn. Petra was taking this the wrong way. Jay tried again. 'Petra, I like you…and I think Jack's a bit of a playboy.'

'And it will all end in tears?' Petra didn't bother to disguise her sarcasm.

'I'm not saying that.' Jay began to wish she had kept her mouth closed. After all, what did it matter to her who Petra liked?

'I can look after myself, thank you, without your advice…which by the way I haven't asked for. I'm not some pathetic innocent. I've practically travelled the world…met all kinds of men…' She brought her face closer to Jay's. 'If you must know, I feel sorry for Jack.'

'Really?' Jay put down her cup.

'Yeah, really.' Petra was back to being sarcastic. 'I'm not going to say any more. It's confidential and if Jack wants to offload he'll tell you himself.'

So Jack had divulged something deeply personal to Petra. But then, Petra knew him – she didn't. It wasn't any of Jay's business so she'd better shut up.

'Anyway, I'm fed up.' Petra threw her head back and let her arms flop on the table. 'It's probably the curse, but there's only so much sea I can take.' She raised her eyes to Jay. 'I'm glad Jack's on the boat – he's fun. But he's also a really kind person. Do you know the reason why he was so late boarding?'

Jay shook her head.

'There was an accident on the motorway. His cab wasn't involved but people were injured and he got out to help. One woman had blood pouring out of her head.'

So that's where he got the blood on his shirt sleeve. Juliet shifted a little in her seat.

'And if you must know,' Petra said, her eyes still fixed on Jay's, 'Louis is perfectly aware that Jack's travelling home with me.'

'It's just that men aren't always aware of the effect they have.'

Petra's expression sharpened. 'On a ditzy blonde? Oh, for God's sake, get a life.' She tossed her head, then looked straight at Jay. 'What about you? *You* obviously think he's drop-dead gorgeous.'

'He's the last man I'd want to get tied up with,' Jay snapped back. 'I've met too many of his type. Besides, he's much too young for me.'

'Don't give me that.'

A cold silence hung between them.

'I'm sorry,' Jay said finally, 'I shouldn't have mentioned it. Forget it. It's none of my business.' She smiled at the younger woman. 'Are we still friends?'

Petra returned the smile and nodded, but the smile was faint.

After a few minutes Jay made an excuse to get some air. She needed to be on her own. Sort out what was going on in her head. How she was going to get through this voyage without upsetting anyone else. She clambered up to the monkey deck but Jack had beaten her. *Damn.* It was too late to retreat. He was leaning over the railing top, looking relaxed, his crossed arms resting along the smooth wood.

'Hello there, Juliet,' he called. 'Come and look at the waves. They've got a soapy edge to them that tells me there's a storm brewing. And look at those clouds. Even heavier than this morning.'

'Hi, Jack.' She kept her voice neutral and took a deep breath.

'By the way, well done on the drill. Not easy, especially in the wind.'

'I only hope we don't have to go through it again,' Jay said with feeling as she tried to stop the wind from sweeping her hair over her eyes.

'What happened to your hand?'

'It's nothing.'

'It's something, or else you wouldn't have put a plaster on it.' Jack took her hand and turned the palm upwards. Blood had seeped through the waterproof coating. 'Was this on the lifeboat?'

She pretended not to feel tiny electric shocks shooting up her arm. 'No, I was fine there. It was when I got back on board and tripped.'

'Hmm.' He stared at her. The gold flecks in his eyes fascinated her. 'If it's not too bad it's better if you can get some sea air on it. Would you trust me to take the plaster off?'

She could only nod.

Gently, so gently, he eased off the plaster millimetre by millimetre until the ugly graze was exposed. He looked up and met her eyes.

'This needs a dressing so it can breathe. I can put one on for you, if you like.'

She hesitated. Did she really want to come across as a pathetic female? She shook herself, feeling stupid. He was only being kind.

'I do have my First Aid Certificate,' he laughed.

'Yes, I...' She'd been about to tell him she knew he was a first-aider who had helped the people in the traffic accident, but she didn't want him to think she and Petra had been discussing him.

'Seems like you need looking after...same as Petra.'

He obviously wasn't saying anything particularly personal. She cleared her throat.

'Talking about Petra...'

Shut up, Jay.

'What about her?' His voice held a cautionary note.

'Jack, can I ask you something personal?'

'Depends what it is.' Jack held his smile but his eyes grew wary.

'She's very much in love with her fiancé.'

'I know,' he frowned. 'What's that got to do with anything?'

'Well, she's a long way away from him in an unusual setting, to say the least,' Juliet's eyes swept over the deck, then alighted on Jack, 'and she's very impressionable.'

'What are you saying?' He studied her face. 'God above, are you trying to warn me off, or something?'

'I wouldn't put it like that, but Petra's vulnerable and—'

'Lay off, Juliet. I'm only too well aware of the fiancé. Petra's not a child, she's twenty-six. She doesn't need *Mummy* to chaperone her.'

Jay flushed, not knowing if it was the acerbic tone he'd used, or whether it was the Mummy bit. She was taken aback when she saw his dark eyebrows knit together and the harsh line of his mouth. In that moment her heart did an unexpected leap.

'I'm sorry you're taking it like this,' she blundered on, 'but I don't want to see Petra hurt, that's all.'

'I'm sure you're acting with the best intentions, but just leave well alone. All you need worry about is getting that hand seen to.'

Jack turned abruptly, and disappeared down the stairs, leaving

Jay to watch his retreating back. *Bugger.* She'd blown it again. She'd upset two people she really liked in less than an hour. Why the hell had she started it? And why hadn't she taken the hint after she'd spoken to Petra and kept her mouth shut where Jack was concerned? But no. She had to stick her nose in. Somehow she'd felt compelled to tackle Jack. And really, was it any of her business if he and Petra were close friends...or lovers?

The sea looked as restless as Jay felt. She stared at it for what seemed like hours, but when she looked at her watch it was only twenty minutes since the row with Jack. She shivered. The waves were definitely gathering force but the *Alexandria* pushed steadily forward with its Herculean cargo. The good thing was that she hadn't once felt seasick, even in the rolling lifeboat. She decided to return to her room, have a read, and maybe a pre-supper G and T to relax her. Perhaps Trevor had got the right idea after all.

Someone had pushed a sheet of paper under the door and she bent down to retrieve it, flexing her back and neck as she straightened. What she would give for a massage. For the first time she wished she was on a cruise ship and could visit their spa.

She read: *Ms Reece, you have received a message on 10.09.2005 at 17.13 as follows:*

Hi Jay,

Hope you're having a wonderful voyage. We're all OK here though I think Lydia is finding it tougher than she thought. Neil is as moody as ever. But don't worry about work – I'm sure Lydia is doing a good job behind the scenes.

I shan't be sorry to see you back, but in the meantime, enjoy, as they say. Let us know how you are.

Love Rachel

Work. At home, she wouldn't have gone more than a day without thinking and planning, but here she felt she was living on a moving island with nothing but sea, and where clients and staff and problems ceased to exist. She gathered herself and read the message again. What did Rachel mean? Why did she say Lydia was probably finding it tougher than she'd thought? And why did she say she was sure Lydia was doing a good job *behind the scenes*? Lydia should be high profile so the team and the clients were aware of her all the time.

Jay frowned. Well, there was nothing she could do about it stuck out in the middle of nowhere. *Damn it.* Was this how the whole trip would turn out – cryptic messages coming at her, demanding her attention? And why had Rachel sent the message through the ship's email instead of direct to her own address? Then she remembered… she hadn't logged on since she'd been on board.

12

La Spezia, Italy

'I'm jumping ship here,' Jack told Jay as they stood on the bridge the following evening just before supper, watching more dull clouds meet and glue together as the *Alexandria* breezed towards La Spezia. 'I'm still a working man...not like some of us,' he smiled, yesterday's quarrel seemingly forgotten.

At first he'd given her a wave from below, but then, as though he'd decided to forget their heated words of yesterday, he'd bounded up the steps. Jay bit her lip as disappointment flooded through her. She'd assumed he was going all the way to Australia. He'd certainly never hinted anything different.

Trying hard to sound casual, she said, 'Oh, so it's business?'

He hesitated. 'You could call it that.'

'In La Spezia?'

'No. Bologna.'

'Are you piloting?'

'No.' His tone had changed, become wary.

She glanced at him. What business could he have if it wasn't work? His tight, almost bitter expression discouraged any further questioning. The wall was there between them again and she wasn't surprised when he changed the subject.

'La Spezia is still a naval base, you know, but it's a perfect starting place to visit the Cinque Terre.'

'They're those special villages I read about, aren't they...built on steep terraces?'

Jack nodded. 'Yes. All five are close together and linked by the train. They're a World Heritage Site now with a national park protecting them. Well worth seeing.'

'Is it possible to see all of them in one visit?'

'Depends how long the captain lets you go walkabout.'

'I'll go mad if I don't get off soon,' Jay said, 'especially as we only saw Hamburg and Rotterdam from the ship.'

'Even if the time's short it's pleasant just to wander in the town or along the seafront. And try the wine. They're famous for it. I'd take you and Petra if I was around.' He looked sharply at her. 'Are things all right between you and Petra?'

It took every ounce of effort for Jay not to go pink.

''Course they are,' she said, averting her face and watching the waves which looked as dull as she felt. 'I'll probably go with her anyway.' Keeping her voice light though she was desperate to hear his answer, she asked, 'Are you joining the ship later?'

'I can't really say. Just depends.'

What the hell did it depend on? She noticed the familiar thinning of Jack's mouth when he wasn't going to elaborate. She saw herself pulling him to her, shaking him, forcing him to tell her *why* he was leaving. What was the matter with her? She caught her bottom lip between her teeth to stop from making even more of an idiot of herself, but the sparkle, as far as she was concerned, had already evaporated from the crossing. She clung onto the rail, still with her back to him. The sooner this bloody voyage was over with, the better.

'Oh, well, please yourself.'

Jack suddenly grinned. 'Come on, Juliet. Relax. Admit you'll miss me.'

She was about to give him a snappy retort when Seraphina floated towards them. Unusually, there was no sign of her husband in tow.

'Lovely, isn't it?' Seraphina gushed as she sidled up, her high-heeled mules somehow managing to grip the deck.

'Evening, Seraphina.' Jay was gratified to hear an irritated note in Jack's tone, hoping it was because they'd been interrupted. 'What've you done with Ronald?'

'I've left him having a bath.' She rolled her eyes and using the back of her hand swept a cloud of pink hair over to one side. 'He always does everything at the wrong time; just as we're coming into another port, or just as the captain is pointing out dolphins or whales, Ronald's nowhere to be found.'

Seraphina stretched out her hands to clutch the rail. Today her nails were crimson and made a vivid contrast to the gold and purple sarong and the bright red jacket. Jay smiled. Seraphina was from another planet compared to Ronald, and she wondered why the two of them had first got together.

'What've you been doing today?' Jay asked her.

'Some washing, and I had a swim this afternoon but the pool isn't big enough to do more than three strokes at a time. Still, it was better than nothing, I suppose. I'm getting so bored on this trip, coming into ports and not being allowed off.' Seraphina fished an artificial rose attached to a rubber band from her jacket pocket and flicked the pink hair back in a pony tail. 'What have *you* been doing all day? Do *you* get bored?'

Jay shook her head. 'Not really.'

'I don't suppose you do.' Seraphina looked at Jay and then more pointedly at Jack. Her tone was more amused than derisive but Jay felt the warning signs of a flush.

'Don't forget Juliet's writing a novel,' Jack reminded her. 'That takes up a lot of her time.'

'Oh, of course…the novel. You probably wouldn't go far wrong writing about all of *us*…' Seraphina laughed throatily, then broke off and looked at Jay with sudden suspicion. 'Or is that exactly what you're doing?'

'I couldn't possibly discuss it with anyone at this stage,' Jay said in a voice as sweet as saccharine. 'So I'm off.' She hesitated and turned to Jack without meeting his eye. 'Have a good trip, Jack.' She spun on her heel and left the two of them together, Jack's mocking laughter singing in her ears.

The captain's announcement came after supper.

'You may disembark at La Spezia tomorrow at 10am and make sure you are back by latest 19.00 hours ready for sailing at 20.00 hours.'

There was hearty applause from Trevor and Seraphina.

'I think I'm going to catch up with a bit of shopping,' Petra told Jay. 'Unless you're going to those funny villages...whatever they're called.'

'The Cinque Terre. Yes, I'd like to. Jack says...' *Damn*. She hadn't meant to say his name but it was too late, '...they're really worth seeing if there's enough time.'

Petra raised her eyebrows but said nothing and Jay, pretending not to notice, rushed on. 'The guidebook says you have to go by train. Do you fancy coming with me? Or would you rather be by yourself?'

'Well, now Jack won't be coming,' Petra's bottom lip pouted, 'I'm not that keen to wander about on my own. So if you don't mind, I'll tag along.'

Jay didn't feel like talking to the others. She told herself she hadn't been sleeping very well and would have an early night. She glanced at her watch. Ages before bedtime. And she wasn't in the mood for any reading or card-making.

Not for a minute did she think Jack was on business in Bologna. She remembered how he'd hesitated before answering. '*You could call it that,*' he'd said. Once again she was acting out of turn, but she was curious to know the parts of his life he refused to discuss. Because that's what this was all about, else why couldn't he come out and discuss the real reason for leaving the *Alexandria*?

What sort of woman did he find attractive? *Get real, Jay. You're years older, for one thing. Flirting with you is just a pleasant way of passing time for him.*

She tried to read Mark Twain, who never failed to make her laugh, but after a few minutes threw it on the bed. *Damn and blast everyone to hell!*

The *Alexandria* nosed its way along the craggy coastline, with its tumble of houses and restaurants, past the naval port and the marina, before it finally docked in the busy commercial port where it joined a line of other ships.

Petra gave a little skip as she took Jay's arm, and Jay was grateful they were friends again. It was heaven wandering along the esplanade. The air was clean with a fresh warm breeze that gently lifted the palm trees. The local people smiled at the two pale-skinned women as they walked by with their hats and cameras. Jay pointed to a table outside one of the bars, and they rushed for it before anyone else had the same idea. To sit in such a quiet and beautiful spot, enjoying the strong morning sunshine, admiring boats of every size, from tiny dinghies to sleek white yachts, was absolute bliss. Jay closed her eyes, trying to pin the memory down so she could recall it when she was back in windswept, gloomy-skied England.

'This view is wonderful,' Petra said, her eye on two young men in shorts and T-shirts, displaying their tattooed arms and legs as they painted their boat. 'And the coffee – it's wicked. I'd forgotten what real coffee tastes like.'

'I'd forgotten what it feels like to be able to walk without staggering like a drunk all the time,' Jay laughed, wiping the crumbs of a particularly crispy croissant from her mouth. 'Doesn't do much for my reputation.'

'Depends what sort of reputation you're aiming for,' Petra joked.

Jay hesitated. 'I'm sorry about yesterday,' she said. 'I was completely out of order telling you how to behave. I don't know what's the matter with me lately.'

'Love means never having to say you're sorry,' Petra grinned, as Jay pretended to cuff her. Her face became serious. 'Juliet, is anything wrong?'

Someone else who'd taken their cue from Jack and called her Juliet.

'I'm concerned about my business,' Jay admitted. 'The main reason for coming away was so I could have a proper break. But now I'm not sure I've made the right decision to let someone else take over.'

'Really?' Petra leaned forward. 'Where *is* your business? London?'

'Close. Kingston-upon-Thames. I only live a few miles from the old family home, and fortunately near my father who's now in a nursing home.'

'Would it help to talk about it? Sometimes another head can see things from a different perspective.'

'It's nothing specific...just a feeling that something's not quite right. But I don't know if it's me being paranoid because I'm so used to being in control.'

'Didn't you say you left someone in charge?'

'Yes.' Jay smiled at Petra a little too brightly. 'But you don't want to hear all my woes and I'd much rather hear about your fiancé. Where did you meet him?'

This was obviously Petra's favourite subject and she talked non-stop for ten minutes. Her enthusiasm was infectious and Jay, who usually found it rather dull when someone was describing somebody she'd never met, was genuinely interested.

'Sorry, Juliet, I'm rabbiting on about me. Tell me about you. Is there anyone special?'

'Not really.'

'I'm amazed.' Petra looked thoughtful.

'My love life is a bit non-existent at the moment. Maybe you can give me some tips. But right now we're wasting valuable shopping time.' Jay leapt up with a smile, slipping her bag over her shoulder. 'Shall we head for the market first?'

They strolled along like...well, Jay decided, almost like aunt and niece, rather than newish acquaintances. Even though Petra's nose was momentarily stuck in a guidebook she'd picked up from one of the stands, she was good company, and for once Jay felt content. Maybe—

She was vaguely aware of the distinct purr.

The sound of a scooter.

Then shouting.

Alarmed, she swung round. The rider was coming from behind them, much too close to the pavement. Instinctively, she pushed Petra further in towards the shop fronts, but seconds later her own arm shot up in the air as a practiced hand jerked her bag from her shoulder. The scooter roared away.

Petra wheeled round. 'Hey, what—?'

Jay's feet refused to move. She stared at her empty shoulder in disbelief. Blinked, desperately trying to focus – clear her brain. She heard Petra yell but couldn't make out the words. *Think what to do.* Her whole body trembled. *Chase him, for God's sake.*

'The bastard. We've got to get him.'

Petra's angry voice yanked her out of her trance. She gathered her wits together and dashed along the pavement, shouting and waving her arms.

'Stop him! Thief! He's got my handbag! Please, oh, please help!'

A few passers-by stared as if they'd witnessed such a theft a hundred times before. Then they lost interest and turned away.

She heard Petra's footsteps pounding behind her. 'Oh, Juliet, I didn't see him. I'm so sorry...I was looking at the map, trying to see where we were going.'

'You couldn't have done anything,' Jay told the girl, furious with herself for not having her hand on the shoulder strap. 'But we need to find a police station – fast.'

'Next junction,' a waiter directed them, 'turn right on *Viale Italia*. You go far,' he gesticulated, 'then big new building with satellite dish. *La questura*. Everyone knows.'

Two policemen were standing at the counter, one bent over a sports paper. They both looked up and flashed smiles as Jay and Petra rushed in.

'Unfortunately, *signora*, this happens sometimes.' The one who'd been reading the paper shrugged. 'They are very clever.' He said it almost as though he were proud of the fact. 'Did you see him?' He took a thick pad of pre-printed forms and began writing.

'No, it happened too quickly. He was young...no helmet... black hair.'

'That describes half the population of this town,' Petra said grimly.

The second officer gave the blonde-haired girl an appreciative wink. Petra rolled her eyes.

Jay tried to hide her anger. Bloody Italians. Couldn't stop flirting, even on duty.

'My bag,' she interrupted.

'*Si, si*, the bag. What is he like, the bag?'

'It's a leather shoulder bag – tan.'

He smoothed back his hair. 'Tan?'

Her eyes swept over the room. 'Like that.' She pointed to a similar-coloured cushion on one of the visitors' chairs.

He nodded. 'How big?'

She drew an oblong in the air.

'And inside?'

'Most valuable thing's my BlackBerry.' The officer raised an eyebrow. 'You know – my hand computer.' He nodded. 'Address book...make-up bag...my—' A hot sensation seeped into her head and took hold. It frightened her. Her lips parted and her breath came out in short darts of pain. She gripped the edge of the counter.

Not my dear little—

Petra grabbed one of the chairs. 'Here, Juliet. Sit down.'

Jay fell into the chair and clung to the arms as if the solid wood beneath her fingers would stop her from sinking through the floor. Sweat poured off her forehead despite the chill inside her.

Calm. Breathe...like Nannie taught you.

'Your purse, Juliet?' Petra prompted.

Jay dragged her eyes upwards. Petra appeared all wavy.

'A red leather wallet.' Jay's voice was dull.

'Passport?'

Jay shook her head. She couldn't speak.

Please get my wallet back.

'We don't have our passports,' Petra answered for her. 'We leave them on the ship for the whole journey. But we keep a copy... in our bags,' she finished lamely.

'Money?'

'Two hundred euros,' Jay whispered.

Keep your eyes on him. Answer the questions. Maybe he can help you. 'Any more else? Any personal item to prove bag is yours?'

Yes. Yes. She wanted to shout it out, but her throat constricted.

Something personal. Something precious. Something I love more than anything. And I've lost it.

The room felt hot. Airless. She stood up on trembling legs. She needed to get out into the fresh air.

'A photograph of my—'

Then her world went black.

She felt sick. Weightless. She must have died. There were voices. She opened her eyes. She was on the floor. She must have had a terrible accident. Three faces were bent over her, watching her with anxious expressions. Two strange men. No, she'd seen them somewhere before. The third face was a girl, blonde hair streaming forward. Petra. *Oh, thank God.* She saw the girl's face break into a beaming smile.

'You're all right, Juliet. You're safe.'

'Where am I?'

She heard foreign voices; strong hands lifted her into a chair. So she was inside somewhere.

'We're still in the police station,' Petra said, in a shaky voice. 'You fainted.'

The two police officers exchanged some rapid Italian, and the older one turned to Petra. 'We leave you for short time. Ring bell if you need.'

'Expect they've gone for a fag and a gossip about two mad Englishwomen,' Petra tried to joke as the policemen disappeared. 'How do you feel?'

'Better, I think.'

'Here.' Petra handed Jay a paper cup of water. 'Juliet, something's upset you badly. Just before you fainted you mentioned a photograph.'

Jay's head throbbed. 'I don't want to talk about it.' She sat like a statue, eyes brimming.

Petra knelt down by the chair, took the cup, and wrapped one of Jay's hands in her own. 'I'm your friend. It won't go any further.'

Jay hesitated. Then she opened her mouth before she could change her mind. 'I have a son.' She spoke slowly, the words un-practised.

'That's wonderful,' Petra said, squeezing her hand. 'How come you haven't told me about him? Does he live near you?'

'No,' Jay said, shortly.

'Where is he?'

'Sydney.'

'Oh, cool. So you're not just following your grandparents but you'll be seeing your son.'

If only.

Jay felt the bile rise in her throat. She swallowed it down.

'I doubt it,' her voice was low. 'He was adopted when he was a baby. His new parents emigrated to Australia. He's never been part of my life.' To her horror she felt the tears start and tried to blink them back.

'Oh, Juliet, I'm so sorry. So very sorry.' Petra put her arms round Jay. 'Was that why you were so upset about losing the photo?' she said softly. 'Was it your son?'

Jay nodded.

'Do you want to tell me about him?'

Jay hesitated. Petra was looking at her with such genuine concern it would have been unkind to reject her. Eventually she said, 'Sorry to embarrass you. I've never told anyone I had a baby – not even my brother and sister. My parents forbade me.'

'That's awful – to have to keep such a secret. Didn't you even tell your husband?'

'No. My parents made me feel so ashamed. I was only sixteen.' She gave a wan smile. 'Believe it or not, you didn't have sex before you were married in those days, let alone get yourself pregnant. And in a Catholic family...well, it was the worst shame. I was sent away to my grandmother's – supposedly for a bad case of nerves. I held my baby in my arms just once...for half an hour. Those were the rules.'

She shut her eyes as she remembered the joy she'd felt when the matron had given her her baby, wrapped like a mummy. She'd unbound him, releasing his arms, and had smiled at the pink plastic bracelet he wore with the label naming him 'Baby Bishop'. She could pretend he was hers forever, that she'd see him take his first steps, leave her on the first day of school, grow up, his first girlfriend, get married, have a family. She remembered as though it were yesterday the smell of talcum powder, stroking his black silky hair, marvelling at his tiny fingernails with their delicate little half-moons. All the while he'd been curled up inside her, waiting until it was time for them to meet. He hadn't cried. Just looked up at her with dark misty eyes. But she'd always been certain he knew she was his mother. How could Petra possibly understand?

But Petra squeezed her hand and whispered, 'Go on.'

Jay took a jagged breath. 'We…Mani…the father…decided to call him Charlie if he was a boy. I kept kissing him and saying his name over and over, telling him I loved him…would love him always. And to be a good boy. And then I was forced to…to…give him back to the nurse and that was the last time…the last time… I handed him over and…' she broke off, tears streaming down her face.

Petra handed Jay a tissue and waited while she dabbed her eyes and blew her nose.

'And the photo?' Petra asked.

'The photo of him in my wallet was the only one I have. It was taken the day after he was born. One of the nurses gave it to me – slipped it into my coat pocket when Nannie and I left the hospital. It was against the rules. I hope she never got into trouble. Doing something like that could cost her her job. And now I've lost it. For good.'

She screwed up her eyes, her hand over her mouth, longing for everything to go back to how it was. For her bag to be by her side. For the red leather wallet to be safely zipped inside, full of euros and credit cards…and her photograph.

'The police might find your bag. They said they'd try.'

Jay shook her head. 'You know I won't get it back. The Italian police aren't interested in something that happens dozens of times a day in their city.'

She brushed the tears angrily with the back of her hand, but still they flowed, spilling from her fingers. After a few moments she lifted her head, her face smeared with grief.

'You must think I'm overreacting, just losing a photograph, but he was the sweetest little baby and now I've nothing to remember him by.' She sobbed afresh and Petra put her arms round her again. 'I only know he was perfect in every way. Black hair...Mani's brown eyes. I fell in love with him immediately.' She had to finish her story now. Maybe the pain would start to ease knowing one other person shared her secret. She gulped and went on, 'Mani never even saw his son. He was only seventeen though I told my parents he was eighteen, and an Indian. That made it worse – having a mixed-race child. Half-caste, they called them in those days. Horrible word.' She looked up, rivers of mascara staining her cheeks. 'Petra, I'd be grateful if you'd keep this to yourself...'

'I wouldn't dream of telling anyone.'

Jay looked at her. There was an odd light in the girl's eyes.

Jay woke, blinking, wondering where she was. She opened her eyes a little more, trying to shake off the deep sleep. Petra smiled down at her.

'Feeling better?'

'I think so.' Jay licked her dry lips, her eyes flicking round the dark space, relieved to see she was back in her room on the *Alexandria*, not recalling how she'd got there. The inside of her mouth tasted sour. It hadn't been a dream. It was real. She'd lost her bag. Lost the photograph. Lost her one precious picture. A chill ran through her body. 'How long have I been asleep?'

'A couple of hours. It was exactly what you needed.'

'I'll get up in a bit.' She looked up at Petra. 'How long have you been here?'

'Just a few minutes. I've looked in twice but you've been still as a log.' She hesitated. 'Shall I come by later so we go for supper together?' Jay shook her head but Petra ignored her. 'Maybe you'll feel like something to eat by then.'

Jay nodded as though to do anything else would take the last of her energy. She closed her eyes again, feigning sleep. She wanted to be left alone.

As soon as she heard Petra leave she stumbled to the shower room, letting the water pour over her and soothe her. She put on fresh clothes but nothing could stop her thinking about her precious photograph. The day-old baby wrapped in a white hospital gown and a shawl Nannie had knitted, his little wrinkled face, his skin the colour of old gold, looking at her with his funny quizzical expression.

'Meet you in the officers' bar in fifteen minutes?' Petra said, when she came to see how Jay was again. Jay was sitting in one of the easy chairs attempting to read a book and glanced up.

'Honestly, Petra, I'm not really in the mood.'

It had been hard enough to try to make normal conversation; she wasn't interested in what the others were talking about, and for the first time she was grateful for Jack's absence.

'Aw, don't leave me with Trev and the Smiths, *please.*' Petra pulled a face. 'And it might do you good, after such a horrible day. Captain says we're staying put overnight which is great news. I'm getting fed up with all the rocking.' She looked at Jay. 'Aw, come on. Do you good.'

'All right,' Jay caved in. 'But I can't guarantee I'll be the best company.'

Music overflowed into the corridor as half an hour later she opened the door. Hesitating, she wondered how she could get through the evening. Seraphina and Ronald were sitting at the bar chatting to Dan, and Petra was talking to a couple of Russian officers who looked bemused but couldn't take their eyes off her cascade of Cinderella hair and low-cut black dress. She broke away as soon as she spotted Jay.

'You look so much better,' Petra beamed. 'What're you having?'

'A glass of white wine, thanks. But don't let me break up your conversation.'

'They don't understand a word I'm saying,' Petra giggled. 'But they're too good-looking to pass up. C'mon, let's go somewhere where we can be a bit more private.' She steered Jay over to a small table.

'Thanks again for being there today,' Jay said. 'You were marvellous. I don't know what I would have done without you.'

'No probs. I'm just glad to see you've recovered. Cheers.'

Jay's hand was unsteady as she clinked her glass to Petra's. She would never recover from the loss of her precious photograph. But she couldn't say that to Petra.

13

Jack

Jack put his foot down all the way to Bologna.

He hadn't wanted to leave the ship at La Spezia, just when things looked as though they were beginning to get interesting between him and Juliet. She certainly was a gorgeous-looking woman, though she didn't seem to know what she wanted in life. She struck him as pretty mixed up. Man trouble, no doubt. And she was too interfering by half. Too quick to take charge and tell people what to do, which must stem from running a business. But it wouldn't wash with him. He snorted. No, she wasn't his type at all. He liked his women more pliant. Yes, Juliet needed to lighten up. He smiled to himself. He'd like to be around when she did. *Mmm.* Juliet letting herself go. Having one glass too many. Throwing her head back and really laughing at something witty he'd just said. Looking at him with those dark seductive eyes over a candlelit dinner. Juliet naked. Lying on her back in his bed, her chestnut hair spread over the pillow, her lips parted… His smile broadened at the image.

He couldn't deny the pure lust he'd felt the moment he'd set eyes on her in the officers' dining room. He should have been looking for Petra but he'd been mesmerised by Juliet. It must have been those eyes which had instantly grabbed him. And from her answering gleam he could have sworn she'd felt the same attraction. That is, until he'd laughed at her name. He hadn't meant to. It had just hit him. God, she'd been furious. She must have thought him incredibly rude. He still flinched at the memory, though she'd seen the funny side when he'd explained.

A scene of the two of them making love on board the *Alexandria* flashed through his mind for the hundredth time. He imagined taking off her clothes, kissing her, caressing her, and it feeling right. Wanting her to enjoy every moment. Women had accused him more than once for being cold-blooded after he'd had them. And they were probably right. But he would never be like that with Juliet, though he wasn't sure why. Jesus, he was hard just thinking about her. But like most women in the end, she probably wanted marriage. He just didn't want any commitment, that was all. Just to think of it made his blood run cold. He'd been down that road and look where it had got him. To a self-centred Italian gold-digger called Isobella, that's where. And sod it, that's who he was heading towards right now.

The only positive thing to come out of that disastrous union was his beloved daughter, Chiara. His mouth relaxed a fraction, then hardened again. Isobella was doing her fucking best to turn his daughter against him.

He wondered idly why Juliet had never had children. After all, she'd been married. She'd have made a bloody marvellous mother. So whose decision had it been? Hers, or her husband's? It was probably too late now for her to change her mind.

The trouble was, he wasn't quite sure what Juliet wanted. He only knew he mustn't hurt her. Something or someone had hurt her terribly in the past and she kept it bottled up inside. It had to be over some bloke. He ignored a wave of jealousy that Juliet had loved a man, but another force, this time of such anger that the bloke had let her down, caused him to grip the steering wheel as though someone were deliberately driving him off a cliff. Of course he was only guessing, he told himself, but sometimes her lovely eyes were desperately sad. She must have been well and truly kicked.

Rather like he'd been last year. Once or twice he'd thought Juliet was about to confide in him. He'd tried to encourage her, but each time the moment had gone. Maybe one day she would trust him enough to tell him. He wanted to help her. Show her how to be happy, though he was probably the last person qualified to do that. He gave a bitter smile. But did he want more than that? To get emotionally involved? Definitely not. This time he couldn't afford to make such a mistake. No, the best thing he could do for Juliet was to hold back. That way, he could be sure of not hurting her.

Several hours later Jack pulled up outside Isobella's nineteenth-century building where she had the penthouse. He glanced in the driving mirror, pulled a face, told himself to get on with it, opened the door, slammed it shut, flicked a button on his key ring to lock it, and purposefully walked up the communal path.

14

The headache had turned into an almighty migraine. Juliet was seeing flickering lights in front of her eyes and her mouth felt like the inside of a furred-up kettle, even though she'd stuck to one glass of wine the night before. She staggered to the bathroom, and not daring to look in the mirror, washed her face and splashed her lids, then opened a small fresh bottle of mineral water, cold from the fridge, and gulped most of it down. Half an hour and two Alka-Seltzers later she felt slightly more human.

But she couldn't stop cursing herself for blabbing to Petra. Could she trust her not to say anything? Not to tell Jack? Or anyone else, for that matter.

Then she remembered how sympathetic Petra had been, how non-judgemental, and for the first time that morning she smiled. If she'd had a daughter she would love her to be like Petra. Her mind drifted for a few moments and then her face clouded. Whatever relief she'd felt when she'd briefly unburdened herself hadn't brought her any closer to finding Charlie. And now she'd never be able to study the little black and white photograph. The police would never be able to trace her handbag. Probably wouldn't even bother trying. She'd have to accept it was gone. She tried to convince herself that his face was etched on her brain and it wasn't necessary to look at a photograph to remember him.

Taking a deep breath she realised it was time to be practical. At least Petra had reminded her to email the credit card people to let them know about the theft, and she'd have to ask the captain if she could email from the bridge. None of the crew had ever said the passengers could do so in an emergency. He might not even allow it.

Stomach rolling, she glanced at her watch. Coming up to eight. She needed to find breakfast.

Wishing with all her heart she didn't have to put up with Seraphina's prattle and Ronald's thin voice saying exactly the same but half a clause behind his wife, she politely listened to their condolences about her handbag, hoping she was smiling and nodding in the right places, all the while longing to get away.

Time slowed down. Jay tried to lose herself in making a card for Will's birthday. Head bent in concentration she glued a cricket bat, a pair of walking boots, a few cans of beer – things Will loved – and for ten-minute chunks at a time she forgot. Then it would come flooding over her like a heavy black cloak and it took all her willpower to carry on with the birthday card.

It was in the afternoon, while she was pacing the deck, drawing in the salty air, and trying to make sense of yesterday, that she bumped into Dan.

'I've been looking for you,' he beamed. 'Captain's got good news. The police found your bag. He says for you to go and see him. He's on the bridge.'

The black cloud vanished in an instant. It was as though someone had soaked her in sunshine. She broke into a broad smile. She hadn't lost the photo of her beloved Charlie after all. Oh, how wonderful the Italian police were. Heart pounding with excitement she took the stairs two at a time.

'I think the captain wants to see me,' she said to the nearest officer, breathing fast.

'Ms Reece,' the captain wheeled round from one of the computers. 'I have your bag, found in litter bin. Police think maybe bomb. Lucky for you they don't blow it up.' He bent under the desk and handed it to her, smiling.

It was badly scuffed and discoloured, and the leather was soaked through, as though it had been thrown in the sea; but she'd got it back, thanks to someone's sharp eyes.

She rushed to her room, wanting to look at the photograph quietly on her own. To prop it up on her bedside table so she could see him the minute she awoke. She opened her bag. No BlackBerry, of course. But everything else was there...and yes, there was the red leather wallet.

Her heart leapt with joy as she unsnapped it with trembling fingers. The money had gone – again, to be expected. She unzipped the secret pocket where she always kept Charlie and ran her fingers inside. It was empty. Strange. She looked in the second compartment and flipped through the credit cards, surprised they hadn't been taken. Not there. She went through the whole wallet again just to make absolutely certain, conscious of her chest becoming tighter and tighter until she felt she was suffocating.

It has to be here, it has to be here, it has to be here. Her fingers slipped with sweat as she shook everything out in a heap on the bed. No photograph. Nothing.

A knock at the door made her jump. She didn't want to see anyone. Wanted only to curl up like a wounded animal until the pain went away. The knock came again, breaking into her misery. Reluctantly she opened the door to see Petra clinging onto the wall, eyes huge in her pale face, her hair hanging in lank yellow strings.

'Juliet, I—'

'Whatever's the matter?' Jay put a restraining hand on her arm as Petra swayed alarmingly. 'You look awful.'

'I've got a terrible stomach pain and I've just been sick.'

'Come and sit down.' Jay led her into the sitting room. 'Let me get you some water.'

Petra gulped it back before Jay had a chance to warn her just to sip it. The next moment Petra retched and flew in the direction of the shower room. Jay followed to find her crouched over the toilet bowl.

'I'm here.' She gently pulled Petra's hair back, then laid her hand on the girl's forehead.

'Oh, Christ.' Petra raised her head. 'I feel bloody awful.' She bent her head again.

Jay waited until the worst was over, then put a hand out and helped Petra to her feet.

'Better?'

Tears and sweat poured down Petra's cheeks. She shook her head. 'God, how embarrassing.' She tried to smile.

'No more than me yesterday.' Jay held her arm. 'Do you want to lie down on my bed for a while?'

'No, I'll be all right. I'll just sit down a minute. Catch my breath. Maybe the smell of the oil's getting to me.'

'Have you taken any anti-sickness pills?' Jay asked.

'Yes.' Petra retched again, and made another dash to the toilet.

'What a couple we are.' Petra gave Jay a rueful smile when she was back in the room. 'You yesterday – me today.'

'Do you normally get seasick on ships?' Jay asked.

'I don't know. I've never been out at sea. I didn't think such a big boat would get as bad as this and the tablets don't seem to be working. Oh, Juliet, I'm scared.'

'What did you have to eat last night?'

'Just some soup and salad. I wasn't that hungry. Nothing for lunch.'

'Shouldn't be any problem there as I had the same. But I do think you should see the doctor because the sea's been quite calm lately, and you haven't been sick before when we've had it rougher.' Jay bit her lip. What was she suggesting? There was no doctor on board. Just Nikolai, the Chief Engineer, who Dan said was trained in first aid and had medical knowledge. Not the same thing at all. 'I think we should get you back to your room, and when you're settled I'll go and tell the captain. I'm sure it's nothing to worry about but I'll be in later to see how you are.'

The girl nodded.

Something occurred to Jay. 'Petra...you're not pregnant, are you?'

'No.' Petra hesitated. 'At least I don't think so.'

17th September 1913, on board the *Orsova*

Until now I've managed not to be sick, but as the days go by the weather is getting worse. One of the sailors said it was a monsoon, which terrified me. What if it tipped over? It's been rolling from side to side like a toy boat, but the pitching is the worst bit. A few hours ago I had to crawl back to my bunk. I was shaking like a leaf as I could hear the cries of women and children every time the lightning flashed and the thunder banged. I wished I could comfort them, but I was too frightened to move.

I don't think I'll be able to write much more as the swell is bad. I'm trying hard not to be sick by swallowing but it's not working. I—

Jay eventually tracked the captain on the deck outside the bridge, quietly smoking a cigarette and gazing out to sea with an expression of pure contentment. The waves swished against the side of the ship, frothing like some giant cappuccino, and Jay wondered how he could still be fascinated with the endless mass of water, day after day, year after year. He smiled at her approach.

'Captain, may I have a word?'

'Please.'

'Petra's sick,' she told him. 'I'm worried about her.'

'Miss Sandys?' Jay nodded. 'What are symptoms?' he asked quickly, pinching out his cigarette before tossing it overboard.

'She's vomited several times, and she's got stomach cramps.'

'Maybe she will have...baby?' He cuddled his arms to his chest and rocked them.

'No, I asked her that and she doesn't think so.'

'I speak to Nikolai.' He paused. 'And you have all in your handbag?'

'Except my BlackBerry…and most of the contents of my wallet.' Her voice wobbled and the captain threw her a glance. 'I was going to ask you if I could check my emails every couple of days.'

'But of course. Better in early morning or late afternoon.' He looked at his watch. 'You may come in two hours.'

She thanked him and he nodded and disappeared.

To take her mind off worrying if there was anything seriously wrong with Petra, Jay decided to take up the captain's offer. She tapped out the first email to her PA.

Hello Rachel

Hope all is well. Thanks for your email. Sorry I've not been in touch. Been so busy learning about ships and emergency drills and talking to fellow passengers, I actually forgot to look at my emails. Can you imagine me forgetting to check my emails?

Unfortunately my BlackBerry was stolen yesterday when we were in La Spezia, so I'll have to use the ship's computer which might not always be convenient for the crew, so don't necessarily expect an immediate reply.

I was a little concerned regarding Lydia. Is she doing OK? Is Neil behaving himself? Did the Braeburn sale go through? Now I'm typing this I'm itching to be there, but I mustn't think like that – you're all capable of doing the job without me for a while.

Let me know if you're really worried about anything. I'll send Lydia an email today too.

Take care.

Jay

Now for Lydia. The difficulty was to find the right tone. Lydia could easily take offence if she thought someone was challenging, or worse, criticising her.

Good afternoon Lydia

 I haven't heard anything from you so presume all is going well. Is it a shock being back at work? It's a shock for me not being there, but I must say I'm having an interesting time. Only a handful of passengers and they're all nice though a bit mixed.

You could say that again.

 I hope the team are giving you their full support. Let me know if there's any info I can give you or indeed, advice. I promise to check my emails regularly, though I'm having to use the ship's computer because my BlackBerry was stolen in town yesterday, and I can't make a nuisance of myself, so it won't be on a daily basis.

 Once again, thanks a million, Lydia. Oh, just one other thing. Has the Braeburn sale gone through yet?

 Warmest wishes

She hesitated. Well, they might as well get used to it. She was going to have to, it seemed.

Juliet

She hit Send and glanced at her watch. Five to six. Time for supper. Maybe she'd feel better with some food inside her.

As she entered the dining room she saw Trevor talking to a figure with his back to her. She gave a start.

'Hello, m'dear. Come and join us. Jack's here.'

Jack looked round and grinned. 'Hey, Juliet.'

She stared at him, her heart thumping against her ribs. He was impossible. A tiny spurt of exasperation shot through her. She pressed it down.

'I thought you'd abandoned ship,' she smiled nonchalantly.

'It didn't take as long as I thought. The captain texted to say you were berthed overnight and wouldn't be leaving until lunch today, so it was my chance to continue the voyage. I've been stuck in my room typing reports all afternoon so it's time to leave off. We were just deciding on red or white. Which do you prefer?'

Pretending to decide what wine she fancied she drew in a couple of slow breaths. Her heart was beating almost normally by the time she slipped into the chair beside him.

'Did you hear Petra's not well?' She kept her voice low.

'Captain told me she wasn't feeling too good.'

'She's been very sick.'

'He'll get Nikolai to look in.' He turned to her. 'Are you really worried?'

'Yes, I am. I just wish there was a proper doctor on board.'

'Nikolai is as good as. I'll go and see her later. Make sure she's okay.'

'Come in,' Petra's voice was weak.

Juliet turned the handle and saw the girl's face had no more colour than the white pillows she was propped up against, but at least she was sipping something hot.

'How're you feeling?'

'Lousy. My stomach feels as though it's been kicked around a football pitch.'

'Has anyone been to see you?'

'Yes, Nikolai. He brought me this ginger tea.' Petra wrinkled her nose.

'And?'

'Suspected appendicitis.'

Juliet gave a sharp intake of breath as her hand shot up to her mouth. If the worst happened and it burst, they were on a ship with no doctor. Petra would be in deep trouble. But she must keep calm. Petra mustn't know how serious this was. She turned her head away, pretending to cough.

'When will he know definitely?' Juliet forced out the question, fearing the answer.

'If the pain gets worse, I guess. Funnily enough I've stopped being sick.'

'Thank goodness,' Juliet said. 'Let's hope it's not that and you'll be feeling a whole lot better by morning.' She paused. 'By the way, someone handed in my bag.'

'That's wonderful.' Petra managed a smile. 'And?'

'The wallet was there...but no photo.'

'Oh, Juliet, I'm so sorry.' Petra looked up with dull eyes.

'I'd given it up for lost, so I'm no worse off.'

'Poor Juliet.' She gave her a wan smile. 'Nikolai told me Jack's back on board.'

'Yes, he is. He's going to look in later. But for now, I want you to rest.'

'He'll know what to do.' Petra leaned back and closed her eyes.

19th September 1913, on board the *Orsova*

I only have time to write a few sentences in my journal. There's an outbreak of smallpox on the ship. It's most alarming. I've met the ship's doctor, a very nice man called Dr Townsend, and although he appeared calm I could tell he was very worried as he called it a crisis. He told me his two nurses haven't been vaccinated against the disease, and had I? I said I had, and he asked me if I would help him in the ship's hospital as he expected there would be several patients who would contract it and need nursing. I immediately said I would.

I hope Ferguson will understand.

As soon as she woke next morning, Juliet pulled on her dressing gown, grabbed her watch which showed five past six, and half ran, half stumbled, along the corridor, feeling the swell under her feet after yesterday's few hours of smooth sailing. Petra's cabin door was unlocked and Juliet went in to find Jack bent over the girl who was lying on her side, knees doubled up, face towards the wall. He straightened up.

'Not good,' he said under his breath. 'I've seen appendicitis before and she's got all the symptoms. It's crucial she gets seen to before it bursts…if it hasn't already,' he finished under his breath.

'Is she asleep?'

'The pain is knocking her almost unconscious. There's only one thing to do and that is to get her into the nearest hospital.'

'But we're hours away—'

'Helicopter,' Jack interrupted, his face grim. 'Captain's ordered one to get here pronto.'

'Is there anything I can do?'

'Not really.'

Petra's eyes flickered open when Juliet gently touched her shoulder.

'We're here, Petra,' she said. 'Jack's here too.'

'I'm scared.' The sound was no more than a whisper.

'You'll be fine.' Jack leaned over to stroke her hair back from her forehead. 'Don't worry. We're going to get you to hospital by helicopter. Nikolai is pretty certain you've got appendicitis. Whip that out and you'll be as good as new.'

Petra gave a thin smile. 'Can you tell Louis? His email is in my address book…in my bag.' She tried to sit up but collapsed back.

'We'll get a message to him,' Jack said. 'Just take it easy.'

'Try to rest,' Juliet urged.

'I can't…pain's too bad. Here it comes again…'and she drew her knees up in agony.

Juliet's brain was racing as she made her way to the dining

room. If Petra's appendix had actually burst she could get peritonitis. It had happened to one of her father's friends and by the time they'd got him to hospital it was too late. Juliet swallowed hard, trying to dislodge the lump at the back of her throat. It mustn't happen to Petra... Every minute would count.

'The helicopter should be here within the hour.' Jack appeared, and helped himself to eggs and bacon. He brought his plate over and sat beside her in his usual place. Juliet marvelled at his appetite; she hadn't been able to eat a thing.

'Didn't hear you.' Trevor leaned forward. 'How's that girl?'

'Not too good, Trevor. She's probably got appendicitis.'

'Rotten luck,' he grunted, stretching over for the basket of toast. He wiped his buttery mouth on his napkin, and popped a large forkful of sautéed potato and bacon between his plump lips.

'An hour seems a long time.' Juliet spoke so only Jack could hear. 'And the wind's got up again. You can hear it, let alone feel it.'

'They'll cope – they're used to bad weather.' He looked at her. 'By the way, Seraphina tells me you had your handbag stolen. That was bad luck. What happened?'

'Kid on a scooter, blast him. But I've got it back.'

'That's great.' He took a mouthful of coffee. 'Was everything there?'

'Nearly everything.'

She mustn't cry. Mustn't.

'Money gone, I expect?'

Juliet nodded wordlessly.

'Too bad. Little sod. I hope he gets picked up.' He patted her hand. 'Never mind, Juliet. It's not the end of the world. As my accountant always says, it's only money.' He speared the last of his bacon and looked at her.

She bit down on her tongue to stop herself from screaming, and swallowed hard.

'Eat something,' he said. 'There's nothing we can do except wait. And you'll feel better with something inside you.' He put a piece of buttered toast on the plate in front of her.

They finished their meal in silence.

'That's better.' Jack wiped his mouth on a paper napkin. His eyes smiled into hers. 'I was starving. Didn't have any supper last night. By the time I came down after waiting for Petra to nod off, Dan had cleared everything away, so I had to make do with bread and cheese.'

She gave him what she hoped passed for a sympathetic smile. At that moment Seraphina and Ronald wandered in, both yawning, and wanted to know if the rumours were true that Petra had appendicitis. Jack patiently explained again. It was somehow reassuring to have everyone's company, Juliet thought with surprise, glad they didn't appear to want to move until there was some news. A half an hour dragged and finally, after they'd drained the third jug of coffee, Dan's tawny head poked round the doorway.

'Helicopter's here.' He rushed out.

Juliet shoved her chair under the table, feeling her legs go wobbly. She clung on to the back of the chair praying they would get Petra to the hospital in time.

Don't think like that.

'Coming?' Jack asked.

Half the crew had congregated by the time she and Jack joined them on the monkey deck. The sky was the colour of dolphins and the sea crashed beneath the deck where everyone was standing. People were craning their necks towards a red and white bird coming closer, making a noise like a roomful of vacuum cleaners.

Juliet had always been contemptuous of people who gawped at the scene of an accident without doing anything practical to help, but now she was doing the same thing she despised in others. But this was the only way she could say goodbye and good luck – to see

Petra taken safely into the helicopter – as though her being there would have any influence. She was grateful for Jack's shoulder, solid and comforting, resting against her own. He was looking through his binoculars.

'Here, Juliet,' he said, handing them to her. 'You never have them handy at the exciting times.'

It's not exactly exciting from Petra's point of view, she was tempted to say, but instead she took them, muttering her thanks.

The bird had turned into a helicopter, its rotors spinning, the noise deafening.

'Will it actually land?'

'No, they hover. Oh, they're bringing Petra now. Poor kid.'

She leaned over the rail where Jack pointed, grateful to feel his hands on her shoulders steadying her. Two of the crew were carrying a stretcher.

'Here comes our man with the basket,' Jack shouted, though Juliet could only just make out the words.

The helicopter seemed to tremble over the bow as Juliet brought the binoculars up to her eyes again. A man appeared at the helicopter door and began to descend from a cable. On a separate hook was a cigar-shaped basket which swung alongside him. It looked to Juliet as though everything was under control, but then to her horror a powerful gust of wind blew the man and the basket sideways. She gasped. The man's legs trod air and she was sure the basket would snap off its cable.

'Oh, Jack...' She thought she would stop breathing.

'It's okay.' He caught hold of her hand. 'They know what they're doing.'

The man dropped the basket off first, then landed on the slippery deck way below the onlookers, and two crew members carrying the stretcher laid Petra in the basket. Immediately she and the helicopter man were winched back up, and through Jack's binoculars Juliet saw the stretcher disappear through the helicopter door.

15

Juliet did her best to read that night in her cabin but the words swam on the page. Impatiently she put her book on the floor and brushed away the tears running down her face. Poor little Petra. Please God let them be in time. She was so young. She mustn't die. The last thing she remembered Petra saying was to let Louis know, and she wondered if Jack had already emailed him.

Jack. Try as she might, she couldn't stop thinking about him. He was disturbingly attractive, but she didn't really know much about him. And when she asked him anything personal he always seemed to clam up.

Why was she working herself up like this? The hospital would sort out Petra and she would never see Jack again after this trip. She dismissed the space inside her head that had got used to being filled with laughing and talking with Jack and Petra. Most of all, she would miss the frisson Jack created when he so much as caught her eye. With a long sigh she switched off her bedside light, then two seconds later switched it back on again to put her watch forward. That done, she pulled up the duvet and pillowed her head, trying to smother the feeling of loneliness.

Juliet woke before five-thirty. Feeling restless, she flung aside the duvet and padded across the living room to look out of one of the portholes. To her delight the sun was edging over the horizon, turning the sky into a riot of orange and crimson. It looked like it was going to be a beautiful day for once. And poor Petra was in some hospital in Italy with no one around who she knew. She must be terrified.

'Get better soon, Petra,' she whispered as she stood quietly for a few moments.

Then her heart turned over again as she thought of the little black and white photo. Charlie's baby face staring up at her.

Flinging on her dressing gown, Juliet slipped out of her cabin and made her way to the outside deck. The air smelt like washing when it was hung out to dry. She lifted her face and breathed in the ozone. Gulls swooped and dived in the distance, showing off as they made their way back to the mainland. Their calls to one another reminded her of when she was a child and her parents had moved to Hunstanton. How excited she'd been when she'd spotted the strip of sea from her bedroom window. This early morning she stood enchanted, her arms hugging her chest against the crisp air. She remembered Will saying she'd soon get bored looking at the sea, but he wouldn't have known at first hand how it altered to reflect its mood. Not just blue-calm or grey-stormy, as she'd always assumed, but often thick stripes of opaque green flowing into a deep turquoise or, as it was this minute, a bright blue shading to a navy-blue stripe on the horizon; then it might change on a whim to charcoal, the waves rearing up in an angry foam.

Now the waves were ruffling innocently against the side of the ship. But it was daft anthropomorphising. The sea was merely itself, caring for nothing or no one, and presumably that was why the captain was still entranced. For some minutes she stood quietly, feeling insignificant but not minding in the slightest, then breathing in a few more lungfuls she turned back to her cabin to make a coffee.

She fiddled with the radio, desperate to hear some classical music, but no matter how she tried to tune it, it growled and whistled. She'd have to ask Dan to show her.

What day was it? It was hard to keep track; one day was so like another. She glanced at the wall calendar above the fridge. The fifteenth. Her birthday. She'd completely forgotten.

'Cheers,' she said, waving her mug in the air, feeling a little silly that she was talking out loud to herself. 'Happy birthday, Juliet.'

After all this time she was now Juliet. Strange. She'd always resented her parents for refusing to call her Jay when everyone else did. And now one man had come along and changed a lifetime's habit.

Telling herself she was losing all common sense, she stripped off and stepped into the shower. As soon as the hot water poured over her and she massaged shampoo into her hair and scalp, she calmed down. She was free for the moment, and she was on her way to Australia – where Charlie lived.

After giving herself a manicure, she flicked through a magazine, being careful not to smudge her nails. Her eyes caught sight of an old sepia photograph of a young, determined-looking woman who reminded her of her Great-Aunt Ruby. As a child Juliet had been fascinated with this aunt, but there'd been no contact with her parents so far as she knew. Ruby had followed her sister to Australia not long after the First World War. She remembered Nannie telling her how she'd sent for Ruby after she and Pop had been in Melbourne a few years. When she'd asked her grandmother more about Ruby – did she get married; did she have children – Nannie had gone quiet, then simply changed the subject. Maybe when she got to Melbourne she could find out what happened to Ruby as well. Somehow she felt there was a mystery surrounding her and it might be fun to uncover it. For all she knew, Ruby could still be alive as she was younger than Nannie. Juliet made a quick calculation. On second thoughts, if Ruby was alive she'd be close to 110.

'Happy birthday, Juliet.' Jack winked at her across the breakfast table.

'How did you know?' Juliet was furious with herself for blushing. With a murmured 'excuse me' she reached across him and helped herself to scrambled eggs, trying not to notice the way a few stray dark hairs protruded from his open-necked shirt. She squashed the temptation to picture the skin and muscles underneath.

He grinned. 'That'd be telling.'

'I haven't told anyone, so I don't see how *you* could have found out.' Why did she have to sound so rude?

Jack raised an eyebrow. 'Were you trying to keep it a secret?'

Was he deliberately annoying her?

'What secret?' Trevor had just come in and caught the end of Jack's question. He plonked himself down next to Juliet. 'Can I be in on it?'

'No, it's nothing.'

'Only her birthday,' put in Jack.

'Your *birthday*?' Trevor's voice rose. 'We need to celebrate. I'll tell Chef—'

'Please don't,' Juliet interrupted. It was the last thing she wanted. 'It's just another day. Jack shouldn't have said anything.'

'Not another word.' Trevor held up the flat of his hand. 'There'll be champagne tonight, I'll guarantee.'

There was no stopping him. Trevor was definitely not the man she'd dreamed of sharing her birthday supper with, but thankfully Seraphina and Ronald appeared and Trevor turned his attention to them. 'Morning all,' he beamed at them. 'Juliet's birthday today,' he went on. 'We should celebrate.'

'Happy birthday, Juliet, and yes, we should.' Seraphina spoke through bright orange lips. She sat herself opposite Jack, smiling archly at him. Today's caftan was fine cotton, streaked with bright orange and a scribble of pink and green, as though a naughty child had painted it.

'Don't worry, m'dear, we'll think of something, the four of us.' Trevor glanced at his watch, and beamed at Juliet.

'It's a pity we're not in a port so we could do something special.'

Seraphina fiddled with one of her hair combs, trying to secure the bright pink wisps.

'Perhaps we'll have to postpone it.' Ronald sounded gloomy. 'But I'll try to think of something, too.'

Juliet cringed to think what Ronald or Trevor would come up with. 'Well, I'm treating it as an ordinary day,' she said firmly. 'I might have a swim, and a go on the exercise bike, then start my jigsaw puzzle for the second, or will it be the third time?' She made herself smile. 'I'm not sure how I'm going to stand all the excitement.' She placed her knife and fork together and stood up from the table.

'I've planned something,' said Jack in an undertone as he got up too.

Her heart missed a beat but she kept her voice casual. 'You have?'

'I thought I'd crack open a bottle of bubbly in my cabin this evening. We can't let your birthday slip by unnoticed.'

'I'm quite happy to, these days.'

'Definitely not allowed,' he chuckled, then looked at her intently with those hypnotic eyes. He seemed about to say something, then changed his mind.

'Wait till you get to my age, then you'll be happy to ignore them.'

Why did she have to say that? Was it just to let him know she was conscious she was older than him?

He had the grace to look puzzled. '*You've* got nothing to worry about.'

She couldn't help laughing. After all, it *was* her birthday and it was time she had some fun. And she'd rather have fun with Jack than anyone.

'What about the others?' she asked mischievously, as they left the dining room. 'Are *they* invited?'

'Do you want them to be?'

'I don't mind.'

Jack looked at her and raised a mocking eyebrow. 'The truth?'

'No, I don't.'

He nodded as though he agreed with her. 'Shall we say five?'

'That would be good.' She prayed she didn't sound disappointed. If only Jack had invited her *after* supper, but obviously all he was suggesting was a pre-dinner drink. She must have got it wrong – he was just being friendly.

'See you in the owner's suite, F deck, at five then,' Jack said. 'Opposite end from you.'

The hours crawled by even though the weather was a dream. All Juliet could think of was how far away five o'clock was. It seemed ages until mid-morning. She went for a swim in the cramped pool and found Seraphina was right – you didn't get any real exercise in such a tight space. She sauntered up to the bridge and an officer nodded towards one of the computers, inviting her to check her emails. Maybe there'd be one from Lydia. But there was nothing from her or any of the team. Oh, she hadn't completely been forgotten. Antonia. She eagerly opened it.

Happy birthday, Jay

How's the trip going? Any gorgeous hunks on board? Anyway, I hope you're not getting seasick like Nannie did.

I'm going travelling myself in a fortnight to see the twins in Rio. I made up my mind on the spur of the moment. You only live once, don't you, so I'm glad now you're following the grandparents and will see Melbourne through their eyes. Do you good to have a break from the business. You deserve it. And I want to hear all about it when you're back.

Don't be too upset if you don't hear from Will. He's going through a difficult time with Miranda and might forget.

140

That's it, darling. Have a lovely day and I'm thinking of you.

All love

Antonia xx

For a split second Juliet wished she was going with her sister to see her nieces, but she knew it was fleeting. She'd a million times rather be where she was. Even so, it was lovely to hear from Antonia on her special day. She read the email again. Strange how her sister seemed to have changed her mind about her going to Australia. She was glad. It was nice to have someone in the family on her side. Suddenly she missed her and made up her mind to keep in touch more often.

Juliet decided not to bother with any lunch. She told herself it was because she wasn't hungry but the real reason, she knew, was that she couldn't face the others, especially Jack, knowing she was invited to his room later in the day. For the hundredth time she wished it was to be after dinner when they could relax and maybe…

Stop it. He's just being his usual charming self and acknowledging your birthday.

No one was about on the lower deck. She removed a plastic chair from a pile and set it near the ship's rail. Smothering her face and legs and arms with sun cream, she pulled on a hat and read until her eyes stung. She looked at her watch. Three-fifteen. She could feel her shoulders beginning to burn. How sexy was that? And there was still another hour and three-quarters to go. What should she wear? She couldn't be too dressed up at such an early hour and yet it *was* her birthday.

She picked up her book and holdall and sauntered back to her cabin. To pass some time away she spread out one of the maps on the coffee table and traced the whole route so far, marvelling at the distance they'd covered and the miles still left to go. Only a few days and they'd be in Egypt. She looked at her watch. That little exercise had taken up all of three minutes. What else could she do? Her gaze fell on the jigsaw puzzle but she was becoming bored with it. She put together a basic greetings card but because it was to no one in particular she couldn't put her heart into it.

What to wear this evening? She opened her wardrobe but her small selection of dresses looked unfamiliar in their new setting, and nothing seemed appropriate.

By the time she'd showered for the second time that day, and washed and dried her hair as slowly as she could without feeling completely ridiculous, it was twenty to five and she still hadn't made up her mind what to wear. Now she panicked. Swiftly, she made up her face, giving it a final dusting of gold powder, and for good luck she brushed the remainder on the tops of her breasts. She gave a wry grin at her reflection. When she'd finished she looked through her clothes yet again and picked out the white dress with the silver belt. She started to unbutton the neckline but put it back on its hanger.

I fancy wearing my lovely new dress, she thought, but it's too fussy for the afternoon. He might get the wrong idea that I've worn it especially for him. But it's hot and I'd feel cool in it. And it *is* my birthday. She took it off its hanger and held it out.

The floaty skirt of silk chiffon, the colour of an aubergine, fell from a fitted purple sequined bodice with plunging neck. She slipped it on. Wisps of chiffon over the shoulders formed small cap sleeves. In the full-length mirror she saw a smiling, glowing woman with generous curves, in a sensational dress. What the hell if it was too dressy. There wasn't time to change again.

She swished her hair up just like Bonita, her hairdresser, had demonstrated, and pinned an evening comb on the side. Yes, it suited her and the new copper glints made her eyes appear brilliant. She applied a deep tawny-coloured lipstick, glanced at her watch and with a satisfied nod to herself, slipped on her silver high-heeled sandals and sashayed out of the room.

16

Juliet tapped lightly on Jack's door. No answer. She knocked louder. She tried the door. It was open and she could hear running water. She paused, then tiptoed in.

His cabin had the air of someone living there permanently. Dozens of books lined the shelves, and a laptop stood on a small desk under the window with its lid open and the screen lit. She wandered through the room into the kitchen area, noticing two used wine glasses in the washing-up bowl. On the worktop stood a stained mug and a carton of milk that hadn't been put back in the fridge. Next to it, in a bucket, with a white cloth round the neck, was the bottle of champagne Jack had promised. The shower stopped running.

'It's me,' she called out.

'Make yourself at home.' Jack's voice came from the bathroom. 'I'll be out in a minute.'

He emerged, a towel wrapped around his lower half, and a smaller one in his hand which he was using to rub his hair. She couldn't help staring at his well-built body – no hint of any paunch, the shoulders broader than she'd realised. Unable to stop herself her eyes travelled downwards where the towel covered him, and in an instant her mind rushed back to Mani. He'd always worn a dhoti around his parents' house in the summer and it had always fascinated her. Dearest Mani. Mustn't think about him. Today was her birthday and she was with Jack. She looked directly at him. His eyes, strangely challenging, held hers.

Her eyes dropped again to the towel which skimmed over his knees. Something was terribly wrong. To her horror she saw his right leg was severely scarred and thinner than the left.

Before she could stop herself she blurted: 'Jack! What happened?'

'An accident,' he said, tossing the smaller towel over the back of one of the chairs. 'You're earlier than I expected.' He nodded towards the wall clock. It was five past four.

Puzzled, Juliet looked at her watch. 'I make it five past five.'

'You must have put your watch on two hours instead of one last night. And there I was thinking you were desperate to see me.'

She felt the heat flush in her face. How could she have been so stupid?

Jack grinned as he sauntered over and kissed her cheek. 'Why don't you sit down and I'll open the bubbly.'

'Isn't it a bit early?'

'It's never too early for champagne. But first I'd better get some clothes on or you might get the wrong idea.' He leered mockingly at her, making her laugh in spite of herself. 'By the way, you're looking absolutely gorgeous. Ravishing, in fact.' He winked and disappeared.

Heart hammering, she sauntered over to the bookcase. Jack had cleverly changed the subject about his leg, passing it off as merely an accident. And, of course, that was why he limped. She wondered if he would elaborate, then shrugged. Let the evening take its course. She turned her attention to the books which were mostly aviation history and biography. She pulled out Douglas Bader's autobiography, *Fight for the Sky*, and flicked through it, not taking anything in but desperate for something to do. All her senses were tuned to Jack moving around in the next room.

'If you turn it the right way up you might be able to read it.'

She swung round. 'It *is*,' she began defensively, then saw the gleam in his eyes.

'Just teasing,' he chuckled.

'Isn't he the pilot who lost his legs in the Second World War?' she asked, desperately trying to convince him she was really taking an interest in his book collection.

'Yes, he was brave, but somewhat foolhardy,' Jack said with conviction. 'Well, I'll leave you to read all about it while I go and get a glass of something.' Looking wickedly masculine in his cream slacks and crisp white open-necked shirt, he set the champagne bucket down on the coffee table next to two crystal flutes, wiped the bottle with a teacloth, and expertly popped the cork.

'Ah...wonderful sound,' he smiled. 'The best. Go and sit down and I'll bring it.'

She hesitated, then went to the sofa. It reminded her of the first night on board when he'd come to her room with a bottle of champagne. Now he was sitting next to her. Too near. She could smell the cotton of his shirt and knew he must have just ironed it. In her nervousness she took far too big a swallow and the bubbles went straight up her nose and fizzed through her mouth, spraying down her chin. Jack burst out laughing and she had to laugh too. It was fatal to try to be cool and sophisticated with Jack.

'You've dribbled your drink before, I seem to remember. In fact, it's the third time. I'm beginning to think you do it on purpose so I can mop you up.'

Before she could open her mouth to protest he turned towards her and took her chin in his hand. Using his index finger he wiped the frothy liquid away. It was the most gentle, affectionate and somehow incredibly intimate gesture she could ever remember any man doing. Her scalp tingled.

To hide her confusion, she said, 'Maybe I should have a bib.'

'I'll make sure to tie one round you at supper,' Jack smiled, still watching her. He was close enough for her to see the flecks of gold spark in his hazel eyes. Then he pulled her to her feet. 'I should give you a birthday kiss.'

Jack held her head gently back, and she felt his fingers on her neck as they supported her. Then soft kisses starting at the corners of her mouth, making her tremble. On and on. She sighed with yearning as she felt the full imprint of his lips on her own, warm with invitation, and more exciting than she had dreamed. Instinctively she searched the inside of his mouth with her tongue, until after long moments he finally allowed her to draw away. She had to. If they'd kissed any longer she would have blurted out something she'd regret.

That she wanted him.

Wanted to feel his skin on hers. The whole length of him. The scent of him. His warmth. Know how he tasted. His tongue. She wanted more. She wanted to feel him move inside her.

She ached with wanting.

She managed a shaky laugh; he laughed too and pulled her close again until her breasts flattened against his chest.

'Mmm. You smell divine.'

'You smell pretty good yourself.'

'Should we try that kissing thing again?' he grinned. 'We might be better at it next time.'

She returned his smile and did something she'd wanted to do since the moment she'd laid eyes on him: she ran her fingers through his hair. He caught her hand, turned it over and kissed the scar she'd got from her fall. Her groin quivered with anticipation. This time his kiss deepened and she felt his tongue explore the inside of her mouth. She wanted him to go on forever and arched her body to fit his, aware of him hardening against her...and the dampness between her legs. She heard him groan.

'I believe you *are* dangerous, Juliet,' he murmured thickly, releasing her. 'Let me know when you're on fire.'

I'm not far off.

Dizzy with kisses, she dropped back onto the sofa and watched him refill their glasses.

'Hope your birthday is to your satisfaction, Madame,' Jack's grin was on the verge of a smirk as he handed back her glass.

'So far, but I'm not going to confirm anything until tomorrow when I'm not tipsy.' Juliet took a swallow of champagne. 'I mustn't have too many of these.'

'It's your birthday, so you're allowed.'

'But I've got to face everyone at supper,' she said, half serious. 'They'll probably think you've tried to get me drunk.'

He sat close to her again and let his arm fall along the back of the sofa, his fingertips lightly touching her shoulder.

'Would it bother you?'

'I hate being out of control...and I will be if I have too much. All to do with work, I suppose.'

'Well, correct me if I'm wrong, but you're not at work.' Jack looked at her, still smiling. 'Sometimes it's good to let your hair down...figuratively speaking, mind, as I love the way you've put it up this evening. It suits you.' His expression altered. 'But am I right that I don't feel you've had a lot of fun lately?'

'Work's quite intense. And now it's weird suddenly doing nothing.'

'So tell me all about yourself and why exactly you're on this trip,' he said. 'The truth now. Is it really following your grandparents' trail? Or something else?' He regarded her intently with those gold-flecked eyes.

Why did he think she had another reason? Most men would have taken what she said at face value. Been glad not to dig further. Not Jack. But she couldn't tell him about Charlie. She didn't know him well enough. And if he was sympathetic, she'd break down.

'I've always wanted to go to Australia,' she said, a little hesitant. 'Everyone I know who's been there loves it. And I've got the connection. My father was born in Melbourne. The grandparents came back to England soon after, and when Dad became an adult he never bothered to go and see what Australia was like when he had the chance. I'm sort of going in his place.' She knew she was gabbling. 'And I have tried to keep a diary,' she said, throwing him a smile, 'which may not be a novel, but at least it's writing. Trouble is, I don't seem to have the patience. I think I'd rather live my life than write about it—' She broke off, feeling a little disloyal to Nannie.

'Me too – even though I love reading other people's,' Jack said. 'My father wrote one during the war.'

'Have you read it?'

'Oh, yes. He was only eighteen when he joined up in '41. Flying aeroplanes at twenty. Doesn't seem possible when you look at some of the youngsters today.' He picked up his glass and took a deep swallow.

'Is he still alive?' Juliet tried to concentrate on what he was saying instead of fantasising about his body.

'No, he died a couple of years ago. But they say I take after him.'

'Is that why you wanted to be a pilot?'

For a moment Jack's face clouded. Then he smiled. 'I guess it was. But Dad did it because he had to. Oh, I think he liked it okay, but it couldn't have been much fun being shot at.'

'Sounds like he was in England.'

'Yes, he was. He wanted to be in on the action – make it count. Don't know if I could ever be that brave. Anyway, let's talk about something more cheerful. Tell me about your brother and sister. Do they live near?' He leaned across her to top up her glass again.

As usual he was asking about her life much more than he seemed willing to tell her about his. She longed to ask him if he'd ever been married. After all, he knew about Gerrard. And did he have children? She half didn't want to know these answers in case it wasn't what she wanted to hear. All men of his age had baggage of some sort. But so what? Jack was still the most attractive man she'd ever known. Funny, intelligent, gorgeous. *For God's sake, just relax and enjoy the moment.*

Her distracted thoughts were interrupted by Jack embracing

her, leaning her head against the back of the sofa, and now his lips were hard and passionate, the inside of his mouth tinged with champagne.

'Juliet,' he murmured, his breath in her ear.

Why had he suggested such a ridiculous hour for this so-called celebration? It must be almost time to go for supper. Why did they have to eat so early on this ship? Well, blow supper. She was prepared to forgo it to stay in Jack's arms.

There was a knock at the door and Jack groaned as he pulled away.

If it's Trevor I shall scream.

She ran her fingers over her smudged lips and looked up. To her surprise it was Dan wheeling in a trolley.

'Happy birthday, Juliet.' Dan's face was one big grin. 'Jack here thought you might like a private birthday supper.' He gave Juliet a conspiratorial wink.

She felt her whole body quiver as she realised Jack had indeed planned a longer evening. That they wouldn't have to step out of his suite until...well...until one of them made a move...

She smiled at Dan, thankful he couldn't read her thoughts.

'Thanks, mate.' Jack took the trolley and wheeled it over to one side.

'Need any help setting up?' Dan didn't seem in too much of a hurry to leave.

'It's okay. We'll manage,' Jack said.

'Well, enjoy your supper. Chef's put himself out for Juliet.'

'Thanks again, Dan,' Jack said as he firmly showed him out of the door.

Juliet was amazed. It was unheard of for Chef to put himself to any trouble like this for the passengers.

'You're not too disappointed that it's going to be *tête-à-tête*?'

'I think I can handle it,' Juliet smiled.

'I wonder.' Jack folded her in his arms again. 'You're sure you can resist me, are you? We'll see about that.' He kissed the top of her head. 'I thought it might be romantic with only the sea for company.' He lifted the combs from her hair so it fell to her shoulders. 'Why… you're beautiful,' he said, in a mock southern drawl, pretending to remove non-existent spectacles.

She laughed. 'Thank you, kind sir.'

'Shall we see what it's like if we eat outside?'

'Outside sounds wonderful if you don't mind eating cold food.' She tried to keep the tone light but it came out as though she was pouring icy water over his suggestion.

'I'm not proposing we drag all this stuff onto the deck. I have my own veranda.'

'You would.'

Jack grinned. 'You're just jealous, I can tell.'

'You're right. It's the only thing missing from my cabin.' She grinned back. 'But I'll be delighted to share yours.'

'Okay. Let's get organised.'

He pulled back the full-length curtains and slid open the glazed doors. 'Madame,' he gestured.

She stepped out onto a small private deck furnished with plastic table and chairs, and a sun-lounger. The light was beginning to fade but the air was thick and balmy from the sun-drenched day. It bathed her bare arms and shimmied over the tops of her breasts as she leaned over to watch the way the ship cleaved through the water, leaving a long thick-foamed trail.

Jack was right behind her. He put his arms loosely round her waist.

'This was all supposed to have been set ready for you,' he murmured in her ear, 'but of course you couldn't wait to get here so you've ruined the surprise.'

'You're not going to let me forget that, are you?' Juliet turned in his arms.

'It's too good to let go.' His eyes gleamed as he kissed her on the forehead. 'Now you stay right where you are and I'll bring the stuff out.'

He grabbed the sun-lounger, folded it and took it inside.

Within moments the veranda was transformed into a tiny private dining room. Juliet laid a white cloth on the table and set out the two place settings while Jack brought out the rest of the champagne and their glasses, then two silver candlesticks holding thick cream-coloured candles. He disappeared again for a couple of cushions for the plastic chairs and finally the trolley which he just managed to squeeze in. He pulled out a chair for her.

'I would tuck this under your chin,' he said, spreading a huge white napkin on her lap, 'to stop you from spilling anymore wine if only you had somewhere to tuck it.' He ran his eyes over her half-exposed breasts. 'Not that I'm complaining, you understand.'

'You're not flirting with me, are you?' Juliet looked up at him with mock enquiry.

'Me?' He pointed to himself with a leer. 'Never.' He filled their glasses and set down the empty bottle. 'Cheers, Juliet.' He clinked his glass with hers. 'I hope you're hungry.' He lifted a couple of the lids and sniffed the contents.

Hungry for you, Juliet wished she were brazen enough to say. What on earth would happen if she did? Her stomach growled and she pressed her hand on it, embarrassed that he might have heard her. She remembered she'd barely eaten anything at breakfast except a piece of toast and a spoonful of watery scrambled egg, and completely missed lunch.

'Ravenous,' she sent him a dazzling smile, trying to ignore the thudding beat against her ribs.

'Me too. There's nothing like champagne and kisses to work up an appetite.' He grinned at her, then struck a match to light the candles. He looked up and held her gaze.

Juliet gave a quick intake of breath, wishing her heart would slow down.

'Well, let's hope you approve of the menu.' Jack ladled out a bright green soup. 'Chef didn't give me a lot of choice. Whatever I chose, he said the others would all have to have the same – he wasn't going to cook different meals.'

'It smells great,' Juliet said, her eyes sparkling. 'I really didn't feel like facing the others tonight. Actually, I was planning to have a quiet evening on my own.'

'Not part of my plan at all,' Jack grinned. 'Much more healthy being in the fresh air.' He blew her a kiss.

Juliet loved the way his eyes never left her. Then she worried he was sizing her up, wondering how old she was today. She was determined not to enlighten him.

'Happy birthday again,' he said, raising his glass.

'And to Petra.' Juliet clinked her glass with Jack's. 'Get well soon, Petra.'

'I'll drink to that.'

They stuck to safe subjects, Juliet being careful that nothing should spoil it. After the soup Jack cleared the bowls and dished out some wild rice onto a plate, balanced a piece of chicken breast on it, and spooned a rich sauce over the top.

'Marsala and mushroom,' he said. 'One of Chef's specials.'

There was a green salad to go with the meal and a good French dressing, topped by another bottle of champagne, courtesy of Chef.

'I never drink this much,' Juliet giggled, as she downed a fourth glass. 'I'm going to suffer in the morning.'

'Not on champagne, you won't.'

They finished the meal with tinned peaches and not a particularly good-quality ice-cream which had already melted to a runny cream, but this evening Juliet thought it the most delicious dessert in the world.

She put her spoon down.

'I want you.' The words dropped from her lips before she could stop them. Shocked at herself, she waited.

He stared at her, long and hard. She lowered her eyes to his mouth. She loved his mouth. Loved how one corner quirked when he smiled. But he wasn't smiling now. Oh, God, had she misjudged him? She brought her gaze back to his eyes, trying to work out his expression.

'I've been thinking of nothing else all through supper.' The gold flecks in Jack's eyes seemed to crackle. 'I could hardly bloody eat for looking at you and wanting you.'

'Then let's not waste another moment,' she smiled seductively, her confidence restored. She took his hand and led him back inside and into his bedroom.

Her only impression was the tidy room and the bed linen which smelt the same as his shirt. After that, everything blurred into Jack.

He sat her on the bed, kissed her, and slowly undressed her. He unstrapped her sandals, kissed each bare foot, then slid his hands under her dress and stroked her between her thighs. Her breathing came faster as he stopped to kiss her mouth, then he raised her arms and gathered up the soft material of her dress, easing it over her head and draping it on the back of the nearest chair. He peeled off his trousers, socks and shirt, leaving only cotton shorts, not attempting to hide his desire for her.

'Lovely,' he murmured, coming back to the bed and looking down at her. 'You really *are* beautiful.' He unhooked her navy-blue lace bra with one practised hand and slipped off her matching silk panties, then lifted her legs onto the bed. He bent to kiss the dark triangle. She lay back on the pillow, giving herself up to him as his fingertips tenderly caressed the damp silky folds between her thighs, on and on...

'Jack. Oh, Jack.'

He stroked her breast, taking her nipple into his mouth, teasing it with his tongue until it hardened, then travelling down to lick the inside of her thighs until she quivered and called out for him, the vibration of the ship increasing her excitement. And when she thought she couldn't stand it a moment longer, she felt him enter her. Something flashed at the back of her mind...nothing between them would ever be the same again...secrets that could blow them apart. But the strength of him...the warmth of him...blocked out... she pulled his hips tight against her groin, hearing him groan as she hooked her legs around his back, arching herself into him, panting, losing control, until she cried out his name.

Afterwards, they lay exhausted, their limbs still entwined, their breathing slowing down in unison, laughing softly.

'Are you all right?'

'No,' she said. 'I don't think I'll ever be all right again.'

He grinned. 'You felt all right to me,' he said, giving her a terrible wink. 'In fact, more than all right. You were fantastic. It calls for a celebration. I think there's enough left in the bottle.' He slid out of bed and returned with two filled glasses, seemingly unaware of his naked body and the effect it was having on her.

'Now, I believe it's my turn.' Juliet raised herself up on the pillows. She took a sip of the champagne and put the glass onto the bedside table.

'If you insist.' He was still sitting on the edge of the bed as he took hold of her wrist, and using his tongue skimmed up to the inside of her elbow. He paused to kiss the soft fold, then bent his head further, letting his tongue travel down. Her breath came in little gasps; her body was on fire again.

'I thought I'd made it clear it was *my* turn,' she laughed shakily.

'I've started, so I'll finish, and *then* you can have your wicked way with me,' he said, not waiting for her reply.

When she thought about him the next morning it was with wild elation and gut-wrenching disappointment. They'd made love as tenderly and passionately as she could ever have dreamed, but although the smell of Jack's skin seemed as familiar as her own as he'd lowered himself onto her, she couldn't read his expression.

It wasn't as though he was detached; no, it wasn't that at all. He'd given her his full attention – every moment – and she hadn't imagined the warmth in his eyes as he whispered her name. But behind the warmth it was as though he was appealing to her... asking her where this was going. Or was this simply all in her crazy mixed-up imagination?

She knew one thing for sure: it would be dangerous to fall in love with Jack Delaney.

17

Damietta, Egypt

The *Alexandria* fought its way towards Egypt over a misbehaving sea which Juliet took great pleasure in watching, hanging on to the rail, the wind whipping her hair across her face, then back again, so her face got the full brunt of the salty spray. But to her intense disappointment Jack made no further move towards her. She might have imagined her birthday evening, she thought wryly, if she'd not had the best sex she'd ever had in her life. She'd never forget it. He'd more or less told her the same thing. So why was he acting like this? His silence could only mean one thing – he was terrified she might start talking about a future together. Or…and she didn't want to dwell on this possibility…he was married.

How could she assure him she wasn't looking for any long-term relationship but that she valued him as a special friend? Make him understand that if a woman is intimate with a man it's nice to know a little about him without necessarily having any expectations.

But was she being scrupulously honest with herself?

'We'll be coming into Damietta at dawn,' Jack announced at the supper table. He glanced at Juliet. 'Make sure you're up really early. You mustn't miss the sunrise. It's magnificent.'

She remembered going through the itinerary in her apartment at home. Then, she hadn't known exactly where Damietta was. Now, in a few hours, she'd be there. At 4.45am her alarm rang. Still half asleep, Juliet dressed quickly; a dab of lipstick, and she was out on the deck. It was beginning to get light and some early gulls were already shrieking and diving, but there was no warmth in the air. She shivered in her too-thin jacket.

'Juliet. Up here.' She turned and craned her neck upwards to see Jack waving from the bridge.

She ran up the two flights of stairs, then tried to steady her breath before she reached him. None of the others had made it. He was alone.

He moved closer…so close she could feel the warmth of his body…could hear him breathing. He put an arm casually around her shoulders, and his touch made her long for him again. Made her want to rip off his shirt and fling him on the deck and—

'See the lighthouse?' his voice interrupted. 'It's a special one. The first one was built in the third century BC and was 400 feet high. Imagine.'

'Did it just disintegrate?' Juliet's voice shook from the force of electricity emanating from his hand. She didn't really know what she was saying – how she was answering.

'One quake after another did for it.' How could he spout all this history stuff when all she could think of was his hands exploring every inch of her body? 'The one you see now is nineteenth century but renewed quite recently,' Jack continued, seemingly oblivious. 'It's still outstanding. The Damiettans were determined to make their port the best one in Egypt.'

As he spoke the sun broke the horizon. The rays spread over the long line of sandy coast dotted with palm trees, touched the rough stone breakwater which protected the entrance to the Suez Canal, until they finally swept across to the tall lighthouse and began to wash up the side of the building, saturating it, then stopped. It was as though the sun was finally satisfied it had illuminated all its best sights for the two onlookers, and by mutual consent the pair stood watching in a comfortable silence. Juliet let out a happy sigh.

'I'll never forget dawn over Egypt.' She turned to Jack, her eyes luminous. 'Thank you for telling me to set the alarm. I wouldn't have missed it for anything.'

He grinned at her. 'I enjoyed sharing it with you.'

From nowhere came a sudden flash of memory. Her father. She was a child.

He'd taken her to London when she must have been about eight. They'd gone to the British Museum, just the two of them. She'd felt so grown-up in her white pleated skirt and brown sandals. It had been one of the hottest days of summer and the museum had felt deliciously cool. They'd strolled around the Egyptian section which had immediately fascinated her; the brightly painted mummies, the pharaohs, the jewellery. She remembered the comforting feel of her small hand being tenderly wrapped in her father's as he explained the ancient kings and queens and their various dynasties. It had been a wonderful day having him to herself. She'd felt almost sick with happiness, looking up at her father every so often to be reassured he was still there.

That one particular day stood out, though they'd probably had similar outings. Her father's love of history, bringing dead people to life, had triggered her own imagination. She could picture herself sitting at a table in the museum café, hardly aware of her sore feet, savouring the last mouthfuls of hot chocolate and her favourite buttered currant bun, hanging on to his words as he answered her questions about the lives of these monarchs.

Well, that was long ago...years before...

'Penny for them.' Jack's gaze was intense.

'Nothing really. Just a childhood memory.'

That's all it was. When she'd adored her father.

'Do you want to share it?'

Juliet shook her head and turned away, her eyes brimming. Jack cupped her chin in his hand and brought her face towards him again.

'Something's bothering you but I won't push it.' He got out

a handkerchief. 'Here. Blow your nose.' He held the cloth to her nose and feeling like a child, she blew.

'There.' He folded the handkerchief and stuffed it into his pocket. 'I don't want you to think sad thoughts after seeing that wonderful sunrise.' He studied her again.

'What? What is it?' Juliet demanded.

'Do you know your eyes are the exact colour of the sea this morning?'

'Are they?' Didn't he have any idea of the effect he had on her?

'Well, now it's got over its tantrums,' he chuckled.

'Are you still talking about the sea – or me?' Juliet laughed, glad they were friends, glad he hadn't let her become morose.

'You choose.' Jack gave a smirk.

'I told you we'd miss it.' Seraphina's raspy voice cut through the moment. 'Hurry up, Ronald, for God's sake.' Her pink head appeared at the top of the metal staircase.

Why did the Smiths always turn up when they were least wanted?

'Did you see it?' Seraphina called as the rest of her body appeared.

'See what?' from Juliet.

'The sunrise, of course.'

'Oh, yes…the sunrise…it was wonderful.'

Jack chuckled. 'It was bloody marvellous. You really missed something, Seraphina.' He turned to Juliet and offered his arm. 'Ready for some tucker?'

By the time they disembarked the sun had climbed higher, and the sky was the colour of lapis lazuli, echoing the darker sea. It was already hot, Juliet thought, consciously breathing the spicy air as she picked her way down the gangplank, a little miffed that Jack had decided not to join them. Emails and reports to write, he'd said. Trevor appointed himself to be in charge as he'd been to Damietta once before, he informed the group. He insisted they all keep together as heaven knows what would happen to women on their own in Egypt. Whisked away by a flowing-robed Arab on a camel, never to be seen again, was Trevor's idea.

'If only,' Juliet couldn't help teasing him, as she took a seat in one of the port buses.

He gave her a horrified snort.

'I'll come and sit next to you.' Seraphina didn't wait for an answer. This morning she'd chosen a sombre brown caftan with turquoise painted leaves. 'That is, if it's not reserved for someone else.' She gave Juliet a pointed look.

'Please do.' Juliet ignored the look. 'Where's Ronald this morning?'

'We're not speaking,' Seraphina confided.

'Oh?'

'He didn't want to come,' she said, using the inside of her arm to swish her pink hair over to one side in annoyance, 'but I made him. He's sitting at the back. But I don't intend missing anything on this trip. Heaven knows, we're chained to the ship long enough.'

Juliet suppressed a sigh. She looked out of the window, pretending to be fascinated by a blurry vision of workers looking like a swarm of busy ladybirds in their red hard hats, as they roped hundreds of containers on and off the waiting ships.

'It's more modern than I expected,' Seraphina remarked. 'I just hate the high-rise buildings, don't you?'

'The port's less than twenty years old,' Juliet said. 'They're apparently very proud of it. The Egyptians finally realised if they wanted to increase their foreign trade they needed a new port to handle more cargo.' She knew she was paraphrasing Jack. 'But Damietta's already famous for all sorts of things. Furniture making, weaving...' she looked at her leaflet, 'a special white cheese—'

'How interesting.' Seraphina put on her sunglasses and stared out of the window.

*

The captain allowed the passengers off the ship for five hours, which was really four when you had to leave an hour's margin for any emergency, like finding a bus or a taxi to take you back to port, Juliet decided. There didn't seem to be any museum. If there was, Trevor didn't take them there. The town was appealing with its palm trees, and she stopped a few moments to watch a handful of men and women sit cross-legged on the street making bread. She would have liked to look in the many fabric shops where you could have anything made up within twenty-four hours, but Trevor insisted they all kept together. Juliet could only give the shopkeepers an apologetic smile. In the end it annoyed her.

'Trevor, please carry on. I'll be perfectly all right on my own. And I can easily get a taxi back to the ship.'

'It's dangerous—'

'Then I'll live dangerously,' Juliet snapped. Trevor's face sagged. 'Sorry, Trevor, but I'm not used to being herded around. I'll be quite safe, honest.'

Trevor sighed and rolled his eyes heavenwards but she ignored him and stood until he gave up and hurried to catch up with the Smiths. She spotted a tall Egyptian, smartly dressed in a western-style suit. He looked like a businessman. He'd be bound to know.

'Excuse me, but do you speak English?'

'You are American?' the man said, his teeth a startling white against the tan of his skin.

'English.'

'Ah, English. I show you good time.' The man's black eyes gleamed.

No way, pal.

'I'm trying to find a shop which sells mobile phones.' Juliet's voice was polite but cool.

'You come with me. I show you.'

He wouldn't be showing her any mobile phones, she'd bet her

161

life. Juliet shook her head. The man shrugged as though it was her loss, and vanished.

She found herself in one of the local markets, so different from anything at home. No mean little packets or jars of spices like you got in the English supermarkets. Instead, enormous baskets of bright yellow, bright orange and earth-red powders, open to the sunshine, jostling with dozens of other colours, were laid out in front of the stalls, their wonderful aromas filling the air. She couldn't help thinking of Mani, but for once she could inhale the smells which so reminded her of him without feeling the old despair. She could even think of the baby they'd created – little Charlie – without her eyes filling, which always happened when she thought of him. An image flashed into her mind of what he would look like today. He'd probably be tall, like her side of the family, but he'd have Mani's golden skin and brown eyes, she was certain. She was equally certain that he was alive and well and happy, and that certainty made her feel more light-hearted than she'd felt in years.

Maybe it was the heat of the sun on her skin, and the cheerful faces of the stallholders, nodding to her and pointing to their baskets, tempting her to buy. Maybe it was simply the sheer pleasure of wandering around an exotic place where she didn't understand the language or the people or half of what they were selling. But she couldn't help smiling back as she turned her head from one stall to another, picturing her son and wondering what he was doing at this exact moment. For a few minutes she stood and watched two women, dressed in the ubiquitous burqa, waiting for their chosen spices to be weighed and wrapped. Did they mind being completely covered in this heat? What must it be like to be a woman here, constantly watched by the moral police? Having your freedom curtailed? She shuddered. It was too horrible to imagine. She wished she could talk to them; ask them why they let their menfolk control them this way. But of course they didn't have much choice. This was a patriarchal society which would take decades to alter – if it ever did. It was all very nice being a tourist, but the undercurrent was close to the surface wherever you looked.

Don't get too heavy, Juliet, she warned herself as she strolled along the various stalls, offering only a brief glance at the usual tourist tat of stuffed camels, cheap jewellery and crudely scratched vases and mugs, pulling a face when she came near a meat stall. The stench hit her nostrils making her feel sick. Carcasses of unrecognisable animals with sad eyes hung from hooks in the blazing sun, and she hurried by, trying not to look. Maybe the burqa gave you some protection against such rotten smells. She wished she could bury her nose in a perfumed handkerchief. Or even a bunch of mint. It was a wonder people weren't lying dead in the streets from meat poisoning in this heat.

Thankful to arrive at a small parade of shops at the end of the market, her eyes were drawn to the carpet shops where they vied with one another. There must have been half a dozen, one after the other, all with a huge display of carpets piled up outside, and smaller rugs had been strung overhead as though on a washing line. She walked over to the first shop and idly fingered a particularly bright-coloured carpet at the top of the pile where a woven pharaoh stared at her.

'All natural dyes,' said a black-haired young man, stepping from the gloomy interior. He came up to her and unfolded it. 'This one is saffron for yellow, and turmeric and paprika for gold and orange, and chilli for red brown. Is beautiful, is it not?'

Juliet was impressed. 'It's lovely.' She thought of her plain living room at home. It would certainly cheer it up and be a wonderful reminder of the voyage. No, she mustn't. She'd never be able to get it back to the ship, let alone on the plane home.

As though he'd read her thoughts he added slyly, 'We send our carpets all over the world. You buy today and we ship it to you. You get in few weeks' time. All safe.' He studied her, his brown eyes gleaming with approval. 'English?'

'Yes.'

'How long you here in my country?'

His lashes were too thick and curly for any man to deserve, she thought, suppressing a smile.

'Only a few hours, unfortunately.'

He widened his eyes in what could only be disbelief, and she thought how ridiculous it was to be in such a fascinating place for such a short time.

'I am Samir,' he said, his long hair flopping over his forehead. 'It mean nice person, good friend.' He held out his hand. 'Very pleased to meet English girl.'

'Nice to meet you, too,' she said, putting her hand in his.

He gave her a deep searching look as he held on to her hand, like some Mills & Boon hero. She bit back a giggle as she shook her hand from his grasp.

'All wool. All handmade.' He jerked his thumb towards the carpets she'd been admiring. 'Come. We have more inside. I show you.'

It couldn't do any harm having a look. He took her hand again and not wanting to seem prim she allowed him to lead her to the back of the shop and up a narrow wooden staircase which opened out into a true Aladdin's cave. The room was stacked from floor to ceiling with every conceivable carpet in every possible design, size and colour. She breathed in the earthy odour of the dyes and the unbleached wool. It smelt good.

'Many choices. And the kilim is not so heavy for packing.' He unrolled one and flung it out on the floor. It had an overall pattern in almond pink and pale blue. Beautiful for a bedroom.

'Even if I wanted one I'd never be able to choose,' Juliet blurted. 'They're all so wonderful.'

'I tell all people so long as size is right, it doesn't matter on colours. They will look beautiful anywhere.'

He was probably right. But just as she was about to ask him

what the shipping costs were he suddenly grabbed her, pushing her up against the wall. He pressed himself on her in a smothering embrace, his erection as strong as the arms that gripped her.

'What on earth—' Juliet tried to wriggle from his grasp but he held on.

'You want this, as me,' he said thickly, forcing his mouth on hers.

Without thinking she shot her hand up and slapped him hard. 'Stop it at once.' She was breathing fast. 'I'm old enough to be your mother. Is that how you would want your mother to be treated?'

He let go immediately, rubbing the side of his face, a regretful look in his eyes.

'I'm sorry,' he said. 'I did not know—'

'Forget it,' Juliet interrupted. Cheeky little bugger. 'But I want to tell you something. English women aren't all on the make, as you seem to think. And you've just lost a customer.'

So much for being a woman on her own in Egypt, she thought, as she left the shop, Samir's apologies ringing in her ears. A burqa would have been quite welcome if this was what she was going to confront every time she took an interest in something. Oh, well, she'd get a taxi to the ship.

She was just making her way back through the market when she walked smack into Trevor.

'There you are,' he said, holding her arm, making her feel like a naughty schoolgirl. 'I've been looking for you.'

She gently extricated his hand. She'd had enough of men grabbing her, even though she knew Trevor was harmless and only trying to be protective. 'Where are the others?'

'They've gone on ahead. I got them a taxi.' He ran his hand through his hair as though the act of flagging down a taxi had been almost too much for him. 'I was worried, y' know. Thought you'd got molested. Know what these Arab chaps are like.'

Juliet gave a wry smile. He didn't know how close he was. 'I'm sorry you were worried,' she said, 'but I'm quite used to looking after myself.'

Trevor would have had a fit if she'd told him what had happened in the carpet shop.

'Not here, you're not,' Trevor said, taking her arm again to steer her away from a pile of rotting vegetables. 'Never know what they're thinking. Did you get your mobile phone?'

'No. And I haven't noticed anyone using one. It's really odd.' She gave him a sideways glance, feeling a tinge of shame for her offhand manner. 'How did you know where to find me?'

'I asked if anyone had seen a tall dark-haired western woman,' Trevor said seriously. 'You stand out a mile from all these black crows. They pointed to the carpet shops and said it's where all the tourists go. I'm glad you didn't get sucked into buying one, like Seraphina.'

So even Seraphina had bought a carpet. And she'd got nothing to show for her escape from the group. No carpet to cheer up her living room and no mobile. It was all rather a disappointment. She wondered if Seraphina had bought a carpet in Samir's shop. But Ronald would have been right there behind her, so no chance for Seraphina to go off the rails. As for a mobile, Juliet might have to wait until they got to Melbourne. She'd need to restrict herself on the number of emails she sent from the ship because it was wildly expensive and the crew weren't that keen on passengers tying up their computers either. She sighed and Trevor looked at her sharply.

'It's just the heat,' she said.

'Drains one,' Trevor agreed. 'Can't take too much of it.'

He was right. His forehead was red and shiny with sweat, and he was beginning to puff. She hoped he hadn't got sunstroke. That was all they needed – another passenger to go down with something.

'We have some news,' the captain said, as he stood at the top of the gangplank to welcome them back on board.

166

Juliet stopped abruptly on the last step. Petra?

'We hear from the mother of Miss Sandys. She is out of emergency and soon to go home.'

Next on the itinerary was the Suez Canal. Juliet found a quiet corner on the monkey deck, well away from Seraphina's chatter two decks below. Bliss. She placed her hands on the warm iron rail enjoying the feel of the early evening sun on the back of her neck and marvelling at the view. Ever since she'd read *The Seven Pillars of Wisdom* and had fallen in love with T E Lawrence she'd been fascinated by the desert, but this was a real meeting of man and nature. Perfect layers of overlapping swirling peaks and patterns formed sandy banks on either side of the incongruous path of water they were skimming through, with barely a foot spare, it seemed, on either side.

It puts all my problems and worries into perspective, Juliet thought, as she strained to see how far the desert stretched. A string of animals crawled along in the distance. Thrilled, she lifted her binoculars, fumbling with the little wheel to bring them into focus before they disappeared. A camel train. She counted about thirty animals. It made her laugh to see how all their noses were at the exact same haughty angle as they swung their hips across the sands like weary prostitutes. You could have all the Bedouins you liked, she thought, but the true kings and queens of the desert were the camels.

A scuffling noise from behind made her reluctantly pull her binoculars away. Trevor was heaving himself up the steep narrow steps. Oh, why couldn't they leave her alone? To her relief Jack followed.

'Magnificent, isn't it?' Jack said.

'I love it.' She wheeled to face him. 'You've just missed the camel train,' she said a little smugly.

'I watched it from the cabin.'

You would.

'Where're the camels?' Trevor, to Juliet's irritation, stepped round to her other side as neatly as a folk dancer. 'Don't see anything.' He squinted out into the distance.

All she wanted to do was stand there, drinking in the atmosphere. *Please go, Trevor.* Jack was polite as usual and chatted to him. A quarter of an hour passed until Trevor finally looked at his watch.

'Nothing happening out there. Time for a G and T. Care to join me, you two?'

'Not right now, Trevor.' Jack gave her a quick glance.

'Juliet?' Trevor queried.

'That would be lovely,' she answered, turning her back to Jack and inwardly cheering that she'd seen his face drop.

'We'll be along in a few minutes,' Jack said. 'Order one for both of us. And one for yourself. On me.'

Trevor beamed, and disappeared.

Juliet heard Seraphina from below saying loudly, 'I can't believe you didn't see the camels, Ronald. You always miss everything. Not that there's been much to look at, but when there is you're never there.'

She heard Ronald mumble a reply and turned her head towards the sea. It was funny. She still hadn't got tired of it.

Jack broke the silence. 'You haven't been your usual self lately.'

What the hell did he mean? She was standing here perfectly happy. *He* was the one who had never once referred to her birthday evening. As if it had never taken place. As though he regretted it.

'I'm fine.' It didn't sound convincing, even to herself.

'When women say that, it usually means they're not.'

'Well, you should know.'

'What's that supposed to mean?'

'What it sounds like. You've known plenty of women so you

have enough experience of our funny little idiosyncrasies.'

Jack frowned. 'So I was right. You *are* mad at me. Come on, Juliet, what's on your mind?'

'It's *you* that's been off with *me*,' she said, her eyes flashing. 'You've hardly said a word since my birthday. And if you must know, every time I try to ask you something personal you put me off. You always say "later" or "now's not the right time". As though you don't trust me. I'm fine for a quick lay and that's all.'

'I don't recall it was *that* quick.' Jack's lips curved in amusement. 'In fact, quite the opposite.'

'You know *exactly* what I mean,' Juliet flung at him. 'Don't try to change the subject. You won't even give me a straightforward answer to your accident.'

Jack's eyes were dark with warning but she couldn't stop herself.

'You don't have to worry about me, Jack. I'm not the clingy type.'

Shut up, Juliet. Just shut up.

'I never thought you were.'

'I just hoped we were friends.'

'We are.'

He still wasn't giving anything away. The same as he'd been after they'd made love that wonderful evening. Tears welled.

'I said I'd explain in my own time.' Jack's voice was emotionless. 'It's not a pretty story.'

She noticed the little lines around his mouth appeared more deeply cut, making him, for an instant, vulnerable. She wanted to take him in her arms, tell him she...well, perhaps not that...but tell him if he needed someone to talk to, that she was a good listener. But as she moved towards him he suddenly said:

'I damaged the leg in a plane crash. I was the pilot. That's it. Simple.'

'Is it? I don't believe it. I don't think you're being open with me and I don't understand why. You opted out of coming with us to Damietta. And you've been so cool since—' She stopped. 'Anyway, we'll soon be in Melbourne. So let's just call it a day.'

'What're you talking about? Call *what* a day?'

'If you can't see it, I'm not going to bother explaining.'

'Juliet,' he caught her arm. 'Don't get so upset. Give me a chance.'

She shrugged away his hand and stalked off.

The voyage was rapidly coming to an end. Juliet spent the time reading, going to the gym, having a swim in the cramped pool which had been refilled, and making a few more cards ready to send to friends. One in particular was for Seraphina and Ronald's wedding anniversary, which they both cooed over and kept propped up all day at their place setting for everyone to admire. She made a point of engaging Trevor in conversation, pressing down any guilt that she might be giving the old boy false hopes. Once or twice Jack tried to talk to her but her pride only allowed her to respond in a perfunctory manner. She ignored the questioning look in his eyes, though the intensity of the brief fling with him grew into a yearning until she thought she would go mad wondering what was going on in his dark head. She hated herself for trying to force him to talk about something he didn't want to. And what did he mean when he asked her to give him a chance? Whatever it was, she'd driven herself into a blind alley and there was no way out.

Back in her cabin she sat in her armchair and tried to empty her mind, resurrecting the mantra she'd once been given when she was learning to meditate, but after five minutes she unclasped her hands and opened her eyes. It was pathetic how she couldn't stop thinking of Jack. Her relationship with him was nothing to get so worked up over. They were just two grown-up people who'd wanted one another and had enjoyed a wonderful evening. That's all. But she felt more lonely than she could remember.

10th September 1913, on board the *Orsova*

I'm not used to doing nothing. When I was working at Bonham Place I was busy from early morning until late evening with one day off. That day I was home looking after my sisters and Dad – cooking for them and mending clothes. This all seems very strange but at least the sea is quite calm and I'm out in the fresh air. Ferguson is thoroughly enjoying himself. He plays deck games with his new friends most days. He told me to come and watch him playing chalking the pig's eye yesterday, but it looked so childish that after a few minutes I got tired of it. I can't understand why he likes it so much. I prefer to find a quiet corner on the ship and write this journal, though it's not always easy as there are so many passengers and crew and we have to keep to our third-class quarters. I wish Ferguson wanted my company more often. I feel lonely even with so many people around me.

It was impossible to believe it was their last night on board the *Alexandria*. What was to have been a means of getting to Australia – be it an unconventional way – had turned out to be more than she'd bargained for. She tried to imagine the trip without Jack – or Petra for that matter – and couldn't. It was illogical and rather silly, but she felt she'd been fated to meet them both.

Dan had lit candles and soft music was playing in the background by the time everyone gathered for dinner. It reminded Juliet again of her birthday and how Jack had gone to such trouble to please her. Her cynical self told her it was to get her into bed, but her heart knew that wasn't right either. Something was bothering him and she'd mishandled the situation. Her eyes pricked with unshed tears.

Trevor gave a whoop of delight at the bottles of champagne Dan brought to their table. Juliet noticed he hadn't bothered to dress up just because it was their last evening, and still had the same tie with splashes of tomato sauce from yesterday's ratatouille. Ronald wore a short-sleeved check shirt, the top two buttons undone to reveal a chicken neck, but his sweep-over was neatly in place. Seraphina shone with pendants and bracelets and rings, all of various colours, which didn't blend with each other, let alone her newest caftan. Jack, sitting opposite her, in jeans and sky-blue shirt, smiled up at Tatyana. Juliet's heart contracted.

'Your good health, one and all,' Trevor beamed as he insisted on clinking everyone's glasses.

'Cheers,' Jack said, to no one in particular, and although his mouth still smiled, his expression was bland.

Chef had prepared a special farewell meal, but after the soup Juliet rose.

'Please excuse me, everyone,' she said, pushing her chair back, not even glancing at Jack. 'I'm not that hungry and I need to find out if there are any emails for me from work.'

She made her way up to the bridge. Ivan was the only officer on duty.

'Good evening, Ms Reece.'

'Hello, Ivan. I wonder if I could check my emails.'

'Please.' He indicated the adjacent computer.

She took the seat beside him and entered her password. Guiltily she opened her inbox, realising she hadn't checked for several days. Nothing from Lydia. Odd. One from Rachel, sent only hours ago. She opened it.

Jay, it's all gone tits up. Lydia and Neil had an almighty row yesterday. Don't know what about but she's walked. Told us she's not coming back. She made some feeble excuse about domestic problems but it's obv to do with Neil. Now he's gone sick. I don't know what's going on. It might be a good idea for you to get back asap.

In haste, Rachel

18

Jack

It hadn't been deliberate but he knew he'd upset her. When would he ever learn? You can't make love to a woman one day and the next show barely a flicker of interest. Behave almost as though it had never happened. Then have the nerve to ask her what was the matter. He bloody well *knew* what was the matter. He'd treated Juliet hardly better than some casual one-night fling. And that's precisely how she must have felt. And that's what made her say, her lovely dark eyes positively sizzling, 'Let's call it a day.'

He squeezed his eyes shut, hearing her voice, and himself giving her the impression he didn't know what she meant.

His mind replayed her birthday. For once, he'd judged it right. Chef had cooked a really special dinner and Juliet had looked sensational in that floaty piece, the colour of purple grapes. She'd arrived an hour early and when he'd teased her about it she'd been mortified. Which had made her look even more desirable. But then he'd kissed her and she'd kissed him back. He hadn't wanted any food the moment he'd set eyes on her. Had she worn the dress especially for him? Or was it just because it was her birthday? Dear God, he'd had to think of anything, anything, to take his mind off wanting her; not making a complete fool of himself. He'd wanted to romance her. But then she'd blown him away completely by suddenly announcing halfway through dinner that *she* wanted *him*.

He hadn't made love with a woman since the accident. Isobella had always made it perfectly clear she would never be interested in a man who was physically flawed. When he and Isobella had first fallen in love he hadn't believed his luck. This beautiful Italian creature desired him as much as he did her, and frequently told him what a perfect body he had. He'd been honoured and thrilled to marry her, and was the envy of all his friends. But they didn't know her. She was always charming to them. One or two of them were still surprised he'd let such a gorgeous creature slip through his fingers.

No, it wasn't just because his leg was scorched that Isobella had turned off him. Things had gone wrong with her years before. The leg had done one good thing, though. It had brought things to a head and she'd filed for divorce. He was certain she'd had another man for some time. If only he hadn't reacted so stupidly when she'd finally admitted it. He should have gone along with her. It would have been easier and certainly a lot cheaper than arguing and delaying. All he wished for now was that the official paperwork would soon be through and he could get on with his life.

Instinctively, he'd felt he could trust Juliet not to back off when she saw his leg. Yes, she'd looked a little shocked when she'd arrived early and caught him with only a towel round his middle, but when he remembered how they'd explored one another's bodies it hadn't seemed to make the slightest difference. She'd just accepted it.

Even thinking about Juliet churned him up. But he hadn't said anything. Hadn't dared to risk letting her know his feelings. How could he when he didn't know what they were himself?

That was the reason he'd decided not to join the group in Damietta. He'd needed time on his own to think. Calm himself down. But Juliet had thought he was snubbing her when he'd made up an excuse that he had reports to write up for work. It was flimsy and she hadn't believed him.

But he was determined to keep his word and take her to the Maritime Museum. He sensed it was an important place for her to visit, and inexplicably he knew he wanted to be with her.

19

'Damn you!' Juliet exploded. Ivan swung round in his chair. 'Sorry, Ivan, I didn't mean *you.*'

'You hear something bad?'

'You could call it that.' She looked at her watch. Just before seven. 'What time is it in the UK, Ivan?'

'Eleven hours behind.'

She made a swift calculation. It would be 8am. Rachel was always in early.

'Ivan,' she turned to him, 'Can I make a couple of important calls to the office right now?'

'Sure. But is very expensive because it comes by satellite. You pay by the minute.'

'I'll keep them short.'

'Is that you, Rach?'

'Jay! Oh, I'm so pleased to hear from you. Where are you?'

'Fast approaching Melbourne. We'll be there tomorrow morning. What's going on?'

'Well, Lydia and Neil didn't hit it off right from the beginning. They were always at each other's throats. Then they had a stand-up row. We could all hear them. Lydia just packed up and said she was leaving. She said something about domestic problems. Bob and Kirsty don't know what accounts she's been working on as she's hopeless at leaving notes on the files. Says she keeps it all in her head. So she's done us no favours at all with her—'

'And Neil?' Juliet cut in. 'Anyone know what's the matter with him?'

'Not a word. He phoned in sick this morning with flu, but he seemed perfectly all right yesterday. I'm sorry if I'm wrong, but I don't believe it...especially as he's been a bit strange lately.'

'Strange? How?'

'Not his usual cocky self. Almost as though he's keeping a low profile. Barely speaking to anyone. Yesterday morning he went into his office and didn't appear until lunch. Then they had the row. Then—'

'Sorry, Rachel, you're breaking up. And I can't hang on.'

The next few words were a jumble.

'We're all sick to death of Lydia,' Rachel continued, when the line was clearer. 'She's got an ego as big as an elephant's arse. And you know I never cared much for Neil. None of us do. But we've put up with him because of you.'

Juliet bit her lip. 'I'm damn well going to get to the bottom of it, if it's the last thing I do. Is Bob around?'

'He's out, and Kirsty's at the dentist.'

'How are they both?'

'They're coping. Neither of them could stand Lydia. Even Jamie couldn't stick her. She ordered him around as though he were her little slave.' Juliet's mouth tightened. 'Oh, before I forget, have you got another mobile?'

'I'm getting a temporary one tomorrow when we dock so I'll email you the new number. And can you give me Neil and Lydia's home numbers? It's driven me crazy since I had my BlackBerry stolen.'

'When do you think you'll be back?'

Juliet's stomach turned. This was all going horribly wrong. She should never have left.

'Are you there, Jay?'

176

'Yes, sorry, line's not very good,' Juliet mumbled. 'I'll get a flight as soon as I can, and let you know when.'

'Sorry to interrupt your holiday when it's barely started, but I've got a bad feeling and I think it's important you're here to deal with it.'

'Don't worry. And, Rach...thanks for everything. Tell the others, too.'

Hell and damnation. Why did Lydia walk out? Juliet always had her down as being ultra-efficient. Conscientious. Tough. It didn't make sense. The woman must have dealt with difficult staff and clients before. She thought of Lydia in the restaurant that night when she'd offered to stand in. Lydia had hinted she was bored; said she'd almost regretted selling. If Lydia was there in front of her she'd shake her until her brilliant white capped teeth rattled for upsetting the staff. God knows what damage she might have done already. But she must be fair. Maybe Lydia had genuinely had enough of Neil's arrogance and had decided she couldn't hack it anymore with him. No, she mustn't make a judgement until she'd spoken to her. And Neil, of course.

She dialled Neil's home number. No reply, not even a recorded message. So unless he was very ill, he should be answering his phone. She let it ring for almost a minute. The phone was ringing in an empty house – she was certain. She thought back. Had Neil ever pretended to be sick? On thinking about it, she couldn't remember when he'd ever called in sick. Even when he had a cold he always turned up for work.

None of this would have happened if she'd been there. But it was no good thinking about what might have been. She needed to get this sorted – fast.

Lydia next.

No answer. She was about to put down the handset when she heard a click.

'Lydia. It's Juliet.'

'Juliet? Who—?'

'It's me, Jay.'

'Oh, Jay.' Lydia's tone was guarded. 'I wondered when I'd hear from you.'

'What's going on?'

There was a pause. Then Lydia said, 'Presumably you've spoken to Rachel?'

'Yes. But I'd rather hear it from you. So why did you—?'

'Before you carry on,' Lydia's voice was now dripping icicles, 'I'd like to explain *my* side of the story. Have you heard from Neil?'

'Nothing.' Juliet's tone matched Lydia's.

'I thought not.'

'Apparently, he's gone sick. But I couldn't get hold of him just now.'

'Sick,' Lydia repeated mockingly. 'He's sick, all right.'

'What do you mean?'

'He had the nerve to proposition me.' Lydia enunciated each word as though to be sure Juliet understood the meaning. 'Said if I played my cards right we could wipe the floor with Jay Reece.'

The bastard.

'I said I would email you what he was up to, and he said he would deny everything and tell you he'd managed to stop *me* from sabotaging the business. That he could twist things to provide the evidence if I didn't play ball.'

Juliet drew in a sharp breath.

'Jay?'

'Yes.' Juliet swallowed.

'Oh, you're still there,' Lydia said. 'Look, I know this is hard for you but you need to know the truth about your wonderful Neil.' There was a pause. 'I said I wouldn't be involved in any underhand stuff and he could go to hell. He threatened to tell Robert I'd come on to him if I didn't back him. I'm afraid I panicked and told Rachel I'd got domestic problems and Neil would have to be in charge.

I went in the following day to pack up my things and hand over the accounts.'

'Why didn't you call me and tell me all this?' Juliet said, feeling sick.

'I sent you a text but had no reply. I assumed you chose not to believe me. I'm not sure you do now.'

'I told you in the last email, my BlackBerry was stolen.' Juliet clamped down her irritation. 'The only way I can communicate is to use the ship's computer and phone, which I'm on now, but it's not always convenient and it's very expensive.'

'Oh, well, whatever's priority, Jay.'

Lydia's voice cracked and the line went dead.

How could she have been such a fool to let some outsider take over her precious business? All she knew was that she'd been exhausted and desperately needed a change. But why had she made excuses where Neil was concerned for so long? Where was her judgement of people? *If* Lydia was speaking the truth, and she had sounded genuine, Neil was more or less threatening blackmail – on top of everything else.

Thank goodness Bob was still there. Dear Bob. Reliable Steady. He would hold it together until she got back – he and Kirsty. And Rachel would keep the office running. But her small team was halved and word must have already got around that Juliet Reece was no longer at the helm.

Her head started to pound. Should she talk to Jack? Although he was perfectly polite, he hadn't exactly been seeking her out after their row. Yet he was the only person she could trust to give her common-sense advice. But what on earth would he think of her? A complete fool, that's what.

Furious with everyone, but most of all herself, Juliet flung her bag over her shoulder, remembered to thank Ivan, and rushed out, her thoughts busy as she half ran down the flights of steps to her room.

Oh, if only she could have a cigarette to calm her nerves.

She needed to find Jack.

After searching the whole ship, Juliet finally tracked him down in his room. She hesitated, then balled a fist and rapped on the door, willing her heart to slow down.

His very presence filled the doorway. Six feet of masculinity. A question in the dark raised eyebrow. Not a hint of a smile. This was a huge mistake.

'This is unexpected,' he said.

She turned to go, but hesitated. Jack stepped aside and held the door wide open.

'Come on in, why don't you?'

In her nervousness she brushed by him, then stopped. The table was heaving with newspaper cuttings and files and photographs. She moved towards it, glancing casually, hoping to see what he was working on, but she was at the wrong angle. Jack stepped in front and quickly gathered everything together. He shoved them in a cupboard.

'I'm not disturbing you?' She turned her head. He was so close she only had to put out her hand to touch him, stroke his face, feel the breadth of his shoulders…so close she could hear him breathing.

'No more than usual.' But he didn't have the old teasing grin.

She tried again. 'Jack, can I talk to you about something confidential?'

A spark of interest flared in the hazel eyes. 'Sure. Make yourself at home. Let me get you a glass of wine.'

He went to the fridge and took out a bottle.

'It's already opened,' he said, bringing her a glass, 'but it should be okay from last night.' He didn't pour one for himself.

Sitting on the edge of the sofa, feeling awkward that he hadn't joined her in a drink, she said, 'Jack, I need your advice. Something awful's happened with my business.'

Jack drew his brows together. 'What is it?'

'Lydia, my stand-in, has walked out. And Neil has gone sick, which is completely unlike him.'

'The woman's bad news,' Jack commented, after she'd finished, 'but you shouldn't believe everything she tells you until you speak to Neil. Hear his side.' He leant forward in the easy chair, seemingly to emphasise his point. 'Thing is, what are you going to do apart from booking your flight?'

'That's the easy part,' Juliet said. 'I just don't know how to handle Neil. If Lydia's not exaggerating and he's really threatening to blackmail her—'

'You *must* speak to him first before you make any accusations.'

Juliet felt the familiar bubble of irritation. 'Yes, I heard you the first time.' She stopped. 'Sorry, that sounded rude, but what if he's really setting out to destroy me? How can I stop him? Employment laws are tricky. You can't get rid of anyone until you go through a messy, drawn-out procedure. It's worse than a divorce and could take months. By then it'll be too late.'

'If he's doing what Lydia seems to think he's doing, you may not have that problem.' He got up and ran the kitchen tap. 'By the way, did you ask your Rachel to check the computers?' he spoke over his shoulder. 'Make sure they've not been tampered with in any way.'

Juliet bit her lip. She was tempted to tell him of course she'd thought of that. But in truth she hadn't. 'I'll get on to Kirsty. She's the whiz on computers.'

'You might need a lawyer.' Jack came back with a glass of water. 'Didn't you say your ex is one?'

'I don't want to involve him.'

'It's going to be difficult to prove unless you find that Neil has been poaching your clients. Presumably they're under contract.'

'Yes. Six months.'

Jack ran his hand through his hair. 'It's possible, I suppose, that he's set up his own company. Maybe told your clients a pack of lies that you've taken a long leave of absence and perhaps they should try him – he may have even offered a discount for changing horses.'

Something else she hadn't thought of. She swallowed.

'Or he could be completely innocent. Genuinely sick – even in hospital.'

Juliet shook her head. 'He's got both parents living nearby and several friends. Someone would have called the office by now.'

'I'm just throwing out ideas.' Jack gulped down his water and put the empty glass on the table. 'Well, you can't do much until we dock. But I wouldn't ask to use the ship's computer or their phone again as this is their crucial time. They won't want any of us hanging about the bridge. Use mine if you need to. We'll be in Melbourne tomorrow, and as soon as you get to your hotel you can get your flight booked. It's a real shame this has come when you haven't even started following your grandparents' trail,' he gave a half smile, 'but there's always another time.'

'You think? I'll never get another opportunity until I finally sell up.' Juliet looked across the few feet separating them. Jack raised an eyebrow as though to ask her a question. 'If, of course, there's anything left to sell,' she added bitterly. 'Fine businesswoman I've turned out to be. And there's so much I wanted to do...' She trailed off, and without warning burst into tears.

She was aware of Jack kneeling beside her.

'Hey, don't get worked up until you know exactly what's going on. And not even then. It's not worth it. Things have a habit of working out. Even terrible things.' His eyes darkened. He gently took one of her hands in his and kissed it. 'At the moment it's only guesswork.'

'It's not just that,' Juliet gulped. 'I wanted to go to Petra's engagement party in Sydney...make sure she's okay...and maybe while I was there see if I could look up...' She froze. *Don't tell him. You mustn't tell anyone – ever.*

'Look up what?'

'The records. To find out more about...my family.' It was a half-truth anyway.

'But your grandparents worked in Melbourne,' Jack persisted.

'No, it's someone else,' Juliet said in a low voice.

Juliet zipped up her overnight bag and glanced in the mirror. Her lipstick was a little smudged from breakfast, and she quickly reapplied it. Strange not to be saying goodbye to Petra, who'd been whisked away so quickly she'd forgotten to ask for her phone number. Would Dan be allowed to tell her? Probably not, but she'd ask him anyway. Or Jack would know. Her heart raced. Looking round her cabin for the last time she remembered him standing in her doorway, holding a bottle of champagne, just as the *Alexandria* slid out of Tilbury docks that first night. Would she ever see him again once they'd disembarked? Was it really just a shipboard romance?

No good thinking like that, my girl. You need to think about home. The business. What you're going to do about it.

Her eyes threatened to brim over and she blinked angrily as she picked up her bags and made her way to the end of the corridor. As she came to Jack's door she hesitated, then marched by. She was aware of his door opening.

'Here, let me help with that.' Jack's voice made her stop. He looked devastating in dark blue jeans and white shirt, open, as usual, at the neck. To show off your bloody tan, she longed to say. He carried his briefcase and grinned down at her overnight bag. On the front was a picture of a dark-haired woman leaning provocatively against her dressing table, clad only in lacy bra and cami-knickers. It had been a present from Antonia. 'Reminds me of a more wicked you,' her sister had laughed.

'You?' Jack winked.

'In my spare time.' She tried to match his banter but her heart wasn't in it.

'Mmm, I like it.'

It was the old Jack, teasing and flirtatious.

'Thanks for the offer but I can manage.' She kept her tone cool, feeling rotten as she did so. It wasn't his fault she'd refused to say more yesterday and left in a hurry. Part of it, she told herself, was the embarrassment about crying in front of him, even though he'd been sympathetic. But she knew it was the mention of 'someone else' that had changed the moment between them.

'Nonsense.' He picked up the bag. 'I'm seeing you off this barge.' He was already striding along the passage as he glanced over his shoulder. 'Heard from Petra?'

'No, have you?'

'Yes. She's back in Sydney with her mum fussing over her, no doubt.'

'How did you find out?'

'She emailed. Sent her love to you.'

So Petra had his email address. Juliet squashed a thread of jealousy.

'Can you give me her address? I need to tell her I can't go to her engagement party and I haven't got her telephone number or anything.'

'Will do. And don't forget, we've got a date for the Maritime Museum.' Jack turned to her. She felt caught in the gaze of those dangerously seductive eyes. So he *did* want to see her again. But her pleasure turned to self-fury for feeling so *grateful*. Then she realised she'd have to cancel that too.

Jack was looking at her curiously. 'Are you okay?' He touched her arm. The sun was already full blown, and she could feel its heat climb towards her as they approached the gangplank.

'Yes.' She stopped; tried not to let him see her bad temper. 'But

I won't be able to go – have you forgotten? I have to go home.'

He turned to face her. 'You might not get a flight immediately – you've probably got a few days. If so, you should make the most of them.' He paused, searching her face. 'I know you're worried, Juliet. But take it easy. You can't make any decisions, do anything, until you get back to the UK. In the meantime, just relax. Enjoy the sunshine. There won't be much of that in the motherland.'

'Easy to say, relax. It's on my mind the whole time. If only I knew exactly what was going on.'

'You won't until you get home. Right now, think about your grandparents. What they must've felt like when they first arrived, just as you are now. Facing heaven knows what.'

She'd thought of that so many times. Nannie plucked out of all that was familiar and dear to her to follow her husband, which in those days, as servants, was a huge undertaking.

'It does feel a bit surreal to know I'm actually here. My grandparents must've felt even stranger. They'd never been out of Norfolk, let alone finding themselves halfway across the world.'

'But they had each other.'

'Yes, they had each other,' she echoed.

13th October 1913, at Amber Bay

We finally arrived in Melbourne. I don't think I'll ever be able to do such a crossing again. It was often so rough and made me sick, and not always able to keep my promise to Dad and write home regularly.

It was strange saying goodbye to Dr Townsend. I felt I'd got to know him a little while working with him. He was wonderful the way he cared for the patients. But I am sure something awful has happened to him in the past as there is often a sad expression in his eyes, even though he always tried to keep cheerful, especially in front of the patients. Sometimes I thought he was about to confide in me but he never did.

Then an embarrassing thing happened at the docklands which I can't even write down. It involved Dr Townsend. Ferguson thought Dr Townsend was criticising him (he was, slightly) and he was furious. And became even more furious with me because I went to Dr Townsend's defence.

I hope things will soon settle down between us as Ferguson is still not speaking to me properly.

Juliet followed Jack down the steep flight of steps, willing herself not to stare at the back of his head where the thick dark hair just brushed the edge of his shirt collar. It was fatal to notice such things. He turned and held out his hand to take her down the last step and she wondered if his skin tingled the way hers did.

She'd made it. She was on Australian soil. Her dream for the last thirty years. Tears pricked her eyes and her mind ran wild with possibilities...then a sickening wave engulfed her when she reminded herself she would have to leave before she even had a chance to visit Sydney. Where Charlie might still be.

The captain, with Alexei, Nikolai, Ivan, and a couple of other officers, were lined up at the bottom of the gangplank to wish everyone farewell. The normally morose Russians looked cheerful for once, and Juliet wondered if they were secretly delighted to be rid of their English passengers. Tatyana and Lena were hugging and kissing the English group as if they were all family.

'Jack,' Tatyana called out. 'You are saying goodbye to me?' She stood on tiptoe and kissed him full on the lips.

Jack laughed as he pulled away. 'Yes,' he said to the pretty Russian girl, then added, 'but you know it's not forever.'

Juliet stood back, taking in the scene, telling herself not to be so jealous whenever Tatyana made a play for him. It wasn't any of her business who Jack flirted with and the sooner she could get it into her head, the better.

Dozens of dockers ran alongside the *Alexandria*, roping it to

Melbourne harbour. Any other time it would be fascinating but Juliet could only think of one thing now: getting to the hotel. She put her hand up to her mouth to stifle a yawn. Tired though she was, she must find out about flights.

'Where are you staying?' Jack cut into her thoughts.

'I need to check.'

As she fumbled in her handbag for the paperwork she was aware of heavy footsteps, half running, behind her. She looked round.

'Glad I've caught you,' Trevor wheezed. 'Did I tell you my hotel?'

'Several times, Trevor,' Juliet said, wishing him out of existence. *Blast!* The address must be in her overnight bag. She bent down to unzip it.

Both men watched her. Why, oh why couldn't Trevor see that he wasn't wanted?

'Say you'll call.' Trevor sounded like a petulant schoolboy. 'Call tomorrow. Want to know you're all right. Which hotel are you in?'

No way was she going to tell him. 'I'll call you, Trevor, when I'm settled in. I promise.'

'Make sure you do, m'dear.' Trevor hovered, then appearing to know when he was beaten, turned to shake hands with Jack. Shoulders hunched, the disappointed figure disappeared into the crowd.

'Well, you might not want to tell old Trevor, but which hotel *are* you staying in?' Jack repeated, as he walked alongside her towards the rest of the group who were already picking out their luggage.

That done, and all the goodbyes said, Juliet was anxious to find a taxi. By the time one materialised she'd found the name of the hotel, hidden in the zipped recess of her handbag.

'I'm at the Mirimar,' she told him.

'Okay.' He gave her a swift peck on the cheek, then closed the taxi door. She watched until his dark head disappeared, then leant forward to tell the driver her hotel.

'The Mirimar, please.'

The driver turned round and tipped back his leather hat. 'It's a new one on me.'

Juliet scanned the confirmation letter. 'It's on the...' She stopped. It was the Mirimar, all right, but the address was Sydney.

PART III

The Discovery

20

Melbourne, Australia

Jack

Usually it felt good to be home but this morning Jack was restless. Back in his apartment he made himself a coffee and took his mug into the sitting room. He stared at the pile of mostly junk mail, all the time thinking of Juliet. It was beginning to annoy him how often she appeared in his thoughts.

Her visit to his cabin just before the *Alexandria* was about to dock had surprised him. He hated the way he'd guiltily bundled up the newspapers and photographs so she couldn't see what he'd been looking at. The very act of gathering up the evidence had made his heart thud. The trouble was, it had become an obsession with him – going over and over the accident, how the media had had a field day with him when he was in hospital, the inadequate letter he'd written to the family of the other couple, let alone to Louis, the reaction of his friends. Worst of all, Isobella's face when she saw his leg. When she reminded him about the other man. That she couldn't continue the marriage.

'Our marriage was in trouble ages before you had the crash,' she'd told him, as if that was meant to make him feel better – or herself, more like, he'd thought bitterly.

Maybe he needed counselling. He'd always pooh-poohed such therapy. Now, he was beginning to wonder. At this rate he was never going to get his life back. Start again without the black cloud hanging over him. Form a closer relationship with his beloved

Chiara. Be a proper father to her. His little girl was almost sixteen. On the brink of womanhood and he wasn't there to love her and admire her and guide her. Make sure she was doing her homework. See that any boyfriend she brought home came from a good family. Some young man who was trustworthy and didn't take advantage of a young girl. Isobella had at least put his mind at rest that Chiara wasn't taking drugs, never had, and he believed his wife because whatever their differences, he knew she would always keep a strict eye on their daughter.

But anything could happen at any time. One of her girlfriends could give her something. 'Just try it this once, Chiara. It will make you feel on top of the world,' he imagined the friend saying. Jack dropped his head in his hands. How could he have any influence over her when he was shut out of her life for most of the year? What exactly had Isobella told Chiara about the crash? He'd only once asked her and she had looked at him, her eyes narrowing and her mouth pulled unattractively tight.

'I told her the truth,' she'd said.

It was all very well his planning to tell Juliet about Isobella, but quite another thing to give her a blow-by-blow account of the crash. If she saw the newspapers she would never give him the time of day. He inhaled deeply and blew out his cheeks, trying to rid himself of the tension. If the worst happened it wouldn't be the end. He wasn't in love with her. She was just fun and interesting and proved, even with a battered leg, that he could still attract a good-looking, sexy woman.

But if she knew why he'd flown against his better judgement, would she understand? He swallowed half his coffee in one go and grimaced. He took the mug into the kitchen and tossed the rest down the sink.

He longed to tell her the truth instead of fobbing her off every time she asked him about his work and how he'd had such an accident. He'd promised he would tell her one day. But not yet. *Don't spoil things yet. You want to see her again. See her dazzling smile. Drown in those navy-blue eyes. Tease her. Enjoy her conversation. Love her...body.*

If he told her the truth she'd reject him.

He'd phone her. Right now. It would be good just to hear her voice. And make a date to see her soon. He felt as though he hadn't seen her for a week and it was only a few hours ago.

He found himself humming a tune, thinking about the next time they would make love. Maybe in her hotel room. She was staying at the Mirimar so she'd be bound to have a beautiful room overlooking the bay. Or she could come here. He'd have to have a tidy up – change the bed, get some decent champagne. Maybe cook for her. He used to enjoy cooking. She might be impressed with his cooking skills. He smiled, thinking about being in bed with her again. Where was the damn phone book? Ah. Shoved in a filing drawer. He pulled it out and looked for the phone number. Flicked the pages back and forth. Strange. It wasn't listed. He frowned. Then it dawned on him. There was no such place as the Hotel Mirimar. She'd given him the slip. Deliberately told him the name of a hotel which didn't exist in Melbourne.

She couldn't have made her message any clearer.

21

Stupid, stupid woman. Juliet flung her bag on the chair in her room at the Sheridan. Jack would think she was a complete idiot. Not being able to get to her business was making her distraught, but she was determined that the likes of Neil and Lydia were not going to tear her life's work apart that easily.

First things first. Get the flight booked.

Leaning forward, her nose only inches away from the hotel's public computer screen, Juliet read the message and swore. Heathrow's Terminal 4 was in the midst of a ground-crew strike affecting all long-haul flights. Both Qantas and BA assured their customers they would post more information when there was any change, but to expect delays for at least a week for those who already had tickets to fly between now and the end of the month. Any new bookings would be in a queue.

Juliet sat for a few moments, elbows on the work station, her head between her hands. She breathed out a sigh of despair. Her return ticket wasn't until the first of December. She'd be weeks behind everyone else unless there were any cancellations.

'Pull yourself together, for God's sake.' Juliet spoke the words aloud and an overweight young woman at the next station turned her purple-streaked head to stare. The girl sent her a sympathetic smile and went back to her screen.

She sent an email to Rachel explaining the situation at Heathrow and that she'd be home as soon as the strike was lifted.

Had anyone heard from Neil? In the meantime, could she and Bob and Kirsty hold the fort?

Recriminations buzzed around in her head and she felt she might actually explode. The only thing she'd made a success of in life was in jeopardy. She had to focus. Daydreaming about Jack was distracting her from her business. Was it because she'd been so used to ignoring her emotions, pressing them down, that now she was faced with a man she had to admit she was crazy about, she was completely unprepared and overwhelmed? And therefore not concentrating?

She forced herself to think of the problems facing her. One, the flight. Two, Lydia and Neil. Three, her father. In that order.

For a few mad moments she wished she could talk to Gerrard. To give him his due, he was pretty sensible at getting to the crux of problems and pointing you in the right direction. It was just all the 'I told you so's' she couldn't stand. Well, she would deal with the practical issues. Take her mind off the emotional stuff.

She filled in the online form to apply for the next possible flight. That done she looked at her watch. Nearly eleven o'clock. It seemed a long time since breakfast. She needed coffee.

She logged off and returned to her room. She'd had so little sleep the night before, berating herself for having put her precious business into Lydia's hands, that a lovely long soak in the bath might be just what she needed. But she stumbled as she unlocked her room door, and without bothering to order any coffee or even undress, she climbed into bed and slept solidly for two hours.

Jack was there, talking to her, smiling at her, telling her to get ready; they would be going out. But she wanted to make love right where she was, and would have gone on dreaming had the phone by her bed not startled her awake. For a moment she couldn't believe it had been a dream, Jack had looked so real. But now he was ringing her. Her heart did a little skip as she snatched up the receiver.

'How are you, m'dear? Settled in? Hope I'm not disturbing you.'

Oh, no, she mouthed silently, staring at the phone in disbelief.

'Trevor, what a nice surprise. I was just having a nap.'

'So sorry—'

'It's all right.' She had a sudden thought. 'How did you know where I was staying?'

'Took a punt, m'dear. Classy lady like yourself – Sheridan's nice and central.' He chuckled. 'To be honest, this was hotel number four.'

She couldn't help being impressed. 'Well, I'm glad you woke me. I need to get going.'

'Wondered if you'd honour me by having dinner this evening.'

Now get out of that one.

Instinct drove her to say no, but she hesitated. What would be the harm with old Trevor? 'How very kind,' she heard herself say.

'Pick you up at eight o'clock sharp,' he said, and before she had time to say goodbye she heard the receiver click. She had to smile. Trevor certainly didn't bother with any niceties.

22

Juliet checked the flight situation on the Qantas website early next morning. No news whatsoever, but at least she should now be in the queue. To be safe, she asked the girl on reception to print it out.

She decided to use every hour and make it count. Just as Jack had advised. At the thought of him she became annoyed. He didn't know her well enough to give that sort of advice. But she knew in her heart he was right. There was absolutely nothing she could do apart from sending an email to Bob. Just for today she'd try to block out Reece & Co. Make straight for the Immigration Museum. The hotel receptionist had been helpful and handed her a leaflet where she'd read over a hurried breakfast that it used to be Customs House; it would have been the first port of call for Nannie and Pop. Now armed with maps and a notebook she stepped swiftly along the street and spotted the tram stop where the porter had told her to wait. A tram was just pulling in.

'Do you go near the Immigration Museum?' she asked the driver. He grinned at her.

'That'll be Flinders Street. Hop on, and I'll let you know when we arrive.'

After several stops he shouted, 'Immigration Museum,' and deposited her right outside. It wasn't on the quayside, as she'd imagined, but she could see the sea sparkling away just beyond the road. Her heart gave a little skip of excitement. She was finally on the trail.

She stepped a few paces back on the wide pavement in order to gain a better view of the building, dodging the shoppers and people on their way to work. The museum reminded her of the fifteenth-century palaces in Florence. As she stared up at the façade, she had the oddest feeling she was inside her grandmother's head looking up at Customs House, as it would have been called, exactly as Nannie must have done nearly a hundred years before. As a child, she had always begged Nannie for more stories about her voyage to Australia, about what she and Pop had done the minute they landed; and now here she was, in front of that same building.

How had her grandmother felt? Overwhelmed; a little scared, maybe, but she saw in her mind's eye the determined set of her grandmother's chin and Juliet knew she would have been ready to tackle anything.

19th October 1913

> Ferguson was very offhand with me after Dr Townsend left us at Customs House. He followed the crowds as they jostled for space through the entrance, whereas I stood in front of the building, looking up at it, trying to take it all in. It was a very grand building and I had the strangest feeling it had a life of its own and was summing me up – deciding whether or not I was welcome in Melbourne. I know it's silly but that's exactly how I felt.
>
> How I wished the registration was over and we were in our room at Amber Bay.

Juliet picked up several more leaflets about the museum and headed for the small snack bar in the corner. Stirring her latte she read about the history of the building. Yes, it was indeed modelled on a Renaissance palace. The Customs House was important because it had been the treasure house of government income as well as a place where the immigrants registered. There was a permanent exhibition at the museum about immigrants and their conditions, from the convicts in the mid 1800s to the present day. Perfect. She gulped the last of her coffee. Time to get cracking.

One of the guides suggested she start on the first floor, so she walked up the grand oak staircase which led to a massive landing with lifts to the second floor. She'd investigate that floor later if there was time, but for now she was intrigued to see a room in front of her adorned with posters begging British workers to come to Australia. One blazoned: 'Australia's offer to the British Boy', implying all kinds of opportunities and adventures. The one next to it unexcitingly offered: 'Australia invites the Domestic Girl'. Yet another poster stated in no uncertain terms: 'Men for the Land, Women for the Home'. The posters were dated between 1901–1945. The usual gender pigeon-holing, she thought with a wry smile. She caught the eye of a smartly dressed elderly gentleman who apparently thought she was smiling at him. He smiled back. She moved swiftly on to the second room.

This one displayed several notices – one of them explained how from 1910 there were reduced passages for domestics, farmers and farm-workers. So Nannie and Pop would definitely have had assisted passages, and that must be why she hadn't found them on any passenger list when she'd Googled the *Orsova* before the trip. Steerage and third-class passengers hadn't yet been listed online.

She came to a map taking up several feet on one wall and stopped to read the route, popular from the 1860s. The starting point was Tilbury, then Tenerife, on to Cape Town, and finally Melbourne. She wondered if there'd been much change from the 1860s to 1913 when Nannie and Pop had travelled. If only Nannie had told her about the ports they'd visited. Or perhaps Nannie had and she'd forgotten.

There were cabinets showing snippets of letters and diaries from some of the passengers. One woman wrote from the SS *Heracles* in 1902: *Terrible seasickness. Gale forces from Table Bay onwards.*

Never get used to being seasick. Another woman wrote in 1912: *No time to say proper goodbyes. Painful to open photo albums of the family now I'm on board and so far away from them all.*

Feeling close to her grandmother and surprisingly, even Great-Aunt Ruby, she bent right over the glass-topped cabinet. Strange how everyone's writing looked identical, as though they'd all been taught at the same school – even when there were thirty or forty years between some of the entries.

She browsed several glass cabinets showing poignant reminders of the various travellers' journeys: purses, pens, jewellery, hats and gloves, spectacles, powder compacts, cigarette cases, postcards, playing cards, jigsaw puzzles, a couple of games she didn't recognise, and various books. There were two or three ancient Bibles and a worn cloth-backed dictionary. Tears gathered behind her eyes as she looked at the photographs; some in albums, and some in silver-coloured frames. Were they of the families left behind, or the voyagers themselves? Or was it possible that a liner had sunk and these were the rescued items? After all, the unsinkable Titanic had gone down the year before her grandparents had sailed. She shivered.

Peering at the various models of ships in use at the time of her grandparents' crossing, she could see no sign of the *Orsova*, and disappointed, she turned to go into the next room.

'Hey, Juliet.'

She whirled round. *Jack! Oh, my God. How the hell…?*

He looked so bloody good.

'How did you know I'd be here?' She tried to exude nonchalance, but as so often when she was talking to Jack, it came out as aggressive.

'You didn't make it easy for me, giving me the wrong hotel. I even wondered whether you'd done it on purpose.' He searched her face and she couldn't tell whether he was joking or not. 'I didn't even have your mobile number.'

'I had my bag stolen, remember? With the BlackBerry.'

And the photograph.

He threw her a sympathetic smile and took her arm. 'Oh, of course. Anyway, I guessed what you'd done and phoned the Sheridan. It's similar to the Mirimar – which is in Sydney, by the way – and yes, you were checked in. Against all the rules they told me you'd asked about the trams to the Immigration Museum this morning. So here I am, at your service, Madame.' His grin was mocking.

'Trevor managed to find me, too.' Juliet couldn't disguise her irritation. 'He rang three other hotels before he got mine.'

'Trevor?'

'He took me to dinner last night. He's actually nicer when he's on his own and not showing off, but...' She didn't quite know how to finish. But he's not exactly *you*, was what she'd almost blurted.

Jack laughed. 'Poor old Trevor,' he said in such a condescending manner that Juliet wanted to defend the old boy. 'Anyway, forget about Trevor. What have you managed to dig up?'

'This room's interesting, but very general. I was just about to go upstairs.'

'Come on then.' He smiled disarmingly, and although still holding her arm in quite a possessive manner, Juliet found she didn't mind in the least. The whole building had suddenly lit up and she couldn't help but beam at him in return.

They wandered up to the second floor of the museum, where it was partly sectioned off to show clever mock-ups of the various cabins for the different classes of immigrants. The steerage passengers had had to put up with appalling conditions in their cramped space with only a narrow bench to sleep on and a filthy old piece of sacking for a blanket. Juliet's heart sank when she pictured her fastidious grandmother sleeping in such a state, until she read the sign that this was a cabin for the first convicts in the mid 1800s. The nearest date of the next mock-up cabin was in the 1920s when conditions had improved considerably.

'Let's hope things were similar in 1913,' Juliet commented as she jotted details in her notebook when something particular caught her interest.

Jack watched with an amused expression.

'Information for that novel of yours?' He gave her a knowing wink.

Juliet couldn't help laughing. He was incorrigible.

'Mmm, that voyage was most interesting,' he said, looking at her and letting his eyes stray to her breasts. To Juliet's annoyance she found herself blushing. Jack glanced at his watch. 'D'you think it's time for lunch?'

'I was going to have a quick sandwich in the café, and then go back to the hotel – see if there's any news. Did you hear there's a strike on at Heathrow?'

'Yeah, it was all over the news. Have they said how long it's likely to be?'

'Not really, but I'm supposedly in a queue.'

'Maybe it's fate to keep you here longer,' Jack said. Juliet gave him a sharp look but he merely added, 'So why don't we stick to the sandwich plan, then go to the Maritime Museum.' He looked at her, the flecks in his eyes like gold leaf.

'I need to buy a temporary mobile.' Juliet tried to drag her eyes away from his. 'I was too tired yesterday to do shopping. And then I must make some calls. Let everyone know my new number.'

'We'll get the mobile on the way to the museum,' Jack said, taking her arm. 'You just want something basic until you get a new BlackBerry, I presume.'

Juliet nodded. 'I suppose a couple of hours can't hurt.'

The Maritime Museum was a good distance from the tram stop but Juliet, who normally hated walking, realised how much she was enjoying matching Jack's long awkward strides, and the warmth of the sun on her face. He seemed even taller now she was in her trainers.

What a wonderful country Australia was. Or at least what she'd seen so far in Melbourne. Friendly shopkeepers and waiters who always had time for a chat, the cleanliness of the city, the architecture, and of course the glorious weather. She wondered idly what it would be like to live here and stole a glance at Jack. His eyes met hers and he grinned.

'Happy?' He tucked her arm through his.

'I would be if I weren't so worried.'

He gave her arm a squeeze. 'Worry never got anyone anywhere. If worry helped you'd see everyone around you with their head in their hands, frowning faces, just sitting doing nothing – except worrying.'

She had to laugh at his nonsense.

'I thought there'd be more boats around.' Juliet looked at the few which bobbed alongside the decked walkway as they approached a group of single-storey buildings.

'Why would anyone want their boat stuck out here?' Jack remarked. 'Though they're restoring a ship which might interest you.' He pointed to an old passenger ship which was undergoing a complete overhaul by the looks of the scaffolding.

'It's the closest I've seen of a ship which reminds me of the *Orsova*.' Juliet was excited. 'Can we go over it?'

'I'll find out.' He strode over to one of the buildings, opened the door without knocking and reappeared almost immediately. 'The museum's closed for a two-year refurb, but they'll let us look inside a couple of the buildings.'

Thinking she was about to look over a traditional passenger ship, Juliet swallowed her disappointment. More cabinets didn't have anything like the same appeal.

'I suppose it's better than nothing,' was all she said as she followed Jack along the slatted wooden walkway to a row of what she would have described as sheds with corrugated roofs.

Lining the low walls were photographs and paintings and

posters of ships from the early 1800s almost to the present day. Wrinkling her nose at the musty smell, Juliet made straight for a display showing liners from 1900 onwards. One of the first ones she came across was a photograph of an impressive two-funnelled ship. Being a more unusual feature of a ship of that era, it was etched on her brain and leapt out at her. The *Orsova*.

'Jack, come and look.' She swung round to see him immersed in some earlier photographs. He strolled over, laughing at her excited face as she pointed triumphantly to the name.

'Fantastic,' he said. 'Maybe they'll have a postcard.'

'I don't need one. I've got two paintings at home…well, I think they're hand-coloured prints that my grandparents bought on the voyage. They're fabulous – this big.' She spread her arms. 'One in calm seas, and the other in stormy. I've got them in my dining room.'

'I'd like to see them sometime.' Jack's grin was on the verge of a smirk.

She willed herself to keep calm. 'It's a long way to go to see a couple of pictures.'

'It might be worth it.' He took her hand.

She felt a tingling shock sweep through her body. Their eyes held. She never wanted to let go of his hand and she could swear he was thinking the same as his grip tightened.

'Are you okay?' he said.

'Yes, of course,' she answered, pretending to look more closely at the photograph of the ship, but as conscious as a besotted teenager of his fingers still entwined with her own.

A thought suddenly nagged her. In her mind she went back to the display cabinets in the museum. Something which had struck her.

Everyone's handwriting looked the same in those days.

'Penny for them.' Jack raised a dark eyebrow and smiled encouragingly.

'I was just wondering about the letters people wrote at the

time. I read a few in the Immigration Museum but I didn't study them all. Now I've seen the photo of Nannie's ship I must go and look again. I might have missed something.'

'Presumably any letters would've been sent back to their families.'

'Not necessarily. It wasn't easy to get anything sent in those days once you were on board. You'd have to wait for a passing ship. A bit hit and miss, I'd say.'

'Want to go back?' Jack didn't sound particularly enthusiastic.

'We don't have time. But I'd like to see the rest of the stuff here – and then I need to make my calls.'

'You can do that in a quiet corner of the restaurant. We're going out for a meal. That okay with you?'

Juliet sent him a steady look. His smile was warm.

'Very okay,' she said, picking up her bag.

The room in the far building, piled with memorabilia that needed to be rehoused, looked like a junk shop. The interior was dimly lit but Juliet could see a display cabinet in the corner. She wandered over. More personal effects similar to those in the Immigration Museum. No letters at all.

There was an adjacent cabinet full of books, Bibles, dictionaries and various papers. She peered through the glass which was smeared with dust and dirt where someone had had a go at giving it a quick wipe, and tried to make out the various objects. A large jewellery box caught her eye. Its lid was open and a well-used leather-bound book was propped up inside it. On the cover were the owner's initials in gold, though badly faded, and she squinted her eyes to make them out. Then her whole body shuddered as though she'd been given an electric shock. The book wasn't open enough for her to examine the writing. She didn't need to. She knew the initials as well as her own. A.E.B.

'Jack,' she called. She felt dizzy. 'Jack.'

'What is it?'

'I think…no, I'm certain…I've found Nannie's diary. Look at this.'

Jack picked his way through the displays to where she was standing, frozen, staring into the dusty cabinet.

'Look. Nannie's initials, Annie Elizabeth Bishop.'

'Don't get too excited,' Jack warned. 'They could stand for "Ada Edna Brown" for all we know.'

'I'm so sure this is my grandmother's diary. Dad said she'd kept one but that it must have been left in Melbourne as he'd never come across it. Oh, we have to ask if we can have a proper look.'

But she was out of luck. The workmen had no authority to open the cabinet and the curator wouldn't be on duty for another week. By that time, Juliet would be back in England.

23

By the time she and Jack strolled back into the centre of Melbourne after visiting the Maritime Museum, people from the town's offices and shops were spilling onto the pavements. It was only just after five o'clock but the restaurants were already busy; it seemed Australians tended to eat early while the sun was still on full beam.

Juliet suggested one of the bistros, where the outside tables clustered haphazardly on the wide pavement. Another time she would have taken it all in, enjoyed the hour, but after a whole day traipsing round museums and the excitement of finding what she was certain was her grandmother's diary, yet not being able to confirm it, she felt as though she'd been squeezed through Nannie's mangle. On top of that was her worry with her business mixed up with her confused feelings for Jack.

Juliet shook her head as though to clear it.

How could her grandmother's diary have ended up in the Maritime Museum? Surely Nannie would have regarded it as precious and taken it back to England with her. Yet hadn't Dad said Nannie had probably left it behind as she wouldn't have wanted Pop to see it? But that was all speculation and in the past. The danger to Reece & Co was real and present. That was what she should be concentrating on. But the diary was taking over.

'You're very quiet.'

'I keep thinking about the diary. How I'd love to get my hands on it. I *know* it's hers. I feel it's been there all this time waiting for me.' She looked at him and gave a half smile. 'I'm being foolish, aren't I?'

'It's understandable. It all adds up for you. The initials and everything. It's a real shame we can't know for certain.'

'The trouble is, it's not just the diary. It's my company that's really crazing me. If I could just be there – get to grips with what's going on. Jack, I really must make those calls. And see if there's any news of Heathrow.'

'Tell you what – we'll have a quick snack and then go back to my place and you can make all the calls you need, and *I'll* find out what's happening at Heathrow. How does that sound?'

'You just want to get me in your lair,' Juliet joked.

'Ah, you're beginning to know me,' he chuckled. 'And,' he took her hand, 'I love teasing you. And best of all making you laugh.' He kissed the back of her hand. 'You know, you're rather bewitching.'

No man had ever paid her such extravagant compliments.

'You're not so bad yourself,' she smiled. 'But I expect all the girls say that.'

'It's not unknown,' Jack grinned, and she had to fight back a spark of jealousy. As if he knew what she was thinking he continued, 'but it's nice to hear it from you.' His eyes held hers and he was suddenly serious. 'Are you really hungry?'

'Not ever so. We didn't have the sandwich that long ago.'

'I want to take you to bed – right this minute.'

'Do they have special rooms here for such demands?' Juliet asked, not wanting to break free of his hand. 'If not, it could be disturbing for the rest of the diners.'

Jack laughed. 'They ought to. They'd make a fortune. C'mon. Let's go.'

They escaped before the waiter came to take their order, and Jack swiftly guided her along the street. Take no notice that the world is tipping, Juliet thought, as she clung like some star-struck teenager to his arm.

Mustn't do anything stupid. Do I need to make him wear a condom? He didn't last time. Surely not now I'm forty-six. Though I'm still regular.

An image of one of her girlfriends sprang before her eyes. She'd got divorced, met another man, and had her third child at fifty. Juliet knew she shouldn't risk it. But what would it be like to have Jack's baby? If it were to happen, by some miraculous chance, she'd keep it. She'd been punished enough. This one they'd never take from her. She closed her eyes. Jack's baby.

Are you insane?

She promptly tripped on a paving stone and would have fallen had Jack not steadied her.

'We can't blame the wine this time.'

'Nor the shoes.' She looked at him, admiring his profile, the slightly hooked nose. 'How far are you?'

'A couple of blocks.'

His apartment block was a colonial-style modern building facing the river. The security guard greeted Jack with a smile and a nod to Juliet. She refused to think how many of Jack's women the security guard had nodded to as they rode the elevator to the sixth floor, but these unhappy images vanished the moment Jack bent his head to kiss her full on the lips just as the doors opened. To Juliet's embarrassment a young couple were waiting outside to go down.

'Looks like you're gonna be doin' all right, mate,' the young man said, smiling and winking at Juliet as he and his girlfriend nudged into the lift.

'If I play my cards right,' Jack grinned at Juliet.

Juliet felt her face flush but she smiled at the couple, took Jack's arm and stepped out onto a wide landing. He swiped a card through the lock on one of the cream-painted doors, and swung it open with a theatrical flourish.

The large sitting room was painted in off-white and cream, and furnished with a pair of mole-coloured suede sofas with soft inviting cushions. An abstract painting hung over the fireplace and one wall was taken up almost entirely by bookshelves.

'Does it get your approval?'

'Very swish,' Juliet had to admit, although she kept it to herself that the abstract painting was hideous. 'Do you own it?'

'No. It'd cost a bomb. The rent's bad enough. But it suits me when I'm here. Which is more often nowadays.' He sounded a little wistful.

The room had huge floor-to-ceiling windows similar to her hotel room, and feeling that she needed to do something, anything, rather than just stand there, she walked over and looked down at the river. Strange, from this angle.

'There's your hotel,' Jack said, slipping his arms round her waist from behind, pulling her to him. She felt his lips part her hair as he kissed her neck, and her scalp prickled. 'Look, over there, just back a bit from that white building.'

She tried to see where he was pointing but everything looked blurry, the sensation of Jack's hands giving her goosebumps. She couldn't think straight. She turned, and he kissed her lips.

'Mmm.' He kissed her again, this time long and sensuously. The feel of his tongue made her want him inside her and she gave a small whimper.

'Jack?'

This time he kissed her with such passion her knees bent like a rag doll. He carried her through to the bedroom, kissing every inch of her face and eyelids and neck and mouth, then gently laid her on top of the bed. He strode to the window and closed the curtains to shut out the still-bright sun, then switched on a bedside lamp which threw soft shadows.

The bed dominated the room. A thought flashed that they should have this size as normal in England. Instead, people were squashed up against each other all night. Then she grinned, admitting there would be nothing she'd like better than to be squashed up against Jack's torso all night and every night.

'You look like the cat that's got the cream.'

'And that's before we've even started,' Juliet quipped. 'It's—'

But he didn't allow her to finish. Instead, he kissed her with a force which left her lips bruised, her body weak. He tore off her jacket, sat her on the edge of the bed, and swiftly unlaced her trainers. Oh, why wasn't she wearing something more sexy? But Jack seemed undeterred. He lifted off her T-shirt to reveal her bra and bent to kiss the top of each breast, then slipped one hand round her back to unhook her.

'Lovely,' he said, running his thumb over each of her erect nipples. He took one into his mouth and caressed it with his tongue. 'Now the other one,' he murmured. 'I don't want it to feel left out.'

He flung the duvet to one side, laid her back on the sheet. It smelt of Jack, masculine and slightly musky, and it was Jack she wanted. He unzipped her jeans, hiking them down and tossing them onto a nearby chair. She struggled to sit up and remove her socks but he pressed her firmly down and took them off himself. Thank goodness she'd worn a matching set of underwear, Juliet thought, as he kissed her stomach while she tried to hold it in as tightly as she could and still breathe. Finally, he slid down her panties.

'You're lovely.' His voice was ragged as he bent over her.

Without thinking she stretched up and grabbed hold of his shirt, trying to rip the top buttons undone, but they held firm. Maddeningly she was forced to undo them one by one, until she came to his bare chest where she buried her face in the dark hair, feeling his warmth, feeling his hands in her hair, repeating her name. She left a trail of kisses on his skin before her hands pulled his arms free and somehow dragged off his shirt. She tried to unzip his trousers but in the state he was, it was impossible. She swore under her breath. Jack laughed and stood up. She tracked his every movement as he yanked off the rest of his clothes, his scarred leg making him seem suddenly vulnerable. Then he sat on the edge of the bed again, naked, facing her, totally at ease. He raised a dark eyebrow.

All right, Jack. This time she'd make sure he'd never forget her. Using all her strength, and taking him by surprise, she forced him down on to the bed. He put up no resistance, but lay there smiling, a kind of question in his eyes, his firm muscular body inviting her. She straddled him, her hair brushing his face; then she raised herself up on her haunches, her hands cupping her own breasts, her lips parted, her breath coming in quick gasps, not bothering to hide her lust for him.

'Do you mind my being older than you?' She tossed her hair back, her smile widening, as for the first time she realised she didn't give a damn about his answer.

He gazed up at her, the bedside light catching the gold flecks. 'Actually, I find it quite amusing,' he chuckled.

'Should I be flattered or offended?'

'I'll let you decide.' He pulled her head down and kissed her neck. 'Anyway, I don't know how much older you are. Could be five years, could be fifteen.' She playfully cuffed him. 'Could be five minutes,' he laughed.

She shifted back a little so she could see his erection. She fingered it lightly, and he gave a deep sigh.

'Mmm, I like it,' she told him.

'Just as well...it's the only one I've got.'

'Jack...I want you now...I want to—'

The bedside phone rang, jangling her senses. To her amazement Jack, cursing, rolled from underneath her, and reached over to grab the receiver. Why hadn't he just let the bloody thing ring? Why? Right in the middle of... Her temper boiled.

'No, I'm sorry...no, I can't...tied up at the moment.'

How she hated that expression. And who could be so important? Jack was listening intently and she caught the faint higher note of a woman. Finally he spoke into the receiver: 'Okay, but I won't be

212

there for at least an hour.' He hung up and turned to her, frowning.

Where was he going? Who was he meeting? She sat up and held the duvet over her breasts like some gawky virgin. 'Why did you have to answer it?'

'Sorry, Juliet, but I've got to leave right away.' He didn't meet her eyes.

She watched in silence as he dressed, his back turned to her like a barrier between them.

'Who was it on the phone?'

He was silent.

'Why all the mystery?'

Still he didn't answer.

'Was it your wife?'

'No.'

'Do you have a wife?'

'An ex.'

'How come you've never mentioned her?'

'I didn't think it was relevant.' Jack buckled his belt, stood up and turned round to face her. 'I'm sorry, that sounded rather rude, but I'm not one to discuss my personal problems.'

'Isn't that what friends are for?'

But she'd never breathed anything to him about Charlie, so what right did she have to try to force information from him? But somehow, she thought illogically, this was different.

'Please try to understand. I have to go. I promise I'll explain, but not now. I'll call you.' He came towards her.

'Don't bother.' She sprang out of bed, blinking back her fury and her frustration.

'Don't go in that mood.'

She glared at him as she threw on her clothes.

'What do you expect me to do, Jack? Lie here naked and wait until you return? She, whoever she is, is obviously far more important. So have a good time. I'll see you around.'

'Juliet, wait—'

Not trusting herself to even look at him, she grabbed her bag and rushed out of the apartment.

What a fool she'd been. As usual, where Jack was concerned, she'd let her heart rule her head.

And she still hadn't made those calls.

24

Jack

It was Jack's personal nightmare that one day he would have to break off in the middle of amazing sex with someone as delectable as Juliet. And it had bloody happened. She'd been furious and he couldn't blame her. But no matter the cheerful face he put on for her and anyone else, his emotions were never far from the surface as he tried to anticipate what Isobella had in store for him. He couldn't bear to leave his phone unanswered as it might be her with some new accusation or scheme he needed to deal with immediately – she was that volatile. And the call might be Chiara needing him. Or his solicitor telling him Isobella's latest financial claim or that he now had diminished access to his daughter. In fact the call *had* been his solicitor. And yes, it *was* about Chiara.

It still didn't excuse him. His life in chaos, answering the phone was so automatic he'd completely forgotten his manners.

Juliet had asked if it was his wife on the phone. Thank the Lord he'd been able to say no. He hadn't wanted to go into any more detail with their emotions running so high, but he'd had to give her a truthful answer to her further questioning that he did actually have an ex-wife. Well, almost the truth. Isobella wasn't quite an ex, but please God, don't let it be much longer.

He couldn't keep the details of the plane crash from Juliet much longer either. He could tell she was hurt that he hadn't confided in her, but the very words he'd be forced to use would blow him apart again, just when he was trying so hard to get his life back together.

He knew Petra and Juliet had become friends on board the *Alexandria* but he had no idea if Petra had mentioned Louis' parents, the Jordans. Dear Petra. She hadn't judged him ever, but then it hadn't been her parents who'd died. Dear God, was he ever going to get over this guilt?

He'd met Petra when he'd flown her and the two other models to Ayers Rock a few weeks before the crash. She'd told him about Louis and how his mother was soon to celebrate her sixtieth birthday. As it was a special birthday she and Louis had wanted to give them both a treat. Petra had asked him if he would fly the couple and their two friends from Sydney to Canberra. They were all mad on Elvis and wanted to see a special exhibition at the National Portrait Gallery by an Alfred somebody, a photographer before Elvis hit the big time. They had to do the trip in one day because Louis' mother was having chemotherapy the next day.

Jack had phoned Louis the day before. He'd still not met him in the flesh, having liaised with Petra about the details, but everything was set to go – except the weather. He looked out of the window as he was talking to Louis.

'The forecast isn't too good,' Jack said, watching a swathe of dark clouds. The wind had got up and the eucalyptus trees which formed the boundary to the apartment block were swaying alarmingly. 'We may have to cancel.'

'Surely it's not much to worry about,' Louis answered. 'Unless, of course, it takes a turn for the worse.'

'I'll have to keep a close eye. It's not just here but at the other end. Even though Canberra's only down the road the weather can be different. If it's bad tomorrow morning we won't go up. Simple as that.'

'I really hope you can,' Louis' voice came over the receiver. 'The thing is, this is about the last treat my mother will have as she has to be admitted to the hospice in a fortnight.'

Jack reached for his diary. 'I've got no gaps for a month,' he said, flicking through the pages. 'But if we can't go up tomorrow I'll put you on the cancellation list.'

'Let's hope it doesn't come to that,' Louis said. 'Shall I ring tomorrow to confirm?'

'No, don't worry. It might blow itself out. If I don't call you, you'll know plans are going ahead. Tell them to be ready at 10am.'

'I appreciate it.'

Early that evening, sitting in a small minimalist apartment he occasionally rented when he was doing events from Sydney, his mobile rang. Jack wasn't going to answer it, but maybe Louis was worried about the weather – which hadn't improved – and had changed his mind.

'Delaney here.'

'Oh, Jack. I'm glad you're in,' came Isobella's sultry tones.

His gut churned. They'd finally agreed on an official separation, though he hadn't given up hope that one day she'd say she missed him and suggest they try to make a go of it again. The worst of it was, he was based in Melbourne and his wife had gone back to Bologna to be near her parents, taking Chiara with her. But it was Chiara, not his wife, he wanted to see every day; his beautiful daughter was growing up without him there, watching over her.

'I'm sorry to have to tell you this over the phone,' Isobella said. 'But it's not easy when we live in two different countries.'

It was your suggestion, Jack wanted to say. He waited.

For God's sake, tell me. Bang me over the head and get it over with.

'I've met someone.'

He was silent.

'Jack, are you there?'

'Yes.' He felt like lead inside.

'He's nice. You'd approve, I'm sure.'

What the fuck was she on about? Approve of what? Some

other fucking man taking his wife and daughter?

'He's very fond of Chiara and she likes him.'

His heart contracted. He didn't want some stranger bringing up his daughter. But he knew in the end he wouldn't have any say. Isobella was her mother, and until Chiara was of age, that's where she would stay. In Italy. She couldn't be any further away.

'I'm very happy for you,' he said flatly.

'Yes, you sound it.' Isobella's voice was laced with sarcasm. 'I'm sorry, Jack, truly I am. But you're better off without me. You'll find someone and—'

'Spare me, please,' he said. 'I don't need you to tell me I'll be happy again one day. Just let me have the papers for the divorce. I won't stand in your way.'

He slammed the receiver down and poured himself a large whisky.

Then another.

And another.

His face grim, he screwed the top back on the bottle and went to bed early before he was tempted to finish it off. The next morning he felt fine, though not in the best frame of mind, so he thought it might be wise to see if another pilot could take them. No one was available. The weather hadn't worsened and against his better judgement he decided to go, not wanting to let everyone down. The trouble was, he would've been perfectly all right if there hadn't been an electrical storm minutes before they were due to land at Canberra Airport, and to compound such bad luck there'd been a technical fault which worsened and he'd been forced to make an emergency landing.

Right up until the last few minutes he thought he was going to be all right. Had plenty of time to land safely. But with such poor visibility the ground rushed up sooner than he expected. He heard one of the women screaming as the explosion knocked him off his seat.

The weeks in hospital were a blur. Try as he might, he couldn't remember exactly what had happened. Only that he blamed himself. No one seemed to know what had happened to the four passengers and because he himself was alive he could only hope they hadn't been too badly injured. He'd clung on to that hope.

For the first few days they hadn't allowed him any visitors. At least, that's what they'd told him, but he'd cynically wondered if the nursing staff were being tactful because his wife hadn't appeared. He'd tried to explain that his wife and daughter lived in Italy but his words were muddled and he'd become upset. Then several days later a smiling nurse put her head in the door. 'Your wife and daughter are here to see you, Mr Delaney.'

His heart had lifted immediately. Chiara came swiftly in, dark hair swinging from her ponytail, her eyes full of love.

'Oh, Daddy, I've missed you so.' She smacked a kiss on his cheek and sat on the visitor's chair, reaching for his hand. He squeezed it and smiled at her.

'I've missed you too, darling. But I'm getting better every day. Look, I'm sitting up for the first time.'

It wasn't quite the truth. Physically he was probably mending okay, but mentally he was in agony. No one had told him about the other passengers. He dreaded what their injuries might be.

He'd looked up eagerly to see his beautiful wife, dressed head to toe in white, except you could never mistake her for one of the nursing staff, staring at him, her expression unreadable.

'Hello, Isobella,' he said, a catch in his throat. 'You're looking very lovely.'

'Hello, Jack.' She took the seat by his other side. 'How are you? We've been worried.' She gave him a perfunctory kiss on his other cheek, even though he turned his mouth to hers.

'I'll be okay.' He couldn't help it. Tears welled up any time someone showed him the slightest kindness or concern. Probably all the drugs. But he'd been wrong about his wife. There was little compassion the way her mouth turned down as though she couldn't bear his weakness.

'Would you like tea, Mrs Delaney?' The cheery nurse popped her head in the doorway again.

'Oh, no thank you. We can't stay long.'

'Mother,' Chiara cried, 'we've only just got here.'

Her mother sent her a warning look which Jack recognised only too well.

The three of them managed to pass fifteen minutes, his daughter doing most of the chatting about school and her music, until his wife rose to her feet.

'When can we come and see Daddy again?' Chiara demanded after she'd kissed him goodbye.

'I'm not sure, darling,' Isobella replied. 'Daddy needs a lot of rest. And he won't get better if he keeps having visitors.'

'I'm not just a visitor,' Chiara muttered.

A few days later he'd had a letter from Chiara telling him she would come again as soon as Mother could bring her. From Isobella, all he received was a get-well card. Love Isobella. During the long six weeks he was in hospital his wife never appeared again. So of course neither did his daughter.

Finally when he was due to come out of hospital his surgeon told him the two couples had been killed on impact. Bile rushed into his throat and he had to get to the bathroom, his bad leg dragging behind. His head over the toilet, he brought up the contents of his gut. With shaking limbs he climbed back into the bed and asked his surgeon if there were any more details. The surgeon shook his head and told him there was nothing anyone could do, and their job was to get the leg fixed up as soon as possible. Apparently the medical staff had been warned to keep the newspapers from him.

The shock that he'd killed four innocent people had been unbearable and for days he couldn't stop shaking. He'd wanted to see Louis immediately. Explain the circumstances. Tell him how sorry…how very sorry… But when he came home and got his hands on the newspaper reports, he'd changed his mind. It wasn't that he was too cowardly but he decided to give Louis a bit of breathing space. Instead, he'd written a short letter and said he would like to see him when Louis felt it was appropriate.

Then the final blow. Isobella had left it for nine months, which she obviously considered gave him enough time to get his life back before she announced she wanted a divorce. The man she'd met was serious and wanted to marry her.

It was over.

And still he hadn't faced Louis.

Surprisingly, Petra had invited him to their engagement party and said that Louis would also like to meet him, and not to get steamed up about the meeting. It was an accident. He'd fully intended to go with Juliet to the party but at the last minute had decided it still wasn't the right time, and warned Petra he might not be able to make it due to work commitments. He must see Louis on his own and not entangled with a bunch of people in a party atmosphere. Especially as it was their engagement party.

But oh, how he wanted to tell Louis he'd never forgiven himself.

And now it seemed that Juliet would never forgive him.

25

Dear Juliet

So sorry to hear you've got problems with your company. But as you haven't yet got a definite date to go back to the UK, isn't there any chance you can come for my engagement party on Wednesday? I so badly want you to meet Louis. He's heard all about you. Please, please come. It will do you good to have somewhere to go instead of mooching around your hotel waiting for news. You can keep in touch while you're here.

I'm hoping Jack's coming too.

Lots of love

Petra xx

Juliet read Petra's email, pulling a face at the mention of Jack. Then she rang Qantas for any news. It took nearly half an hour to get through to a real person and she had to stop herself from screaming when she was told to ring yet another number. After she was told that her call was important, she was forced to listen to the first few bars of a piece of classical music, tinny and electric, over and over. When a voice finally answered it made her jump.

'Can you tell me the latest on flights from Melbourne to Heathrow, please?'

'No chance at the moment. The strike's still on, though they're hoping to resolve it by the end of the week.'

A thought occurred to her.

'Would it be any easier if I went back to England from Sydney?'

'It won't make any difference.' The man's voice was weary, as though he'd just pressed a button and let his recording do the talking. 'It's not this end that's the hold-up.'

'What about other UK cities? Manchester or Birmingham...or Glasgow.' She was trying to think. 'It's only for one person. Juliet Reece. There must be space somewhere. I've got a ticket but it's not for a few more weeks. I need to get back to England now, on an emergency.'

'Sorry, ma'am. Because of the strike all other flights are full.' He paused. 'One moment, please.' The phone went silent and after a long minute when she thought he'd forgotten her he came back. 'I see you already have a ticket booked for the UK on the first of December.'

'Yes, but I need to return now,' Juliet repeated, drumming her fingers on the edge of the bedside table of her hotel. 'I've been told I'm in a queue but how long will it take to clear?'

'There's no telling.' The man's tone was becoming impatient. 'We'll let you know the first available flight.'

'Can you see my name in the queue?'

'Yes, I've got your name here.'

'And there's no way round it?' Juliet persisted.

'Not at the moment.'

'What about going from Sydney to Paris, or somewhere else in Europe? Then I could get back to England on the train.'

'Most of those flights got booked immediately when the strike began.' He paused. 'I'm just looking for you.' She waited, heart in her mouth, willing something reasonable to come up on the computer that she could take. 'No, I'm sorry, Ms Reece. Nothing at the moment.'

She could have kicked herself for not thinking that way round the problem before. And she was equally annoyed with Qantas for not having suggested any alternatives earlier when she might have had a chance.

'Can I help you with anything else?'

'Yes,' Juliet said quickly before she could change her mind. 'I'll book a ticket to Sydney to leave tomorrow afternoon.'

'No worries, ma'am.'

All was going according to plan when it happened.

For one thing, Sydney Airport was smaller and older than she had imagined, and extremely crowded. Standard royal-blue carpet contrasted harshly with the parallel shiny cream floor. She made her way through to customs. Twisting round on one of her high heels to get out of the way of the other passengers who were waiting to collect their luggage, she tripped over a wheel which protruded from one of the carts. She heard a muttered apology as she went headlong. *Ahhh!* Her hands flailed, and she lost her grip on her flight bag which slithered in front of her along the shiny tiled floor.

Several people rushed to help her up; one woman brought over her bag.

'Thank you so much.' Juliet struggled to sit up and gratefully took it.

'You went down with quite a wallop,' said a rather short, aging Englishman wearing an Australian hat. 'Here, hold on to my arm if you can.'

She was worried she'd pull him over but he was stronger than he looked and hauled her to her feet.

Juliet sucked in her breath with the sudden pain.

'Are you hurt?' He sounded concerned.

'It's just my wrist.'

'You need to get it checked,' the man said, glancing at her left hand. 'It might be broken.'

'Oh, no, I don't think so.' It was swelling in front of her eyes but if it was broken it was a first. No, although it was painful, it wasn't painful enough for a broken bone, she was sure. And she could still move it.

'Well, I would in any case – just for your own peace of mind. And get an icepack on it as soon as you can.'

Elvis's voice throbbed in tune with Juliet's wrist as he sang a 'Heartbreak Hotel' welcome while she edged into the revolving door of the Hotel Morello, trying to protect her wrist. A porter directed her to the first floor where the noise of a party-going crowd led her to one of the rooms.

Everyone appeared to know one another and she couldn't very well push into one of the groups. Where was Petra? Heart beating a little faster she suddenly wished she hadn't come. *Don't be silly. Pretend it's a business networking event. You're good at those. Just count to ten. Breathe in slowly.* She drew herself up and immediately felt more confident. She'd be fine. She was debating which group to infiltrate when a cheerful waiter came over and handed her a glass of champagne. At the same moment she spotted Petra's blonde head.

No sign of Jack.

Petra was chattering and laughing in a small group. Before Juliet could put her hand up to catch Petra's eye and wave she felt her heart squeeze, the sudden contraction making it impossible to move. She clutched her hand to her heart, wondered crazily if she was having a stroke. *Dear God, it can't be…it can't possibly be…*

She looked again at the man standing next to Petra, his head bent to hers, as though not wanting to miss one word of what she was saying, his arm pulling her close. Shiny black straight hair. Same slim build. But taller. Much taller. Drops of cold perspiration ran down her back. With every effort she tightened her stomach, made herself take more deep breaths.

A tiny toffee-coloured face and brown eyes flashed in front of her. Her eyes filled with hot sudden tears at the memory but she forced herself to steal another look, her heart pounding out of control. His back was now turned towards her but it made no difference; even the shape of his head looked familiar.

'Are you all right?' A woman about the same age as herself, wearing a smart black shift dress and a bright green and blue necklace, came into view. 'You look like you've seen a ghost.'

The woman's words were perfectly clear but Juliet's head felt like it was going to burst.

'You haven't touched your drink,' the woman observed.

Juliet forced herself to focus on the woman. 'I'm sorry...I was miles away.'

'Name's Sarah,' the woman smiled, holding out her hand.

'Juliet.' The woman's hand felt warm and friendly, but all Juliet wanted to do was stare at the back of the man standing by Petra.

'Well, Juliet,' Sarah broke into her thoughts again, 'are you a friend of Petra or Louis?'

'Er...Petra,' Juliet managed.

'Well, I'll take you over,' Sarah said. 'Have you met Louis?'

'No...no I haven't,' Juliet stuttered. She'd have to go over to them now. No way to slip out of the door with Sarah holding her arm so firmly. She felt as though she were in a film, in slow motion. The next thing she knew, Petra was flinging her arms round her. The man with the straight black hair had wandered over to a nearby group.

'Juliet. I'm so pleased to see you. You look great.' Petra's sharp eyes flicked over her. 'But what have you done to your wrist?' Her expression was horrified as she lifted Juliet's hand. 'It's terribly swollen. What happened?'

'I fell. Stupid thing to do...yesterday at the airport. It's nothing. I've put ice on it and I don't think it's any worse.'

'Have you seen a doctor? No, of course you haven't. Sarah, have you seen Juliet's wrist?' Petra turned to Juliet. 'Sarah's a doctor.'

'Let me see.' Sarah took her hand and gently ran her fingers over the angry swelling. 'Mmm. You should have it X-rayed.'

'Is it broken?' Petra looked anxiously at Sarah.

'Could be,' Sarah said. 'Why don't you call the hospital first thing tomorrow? Ask to be put through to me. Here's my card.' She delved into her small velvet bag and handed it to Juliet. 'In the meantime take painkillers and don't use that hand if you can help it.' She turned to Petra, her smile lighting up her plain features. 'I'll leave you to catch up with Juliet then.' She disappeared.

'What a nice woman,' Juliet said, her heart still racing, desperately trying to concentrate on Petra. 'Let me have a proper look at you. You look fabulous. Rather different from the last time I saw you.'

Petra gave a twirl of her dress, a silver concoction, sprinkled with tiny coloured sequins which glittered under the light of the hotel's chandeliers. The only jewellery she wore was a pair of diamond earrings to match her engagement ring. A present, maybe, from—

Juliet was aware of his presence even before Petra introduced them.

'Darling, this is Juliet who I've told you loads about. She looked after me on the boat when I thought I was dying.'

'It's true, she's told me all about you,' Louis smiled, showing perfect white teeth, and Juliet found herself looking straight into the most melting brown eyes she had ever seen since she'd last looked into Mani's.

Juliet didn't know how she'd got through the rest of the party.

Louis had offered to drive her back to her hotel but she told him she'd already ordered a taxi. The thought of being alone with him made her tremble. How mortified she'd feel if she blurted out anything. Because, of course, there was no way he could possibly be Charlie. Safe now in the taxi she inspected her wrist which was still throbbing gently. Thankfully she'd be seeing Sarah, that nice doctor, tomorrow. A strap on one of her sandals pinched and she kicked them off for a few minutes' respite, just like she used to when she was working.

Work. Oh, God, she hadn't thought about work since morning. Too much had happened in the space of forty-eight hours. First, the wrist. Then seeing Charlie. She shook her head angrily...Louis... it's Louis. Oh, God, I'm going mad. He can't be Charlie. She bit her lip. Must focus...one thing at a time. If she didn't get Reece & Co sorted she'd had it. All that she'd built up. As soon as she got back to her hotel she'd find out if there was any news about Heathrow, and try to speak to Bob or Kirsty.

The taxi driver was edging close to Sydney Harbour. Juliet looked out of the window and gasped. The bay was encircled by lights, the Opera House just coming into view; then it seemed to sail right past the taxi's windows. Would there be time to look inside? She'd always dreamed of seeing an opera in the iconic building but how could she enjoy anything now? And she was only here for a couple of days anyway. Everything would be booked up. There simply wouldn't be time. It just wasn't fair, she thought childishly.

She leaned her head on the back of the seat, closing her eyes, aware for the first time of another woman's perfume. Presumably the driver's last customer. Was the woman with anyone? Or on her own? Was she happy or sad? Did she enjoy her life or was she, too, swamped with insurmountable problems?

Somehow it felt important to know that she wasn't the only one with problems. Her eyes flicked open as she replayed in her mind for the countless time Petra's engagement party. Petra had been the perfect hostess, making sure Juliet was introduced to her parents and friends. Her mother and father had been charming and thanked Juliet profusely for looking after their girl. They were hardly older than herself, both attractive, and were delighted when she'd told them she could see where Petra got her looks. But all the time Juliet's concentration was on someone else, and she could never stop searching the room for him, finding all kinds of connections that would be laughable if they weren't so heartbreaking.

She saw herself asking Petra if Louis' parents were at the party. Petra had said crisply, no, unfortunately they'd been killed in an aeroplane crash last year. That had been another shock as she'd always imagined them still very much part of Charlie's life. If, of course, Charlie was Louis. But she couldn't bring herself to ask Petra if Louis was adopted. Now in the taxi she played around with the irrational thought that as he didn't have his parents any longer he might be pleased to think he had a natural mother. She flicked her eyes open impatiently. Who was she kidding? That scenario only happened in fairy stories. If it truly was him she'd better be prepared for him to hate her for giving him up. So the sooner she got rid of the idea that Louis was anything but Petra's fiancé, the better.

'We have the results.' Sarah pointed to the X-ray, clipped to the lightbox. 'You're lucky. It's a moderate sprain which means moderate damage.'

'Thank goodness. I was beginning to think I'd broken it, it's so painful.'

'The pain can be as bad as a break,' Sarah said. 'Especially as you've partially torn some ligaments. I'll give you some strong painkillers.' She wrote out a prescription. 'But it needs bandaging to get the swelling down and then a sling to keep it elevated.' She put her pen down and pressed her intercom. 'You may or may not need a splint but we'll try you without to start.' A man's voice answered. 'Oh, Tim, there you are. I'm sending Juliet Reece for bandaging. Grade two sprained wrist – left.' She paused. 'Okay. Fifteen minutes.' She looked at Juliet. 'He's just finishing his last patient. Would you like another coffee?'

'I won't, thanks. It sounds as though it's going to be a nuisance.'

'The first forty-eight hours are crucial, which is when you

should have rested it, but we'll keep an eye. You should be fine.'

'How long will I have to keep the bandage on?'

'Shouldn't be more than a week.' She gave a friendly smile. 'How long are you here?'

'Not long. I have to get back to England straight away. I've come to Sydney on a flying visit to see Petra…and meet Louis.' Juliet paused, feeling her heart turn over. She asked the same question Sarah had asked her at the party: 'Are you a friend of Petra or Louis?'

'Petra's. She's a sweet girl, isn't she? Her parents are patients of mine – have been for years. Louis, I've only met once before last night.'

'Do you think he'll make her a good husband?' Juliet couldn't stop now.

'He's a few years older than Petra, who's never really grown up. But maybe that's exactly what she needs. He seems a steady sort of guy, and they appear idyllically happy. But what an odd question.' She took her glasses off and Juliet felt Sarah's eyes, with or without the glasses, missed nothing.

'I'm just curious. I haven't known Petra long. She was on the ship with me from England.'

'Ah, yes,' Sarah said. 'Since the crash when Louis' parents were killed she's got a phobia about flying. Not very convenient in her line of work'

'She mentioned that last night. How awful. I didn't like to probe at the party, but I understand there were four passengers. What happened to the other two?'

'Killed outright. It was only a light plane – five-seater. Only the pilot survived.'

'That must have been a miracle,' Juliet said. 'Did they ever find out what happened?'

'There was a big investigation. It burst into flames on landing. It was in all the papers for days.'

'Was it engine trouble?' Juliet was hungry to know everything she could to piece together Louis' background, however inconsequential.

Sarah glanced at her as though surprised with her new patient's questioning about a complete stranger. Juliet shifted in the uncomfortable patient's metal chair.

'The weather was pretty appalling,' Sarah said eventually, 'but I can't make judgements. It was a complicated case.'

'How terrible to have that on your conscience. Being the only one to survive, I mean.'

'Well, he was quite badly injured – nearly lost a leg, I believe.'

A tiny curl of dread started in the pit of Juliet's stomach.

'Do you know his name?'

Sarah frowned. 'An Irish name, I seem to remember.' She shrugged. 'It'll come to me as soon as you've gone.' She doodled on her pad for a few seconds, then looked up. 'I think it was Della something.'

'Would it...' Juliet swallowed, trying to dislodge the lump in her throat, 'would it be...Jack Delaney?'

'Now that you mention it, yes – that's the guy. Jack Delaney.'

26

'What's the matter, Juliet? You look terrible.'

Juliet struggled with herself. She looked at Sarah, whose grey eyes were wise and genuinely friendly. Hell, she was a doctor. You could say anything to doctors and be sure it was kept confidential. 'I know Jack,' she said, finally. 'I met him. He was on the same ship as Petra and me. They knew one another but Petra would never let on how. And she'd get ratty if I asked her. She just said once that she felt sorry for him.'

'Good God.' Sarah looked startled. 'What's he like? I've only ever seen a photo of him in the newspapers. He looked rather attractive.'

'He's *very* attractive,' Juliet blurted. 'And charming with it.'

'Looks like he made quite an impression on you.' Sarah scrutinised her. 'Tell you what, why don't we meet next door for a sandwich after my clinic. Tim should be ready for you now. Shall we say...' she glanced at her watch, 'quarter to one?'

'I'd like that,' Juliet said as the nurse came to fetch her.

Tim's round face dimpled as he smiled and chatted non-stop while bandaging her arm, but her attention wandered. Jack crowded her brain. So he was the pilot of the plane that killed Petra's in-laws to be. That was why Petra had felt sorry for him and wouldn't discuss it with her. And Jack had spoken very little about his career...and nothing about how he knew Petra. One piece of the jigsaw puzzle had fallen into place. Sarah said the weather had been dreadful but there'd been an investigation. Well, there would have been, without doubt, over such a tragic accident. Juliet wondered if there'd been any further developments to prove anything conclusively, or had they simply closed the file? A vision of Jack's cabin swam in front of her. Was that what he was doing that day? Going through all the reports of the crash? It must still be raw for him and maybe he could only deal with it if he shut himself away. He obviously didn't trust her enough to confide in her.

'All done,' Tim said, cutting through her thoughts. He'd bandaged as far as her elbow. 'Move your fingers.' He pulled up a table and carefully laid her arm on it. She wiggled them in the air. 'Good. Doesn't feel too tight?'

'I don't think so, though I don't know how it's supposed to feel.'

'Firm and supported. But I'm going to put a sling on you to remind you not to use it.' He handed her some swatches. 'Here, choose a colour.'

'You choose. I can't make any big decisions like that on the spur of the moment.'

He grinned. 'Go for the purple.'

It was lilac but she couldn't be bothered to argue.

He tied it on with a professional flourish and raised his eyes to hers. 'How long are you in Oz?'

'Not long.' She rose from the chair. 'I've been called home urgently, except there're no flights because of a strike at Heathrow.'

'Sorry to hear that. But the important thing is to keep your sling on so the arm stays stable and gives the wrist a chance to heal. And at night,' he threw her a saucy grin, 'the only thing you need to worry about being elevated is your arm.'

Green Bean was a sandwich bar where the A-board outside announced all its sandwiches were organic and freshly made to order. It was packed when Juliet stepped through the door, grateful to the young woman who kindly held it open, but by the time Sarah arrived Juliet had managed to find a table for two.

'Excellent,' Sarah said as she undid her jacket. 'Sometimes you end up sitting on a bar stool, and I hate that.' She took the chair opposite. 'How's the wrist?'

'Hard to tell,' Juliet smiled as she handed Sarah a menu, 'but at least the painkillers have kicked in.'

'That's good.' Sarah put her elbows on the table after they'd ordered, fisted hands under her chin, waiting.

Juliet knew exactly what Sarah was waiting for but she raised an eyebrow in question.

'Jack,' Sarah said. 'Tell me about him.'

'He never says much about himself.'

'Did you have a fling?' Sarah threw her a wicked smile.

These Aussies. They were not in the least embarrassed about asking personal questions, Juliet thought. She'd been brought up with so many secrets she'd never learned the art of confiding. Now here was this doctor, not behaving at all like a doctor, wanting a gossip.

'Well?'

'You obviously guessed I did.'

'And?'

'There's no "and". I doubt if I'll ever see him again.'

'Why do you say that? Have you seen him since the ship?' Sarah's eyes were full of friendly curiosity.

'Once or twice.'

'Sounds promising.'

'Not really. The last time I saw him in Melbourne we had a row. I walked out.' Juliet lowered her voice, reluctant to continue the subject.

The waiter brought their lunch and for a few minutes they were silent.

Sarah bit into the second half of her sandwich and said, 'Something's bugging you.'

'I was wondering if they'd found anything more about the cause of the crash in the investigation?'

'Was Jack at fault, do you mean?' Sarah's eyes scanned her as though she were reading one of her X-rays.

'Not really,' Juliet replied, untruthfully. 'I just wondered what the papers said. The way Jack is so secretive, it feels as though he's hiding something.'

'It was never proven that it was Jack's flying ability, or rather lack of it, that was the cause, Juliet,' Sarah cautioned her. 'There was a big inquiry about something mechanically wrong. And the awful weather. So don't go looking for something that isn't there. And don't forget – he was acquitted.'

Sarah was right. If it had been his fault he wouldn't be allowed to continue to fly. Juliet hated herself for such doubts but how could she help speculating when no one seemed to know the whole truth? Or if they did, they weren't telling her. And how did Louis feel about all this? It was a question she'd never be in a position to ask, and a relief when lunch came to an end.

'I can't believe the time.' Sarah looked at her watch. 'I've got a two-fifteen, so must dash. It was lovely to meet you. I know you're going back soon but keep in touch.' She bent down and kissed Juliet on the cheek. 'I want to hear the next instalment of Jack,' she said over her shoulder, to the amusement of the other diners.

Juliet hadn't reckoned on falling in love with Sydney as she wandered through the city that afternoon. So this was where her Charlie had grown up. What was he doing right now? Because of course he wasn't Louis. She wondered what career her son had chosen. If he'd stayed in Sydney or settled somewhere else. Had he ever come to England? If he had, maybe he'd tried to trace his natural mother. And she'd been there all along…not knowing. She shook her head, pressed her lips together, trying to dispel such a depressing thought.

She trudged the length of Sydney Harbour Bridge and took

a ferry from Manly to Circular Quay, admiring the boats as they skimmed across the water. They docked at the Opera House and she thought she might as well join a group on a guided tour of the building. It would probably be the only chance she'd get to see the inside, but it turned out to be unexciting compared with its innovative exterior. She lagged behind the group, reading the posters advertising forthcoming operas and ballets, disappointed that she wouldn't be able to see their forthcoming production of *La Bohème,* to be performed the following week.

Back at the hotel she phoned for news of the strike and was told it was likely to be resolved in the next couple of days. She was still in the queue and would be notified when there was a seat. Was there no end to this wait? She gave them her new mobile number and also the hotel's.

She'd finally made all her calls to let Rachel and Lydia know her new number, and Antonia and Will, but she'd had to leave messages for all of them as the timing hadn't been right. So far she hadn't heard back from anyone. She was in two minds to phone Jack but in the end she left him a message too, half disappointed, half relieved he hadn't picked up.

This evening she would eat in the hotel restaurant. It was only half full and those diners already seated were all couples, or girls having a night out. Usually that wouldn't have bothered her at all but this evening felt different. She wanted someone to talk to – offload her fears for the future. When she'd started the business in her late thirties she'd had plenty of energy and enthusiasm but if she was honest, heading towards fifty was another matter. And what about finances? If Lydia and Neil had buggered things up and she'd lost some clients, there was an emergency sum in her business account, but that wouldn't last more than six months by the time she'd paid out salaries and all the overheads. *Mustn't think like this.* If she could just get home, of course she could pull her company round.

*

236

After her meal she phoned Qantas for the third time that day.

'Yes, the strike's lifted,' said a low-pitched female voice in a bored drawl.

Thank God. Normally, she would have torn the woman off a strip for Qantas not having contacted *her* but she didn't dare show any sign of irritation that might go against her.

'Your name, please.'

Juliet went through the same rigmarole as before but the Qantas woman said she had gained some places up the queue and to keep in touch. It should only be a matter of a few days now.

Meanwhile, anything could be happening to her business.

She must *do* something to take her mind off home or she'd go mad.

Charlie. Now was a perfect opportunity for her to look for him. Up until now she'd told herself she'd just been happy to be in the same country, but if she were honest it wasn't nearly enough.

Her stomach fluttered with nerves, reminding her of when she'd been carrying Charlie and felt the featherlight movement for the first time. Nannie had told her it was the quickening. And later he'd kicked her unmercifully as though he was hammering to come out and meet her. Sometimes it had been quite brutal but she'd loved it, knowing her child was alive and somehow everything would be all right. Unconsciously she put her hand over her stomach, a bittersweet smile curving her lips at the memory.

Admit it, Juliet. You're scared. That's your trouble. You can handle all the business stuff thrown at you but when it comes to emotional stuff you go to pieces.

But if she didn't do anything, how would she feel when she was back in England? Wouldn't she beat herself up for not trying to make a proper search? And hadn't this search been at the back of her mind right from the beginning? Right from when Lydia first said she'd take over?

It was tempting to leave well alone as she had for all these thirty years. Yet what was the point of being in Sydney if she didn't try to find out what had happened to him? Surely she was meant to be here. She chewed the inside of her mouth, desperately trying to make a decision.

She went to the bar and ordered a brandy. She would do her level best to find her son. She'd need to be systematic. Go up every possible path. But where to start? She frowned. They must have some sort of Citizens Advice Bureau who could point her in the right direction. And then she'd be able to confirm once and for all that Louis wasn't Charlie. Her heart raced and she swallowed a mouthful of the warming liquid, trying to gain courage as it slid down her throat.

Maybe she could start with the newspaper archives and find out about the plane crash. It wouldn't be anything to do with checking up on Jack, she told herself. Nothing to do with being disloyal to him. No, she wanted to see if there was a photograph of Louis' parents. If Louis *was* her son – and she couldn't get it out of her head that he really might be – then she dearly wanted to have a glimpse of the people who had brought him up. Given him a home and education. Loved him as though he were their own son. She wanted to see if they looked like nice people. Would she have chosen them herself? That way, she didn't have to probe into Louis' life if all she did was look at a few photographs.

Sarah said the crash had been in all the papers and it only happened a year ago, so it shouldn't be too difficult to find. She squashed a tinge of guilt. Too bad if Jack found out. Well, if he valued her as a friend he would have told her about it, wouldn't he? She couldn't go on any longer wondering if it was the engine or the weather or both...or...something else. And anyway, she was doing this for Charlie.

The next morning was overcast, in sharp contrast to the beautiful sunshine they'd enjoyed over the last couple of days, and by the time

Juliet left the hotel it had started to rain heavily. The perfect day to carry out her investigations. She'd looked up the *Sydney Morning Herald* on the hotel's map and found the address, which she jotted down. But she'd go on the tram. And not bother to ring – she'd just turn up.

'I wonder if you could help me,' Juliet asked the receptionist, whose make-up would have been more appropriate for a sultry film star. Thick, dark shoulder-length hair, with matching fringe covering her eyebrows, and full lips the colour of ripe plums.

'I'm trying to find a news item from about a year ago of a plane crash.' The girl raised a black-pencilled eyebrow. 'It was a light aircraft and the pilot's name was Jack Delaney. I'm not exactly sure where the plane crashed but he took off from Sydney Airport.'

As soon as Juliet said his name she felt utterly disloyal. It was as though she were betraying this man who she wanted to be near, wanted to talk to, wanted to see smile at her. But the way she was carrying on she didn't in all honesty deserve to. Surely if she really valued him as a friend she wouldn't be checking up on him like this. She gave her head a little shake. She was here now. Best get on with it. She gave the receptionist a tentative smile.

'Do you think it would be possible to look it up without knowing the place he landed?'

The girl threw her a look as if to ask where she'd been these last years. 'All we have to do is look up his name on the computer,' she jerked her thumb towards a screen, 'and it will tell us the exact dates he was mentioned. Where he landed. What headlines he made in which newspapers. Everything.'

Dear God, it was too easy.

The receptionist glanced at Juliet. 'Wouldn't you rather do all this on the computer? It's so much quicker and easier and you'll get the full story in one go.'

'No,' Juliet answered. 'I want to read it as it happened in the actual newspapers, if possible.'

The girl rolled her eyes and motioned for Juliet to follow her into one of the rooms off the main reception area and told her to take a seat. There were extensive work tables set in rows with a handful of people using their laptops or writing furiously. No one was speaking and the only sound was of the newspapers being quietly turned over, page by page, or folded and put on various piles.

'I won't be long,' she told Juliet, and true to her word she came back presently bearing an armful of newspapers. 'You're in luck. Your Mr Delaney made the front page on the first day. There's more news of the case over the following days, and then after the court case it dwindles down to a couple of paragraphs.' She set the pile in front of Juliet. 'They're all here. Take as long as you want. And if there's anything you want to have photocopied come and see me.'

Juliet muttered her thanks and found herself staring straight into Jack's eyes. A wing of hair had flopped over his forehead and he looked relaxed, though unsmiling. Huge letters swept across the width of the paper:

PILOT CRASH LANDED AT CANBERRA AIRPORT
ALL 4 PASSENGERS KILLED

With hammering heart she looked at the second photograph of the two couples just before they'd boarded the plane. The first couple, Mr and Mrs Morgan, looked happy. He had his arm round her and they were both grinning at the camera. She peered more closely at the couple standing next to them – Mr and Mrs Jordan, aged sixty-four and sixty. Mrs Jordan looked a little too thin in her flowered shift dress and a matching turban with not a wisp of hair showing, and although she was smiling for the camera her eyes seemed deep and sad. Her husband was a larger man with a toothy grin. Juliet's eyes brimmed as she studied them. They'd had no idea that morning when they got ready for their celebratory flight that it was to be the last thing they would ever do. She swallowed hard. Mr and Mrs Jordan might have been the couple who brought up her Charlie – a normal, nice Australian couple who loved him as the son they'd never had. Blinking to hold back the tears she began to read the editorial.

One eye-witness at Canberra Airport said the landing appeared clumsy. Seconds later the plane burst into flames. There has been no conclusive evidence but it may have been caused by a technical problem. Mr Delaney, the pilot and only survivor, was pulled out but was badly injured. He was admitted to hospital, but the investigation will go ahead with the hope that it won't be too long before Mr Delaney is able to give his own account. Mr Delaney is married with one daughter.

Married? Frowning, she read the last sentence again. He'd told her he had an *ex*-wife. Still, this report was a year ago so they must be divorced by now. But he had a daughter. Why hadn't he mentioned her? What was the daughter's name? How old was she? Elbows on the table she cupped her cheeks in her hands, her fingers pressing under her eyes, trying to absorb it all. So many questions. Her left arm began to itch and she used her pencil to poke it inside the bandage but the spot was impossible to reach. For a few minutes she sat there, the arm tormenting her, wishing to God she'd never heard of the *Sydney Morning Herald*.

Then common sense took over and she knew she couldn't continue any relationship with Jack if she was wondering all the time what he was keeping hidden. Even when Jack was making her laugh, making love to her – *no, don't think of that* –he would close up when she wanted to know more about him. Everything seemed to be on his terms. When *he* decided. No, no matter how painful, she had to know the truth. So he had a daughter. She briefly lowered her lids, thinking how lucky he was. A beautiful daughter with her father's dark hair and gold-flecked hazel eyes.

Juliet forced herself to pick up the following day's paper. There was no mention of Jack or the crash on the front page. She carefully laid her bandaged arm on the paper to steady it, and turned the pages with her good hand. When she eventually found a report it merely said that Delaney's leg had been severely burnt, and that the investigation of the crash was still being carried out at the scene of the accident. Same sort of report on the third day…and the fourth. She added the papers to the small pile and took up newspaper number five. She didn't have to turn over any pages. The headlines once again shouted from the front page:

WAS THERE ALCOHOL IN CRASH PILOT'S BLOOD?

It was the first mention of anything untoward. Feeling sicker by the minute Juliet skimmed the report, her eyes flying to the end where the article didn't appear to conclude as to whether Jack had or hadn't been found guilty of alcohol in his blood before he took the plane up. She was forced to go back to the beginning. To read it slowly.

Mr Delaney is making fair progress and the burns on his leg are being treated at the Canberra Hospital. He will require skin grafts but for the moment is said to be comfortable. Blood tests are being carried out as it is thought he had been drinking alcohol the night before. It will be the responsibility of a medical expert to decide whether or not it would have had any effect on Delaney's skill and judgement when attempting to land. The Civil Aviation Safety Authority rules states no alcohol is to be consumed at least twelve hours before a flight.

Had it been within the twelve hours when they would have to prosecute, or was Delaney in the clear because more than twelve hours had passed? And so it went on. She laid the newspaper on the table. There were several more left to read but she couldn't face them.

Newspapers often distort things, exaggerate to sell papers, she kept telling herself.

Alcohol in his blood. Surely Jack was not so irresponsible as to risk other people's lives even if he didn't bother about his own. Which she knew he did. When he was in an 'open' mood (she called it to herself) he was fun and spontaneous, but he had a serious, caring side to him. Surely they weren't the characteristics of an irresponsible person. Unconsciously she shook her head. And would he risk his licence? But what if there was a grain of truth? He'd be someone you couldn't really trust. But Petra wouldn't have invited him to her engagement party, let alone travelled back to Australia with him if there'd been any doubt. He'd been acquitted – Sarah said so. And it must be true because he was still flying.

But whatever the outcome he must feel guilty. He was the pilot in charge, after all. No wonder he hadn't shown up at Petra's engagement party. He couldn't face Louis. But she was running away with her thoughts – speculating – and that was dangerous. Jack's case was obviously closed.

'Anyone need any help?' a young man enquired to the room in general. Everyone shook their heads except Juliet who sat staring in front of her, too miserable and numb to make any sign at all.

To her intense embarrassment her new mobile rang. The young man frowned and pointed to a notice, but by the time she'd scrambled in her handbag with her good hand it had gone to answerphone. She scrolled to see who the number was but before it came up the mobile rang again, making her jump.

'Juliet, is that you?'

She couldn't quell the warm shiver which ran through her at

the sound of his voice, deep and full of life. She felt like a stick of wax that had started to melt. Then everything tumbled together – the traces of alcohol...the wife...the daughter.

'I can't speak at the moment. I'll call you back.'

Her stomach gave a sickening roll. If Jack could see where she was and what she'd been reading he'd be furious. There'd be no possibility of building any trust in the future, that was for sure. She tucked the phone in her handbag and gathered her things together. Quite frankly, she'd had enough for today.

Her brain buzzing she stepped outside. She tilted her head to the sky where dark grey clouds hung heavy though it had almost stopped raining. What did she want? To break off with Jack – whatever there was to break off? Was that really what she wanted? Drops of rain splattered on her hair and she opened her umbrella. Her mobile rang again. *Damn him. Let it ring.*

It rang three more times before she got back to her hotel room. On the fourth time she sat on the easy chair and pressed the receive button.

'Who's speaking, please?' She might have been talking to a client.

'Jack. Remember me? Jack Delaney. How soon they forget.' His tone was light with a hint of amusement.

'Oh, Jack, sorry I couldn't take your call.' Her voice was cool. Let him make of it what he would. 'We missed you at the engagement party.' Actually, she wasn't certain his name had been mentioned, but perversely she wanted to keep him talking.

'Yeah, great pity I couldn't make it. Go well?'

'Very well.'

'And her fiancé...Louis?' There was a pause. 'How did you find him?'

Why did he want to know her opinion of Petra's fiancé?

'I liked him a lot. He's perfect for Petra.'

Stop the conversation. Hang up. Tell him you have to go. It's not convenient. Anything.

Ignoring the voice in her head she rushed on: 'Funny, his parents naming him Louis when their surname is Jordan. Apparently, his mum—' She stopped. To say the word 'mum' in the same breath as Louis was almost more than she could bear. 'His mum,' she repeated firmly, 'was a keen fan of Louis Jourdan, the film star, and as their surname...' her voice wobbled, 'is...was...Jordan...' Oh, God, she couldn't remember whether she was supposed to know Louis' parents were dead. There was a long silence. Her eyes stung. Trying to control herself she said, 'But you're not ringing me to discuss Petra's engagement party.'

There was a long pause. Then she heard him say, 'Is anything wrong, Juliet?'

'Why should there be?'

'You tell me. You just sound a bit strange, that's all. Are you still angry with me?'

How was she to answer that? *Yes, damn you. Why didn't you think enough of our friendship to tell me you had a daughter? And what's more, that phone call was obviously more important than what we were doing. And it was definitely a woman on the other end. Was it your ex? Or is she still your wife?*

Oh, but how she wanted to confront him. Tell him she'd deliberately gone to the *Sydney Morning Herald* and dug something up that he hadn't wanted to discuss. But that would set up another row, no question of it. And then she'd have to bear his cold fury. His mouth hardening. His eyes bereft of the gold-leaf sparkle. She shuddered at the new imagined picture of him.

'Why should I be angry?' She fought to keep calm.

'Can't hear you very well...you're breaking up. But when are you coming back to Melbourne?'

'The day after tomorrow.' She hesitated. 'By the way, the strike's over.' It was impossible to finish with him over the phone. She'd have to tell him in person. She'd never been a coward and she wasn't going to become one, no matter how ugly it got.

'Yes, I heard.' Jack's voice was faint. 'And if I can wangle any favours, you know I will.' The line went dead and Juliet thought he'd ended the conversation. She was about to switch her mobile off when she heard him say, 'I've got something important I want to talk to you about. Can you come tomorrow?'

'No, I already have my ticket for the day after. And I couldn't anyway. I've sprained my wrist. I'm supposed to rest it for forty-eight hours.'

'How did you do that?'

'I fell in the airport.'

'Oh, no. You see what happens as soon as my back is turned?' He gave his hearty laugh. 'See how you need me to take care of you?'

Empty words.

'I'm pleased you find it so funny.'

He laughed even louder and she had to hold the receiver away from her ear.

'I have to go,' he said. 'I don't want to say this over the phone. But tell me what time you arrive and I'll meet you in.'

It was going to be more difficult than she'd imagined, saying goodbye to Jack.

That evening there were four messages for her. One was a plaintive message from Gerrard enquiring why he hadn't heard from her, and whether everything was all right, and the rest from work.

Hi Jay

You've probably heard from Lydia by now. No one has heard anything from Neil. He must be really sick (or dead, and I don't suppose for a minute that's his excuse!). Please try to come as soon as this stupid strike at H'row is over.

Love Rachel

From Bob, sent two hours later:

Jay, sorry not to have been in touch but I know Rachel has kept you updated. As you can imagine we've been a bit busy. Rachel's told you that Lydia walked out and we've not heard a dickybird from Neil. If he was really sick I'm sure he'd ask one of his many girlfriends to get in touch as a matter of courtesy.

Have you managed to get a flight? You're really needed.

Regards, Bob

Juliet rubbed her forehead which had begun to throb worse than her wrist. She hunted for two more painkillers and swallowed them with a full glass of water, her mind flitting with questions that had no answers. Was Bob hinting at what had already crossed her mind? That Neil and Lydia were somehow working together. She gulped and reread it, blinking back the tears. Why had she been such a fool? Why hadn't she listened to her instincts not to put her precious company into a stranger's hands?

Fury, like bile, rose in her throat, as she opened Lydia's.

Jay, I'm sorry we had such a difficult conversation when you phoned, but this is to tell you that I have formally left the company. I found it impossible to work with Neil. I don't know how you stood it all these years. He tried to make my life miserable and I don't need to put up with that sort of behaviour at sixty! And to stoop to blackmail – that was the end, so far as I was concerned.

I'm quite sure he is setting up his own business using your list of clients, which I think is despicable after you've provided him with a good position in the company all these years. I'm all for anyone climbing the ladder but not when they stick the knife in to do so.

I would have gladly carried on if I'd had his support. Bob and Kirsty and Rachel were super. They are 100% loyal to you, which is how it should be.

Maybe once you're home and get work sorted out we can have lunch or something and I can tell you in more detail, but it doesn't make a very nice story.

All the best

Lydia

Juliet's lips set in a grim line. She didn't know whom to believe.

27

Melbourne

Juliet spent most of the flight from Sydney to Melbourne worrying about the business, beating herself up for having left it in the first place. Lydia's email had sounded so plausible that maybe she'd misjudged the woman. Maybe Neil really had made Lydia's life impossible. Lydia might be a lot of things but somehow being in cahoots with Neil seemed totally out of character from the little she now admitted she knew about her. Juliet's thoughts whirled, but knowing there was nothing she could do to alter whatever the situation was at Reece & Co until she got home, she pulled out the flight magazine in front of her and idly flicked the pages.

Travel articles which would normally grab her interest were suddenly uninteresting. She turned over a few more pages but even luxury spas in exotic countries failed to entice her. She needed to get back home before it was too late. If it wasn't already. A sensation of dread slipped around her shoulders as palpable as a cloak and she gave an involuntary shiver.

Think of something nicer, Juliet thought, just as she used to when she was a child and her mother was reproaching her for not getting such good grades as her older siblings. She saw her mother's mouth turning down at the corners with regret as though it were yesterday. Juliet gave a wry smile. She wasn't that child any longer but she could remember the shame. She wondered what Jack's childhood had been like.

Jack. He was an enigma. She remembered what she'd said to

Lydia about not wanting to get involved with a man – they had too much baggage. Well, Jack certainly had more than his fair share.

She wanted an uncomplicated relationship or none at all. But when you reached her age weren't all relationships complicated? She closed her eyes, resolved not to carry on seeing Jack – so why was she even worrying about complicated relationships?

He was standing at the front of the barrier holding up a card with JULIET REECE handwritten on it as Juliet exited through the Arrivals gate, still not having worked out what she should say.

'How did you know I've always wanted to be met by someone holding up a grotty piece of cardboard with my name written with a black marker pen in shaky letters?' In spite of herself she couldn't help laughing.

'Well, you seemed to have difficulty in recognising me when I called you yesterday,' Jack grinned, 'so I thought it the easiest way for you to pick me out as your chauffeur. At your service, Madame.' He kissed her lightly on the cheek.

She wouldn't tell him she'd instantly be able to pick him out from this whole airport crowd. The shape of his head, his profile, his easy confident walk – albeit with a slight limp – not only all those things but the very aura of him. In her nervousness she turned abruptly and the strap on her shoulder bag slipped to the elbow of her good arm.

'Here, let me,' Jack said, taking her flight bag and readjusting the bag on her shoulder. 'I see you went for a purple sling. Very fetching.'

'Lilac,' she corrected. 'To coordinate with my blouse.'

'So it does.' He gave her his warm smile. 'Great to see you, Juliet. How was the flight?'

'Fine.'

It seemed like a year since she'd seen him.

'Let's get out of here.'

He was a skilful driver which made her wonder again about

him as a pilot. Had he taken the plane up when he shouldn't? Juliet shivered slightly in her denim jacket.

'You okay?' He turned his head briefly to look at her. She nodded. 'I've booked you into your same hotel.' Jack's hands held the wheel of the Mercedes lightly yet firmly as he negotiated the traffic.

'Just as well. I've left my other stuff there.'

She tried to watch him surreptitiously, but he caught her gaze.

'It's good to see you, Juliet.'

'You, too.'

She wished he'd invited her to stay in his apartment for a couple of nights, then remembered this was definitely not part of her plan to finish it between them. But at least they would have had some privacy. Be able to be open with one another for once.

'Unless, of course, you'd rather stay with me! You might need some extra help getting undressed with that arm.'

Juliet started. He had an unnerving habit of reading her mind. She turned towards him and caught him grinning.

'Sounds tempting,' she said. 'But I think I'll stick with the hotel.'

'Don't say I didn't offer.'

Juliet had no idea whether he was disappointed or not.

The journey seemed to take forever but although Jack appeared perfectly relaxed, Juliet felt an awkwardness between them. It wasn't anything she could put her finger on. He asked her if she was comfortable. If the arm didn't hurt too much. If the air conditioning was set too high. No, it was probably all her own making. Guilt. She knew too much and she couldn't un-know it now. Once again she cursed the fact that she'd checked up on him. But she hadn't gone to the newspaper archives specifically to do that. She'd wanted to see who might have been Charlie's adoptive parents. But she had to face the fact she'd known she was bound to uncover some information about Jack at the same time.

Now that twenty-four hours had passed she realised it was

pretty despicable. Imagine if he'd done the same to her. She would never have forgiven him for not asking her face-to-face to explain. But he always avoided those kinds of confrontations and was adept at changing the subject, saying he'd tell her later, and not to spoil the moment. And she would never have found out the truth. That he might even still be married, that he had a daughter who he'd never mentioned. He'd built a wall around himself for all his casual cheerful manner, and woe betide any woman who tried to close in.

Purely for something to say to break the silence, she said, 'Anyway, what's this mysterious news you've got to tell me?'

'Later,' Jack said. 'At supper. I'll pick you up at eight o'clock. That suit?'

It probably made no difference whether it suited or not, Juliet thought, as he drew up outside the Sheridan. She waited for him to come round and open the car door for her as the last thing she wanted was to put any added strain on her wrist, and she couldn't help noticing how his eyes flicked down to her legs as she swung them round and onto the pavement.

'Thanks for meeting me, Jack. I'll look forward to supper.'

'Dress up.' Jack got out and retrieved her flight bag from the boot, handing it to the bellboy. 'Not that you don't always look stunning. Even with a sling,' he added, mischievously. 'But we're going to a special restaurant. To celebrate.'

'Celebrate what?'

'I'll tell you at the restaurant. Y'know, it really *is* good to see you,' and he kissed her swiftly on the lips. 'See you at eight.'

She logged on to the hotel's computer to get the final update before getting ready to go out. BA and Qantas websites both told her the same – the strike was officially over but there was still a backlog at all the main airports from Australia to Heathrow. Again, both sites announced all passengers in the queue still waiting to fly in and out of the UK would be notified.

Juliet fixed the hotel's plastic laundry bag on her bandaged arm and secured it with a rubber band, ready for her shower. Everything you took for granted was difficult. But it could have been worse. She might have broken her wrist and be encased in plaster, but it was still awkward just getting the tops off the shampoo and conditioner, and actually washing your hair with one hand was a major feat.

She looked in the mirror, outlining her mouth with lip pencil and filling it in with a creamy coral lipstick. Instead of her make-up taking the usual five minutes it took at least twenty; trying to squeeze out her moisturiser and foundation cream, keeping an eye-shadow compact level with the fingertips of her bandaged arm while she applied the colour with her right. Getting dressed would be tricky.

She decided on a flared black and white knee-length skirt, defying Joan Collins who always said no woman over forty should wear anything with an elasticated waist. *Sorry, Joan, but it's going to be much easier than doing buttons and zips.* Smiling at the thought of Joan's horror she chose a silky black top with loose-fitting sleeves and deep V neckline. It was a struggle but it finally slipped on. And with some effort she managed to put in her amber earrings, supporting the bandaged arm on the dressing table as she threaded them through the lobes.

Amber. That was it. That was the name of the house where Nannie and Pop had worked. Amber Bay. It was bound to be there still, and probably under the same family name, which she couldn't for the life of her remember...except the children's names. It was all coming back. Russell, who Nannie had told her got killed in the war, and the two girls, Louise and Daphne. They'd be old ladies now if they were still alive, but they'd probably married and had children. How wonderful if she could find one of them, speak to them. Ask them if they remembered her grandparents. Or had even heard of them. Her heart beat with excitement at the thought of picking up the trail again.

Juliet's hair shone as she brushed it. She had to admit she rather liked her hair longer. She'd have to ask Jack to help her make a sling of her silk scarf, which didn't exactly conjure up the image of the sexy woman she wanted to be. She pulled a face in the dressing table mirror. How would this evening turn out? She got up suddenly and felt her knees almost give way. Should she make an excuse? Get a headache? Or say her arm was playing up? But that wasn't her way. Not how she'd been brought up, and certainly not how she ran a business. *Oh, God. The business.* But first...her heart hammered... this evening.

At two minutes past eight, and feeling a shade self-conscious, she walked the length of the hotel foyer, high heels clicking on the ceramic-tiled floor, to find Jack waiting. He was sitting on one of the leather sofas flicking through a brochure, impeccably dressed in a navy suit, blue-striped shirt, and a navy tie dotted with bright green parrots. He rose to his feet and smiled and her heart skipped a beat. He was so damned attractive. Better than handsome.

'Can you tie this thing into a sling?' she asked, handing him the scarf and a safety pin.

He kissed her cheek. 'Sure.' He tied it almost as deftly as Tim had done at the hospital. 'Now let's have a look at you. Mmm. You look terrific,' he said, slipping her jacket around her shoulders, then bending to retrieve his laptop case. 'Ready?'

The restaurant was on a lower street level than the Sheridan. Jack held her good arm firmly as they descended two flights of concrete steps. He caught her looking at him and grinned.

'I shall have to take good care of you this evening, won't I, darling?'

Juliet's spine tingled at the endearment. It was the first time he'd used it.

'Sounds good,' was all she could manage.

'It's quite close,' he said. 'I didn't want to drive so we could have a few drinks.'

She took in a quick breath at his words and he looked at her sharply, but said nothing.

'It's Italian,' he said as they approached the restaurant. She noticed there was no outside menu. 'Is that okay?'

'Perfect,' Juliet smiled.

A maître d' greeted them, and directed a waiter to show them to a table by the window with a view of the Yarra River, twinkling like a string of diamonds.

'We'd like a bottle of champagne.'

'Certainly, sir. May I recommend the Clicquot?'

Juliet attempted with her one hand to open the heavy cover of the menu but each time it flopped back.

'Would you trust me to order for you?' Jack looked up as another waiter approached.

No man's ever done that.

'Well, it would save me trying to turn these blessed pages over.' She laid the menu down and looked at him, wishing he didn't make her feel so light-headed. 'That didn't sound very gracious, did it?' She sent him a dazzling smile. 'I'd love you to order for me. I'll just sit back and relax. Just don't choose kangaroo or crocodile.'

'You don't know what you're missing,' Jack laughed as he flicked back a page. His eyes ranged over the menu and then he nodded in a triumphant way and smiled across at her as he laid it down. 'We'll have the bouillabaisse to start,' he told the waiter, 'followed by the double-baked cheese soufflé, sautéed potatoes, roasted vegetables and a green salad between us.' He looked at Juliet. 'Is that to your taste, Madame?'

'I couldn't have chosen better myself.' She loved the way his mouth quirked.

'We'll see how we feel about dessert later.' Jack gave a mocking leer.

'Stop it, Jack. People will think you mean it.'

'I do.'

'Anyway, desserts aren't part of my diet.'

'You, dieting? You've got a fabulous figure. Don't dare get skinny.' His eyes travelled over as much as he could see of her above the table and Juliet couldn't help laughing.

'Don't worry. I'll never be that. Come on, Jack. I'm dying to know. What's all this about?'

Before he could answer, the wine waiter appeared and poured the champagne.

'To your grandparents,' Jack said surprisingly, clinking her glass with his. 'If it hadn't been for them I wouldn't have had the pleasure of meeting you.'

He made the slightly formal words sound incredibly personal, especially in his laid-back Australian accent. Juliet noticed the gold flecks in his eyes sparkled quite as much as the champagne.

'Excuse me a second.' He bent down for something in his case. 'I believe this is what you've been hoping to hold in your hot little hand.'

He slid a leather-bound book across the table in the space between them.

28

Juliet gaped in amazement at the book. A smell like an old attic filled her nostrils. But its most remarkable feature leapt out at her.

'I don't believe it!' She ran her fingers over the tarnished gold-coloured initials – AEB. 'Annie Elizabeth Bishop. It *must* be hers.'

'It is,' Jack said. 'Something on the first page tells me your instincts were right.'

He reached across the table and lightly held down the cover of the book so it didn't slide around while Juliet fumbled for the first entry with her good hand. With bent head she gave a swift intake of breath. There it was. Hardly realising what she was doing she read it aloud in a low husky voice, almost oblivious of Jack's presence.

'"Wednesday 3rd September 1913, on the *Orsova*. I'm keeping my promise to Dad and starting the diary. It's not the first time I've written things down if they were important. And nothing is more important than today and the future with my dear Ferguson..."'

Her beloved grandmother was talking to her. Wanting her to know she was still near. Juliet's scalp tingled and the words began to blur. She couldn't read any further. Dazedly she looked up, remembering where she was, her face aglow. 'Jack, how on earth did you get it?' Her voice stuttered in excitement.

'You don't need to know the details.'

'Not stolen, I hope?' she laughed.

Jack's eyes danced. 'More or less,' he said.

'What? Don't joke. Come on, Jack – I'm dying to know how

you talked them into opening up that cabinet. How long are you allowed to borrow it?'

'Indefinitely. But don't mention it to anyone.'

'The bouillabaisse, madam...sir.' The waiter set down two steaming white soup plates. '*Bon appétit.*'

'*Bon appétit*, Juliet.' Jack raised his flute to toast her.

She was speechless. Surely he was playing games. No, he looked perfectly serious though his mouth quirked as though he was trying not to laugh.

'You *stole* it?'

'There was no other way. I was just as sure as you it was your grandmother's. After all, she landed in Melbourne, we were in the Melbourne Maritime Museum, the initials were the same...and what were the chances of a diary with those same initials in that exact order?'

'Only someone named Alice Evelyn Baker,' Juliet quipped. 'Or those other names you came up with.' Then she realised the enormity of what Jack had done. She looked him full in the face. 'Jack...isn't it a criminal offence?'

'If I get caught. And I'm not planning to.' He chuckled. 'I'll guarantee it won't be missed.'

'But it'll leave a space.' She tried to turn another page but it was difficult with one hand, especially one that was trembling so much. Frustrated she closed the book, but couldn't resist running her fingers over the worn leather cover, now mottled with mould, needing to touch it, to make sure it wasn't a figment of her imagination.

'No, it won't. I've put something in its place.'

Juliet's head shot up. 'What do you mean?'

'A pilot's diary from the Second World War. Lieutenant Jonathan Delaney's. My father. I told you he kept one. I looked it out and went back to the museum the next day.'

Was there no end to Jack's madness?

'How on earth did you get into the cabinet?'

'Easy. It wasn't locked. Remember everything was in chaos when we went in that room. The guy we met was probably little more than a caretaker. Anyway let's not call it *stealing* – let's think of it as being on loan. You've got your grandmother's diary and they've got Dad's wartime diary. Fair exchange is no robbery.' He grinned.

She shook her head in disbelief. 'They're bound to discover it sooner or later. And you can't call it "fair exchange". Your father was a pilot. You've put his diary in the *Maritime* Museum.'

Jack was still grinning. 'Ah, that's the beauty of it. He was a *naval* pilot in the RAN.' Juliet raised an eyebrow. 'The Royal Australian Navy,' he explained, 'so it's perfectly appropriate.'

'You're crazy.'

'But that's why you like me.' His expression reminded Juliet of a mischievous schoolboy. 'Don't look so shocked. You're letting your soup go cold. Which is a pity – it's delicious.'

Jack had committed a theft. The diary wasn't hers...and yet... it was as though it had been waiting for her to find it all these years. That Nannie had ordained it.

Jack reached across and stroked her fingertips which poked out of the bandage. 'It's only on loan, remember?'

'I'm worried you'll...we'll get into trouble,' she whispered, trying to ignore the sensation of his touch. 'On loan, or whatever you call it, is just a euphemism for stealing. And I don't feel comfortable. It's my strict upbringing, I guess. All I know is – we'll have to own up.'

'Read it first,' Jack urged, 'before you decide anything. We can always smuggle it back later if you still feel bad about it.'

Be sensible. Jack wouldn't do anything to jeopardise his reputation. Then the unwelcome thought crept into her mind that maybe his reputation was already shot, so anything else wouldn't really matter. She pushed the thought away. He'd done it for her, thinking she'd be delighted.

'All right,' she gave in. 'It was a fantastic risk you took. I do appreciate it, really.'

She was rewarded by Jack blowing her a kiss. 'Anything for you, Ms Reece.'

Juliet dipped her spoon into the bouillabaisse and tasted it. Jack was right. It was delicious. The whole world was suddenly delicious. She couldn't help it. A beam spread across her face.

'That's better,' Jack said. 'I love it when you smile. You really light up.' He grinned back at her. Then his grin dropped. 'But you must promise to come and visit me every day when they put me in prison.' He bent his head and wiped a chunk of bread round his soup plate.

'Jack, they couldn't—'

'I'm joking.' He glanced up from his soup plate and winked. 'You should see your face,' he laughed. 'Don't worry. It'll be fine. But leaving the diary aside for the moment, what was that about your strict childhood?'

'They were definitely not the happiest days,' she said, letting her shoulders relax. 'My mother was Catholic and though she never completely converted my father, they brought me up as a Catholic. Both of them worked. And even though Dad was at home writing he might as well have been in an office in the City. I had to look after myself, more or less. I was quite a moody child, always trying to get their approval. But you don't want to hear all this.'

'Yes, I do.' Jack was serious now. 'Go on. What about your brother and sister?'

'They're a lot older than me. When I was a teenager they were grown up and married.'

'Too bad.' Jack took a mouthful of champagne. 'Do you see much of them?'

'Not really,' Juliet admitted. 'Antonia – she's in Canada – has twin daughters who I used to see regularly before I started the company. Now they're older and in the fashion business they're always travelling. As for brother Will...' She paused. She wasn't used to talking about her family in such detail but Jack's expression was sympathetic. 'He's a workaholic like Dad. It's ruined his marriage. Besides the fact that I have a sneaking suspicion he might be gay... though he's never come out and said.'

Jack laughed. 'What an illustrious family you have.' He looked at her quizzically. 'And *you*, Juliet – you've never wanted kids?'

Here we go again.

Why did people assume if you weren't a mother you didn't ever want children? They never stopped to think it might not be medically possible, or might not have worked out. People never seemed sensitive enough to realise they could be treading on dangerous territory. Jack was looking at her questioningly. She was always accusing him for keeping secrets but she was doing the same. But how could she tell him her deepest one? And the reason why she'd never had more children. That she couldn't bear it if one day Charlie found her, all happy with her new family, his knowing she'd given him up, her firstborn. No, by not having another child she'd remained loyal to Charlie...but how could she explain that to Jack?

'Juliet, what's wrong?' Jack interrupted her thoughts. 'Tell me. I know you've got something important on your mind.'

Not yet.

'What about *you*?' she asked instead. 'You're always asking about me and I still know nothing about you...' she paused, 'except you say there's an ex-wife.' She watched him closely. Here was his chance to say, 'Actually, I'm still married.' But he didn't. There was a moment of silence and the only way she felt she could continue naturally was to ask him, 'Do *you* have children?'

A shadow passed over Jack's face. Juliet held her breath. 'Yes,' he said at last. 'I have a daughter. Her name's Chiara.'

As his lips formed his daughter's name, for a fraction of a second it seemed as though he was smiling, but his mouth immediately dropped, his expression darkening. She felt her stomach lurch as she pretended to assimilate this information for the first time.

'Sounds Italian,' she managed.

'It is. Her mother's originally from Rome.'

Juliet hated the mother immediately; hated her long black shiny hair, her wide smiling mouth, her model-thin body, exquisitely dressed. She fought to block out the image as the waiter collected their soup plates.

'How old is Chiara?'

'Fifteen. She's beautiful. Like her—'

'Mother,' Juliet finished, desperately trying to keep her voice neutral.

'Actually I wasn't going to say that,' Jack said. 'She's the image of *my* mother.'

Was he being tactful or truthful?

'Do you see her?'

'Not very often. She lives in Bologna with her mother.'

'Was that why you got off in La Spezia?'

'Yes. Her teacher let me see her for a couple of hours. Too bad her mother doesn't have the same generous nature.' His voice had taken on a bitter edge.

'It's a pity your daughter lives so far away.'

'I've been trying to get her to Melbourne. To go to school here. She's bilingual as her mother insists on speaking to her in Italian all the time...probably no bad thing but I don't want her to lose her English.'

'Did you all live in Melbourne before...' Juliet wondered how to put it without mentioning the crash, '...things went wrong between you?'

'Yes. Her mother took Chiara back to Italy a couple of years ago.'

Before the crash.

'Is there a chance Chiara could come out for a few months at least?'

'Maybe.' Jack hesitated, then said, 'That's what part of that phone call was about...the one that interrupted us before you went to Sydney.'

Juliet felt a flush creep up her neck to her cheeks.

'It was my solicitor,' he explained. 'She wanted me to meet her to give me the update and sign some papers.'

So that was the woman on the phone. A thought struck her.

'Were they divorce papers?'

Jack nodded.

'Why didn't you tell me at the time?'

'I just didn't want to go into it right then,' Jack said. 'Particularly as we were enjoying one another so much.' Juliet quivered at the memory. 'You might have been upset that I was still legally married and hadn't told you. I thought it best to say I'd explain later.' He looked at her. 'I'm sorry – I was wrong. I just didn't want us to fall out.'

She was astonished. It was the first time he'd made such an admission. *I was terribly hurt,* she wanted to say, but thought better of it. She took a deep breath. 'I was annoyed at the time, but that's past. More important – what did the solicitor have to say?'

'The soon-to-be-ex wants Chiara to go to a private school in Rome and lodge with one of the aunts, presumably so she doesn't have a teenager spoiling her fun. But Chiara's not used to being away from home and she'd be really unhappy. Her teacher's very concerned...and so am I.' He snapped a breadstick in half. 'Trouble is, I'm away a lot, so if she came here she'd have to board, and she's probably lost contact with her Australian friends. I just don't know what to do for the best. Still,' he looked at Juliet with a flicker of a smile, 'things might change now her mother's serious with someone who apparently wants to marry her. Good luck to him, I say.' He downed the rest of his drink.

She noticed Jack never once mentioned his wife's name. But this was the first time he'd ever admitted he had personal problems, let alone discussed them with her. Somehow it made her feel they had become real friends. That he trusted her. She glanced up and caught his eye, and before she could stop herself she put her hand out and gently took his. He pressed hers in return, giving her a rueful smile. And it was in that moment – that very moment – that it hit her. Her feelings for this man ran much deeper than friendship. Deeper than she could ever have imagined. This wasn't just a flirtation. It wasn't just sex. She loved him. Unequivocally. With all her heart and soul, body and mind. She was in love for the first time since Mani. It was almost laughable. Love like this knocking her off her feet at forty-six. She would never have believed it. Her pulse raced. She longed to tell him. It was on the tip of her tongue to say something. But she must never let him know, because it would all end before you could say…well, before you could say 'Jack'.

She felt him giving her a curious gaze. He often tapped into her thoughts. She tried to rearrange her expression from the exhilaration of her discovery. Dear God, he mustn't tap into her head this time. She cleared her throat, desperately trying to remember what she had been about to answer – oh, yes, his daughter – when he spoke.

'Changing the subject, have you heard any more news about your company?'

'I've sent everyone more emails this afternoon to phone me urgently.' Juliet bit her lip, her teeming mind reluctantly being dragged to her business. 'But they wouldn't have got into work with the time difference. I'm hoping I'll hear when I get back to the hotel. The whole thing's a nightmare with not being able to go home and sort it.'

'I did ask my contacts in Qantas but their hands are tied. They've promised to let me know as soon as they get anything to report. I'll keep on top of it.'

'Thanks. It's kind of you.' She paused. It was now or never. She had to know from him. 'Jack…'

'Yes?'

'You've never told me much about your career as a pilot. The sort of things the public are never told.'

'What do you mean?' His voice was measured.

'It must be dangerous occasionally.'

The gold flecks in Jack's eyes dimmed. 'Occasionally. Why?'

'Petra hinted at something...' Her heart raced. Oh, God. She should have kept quiet.

'Did she?' Jack's features visibly hardened. It should have made him less attractive but it had quite the opposite effect on her.

'She didn't tell me anything – just that if you wanted to offload, you would. But let's drop it. Here's probably not the place for spilling secrets.'

'What are you insinuating?' Jack demanded.

'The plane crash, if you must know,' Juliet blurted, then wished to God she hadn't.

'What about it?'

'Your soufflé, madam...sir.' The waiter seemed to have a knack of arriving at an awkward moment, Juliet thought, or might he be saving the day? 'Be careful – the plates are extremely hot.'

'Thank you.' Jack turned to Juliet, his eyes narrowing. She cursed herself. He seemed to be wrestling with something in his mind. A full minute passed. The whole restaurant seemed to be holding its breath. Then to her amazement he smiled and said, 'Let's not get heavy. We don't want to ruin the evening. But I promise I'll tell you one of these days.'

But she pressed on. 'This is what you always say. And it just leaves me guessing. How can we be true friends if we're not honest with one another?'

'Can a man ever be friends with a woman?' Jack said. 'There's always bucketfuls of emotion to deal with...misunderstandings... certain expectations on either side. That's the downfall, in my opinion, of most male–female relationships.'

It was the first time he'd ever touched on the subject of emotion so perhaps that was progress of a sort. Maybe she shouldn't push it any further tonight.

'Don't ruin the evening,' he repeated. 'I wanted this to be lovely...with your grandmother's diary and everything.' He half rose, leaned across the table and kissed her full on the lips.

He was right. She mustn't spoil the moment. Especially now she knew she loved him.

'Mmm,' he murmured. Then using the edge of his napkin he picked up her plate.

Juliet watched as Jack carefully cut up her whole dinner. It was almost worth the accident to have such loving attention, even if he was only being well-mannered.

'Tell me more about the engagement party.' Jack set her plate in front of her.

Dangerous waters again – this time for me, Juliet thought, her blood racing as she answered lightly.

'Louis seems a nice chap. A little older and seems steady, which is good for Petra. And you can see he adores her.'

'I'm glad,' Jack said as the waiter appeared and filled their glasses. 'To you.' He clinked her glass. 'Are you happy?'

He'd asked that question once before.

'I'm happy just to be here...in Australia,' she added hastily.

'Just "happy to be here" will do,' he grinned, 'and if you add, "with you, Jack", that's even better.'

Why did he always make her feel like a love-struck idiot? She knew he was only teasing to get a reaction and she gave it every time. She was annoyed that her face felt warm.

'Even though my time's been cut short,' she continued, ignoring his smirk, 'it'll be a good excuse for me to come back. But I can't relax with the business hanging over my head.'

'Try to let it go for this evening,' Jack said, serious again. 'There's not a thing you can do until you get your flight confirmed. Once you're in the UK you can find out exactly what's going on.'

He turned his hazel eyes to her. 'I just hope you find what you're looking for.'

What a strange remark. She tried to work out what was behind it but Jack was giving nothing away. To cover up her confusion she said:

'It looks like you've already found what I've been looking for.' She stroked the diary once more and suddenly gave a deep sigh. Here she was in a beautiful restaurant sharing a bottle of champagne with a beautiful man who had gone to such trouble to *borrow* (she decided to call it) something so precious for her.

'I've found what you've been looking for?' Jack raised a dark eyebrow 'I think that's only the beginning.'

It had been an unpredictable evening, Juliet decided, as she lay curled around Jack's body in her king-sized hotel bed. She'd barely slept as she wasn't used to someone there, breathing, lightly snoring. Jack was a restless sleeper, but she was perfectly willing to be deprived of sleep for the novelty of making love twice in one night. She smiled in the darkness, remembering the warmth of his skin, how he'd made her laugh.

He was an unselfish lover – had taken his time. Once he'd even called out her name and she loved him for it. Love. She must stop using that word. There was no future in it...only heartbreak. *Keep it friendly, sexy, romantic, passionate even – but do not love. Don't look for anything more.* But how could she possibly take back her love? Suddenly switch it off. Stop loving him. It was impossible. *Fair enough, but don't make* him *feel guilty. Simply enjoy it for what it is. Whatever it is.* Lazily, she let her good hand caress the back of his neck, threading her fingers upwards through the dark silky hair until he grunted and turned round to face her. Opening one gold-flecked hazel eye, he grinned.

'Good morning, darling. Sleep well?'

'Fantastic,' she lied, loving the way he'd called her 'darling' for the second time. She smiled at him, her eyes stinging through lack of sleep, praying they weren't bloodshot. Then she laughed. 'Not a wink actually.'

'Oh, no. Did I snore?'

'Not really. But you're very twitchy when you're asleep.'

'I'm sorry I kept you awake. I'll just have to cheer you up somehow. Let's see...I don't think you thanked me properly last night for pinching the diary.' He pulled her on top of him, being careful with her bandaged arm, and kissed her mouth; a lingering kiss, gentle and probing.

'I haven't looked at the diary properly,' Juliet said as she ate her porridge.

They were in the Sheridan breakfast room.

'Wait until you're on your own.' Jack buttered his toast. 'Your grandmother wrote it in private and you need to read it in private. But I'd love to hear about it later.'

That's why I like him, she thought. He's genuinely interested in people, whether he knows them personally or not.

'And I remembered where they worked,' she said. 'It was when I was putting in my earrings.' She pointed to one of them. 'Amber earrings – Amber Bay. From what Nannie described, it sounds like a gentleman's residence...if they have anything that grand here in the outback,' she teased.

'We've got it all here, babe,' he grinned. 'Gentleman's residences, maritime museums, diaries that go walkabout...'

'All right.' She pretended to smack his wrist. 'But I'd love to find the house. Though it's going to have to wait until I come back.'

'I'll make sure it's a date in my diary.' His eyes danced as he grabbed her right hand and turned it towards him, kissing the small white scar from her accident on the *Alexandria*, sending a thrill up her arm. 'If you want my company, of course.'

'I can't think of anything nicer,' she said.

*

Juliet sat up in bed, her bad arm resting on a pile of pillows. She and Jack had taken the lift up to her room after breakfast and they'd made love again. This time he'd surprised her with his tenderness. She snuggled a little further down under the duvet, unable to stop smiling. Jack had left her, promising to ring later when she'd had some sleep.

She picked up the diary, savouring the moment when she would learn more about her grandmother, wanting to share the journey Nannie had undertaken, both on the voyage and her growing up as a young wife.

She turned to the first entry, the one she'd started to read to Jack in the restaurant. Nannie had gone into some detail about her fellow passengers, especially Adele. Her grandmother was a natural writer, she realised, as she began to live the voyage with the young Annie. She frowned as she detected a slightly negative tone on occasion when Annie wrote her thoughts of Ferguson. Juliet put the diary down on the duvet. It was strange as she couldn't remember ever hearing Nannie speak a bad word about Pop.

She glanced at the clock. A quarter to twelve. She picked up the phone and rang reception.

'Would you please bring me some coffee?' she asked the young man on the desk. 'And a couple of croissants.' Blow the diet. Today was special.

'May I bring you a glass of Buck's Fizz, madam, to go along with the croissants? The two go so well together.'

His cheek made her smile.

She made a half-hearted attempt at straightening the bed and Jack's crumpled pillows, then decided not to bother. It was too lovely a reminder of him. While she waited for room service she dragged a comb through her tangled hair, then slid back under the duvet.

There was a knock at the door. Without waiting for an answer a young girl came in bearing a tray. She set the glass of Buck's Fizz on Juliet's bedside table.

'Shall I pour you a coffee?' she said, glancing at Juliet's arm.

'Yes, please.'

The girl put the tray on the bed, wished her good day and disappeared.

Juliet leaned against the heaped pillows being careful not to disturb the tray. She stretched out her good arm for the Buck's Fizz, toasted the air, drank it down in five delicious gulps, and bit into a croissant. It flaked into her mouth in a heavenly buttery crispy dream. She took a sip of the rich Arabic coffee and gave a blissful sigh. A smile played about her lips. The caffeine was having the opposite effect and she sank back, feeling her eyes grow heavy.

It was gone three by the time she woke up. Feeling decadent she couldn't help grinning. Her stomach was flatter than it had been in years. Takes a younger lover, she smiled to herself. Much more fun than dieting. She felt a tingling over her body, a longing for him again. Her stomach growled and she picked up the phone and asked room service for a smoked salmon sandwich and a fresh pot of coffee.

To get her mind off Jack she picked up her grandmother's diary again. Except it wasn't a diary as she'd first thought, but more of a journal spanning several years with long gaps between some of the entries. Within seconds Juliet was plunged back into Nannie's world which was right here in Melbourne. She wondered how much Nannie would recognise if she could come back.

They'd been married less than a year and Nannie was already showing signs of not being so happy with her husband. Juliet's mouth tightened. Her grandfather's lack of enthusiasm over the coming baby must have put a terrible strain on their relationship.

Reading on, it was as though her grandmother was speaking to her over the intervening years, wanting Juliet to know the truth… though the truth about what, Juliet had no idea.

A knock at the door snapped her out of her thoughts and she laid the diary back on the counterpane. The same young girl from the morning appeared with a tray. 'Your lunch, madam, and this was left for you at reception.' She handed Juliet an envelope and vanished.

Juliet stared at the writing. She didn't recognise it. She tore it open and brought out a simple white card. Her eyes darted to the signature. Jack.

Juliet, I didn't phone in case you were sleeping. One of the pilots has asked me for a favour so I'll be caught up for the next couple of days taking over her training sessions. Really sorry as was looking forward to hearing more about Annie. And to lie with you again.

Good luck on getting your flight. Will call you.

Love and xxxx

Jack

Her heart plummeted with disappointment while her body quivered with the thought of lying with Jack again. Somehow she felt they'd reached a new level in their relationship. Something more honest. She hoped she wasn't imagining things. That he felt the same. But it didn't stop her being fed up that he wasn't going to be there when she was bathed and dressed. She turned to Nannie's diary again.

Her stomach complained even louder and she took a bite out of one of the sandwiches. Almost wolfing down the rest of them and munching the garnish of crisps, she read on.

When she came to the part about Annie finding out that Adele owned her own hotel she stopped reading and lay back on the pillows, closing her eyes so she could picture the scene. It must have been highly unusual for a woman to own a commercial property as far back as 1913. Good for her. Juliet felt herself warming towards

Adele, though she still couldn't work out how the two women came to be friends. What could they possibly have had in common?

Thinking about Adele's business brought her back sharply to her own business and the awful position she was in. Heart beating rapidly she abruptly closed the diary. She needed to get dressed right away and find out the latest. Surely she would have had an email from them by now.

There was nothing from Qantas or BA. But there were emails from Petra and Will.

She opened Petra's.

Hi Juliet, hope all is well and the wrist is better. Louis has taken some time off and we plan to come to Melbourne very soon, so hope to see you. Are you still at the Sheridan?

Lots of love from us both. Petra xx

The second message was from Will.

Jules, I wouldn't normally bother you but Dad's ill. He had a minor heart attack just after you left so I didn't worry you, but unfortunately he had a more serious one yesterday. He's in intensive care, but they think he's got a reasonable chance. I know there's been a strike at H'row but try to come home as soon as you can.

All love, Will

No! Juliet's heart beat hard as she read her brother's words. Sick with anxiety, her hand shaking, she picked up the phone. For the first time in a week she was miraculously put straight through to bookings.

'Please, I need to book a flight from Melbourne to London immediately. My father's been taken seriously ill.'

'We can't get you on anything until the end of the week, I'm afraid.' The voice was annoyingly smooth, as though he'd repeated this a dozen times already this morning. 'Friday's the earliest.'

'I can't wait that long.' Fear made her voice rise. 'What about First Class?'

'Fully booked. You're probably aware of the problems Terminal 4 has had with a ground crew strike. This is the best I can offer you and you need to decide now.'

'I'll take it.'

There were still five days to go. Five bloody days. By then it might be too late.

29

Petra's reply to Juliet's came in the early evening:

Of course we'll come and see you. We'll be at your hotel
Thursday at noon to take you out for some lunch. Catch up
then. Lots of love, Petra xx

She'd see Louis again. Maybe he'd say something that meant
she would know for certain, either way. Against her will she pictured
him. As she had done so often in her dreams but now she had more
than a hazy image.

The age is about right although that's just chance…but you
couldn't dismiss those same polished mahogany eyes. He was nearly
a head taller than Mani, but then she was tall, and so were both
her parents. Louis might easily have Asian blood running through
his veins, even if his skin appeared merely to be healthily tanned
by the Australian sun. All she had to do was ask Petra his date of
birth. But if she knew for sure, would it really bring her any peace
of mind?

*Dear God, don't let me keep asking the same question over
and over.*

If she started asking questions and he wasn't Charlie, he'd
know she'd given her baby away, and she couldn't bear to see the
disgust in those eyes. No, it was better to remain silent.

She let out a deep sigh. First things first. Enjoy seeing the two of them again without keep worrying. Then get back to England and visit Dad before it's too late, and finally tackle Neil and Lydia.

The following afternoon Juliet checked out of the main hospital in Melbourne. As she cautiously flexed her wrist she realised how wonderful it was to be able to use both arms properly. Planning what she would wear to tomorrow's lunch she quickened her pace along the path at the edge of the river. Sunlight glinted on the half-clad bodies of the boat owners, and two or three of them waved as she passed by. One even wolf-whistled – something that hadn't happened for years – and she couldn't help smiling back, even though she'd been brought up to ignore such behaviour.

Back in her room at the hotel, in one of the comfortable armchairs, she took up Nannie's diary again. She'd abandoned it by her bed for the last two days and she tried to work out why. Though desperate to read her grandmother's entries, to absorb every word, she was beginning to feel uncomfortable reading such a private account, even though that person was dead. And at the back of her mind she dreaded reading something she'd rather not know.

She'd already read about Annie's joy on having Ruby come to Melbourne and finding her the job that Ruby ended up hating. But the next passage was over a year later. She frowned. *What...?* Then she realised there were pages missing. Quite a chunk, in fact. Why? Had Annie got upset about something and torn them out? Or had someone else? She hoped she'd be able to pick up the thread. Just as she found the place where she'd left off, her mobile rang.

'Juliet?'

How she loved the warmth of his voice.

'Hello, Jack. Thanks for your message.'

'How's everything?' Without waiting for an answer he went

on: 'Have you finished your grandmother's diary?' He chuckled. 'Found any interesting skeletons?'

'Too many to talk about over the phone,' Juliet said, wishing she could joke back.

'You sound serious.' Jack's voice instantly changed.

'Dad's had a heart attack and I can't get a flight until Friday. I'm worried sick.'

'Oh, Juliet, I'm so sorry – thank God you've got your flight. What's the prognosis for your father?'

'He's in intensive care,' she gulped. 'They think he has a reasonable chance. Apart from that, I know very little.'

Juliet squeezed her eyes shut, imagining the worst. Her dad lying in a coma. She *had* to get back to him before it was all too late. Talk to him. Tell him...tell him what? She didn't know. She only knew she had to see him.

'I wish I was there but I'm in Adelaide, of all places. Back Wednesday.'

Juliet swallowed her disappointment. She'd been hoping to spend a few hours alone with Jack. To try to explain about her relationship with her father. Jack was a good listener. She felt he'd understand. And maybe...maybe even tell him about Charlie, and her suspicions. But that would bring the conversation round to Louis which would lead to the plane crash.

'So what's the plan in the meantime?' Jack cut into her dangerous train of thought.

'Petra and Louis are coming to lunch Thursday to say goodbye, so if you're able to join us that would be nice.' She felt her voice go all formal without meaning to.

'It's a definite date.'

As she put the receiver down she realised with a start it would be the first time he and Louis would meet. Jack hadn't hesitated. But would it be embarrassing? She decided to email Petra to warn her Jack would be there.

Petra's response was immediate.

Hi Juliet, Louis has never met Jack – he was supposed to meet him at our engagement party – so it will be a perfect opportunity. Lots of love, Petra xx

Petra wouldn't know about her conversation with Sarah – that Sarah had been the one to tell her Jack was the pilot in the crash that killed Louis' parents. Juliet blew out her cheeks.

Oh, well, bring it on, as they say.

She turned back to Nannie's diary. Her eyes widened in shock as she began to read the longer entry than usual.

19th November 1920

Everything has gone so very wrong. My head will burst if I don't write this down. I sometimes think I'm going mad.

I was sick for much longer with this baby and suffered badly from headaches. Ferguson tried hard to be patient. I know he hoped the new baby would bring us closer. I was sure it would be a boy this time. I went back to the same hospital, longing for it to be over, longing to see my new baby – the only good to come of this whole rotten mess.

The hospital smelled of disinfectant and blood and turned my stomach. The doctor was much older than Alex, with a stern face, but the nurse I had this time was very kind. I was in labour for sixteen hours. When I thought I couldn't stand it a moment longer the doctor used some sort of instrument. It was as though a red-hot poker had stabbed me. I heard screaming. Was it me, or one of the other mothers? I bit down on something that tasted like rubber, and clung on to the nurse's hand. I felt the sweat run into my eyes. It would all be worth it, I kept telling myself, as the doctor clamped a gauze pad over my mouth and nose.

The next thing I knew Ferguson was sitting by the bed, holding my hand. His eyes were bloodshot.

How long have I been asleep? I asked him.

About four hours. His voice was unusually gentle.

Have you seen the baby? Is it a boy? What you wanted—

Yes, Annie, a beautiful baby boy.

A son. We'll call him Harry. I couldn't help smiling. I looked at Ferguson. Maybe we could repair some of the hurt. I could tell he had something important to say to me but he seemed to be having difficulty getting the words out. He squeezed my hand so tight my engagement ring cut into my finger.

Annie, the baby—

Where is he, Ferguson? I haven't seen him yet. Is he asleep?

Ferguson's usual ruddy complexion had turned pale.

Ferguson?

Annie, dearest, you have to be very brave—

A coldness crept through every part of my body until I was numb. I turned my head to see him properly. His Adam's apple was jumping up and down and I watched it, hypnotised.

The baby was stillborn, Ferguson said.

Then he squeezed my hand again, even more tightly, but this time I didn't notice any pain.

There must be a mistake, I said. They were talking about the wrong baby. My baby was just asleep.

Ferguson looked like death.

No, no, oh please God, no. I began to shake. My head started to swim and bile came up in my throat.

You mustn't upset yourself, Annie. There was nothing anyone could do.

I wanted to scream. To hit out at him. My beautiful baby.

Alex – if he'd been here he would have saved my baby. Where was he when I needed him?

I must have said those words aloud because Ferguson

frowned, though all he said was that I must get some rest and he would be in to see me again tomorrow. Then he kissed me on the forehead and left me.

Left me with my demons. The hospital. My baby. Ruby. Ferguson. Even Alex.

With trembling hands Juliet closed the diary. She leaned her head on the back of the armchair and shut her eyes tightly, but the tears squeezed through and trickled down her cheeks. Poor, dear Nannie. No wonder she'd been so understanding when she'd become pregnant with Charlie. What painful memories it must have stirred for her. Juliet could see herself, one month off seventeen, head on the hospital pillows, and Nannie close by her bedside wearing an expression of pure grief. She'd thought at the time Nannie was upset for her only, but it must have brought back all the sorrow of her own loss. And she'd had no idea.

Juliet read the last sentence again. Left me with my demons. The hospital. My baby. Ruby. Ferguson. But why had her grandmother written that her sister was one of her demons? And the most mysterious one of all: Even Alex.

30

Jack was the first to arrive. Juliet was waiting in the foyer and her heart somersaulted the moment he strode in. He wore his usual white shirt, but today with cream slacks and navy linen jacket. He looked very fanciable – if that was such a word. She couldn't help smiling. As soon as he caught sight of her his grin lit up his strong features. She swallowed. He really was the most magnetic man she'd ever known. The one she felt more alive with than anyone.

'Great to see you, Juliet.' He swept her into his arms and kissed her. 'Missed me?'

'Desperately.' She tried to sound mocking as she drew away and searched his expression, loving the way he smiled down at her, making her feel special. It was an odd feeling. Then she burst out laughing. If she wasn't careful she'd turn into a Mills & Boon heroine.

'Tell me the joke.'

'The important thing is,' she was being uncharacteristically flirtatious, 'have you missed *me*?'

'I can't be sure until I kiss you again.'

He slipped an arm round her waist and pulled her into the side of the lobby where there was a bank of tall plants in pots of gravel. This time his kiss was not a cheerful greeting. He began with little kisses around the edge of her mouth, his tongue softly licking into the corners, teasing her until she felt an ache between her thighs. She put her lips firmly on his and immediately Jack smothered her in a passionate embrace, his tongue exploring the inside of her mouth, and she felt his body harden against her own. God, how she wanted this man.

'Not here.' Her voice was husky, teasing. 'We're in a public place.'

'We are?' He grinned, holding her away from him but keeping his hands lightly on her shoulders. 'And you've finally got two usable arms.' He ran his fingers along the arm that had been bandaged and her skin tingled. 'When did it come off?'

'Yesterday. It's heaven to be free of it.'

'When are the others arriving?'

'Any minute.'

'No time to go upstairs, then.'

'No time at all,' she laughed. 'So that's the reason you're here? If so, it's a fabulous reason and I promise to take you up on it.'

'I'll keep you to that.' Jack's eyes gleamed. 'By the way, any news of your father?'

Before she could answer Petra whirled through the revolving door with Louis behind her, smiling, and carrying two small cases.

'There you are.' She rushed to Juliet, hugging and kissing her, and Juliet, usually embarrassed by such a display of emotion from a woman, decided this time she rather liked it. Jack embraced Petra and Juliet was taken in Louis' arms where he soundly kissed her on both cheeks.

'Good to see you again, Juliet,' he said, his smile showing off his beautiful teeth.

'You, too, Louis.' Juliet had difficulty keeping her voice even.

'Jack, this is my fiancé, Louis Jordan, but more handsome than the famous film star, so Mum tells me.' Petra laughed. 'Louis, Jack Delaney.'

Juliet watched the two men closely, holding her breath as they shook hands. She released it when Louis smiled.

'How're you doing, Jack?'

'Okay. It's good to meet you at last, Louis,' Jack replied.

It was as simple as that.

'I can't believe you're going back to England,' Petra said, linking her arm through Juliet's as they went outside. 'Just when I'd got used to having you around.'

'I don't want to go, but Dad's ill.'

'Oh, my God. It's all happening at once, what with the business and everything.' Petra ground to a halt, her hand on Juliet's arm. 'What's the matter with him?'

'Heart attack. His third. Second since I've been away. My brother needs me but there's been a strike at Heathrow. I've only just been able to get a flight tomorrow.'

'I'm so sorry about your father,' Louis said. 'Presumably he's in good hands.'

'Probably the best...in intensive care.'

'Have you managed to sort out your problems with your company?' Louis asked.

Juliet rarely discussed her business with anyone outside the staff but Louis' brown eyes showed only concern.

'Can I tell you over lunch?' she said. 'I'd value everyone's opinion.'

'Sounds like it's worse than you'd thought.' Louis stretched out his long legs and drained the last of his beer. He set the glass on the wooden table top and looked at Juliet. 'And that woman – Lydia – I don't think she's done you any favours, going to pieces and walking out. Did you know her before?'

'Yes. A few months. I sold her chain of estate agents.' A warm breeze lifted Juliet's hair as she spoke, and she remembered England in autumn. She'd be back home in two days. Back to England's damp, dreary, cold, miserable weather. She pulled herself up straight, telling herself not to be so pathetic.

'It's not easy taking over another business.' Louis frowned, running his forefinger down his nose.

282

Juliet caught her breath.

Mani used to do that when he was thinking.

Jack slanted her a curious look but she pretended not to notice.

'Lydia persuaded me it would be similar. And she *did* run a very successful company.'

'Or her staff did.' Jack's tone was cynical.

'That's more likely,' Louis agreed. He turned to Juliet again. 'Is there anyone at home who could advise you? Petra says you're still friendly with your ex. Isn't he a lawyer?'

'Gerrard? Well, yes, but I rarely confide in him about the business unless it's legal stuff. No, I'll have to sort it myself.'

'Are you coming back to Oz?' Petra asked. She glanced at Jack as she asked the question, and then her gaze fell on Juliet again. 'You've barely had a chance to see anything.'

'Not in the foreseeable future. I'm going to be a bit busy by the looks of things.' She drained her coffee which suddenly tasted bitter.

'I'm booked for a conference in London next week,' Louis broke in. 'D'you fancy meeting up? Sometimes it's good to chat things through.'

She wasn't prepared for this. She swallowed hard. 'Are you sure?'

'Sure I'm sure,' Louis grinned.

'Then I'd love to. When do you arrive?'

'Monday. Ready for a meeting Tuesday.'

'Where exactly is the conference?'

'It's being held outside London. In Richmond. Is that anywhere near you?'

Juliet laughed. 'Only the next-door neighbour. I'm in Kingston-upon-Thames.'

'It sounds awfully grand,' Petra said teasingly as she put her knife and fork together neatly on her plate.

'I think it used to be. Nowadays I'm not sure.'

'Do you want to let me have your mobile number so we can arrange something?' Louis said.

To Juliet's embarrassment she felt her eyes prick with tears. As though Jack could tell how she was feeling, he handed her a handkerchief and put an arm around her shoulders.

'Are you okay?' he asked under his breath.

'I'm sorry.' She gave him a weak smile. 'Stupid of me.' She blew her nose.

'You're here with friends,' Petra said warmly. 'It's good for you to have a cry. You're going through a bad time with your dad and everything.' She turned to Louis. 'I think it's a great idea for you to meet up. Be supportive.'

'Can you come too, Petra?' Juliet said. 'I can easily put you both up.' She paused. 'Well, that is, if you don't mind sharing the same bedroom,' she added with a straight face.

Petra chuckled. 'Oh, we couldn't possibly share,' she said laughing. 'But I'll take a rain check on the offer.' She shook her blonde mane. 'I try not to fly, remember? Especially long haul. You're lucky I got on the plane to come and see you today.'

Juliet was about to answer when a shadow loomed over the table. Her heart sank as she heard a jocular voice.

'Hello, m'dear. Thought it was you. And little Petra. How are you, m'dear, after your ordeal? And what do you know? If it isn't Jack. Mind if I join you?'

'How nice to see you again, Trevor.' Petra bounced up and kissed him. 'Of *course* you can join us. Grab a chair. We've nearly finished but we're just about to order some more coffee. Have you eaten?'

'Yes, yes. Don't you worry about *me*. I put my glasses on to see the bill. Looked across. There you all were.' He beamed round. 'Well, if this isn't a pleasant surprise. And presumably this is your fiancé.' He shook hands with Louis, then flopped down in the basket chair and mopped his face. 'She never stopped talking about you on the ship, y' know.'

Louis looked bemused.

'Louis, this is Trevor who we met on the boat. I told you about him. What have you been up to since we last saw you?' Petra smiled at the older man encouragingly.

'Seeing Mother,' Trevor explained. 'She's in a nursing home. All a bit sad.'

'I know what you mean,' Juliet said. 'I think I told you, Dad's in one at home. He's had another heart attack so I've got to get back to England. I'm off tomorrow evening.'

'Bad luck, m'dear. Is it serious?'

'My brother says it is. He's had a couple of others but they were mild. I think my brother's trying to prepare me.'

'Dear oh dear. Is your father all about? Got his marbles, I mean.' Trevor tapped the side of his forehead with a nail-bitten finger.

'He was when I last saw him.' Juliet hesitated. She couldn't believe her father would be anything but compos mentis.

'My mother's ninety-five. She's all there. Not like some of them years younger. Doolally, if you know what I mean.'

'Has she made any friends in the home?' Juliet asked, feeling guilty that she'd never bothered to find out if her own father had.

'Only one old dear who's always going on about the family who abandoned her.'

'How awful.' Petra leaned forward to enjoy a bit of drama. 'What happened?'

Trevor looked pleased with the attention. He sat back and raked his hand through his curls. 'Well, her sister and husband came to Oz first, apparently. Around the time of the Great War. They sent for the young sister – this one who's in the home – then left her more or less stranded when they buggered off back to England.'

Juliet jumped as though someone had doused her with cold water. Her eyes darted round the group. Thank goodness no one appeared to have noticed except Jack, who caught her eye and raised an eyebrow.

'How cruel,' Petra cried. 'Poor thing. And she stayed in

Australia all these years? Never went back even to visit?'

'Oh, I don't know the ins and outs.' Trevor trumpeted his nose. 'Get fed up listening to it all. Women nattering on.' He looked round apologetically. 'Present company excepted, of course.' He gave a short bark. 'Now then – what are we all having for a drink? Surely not coffee. How about G and Ts all round? On me.'

'Bit early for that,' Jack said. He settled back in his chair. 'Tell us more about the old lady. She sounds a character. What did you say her name was?'

Juliet found she was holding her breath.

'I didn't. Not really interested.' He summoned the waitress. 'A gin and tonic, please, dear. Ice, no lemon.' He watched her walk away. 'Gem of a girl,' he said, admiringly. He paused, as though trying to keep abreast of his train of thought. 'Yes, that's it. The old girl's name is Pearl...no, Ruby...yes, it's definitely Ruby.' He beamed at the group.

Juliet's thoughts raced. You didn't often hear that name. *Should I—?* She stopped herself. *Should I what? Start probing?* Like she'd done with Jack and wished she hadn't. Like she'd been tempted to with Louis. Was she becoming obsessed with trying to find out who people really were...or who she wanted them to be? She was trying to make a couple of coincidences become fact, which was ridiculous in this case, as she could never imagine Nannie abandoning her own sister. Besides, Ruby must have died donkey's years ago.

'Ruby?' Jack, who was sitting close enough to Juliet for her to feel his thigh warm against hers, turned his head towards her. 'Wasn't that the name of your grandmother's sister? The one who followed them out to Australia?'

'You've got a good memory.' Juliet bit her lip. She nudged his foot under the table hoping he would understand not to mention the diary in front of the others. 'But it can't possibly be the same person.'

'Why not?' Petra intervened, shooting a look at Juliet while dabbing her mouth with her napkin. 'Weird things are always happening in life. Why don't you check her out?' She put down her napkin. 'Oh, sorry, that sounds awfully rude.'

'It can't be her because she'd be a hundred and ten.' Juliet laughed at Petra's disappointed expression. 'And my grandmother would never abandon her sister – not in a million years. But you're right, Petra, I *should* go and look her up, if only for interest.' She looked across at Trevor who was tipping back in his chair and gulping his gin and tonic as though he'd just come from the desert. 'What nursing home is your mother in, Trevor?' she heard herself saying. 'If it's not too far I'd be happy to go with you and visit her, but it would have to be first thing tomorrow morning.'

It would be a rushed visit but at least she would have tried, she told herself.

Trevor cupped his hand to his ear. 'Didn't catch you, m'dear.'

'I said I'd go and see your mother – make a change for her. And meet her friend Ruby.'

'Would you really?' Trevor beamed as he put down his empty glass. He raked his hair. 'How awfully decent of you.'

31

Trevor shoved the gear lever into reverse, backed and stalled, taking up two parking spaces at the side of the nursing home. Juliet rubbed the back of her neck, resolving after today never to ride in a car again with Trevor at the wheel.

'Righto,' Trevor said. 'Into the fray.'

She followed him into a low modern building where two unsmiling women behind the reception desk greeted them. He signed the visitors' book and moments later they were sitting in a Victorian conservatory chatting to Trevor's mother who was busy knitting an indeterminate multi-coloured shape.

'How long have you known my Trevor, dear?' the old lady inquired, her needles flying.

'Met on the ship coming from England,' Trevor said before Juliet had a chance to open her mouth. 'Friends from the start.'

'How nice, dear.' She gazed at her son adoringly, then turned to Juliet. 'My boy needs a nice lady friend. He's no good on his own.' She gave Juliet a conspiratorial wink as she laid her knitting on her lap. 'I'd like to see him settled before I go.'

This was not the turn of conversation Juliet had envisioned. She was about to change the subject but Trevor's mother beat her to it.

'What brings you to our fine country?'

'I needed a change of air. A holiday. I was working too hard.'

Mrs Manning gazed at her son. 'Trevor tells me you have your own business back in England.'

Juliet wondered what else Trevor had told his mother, but she said lightly, 'That's right, but I'd rather not talk about it, if you don't mind. I have to fly home this evening to deal with some problems so this is my last chance to forget it for a few hours.'

'I'm sure my boy would be only too glad to help out.'

'That's very kind, Mrs Manning, but I—'

'Oh, do call me Barbara,' the old lady smiled, showing rotting brown teeth.

Juliet shuddered. 'Have you been here long, Mrs...er...Barbara?'

'Too long,' Mrs Manning snapped, picking up her knitting again. 'And Trevor only comes to see me once a year since he moved back to the Old Country. It's out of sight, out of mind, isn't it, dear?' She turned to her son. 'Forgets he's even got a mum half the time.' Her fingers briskly finished the row. 'There's no company in this place. They're half-baked, most of them. All they do is sit in a circle with their heads lolling and their mouths hanging open. Look like a load of doped fish.'

'I thought Trevor said you'd made a friend here,' Juliet said encouragingly. *God, what a woman. Poor old Trevor.*

'There's no one here I'd want to be friends with.' Mrs Manning didn't bother to lower her voice.

'What about Ruby?' Trevor said, clearly relieved that the conversation had turned from his shortcomings where his mother was concerned.

'Oh, Ruby.' Mrs Manning screwed up her eyes. 'Yes, she was the only person around here with any sense, but she's gone.'

'Oh, I'm sorry,' Juliet said automatically. *Damn.* Just as she'd thought she might be on to something the old lady had died. If only she'd come a few weeks ago she might have had the chance to find out exactly who this Ruby was.

'I'm sorry you've lost your friend,' Trevor said, wiping the sweat off his forehead. 'She was here last time I came. When did she die?'

'Oh, she didn't die.' Mrs Manning began to cough.

Juliet jumped up to pour her a glass of water from the carafe on the side table. Excitement fizzed through her that all might not be lost. She tried not to show her impatience as Mrs Manning gulped some water, spluttering as she motioned to her son to pull her further up in her chair.

'Yes, put the cushion behind my head, Trevor,' she instructed, then turned to Juliet, woman to woman. 'I didn't realise it at the time but Ruby was only going to be here for six weeks till they finished the decorations and such at her own nursing home.'

'Where's that?' Juliet tried to sound casual.

'Why do you ask?' Mrs Manning sounded suspicious. 'I thought you'd both come to visit *me*.'

'Of course we have,' Juliet said. She'd have to humour the old girl and when the visit was over she'd find out at reception the name of the nursing home Ruby had gone back to. In fact, she'd go and find out right away.

'I'll just have a wander round,' she told the mother and son, 'while you have a nice chat together on your own.'

The two unsmiling women in reception had changed into one bored-looking girl filing her nails, who'd never heard of Ruby.

'I'm only a temp. The person you need to speak to is on early lunch. She should be back in...' she looked at her plastic watch, 'about half an hour.'

'Would you mind finding someone who *would* be able to tell me?' Juliet persisted. 'It's really important.'

'I'm not allowed to leave reception.'

'I'll wait here until you come back,' Juliet told her, using her business voice.

Ten minutes later, with the name and address of Ruby's nursing home now safely in her bag, she wandered round the shop until Trevor came to find her.

'Oh, there you are.' He sounded a little peeved.

'I thought you should have some quality time together,' Juliet said. 'I know mothers can be a bit overprotective, particularly where their only sons are concerned. She just wants the best for you.'

'Never know what to talk about with the old girl.' Trevor took her arm. 'Just come and say cheerio and then we'll buzz off. By the way, did you find out where Ruby went?'

'Yes, she's not far from here.' She showed him the address.

'I know it,' Trevor said, taking her arm as they left the building. 'Looked at that one first for Mum. We can be there in two ticks.'

No way. Not with your driving.

'Thanks, Trevor, but you've had enough of nursing homes lately. So have I, for that matter. But I must follow the trail, just in case Ruby turns out to be my great-aunt. Wouldn't that be amazing? I know she's not a hundred and ten like I told Petra but she's not that far off, unless my calculations are completely wrong.'

'Might finish her off,' Trevor snorted.

Juliet couldn't help laughing. 'I hope not, but if it does, and she's as old as I think she is, I shan't take the blame.'

'Lose touch, did you?'

'More or less. Her name was rarely mentioned at home as though it was a taboo subject. This Ruby, whoever she is, might not be happy if I suddenly turn up out of the blue, but I'm going to take the chance.'

Trevor had told her it was only a ten-minute walk but she decided to save time and hail a taxi. Now was not the time to study street maps. The driver rolled his eyes when she told him the address, but she ignored it and stepped in. Three minutes later he dropped her outside a building not dissimilar to the one she'd just left, and after giving him an overly generous tip she found the entrance. She rang the bell and heard a buzzer inside which connected to the front door. She pushed it open.

The interior didn't live up to Mrs Manning's nursing home at all. Juliet wrinkled her nose. Underlying the smell of the fresh paint was the unmistakable odour of urine. The new paintwork only thinly disguised a narrow, old-fashioned hall with well-worn carpet. This led to the reception area where a large, harassed-looking woman, maybe only a few years older than herself, greeted her from behind the desk.

'I'm visiting Ruby Jane Ring.'

'The only Ruby we have is a Mrs Winters.' The woman looked worried that she wasn't going to be able to produce the right Ruby to this new visitor.

Of course – Ruby had married but she'd never known her great-aunt's married name. This was even more of a shot in the dark.

'It could well be Winters,' Juliet said. 'Is it possible to see her?'

'Follow me,' the woman said, struggling from her post.

The corridors reminded Juliet of a seedy hotel. Just as they entered the communal lounge where groups of residents were sitting at various tables Juliet's ears pricked.

'Come on, Ruby, time for your cuppa.'

She saw a plump young nurse trying to force the spout of a plastic beaker between one of the resident's lips.

'I'm not ready for it yet,' the old lady answered in a determined fashion. 'Come back in half an hour. And don't forget to put a tablespoon of whisky in it.'

The nurse pulled a face behind Ruby's back and spun on her heel.

Juliet was fascinated. This tough old bird wasn't going to be forced into doing anything she didn't want to do. She had to admire her but she didn't think this Ruby was anything to do with the family. For one thing she couldn't be more than ninety, tops. But she was here now. She closed the gap to where Ruby was seated, staring crossly after the departing figure of the nurse.

'I keep saying I'm Mrs Winters to her,' the old lady muttered, 'but they take no notice.' Then she strained her neck up. 'Oh. A visitor, no less. And who are you, may one ask?' The voice was cracked but decidedly strong.

'I'm Juliet, from England.' Juliet smiled and held out her hand to take the small claw-like one briefly in her own. The skin was like a piece of greaseproof paper which had been screwed up tightly and roughly opened out again. 'A friend of Mrs Manning's son.' Ruby frowned. 'In the Clanricarde where you stayed for a few weeks while yours was being decorated.'

'I didn't want to leave. Better than this dump. But who cares where I am?'

Juliet decided to bring the subject back to safer ground.

'Mrs Manning sends her best wishes to you. She said you were the only one she could have a proper conversation with.'

'Barbara?'

Juliet nodded.

'Only sensible one there. I met the son too.'

'Yes. Trevor. I came with him today.'

Ruby peered at her. 'He's too old for you.'

'Oh, it's nothing like that,' Juliet protested, pleased that at least Ruby recognised the unsuitability of such a pairing. 'We're just friends. But Trevor told me a bit about you through his mother and I was curious.'

'Curious? What about?' The old lady's tone was suddenly sharp.

'Trevor tells me you've led a fascinating life.' Juliet realised she was invading the old lady's privacy, but before she could make her apologies, Ruby said:

'Sit down then, Juliet from England. It's nice to have a visit from someone from the Old Country. You're the first.' Ruby's fingers clutched the crocheted shawl over her knees.

Juliet pulled up a visitor's chair and sat by her side.

'So you're Juliet. It's a beautiful name.'

Ruby's eyes met hers; inside the delicate folds of skin around the sockets they were a penetrating navy-blue.

Her eyes. They're the exact colour of mine.

'Well, child, what do you want to know? I'm the oldest one here. Born in 1898. They tell me I'm 107 my next birthday.' She cackled.

Unbelievable.

'You look fantastic,' Juliet said before she could stop herself. 'Sorry, I didn't mean to sound patronising.'

'It never hurts to have a compliment,' was the unexpected reply, 'no matter how old one is.'

She looked at Juliet and for a brief second there was a gleam in those eyes. Was Juliet being fanciful or was there a kind of recognition?

'I'd love to know about your family,' Juliet said. 'Why you came to Australia. Trevor told me you lived in England when you were a teenager.'

'We weren't called "teenagers" in those days. We grew up before our time. Worked from the time we left school at twelve. Up at dawn blacking grates, scrubbing floors. You young ones don't know you're born.' She glared at Juliet.

Juliet shifted position, feeling slightly uncomfortable. Ruby was certainly a dragon and she wondered briefly why Barbara Manning liked her so much. The nurse came back with Ruby's drink and this time Ruby took it graciously with a charming smile. She must have been stunning when she was young. Even at such a great age you could see she had good cheekbones. There was no sign of the flame-coloured hair Nannie had described, but Juliet could imagine it.

'I know we've had it far easier than your generation, Mrs—'

'Call me Ruby. Everyone does, whether I mind or not.'

'What I'm trying to say—'

'You don't have to explain, girl. I've heard it all before.'

Juliet tilted her head towards her. 'I'm interested to hear why you came to Australia because my grandmother came out about the same time.'

'Did she indeed?' Ruby's tone betrayed some curiosity for the first time. 'Why?'

'She was very young and newly married. Her husband – my grandfather – wanted to improve life for them. He persuaded her to emigrate with him. So they came here.'

'What did you say your surname was?' Ruby's eyes, the only colour in her old face, were suddenly alert.

'I didn't. It's Juliet Reece, though that's my married name. I use it professionally as I like it better than Bishop.'

'Juliet Bishop.' Ruby tested each syllable as if trying to see whether it fit. Then she said slowly, 'Your grandfather wouldn't happen to be Ferguson Bishop, would he?'

32

Ruby

So you're my granddaughter.

I never thought I would set eyes on you. I sit very still and upright, feeling more than a little shocked. What's giving me the shivers is that if I'd died at a normal age I would never have met you. But maybe that would have been for the best.

I knew about you, of course, but only as a child. Or was it your sister? I get so muddled these days. Annie and Ethel kept in touch. Sent me letters and photographs of the family for years, right up until they died, though I usually only answered with a birthday and Christmas card. I'd made a new life. I had to wipe Harry from my mind. I didn't even tell Ted about him. After all, I never saw Harry again after Annie and Fergus took him away from me. I close my eyes against a stab of pain. Be honest. It's far too late to lie to yourself. I knew what I was doing. I used Harry as a pawn to get my own way. I didn't want to be lumbered with a baby. Life was far too exciting in Melbourne and I loved my job at the Esplanade too much to give it up. All I'd really wanted was to have Fergus for my husband. He would have been far better suited to me than Annie. Me, who loved adventure and excitement as much as he did. But if I couldn't have him I wanted to be like Adele. Independent, with no ties. When I set foot in Australia I was free for the first time in my life.

But now I'm an old woman. Has it been worth it? Did I miss something in not keeping my baby?

People say, how do you miss something you've never had?

But that's not strictly true. All through this old life of mine there's been a space inside me I know will never be filled. Even my marriage was a disappointment, but it was because I never loved him like I loved Fergus – and Ted knew it.

It's only now, this moment that I've set eyes on you, Juliet, who I know is my own flesh and blood...*my* granddaughter, not Annie's...I feel almost happy. And proud. At least something good has come from it.

What a beautiful woman you are. So assured. I imagine that husky voice turns men into marshmallow when they hear it. And your eyes – exactly the colour of mine, though a pity you've inherited Annie's nose. Though it's not much consolation to remember I was the prettiest.

I open my eyes. A cold feeling creeps over my heart. I can never tell you the whole story. I'm doomed in this nursing home. How much longer can this old heart beat? Is this to be my punishment? That I'll go on forever?

I hear you give a sharp intake of breath. Then you say, 'You really *are* Great-Aunt Ruby. I can't believe it.'

Then don't believe it because it's not true, the voice snaps in my head, but I manage to bite back the words. I wonder what Annie has said about me – it's obvious you haven't been told that I'm your real grandmother.

'And you never came home,' you say, more as a statement than a question.

'No, I never came home,' I repeat her words. 'There wasn't much point. I'd made my life here. I married a sheep farmer – did you know that? He died at seventy. Adele was here. She was a good friend to me and...Annie. Adele lasted the longest, bar me. Ninety-one when she died. There was no one in England. Father was long dead; Annie and Fergus were both dead.' My voice wobbles as I say their names for the first time in decades. 'Ethel, the youngest, died

first. There was no one. What was the point of me coming back?'
I look at you.

'I suppose there was only my aunt Frankie and Dad,' you say.
'Your niece and nephew.'

'Yes, little Harry…' I linger on his name. 'He was a baby when
I last saw him.'

Any minute now I'm going to break down. I feel like screaming.
To shout: *Harry was my son, don't you understand? And I gave
him up because your grandfather wouldn't marry me. Wouldn't get
a divorce. Said he would always love Annie. But it was* me *he loved.
Me. I know it was.* I can't stop my feeble old hands clutching the
shawl, pushing my bent old fingers in and out of the crocheted holes.

'Tell me about your father.' My voice sounds far away to my
ears. A shadow has fallen across your face. Instinct tells me you two
are not very close. Now I'm really curious. 'Juliet?'

'Dad's in a nursing home,' you answer.

I'm incredulous. How can my son be old enough to go into
a nursing home? I try to calculate his age.

'He's just had a heart attack and I'm worried about him. Will
– that's my brother – says it's serious, so I'm booked to go home this
evening.'

I swallow my disappointment. Just when I've found her she'll
go. I'll never see her again.

'I'm sorry to hear that,' I say. My God, I might outlive my
own son by the sounds of things. I can't bear this. 'When you see
him, will you tell him you've met me?' I barely breathe, waiting for
your answer. I can't believe how important this is to me that Harry
knows I'm still alive. His mother.

'If you want me to,' you say.

You sound reluctant. I catch your lovely eyes with mine. 'Tell
me, Juliet, were you fond of your grandfather?'

You frown. I know it seems an odd question. That I want to
know about my brother-in-law and not my sister.

'I wasn't as close to him as I was Nannie – that's what I called your sister,' you say. 'Pop died at sixty-eight. It was his heart. It must run in the family.'

It is as though a black solid mass has covered my own heart. I knew he died a very long time ago but the pain is still as raw.

'His heart was strong enough when I knew him,' I blurt.

You look surprised. It was a stupid thing for me to say.

'He was very overweight. Nannie told me he ate himself to death.'

Now it's my turn to be surprised. Then I say, 'It doesn't sound as though your grandfather was a happy man.'

You look at me sharply. 'What do you mean?'

'People who overeat usually do it to compensate for something. Were your grandparents happy?' I think this is what they call a loaded question but I must know the answer.

'I never heard Nannie say a bad word about him.'

No, Annie wouldn't. But I didn't ask the child that. I asked if they were happy. I give a tiny smile, so tiny she doesn't notice. She's told me all I want to know.

'Did she ever mention a man called Dr Alex Townsend?' I watch her face.

'He was her doctor, wasn't he? He delivered my father, I believe.'

'You believe wrong. He delivered Frankie. *I* was at Harry's birth…it's important for you to know that…you'll have to ask your father. I was always the black sheep. One day…perhaps…' My voice trails off. I know I'm not making sense.

'Why is it important for me to know?' you persist.

'Nothing…no matter. Just the ramblings of an old woman.' But you don't look convinced. Then I ask, 'Do you have children?'

Your lovely face crumples. Dear Lord, whatever have I said? It was an innocent question.

'N-no. Yes.'

'It can't be both,' I say, patting your hand.

You go so white I'm frightened you're going to faint. I try to fumble for the chord to ring for a nurse but you stop me.

'I'm all right,' you say. But I know you're not.

'Didn't Nannie ever tell you how she looked after me when… when…?'

I see you gulp. It's painful to watch.

'Go on,' I try to encourage.

'When I was sixteen…I had a baby. A beautiful son. Charlie. Mum and Dad made me have him adopted.'

Oh, my poor love. You lost your baby the same as I lost mine. But at least my baby stayed in the family.

'It must have been a dreadful time for you.' I don't want to sympathise too much. That would open the floodgates – for both of us. 'Do you know where he lives?'

'In Sydney.'

'Is that why you came to Australia? To find him?'

You nod. 'I may have found him already,' you stammer, 'but my rational mind says it can't possibly be.'

I'm amazed. 'And…?'

'He's a lovely man. I'd be proud if he *was* my son but I'm too frightened to ask in case I'm wrong…or worse, in case I'm right.'

I want to take you in my arms. I'm trying to work it all out, what you're saying. I don't want to but I'm closing my eyes again. All I know is one thing.

'Don't leave it too late,' I manage to tell her. 'Be brave. Ask this man the right questions. If you don't, you'll always regret it. Believe me.'

You look thoughtful. Now I'm very tired. I would love to talk to you all day but I have to let you go. It's doubtful I'll be here next time you come a-calling. If you bother. I've turned my back on the family and I have to live with it – God forbid, not for much longer.

'Will you be coming back to Melbourne, Juliet?' If I could just feast these old eyes on you once more – my beautiful granddaughter.

I wait for your answer which seems to take forever.

'I hope to...one day,' you say softly.

'Don't leave it too long,' I say, 'though I shan't be here.'

'Who knows,' you smile. 'You've made it to an incredible age so far.'

I smile back but keep my mouth closed. Very old people look terrifying when they smile and I don't want you to be frightened.

'I mustn't tire you, Great-Aunt Ruby,' you say, getting up to go, and it sounds like music to me that you're acknowledging me as family but I want you to call me 'Grandmother'. My rightful name. But then in my mind I can hear you say: 'I'm sorry, Great-Aunt Ruby – because that's who you'll always be as far as I'm concerned – it isn't necessarily the direct bloodline, but the one who nurtures you, who loves you unconditionally, who's there for you if you're ill, who's proud of you, who my father has always told me was the best mother a boy could have, and to me the best grandmother in the world.' I see your lovely eyes turn black with anger that you were so misled. Nothing I could say would win your sympathy. You'd just see me as a vile old woman. No, I couldn't stand that.

You bend over to embrace me. I smell your hair, your skin, your perfume. It's like a breath of sea air. Your lips touch my cheek. My vision blurs. I can't let you go like this. I make up my mind.

'Juliet, there's something I must tell you.'

'What is it?' You straighten up, smiling, waiting.

'I'm not your great-aunt.'

There. I've said it. Now make of that what you will.

'But...' You look puzzled.

'I'm your grandmother...your *real* grandmother.' I raise my voice and I see out of the corner of my eye that one of the residents has come out of her stupor for a few seconds and is watching me curiously.

'But Nannie...'

You stop; shake your head in bewilderment. Should I have kept quiet? It's too late now.

'How can you be?'

'Your grandfather and I...' My throat fills.

'You and Pop...?'

I nod. Maybe it was selfish of me. But you're strong, like me. You'd rather know the truth. 'I'm your father's mother,' I add, unnecessarily.

We just look at one another. Shocked. You sit down on the chair again.

'Does Dad know?' you finally ask.

'I believe Annie told him the truth years ago, when he was a young man.' I look directly at her, beseeching her to understand. 'I loved your grandfather, and he loved me, but he kept loyal to Annie. It was impossible for me to bring up a bastard child.' You flinch. 'That's what they called them in those days. I gave away my son...gave him to my sister.'

I feel my voice tremble, and then your hand stretches out and closes over mine.

'Annie had just lost her baby, you see,' I try to explain. 'She'd already decided to call him Harry if he was a boy. And he was, but he was stillborn. So I told her to take mine and bring him up as her own, and call him Harry.'

You squeeze my hand and I hope it means you understand, but you've gone very pale. We sit for several minutes, saying nothing. I don't know what to think. Juliet, can you forgive me? You press my hand again and get up for the second time, saying you must go. You have a flight to catch. You don't want to tire me. As if that matters at my age. Then something wonderful. At the doorway you turn back and smile.

The most beautiful, loving smile.

'Goodbye for now...Grandma. You know I'm going back to England this evening, but I'll write.'

I nod, but I feel so weak I'm not sure whether she will have seen it. But I'm happier than I've been for a very long time.

I lay my head on the back of the chair and shut my eyes, knowing I look like all the other old girls at this moment except at least I've got my mouth closed. But I'm not napping; my mind's reeling with thoughts and regrets and lost memories. Memories I've never had of my own son. Oh, yes, a few photographs during the first years when Harry and Frankie were growing up. Ethel and Annie were scrupulous about keeping in contact but I rarely answered their letters. I always told myself it was for the best. No point in raking things up. Then there was Dr Townsend. Ethel wrote to me, told me about Fergus. If only I'd known sooner I wouldn't have married Ted...I'd—

A clear young voice cuts across my ramblings. 'Mrs Winters, are you all right?'

'Course I'm all right.' I know I sound irritable. I open my eyes, one at a time, and meet those of a young trainee. 'I'm not dying yet, if that's what's bothering you.'

The young girl blushes. 'No, of course not. I just wanted to make sure you didn't need anything.'

She looks scared. My God, am I that unpleasant? 'I'd like a drink of apple juice...please,' I say, mostly to get rid of the girl for a few minutes.

'Right away, Mrs Winters.' The girl flies off.

Poor little blighter. I gaze after her. She reminds me of Ethel, trying to please. Thank goodness I was never like that. Far more spirit. But Annie was always the strong one.

I suddenly feel myself grow hot with shame at the way I treated my sister. Annie, who always showed me such love and protection. Defended me when Pa was unduly harsh...looked after me when I had the chicken pox and mumps...comforted me when I discovered blood in my drawers and told me it was the start of womanhood. She tried to take the place of our mother and never complained. It was only that she was so lucky to meet Fergus and make a new life in Australia. It was as though she made my own dream come true, but it was happening to her and not me. And however much I pleaded, Fergus held firm – even when I warned him I would tell Annie I was going to have a baby, and who the father was. And Annie, even when she was told the truth, remained steadfast. And found a solution.

33

The plane was delayed a couple of hours but to Juliet it was small fry considering the wait caused by the strike. She slipped off her heels and swapped them for a pair of mules, and the woman sitting across from her sent a sympathetic smile.

'It's a long one,' the woman said. 'I think you're wise. I usually have my flight socks, but I forgot them this time.'

I'm glad for the company, Juliet thought, as the woman who introduced herself as Tina chattered on. *Too many things going round my head.* Even though she'd thought of little else these past few hours it was still difficult to take in the fact that Ruby was still alive, let alone her astounding confession. The old lady had made no excuses for herself, only that she'd loved Fergus, as she called him.

Yes, Juliet remembered reading in Nannie's diary about her baby being stillborn, but she'd just assumed Nannie had had another baby a year or so later.

'And do you work? Kids? Or lady of leisure?' Tina enquired.

Juliet jumped. 'Sorry, I was miles away. I didn't mean to be rude.'

The flight was one of drinks, meals and films, then more drinks, more meals and more films with some chat with Tina in between. Juliet was thankful she had managed to get business class after all. She finally donned the complimentary eye mask, and in spite of the constant droning soon fell asleep.

The plane refuelled in Hong Kong and then took off again for the last lap of the journey. It's going to feel strange being back in England, Juliet thought. And seeing Louis there. Thinking about him, she felt a glow of pleasure.

She pulled her Nannie's journal out of her overnight bag, remembering how Jack had stolen it – no, substituted it with a diary of his father's. Risking such a deception, purely on her behalf, must surely mean something. She fingered the soft leather, then carefully, as though handling a priceless artefact, and still not sure whether she would return it or not, she turned to the last few pages.

We have had the decision made for us – to return to England. I am so ashamed and angry.

Something terrible must have happened to have forced them to return to England.

The following entries were almost as though someone else had written them, there was such a lack of feeling. She'd become used to reading about a young woman who poured out her thoughts and emotions. Juliet trembled as though she'd just tackled a dive which was far deeper than expected. What was going on? Had Nannie had second thoughts and decided she'd been too candid? Was she worried the wrong person would get hold of the diary? Such as her husband? If only so many pages hadn't been missing.

She came to the final page.

15th January 1921

This is the last time I intend to write in my diary. When I look back to the voyage over here and my feeble entries I wonder why I am taking the trouble. It served me well when I was going through *that time* but now it is of little use. There's only me to read it. And I don't want to be reminded of any of it.

Juliet shut the book feeling uncomfortable, and altered her seat position so she could lean back. Would Nannie feel her privacy had been violated if she'd known her granddaughter, or rather her great-niece, as Juliet now knew she was, would one day read her diary? Would she understand Juliet needed to know; to somehow find her own place in the world? To understand her own character and perhaps one day forgive herself?

Somehow she knew that whatever Ruby had done, Nannie was her sister and would never have stopped loving her. She hadn't abandoned her as Ruby liked to say. It had been Ruby's idea to give her baby to the young Annie to bring up.

She closed her eyes, feeling as near to Nannie as though she were sitting beside her. Nannie had put her trust in those she loved and they'd let her down, big time. Strange that Nannie referred to their betrayal as 'that time' – the same words Juliet used when she thought about how she'd been forced to give away little Charlie. And if Ruby hadn't been alive to confess, she wouldn't have understood what Nannie had meant by 'that time'. Nannie must have written about it in her diary and later torn the pages out; maybe she'd been worried that Pop might come across it and be upset.

'Juliet, are you okay?'

It was Tina.

'Yes, yes, I'm fine. Not crazy about the turbulence though.'

'It's been as smooth as a millpond.' Tina sounded puzzled.

'Oh, dear. I'm not much company, am I?'

'Don't worry.' Tina opened her paperback. 'I've got plenty of reading. So long as you're all right.'

Juliet was about as far away from 'all right' as she'd ever been in her life. But somehow she felt as though the questions in her past were slowly being answered. If only the ones in her present were as clear.

34

Jack, Melbourne

Jack slumped on the sofa in his apartment, a coffee untouched on the table beside him and a newspaper in his hands that he willed himself to concentrate on, all the time wishing Juliet had asked him to go back to England with her, and not Louis. To be fair she hadn't asked Louis, or even hinted. Louis had offered. And it was natural. Louis was already going to London to some dentists' conference or other. It wouldn't have been easy getting the time off, but face it – it wouldn't have been impossible. So why hadn't he spoken up? Because he was a coward, that's why. He couldn't bear it if she'd said 'thanks, but no thanks'.

He still couldn't work out what his feelings were for her; only that as soon as he waved goodbye to her at the airport, and probably out of his life, he hadn't been able to shake off a feeling that things didn't feel right. But whether it was Juliet he was referring to, or himself, he didn't know.

The only good thing was that Louis had been generous enough not to allow him to make any apologies for the accident. Jack had managed to appear reasonably calm as he shook Louis' hand though he was trembling inside. He'd tried to put everything into that handshake and Louis had squeezed it briefly, then brought his other hand up over it, as though to let him know he understood. What a decent bloke. As Juliet had once said, perfect for Petra.

But although she'd suspected something, Juliet had gone home still not knowing the full story of the accident. The way the media had portrayed him. The question as to whether the whisky he'd drunk the night before really did have any influence as to how he'd handled the descent. The trouble is, when you're older and the other person is older, and you've only known one another a short time, there's so much in the past which needs to be explained. If it's pushed further back it just pops out when you least expect it. He grinned at the sudden image which he hadn't meant at all.

Juliet had her family problems but he longed to help her solve unanswered questions, follow trails, see her lovely eyes light up, hear her laugh.

He shrugged and folded the newspaper that he hadn't read. More than likely he'd never see her again so why was he worrying? But if he never saw her again what would be the point of all they'd gone through? All they'd shared? To let her go would be madness. But she didn't want commitment any more than he did. At least that was the impression she gave him. Yet he was sure the friendship meant as much to her as it did to him. Surely she wouldn't forget him.

But there was something about some man in her life that was still upsetting her. Could it be her ex she was still in love with? Yet she'd seemed perfectly genuine when she'd spoken about him. That she'd married him because he seemed kind and her parents approved, him being a lawyer. But their approval of their son-in-law was not enough for her in the end. He gathered Gerrard was quite a few years older than Juliet and a bit stodgy, though she'd never spoken of him in a disloyal way. So why would she still carry the torch? If it wasn't Gerrard there must be someone else.

He thought of how he and Juliet were together. Her hair sliding through his fingers. Those eyes, luminous as she looked down at him that time when she'd pushed him back on to the bed, shaking her breasts to tease him... He felt himself harden at the image and impatiently reached for the mug of coffee, barely lukewarm, swilling back the contents in one go, grimacing as he put the mug back on the table. He frowned. Juliet had certainly made life-changing decisions on account of pleasing her parents. He wondered again why she'd never had children. He'd tried to ask her once but she'd seemed upset. Maybe she couldn't have them. Some women were dead unlucky in that department.

So about this guy in Oz she'd only hinted at – was it that she hadn't seen him for a long time? A childhood sweetheart? Or was he married? Was she still in love with him? He didn't want to think about Juliet being in love with someone. Thinking about another man making love to her. Doing the same things he and Juliet had done in bed.

Cursing under his breath he left the apartment, slamming the door. He needed a long hard walk. But it was only when he found himself striding in the direction of the Maritime Museum that he felt a strange pricking at the back of his eyes.

PART IV

The Return

35

Kingston-upon-Thames

'Will, it's me. I've just landed. I'm on my way home.'

'Jules. Great to hear you.'

'How's Dad?'

'He's back in the nursing home. Apparently he's not too bad but it's slowed him right down.'

'Have you seen him?'

'I went last week when he was in hospital. I could only stay a couple of days. The divorce is getting a bit hairy. He asked if you were still out in Oz. I told him you were coming back soon but I didn't mention it was because of him. Didn't want to alarm him in case he thought he was on the way out.'

She strained to hear her brother's words. It wasn't the best connection in the back of the taxi. Dear Will. Always sensitive to others' feelings.

'I phoned the home an hour ago to tell them you'd be back today,' Will continued, 'but they said not to go in till this afternoon. He's quite comfortable, but tired.'

'Okay, I'll see him later.'

Juliet put her key in the lock of her apartment but felt no sense of joy. Where was the happiness everyone talked about when they'd had a super holiday but oh, how good it was to be home? She felt nothing as she set the plastic bag on the worktop, the few bits she'd picked up from the airport supermarket. Was it the jet lag making her head swim or the emotions of the last two days? Feeling decidedly shaky she filled the kettle.

Taking her mug of tea into the sitting room she picked up the phone to make the call she was dreading.

'Good morning, Reece & Co, Rachel speaking.'

'Rachel, it's—'

'Jay!' Rachel cut in. 'Where are you?'

Strange to be called Jay.

'I'm back, and nearly beside myself with worry. How's everything? Any news of Neil? Or Lydia?'

'Zilch. When are you coming in?'

Juliet looked at her watch. 'Give me an hour. Can you pick me up a sandwich from the deli?'

She took a few more gulps of tea, then dialled again.

'Hi, Gerrard.' She couldn't help smiling. Gerrard hated Americanisms.

'Who's that?' Gerrard sounded puzzled.

'It's me.'

'Jay! Where are you? You sound like you're just round the corner.'

'I am. I'm home.'

The very word made her feel odd. Was this really home? She looked around her sitting room as though seeing it for the first time. Everything was as she'd left it but somehow duller. She'd had it painted in neutral creams and whites to lighten the place when she'd first moved in, but now she realised the result was bland. In Australia everything had been brightly coloured. Aboriginal carpets and cushions zigzagged their way into hotels and restaurants as a vibrant contrast to the less flamboyant designs of Britain. And the sunshine. Those fabulous bright hot days. She felt depressed already. Glancing out of the patio doors to the balcony where water was pooling she noticed how grey the Thames looked. Yes, the view was wonderful – it was the reason she'd bought the apartment in the first place. But today it had lost its charm.

'Good God. When did you get back?' Her ex-husband jolted her into paying attention.

'Half an hour ago.'

'You might have told me you were coming.' He sounded peeved. She ignored it. 'How've you been?'

'Well, you know me. Just the same as when you left. When do I get to see you?'

'In a few days. I'll come over one evening. And I might have someone with me.'

'Oh, yes?' Gerrard's voice was guarded. 'Who might that be?'

'A man,' Juliet said. She heard his sharp intake of breath. 'But nothing to get excited about. He's young enough to be my son.' She managed to keep her voice even.

'I wanted to speak to you in private.'

'Anything in particular?'

'*I* think so.'

'Can you tell me on the phone?'

'No.' He sounded impatient. Then his tone changed. 'Why did you cut your holiday short? I didn't expect you back until the...' He must be looking at his calendar, Juliet thought. '...first of December.'

'Dad's ill again. Another heart attack—'

'Oh, I'm sorry to hear that. Is there anything I can do?'

'Thanks, not at the moment. The other thing is that the business is in trouble.' *Hell and damnation.* She hadn't meant to tell him. Her free hand clenched into a fist and she shook it at herself. *Here goes. Wait for it.*

'What kind of trouble?' Gerrard's voice was suddenly alert.

'Lydia walked out and—'

'*What?*'

'Exactly what I said.' Juliet blew out her cheeks with exasperation. It was her own fault for not keeping quiet. 'I think in the end she couldn't cope.'

315

'Well, you'll be back at the helm in a day or two and sort it out, no doubt.'

She might as well finish the story now she'd got this far. 'It isn't that simple. Neil's off sick and I can't get hold of him. I'm going over now to find out what's been happening.'

'I told you the woman was bad news. You were bloody daft letting her take over.'

When Juliet trudged into the small reception area of Reece & Co she felt as though it was closing in on her. Had Pop felt suffocated like this when he was a footman? Wanting to break free? Have an adventure?

'Jay!' Rachel flew out from behind the desk and hugged her.

'It's great to see you, Rach,' she said, returning the hug warmly. 'But what on earth's that ugly tank doing here?' She pointed to a glass cube containing one evil-eyed monster of a fish.

'Lydia made a few changes.' Rachel rolled her eyes. 'Wait till you see your office.'

Juliet frowned. Her office was sacrosanct. The only one to make changes was *her*. And she rarely did. 'What time will the others be in?'

'Bob'll be here shortly. He's been out to look at a business. Kirsty's just gone on a late lunch. Jamie's...oh, here's Jamie now.'

'Hi, Jay.' Jamie gave her a broad grin. 'How was Oz?'

'Just like on the telly,' Juliet told him impatiently. 'Jamie, can you hold the fort while Rachel and I have a chat in my office?'

'You bet.'

At the top of the stairs Rachel said, 'Jay, you need to be prepared. Bob's been phoning—'

Juliet opened her door and gasped. 'What the hell's going on?'

All the furniture had been moved. A plant, which would have been more at home in a jungle, hogged the space where one of her filing cabinets had been; her desk now faced the door, looking sleek but empty with only a large open diary and a telephone. Where was the computer? Where were all the files and other paraphernalia? Pictures had been removed from the walls leaving pale oblong patches. The room was unrecognisable.

Rachel stood beside her. 'She's into feng shui big time.'

'She can feng shui it back again,' Juliet said. 'This is all nonsense.'

'Really?' Lydia's voice was almost a drawl.

Juliet whirled round to stare straight into Lydia's cool green eyes. A bubble of anger stormed in her head but she was determined not to rise to the woman.

'Come on in, Lydia,' she ushered her into the office. 'You might as well join the party.'

'I'd like to talk to you alone,' Lydia said, looking directly at Juliet. Her green eyes were unwavering. 'No offence, Rachel, but some of the issues I want to discuss with Jay are sensitive.'

What a nerve. Acting as though she hasn't abandoned the company.

Juliet bit the inside of her mouth. She must keep calm. Be the one in control. She caught her PA's anxious gaze. 'I'll see you later, Rach.'

As soon as Rachel had closed the door behind her she turned to Lydia.

'So, what's been going on in my absence besides wasting time changing my office around to suit your silly superstitions?'

'I'll ignore your last remark.' Lydia's voice was frosty. 'To answer the first part, it's not quite how you think it is.'

'I can't wait to hear.'

'Cut the sarcasm,' Lydia flashed. 'And don't interrupt me.'

It was hard to refrain from slapping the woman. Instead, Juliet sat straight-backed behind her desk and gestured Lydia into the other chair.

'Well?' Juliet's voice was cold.

'Everything was going fine...except with Neil, of course. Like I told you on the phone, he was very anti. Then a couple of weeks in he changed his tune...became friendly. I just thought he'd decided it was the easiest way. Then a few days later he came into my office saying he was sorry for being so offhand at the beginning but his nose had been put out of joint with me taking over. Then he said...' Lydia fixed her gaze on Juliet, 'wait for it, Jay, "It was always understood Jay would offer me a partnership."'

'I said nothing of the—'

'Let me finish.' Lydia put her hand flat in the air as though she were admonishing a wayward employee.

So this is what the others had had to put up with.

'He asked me if I'd invested the money I'd made in selling up. I said I was looking at the options, still talking to my financial adviser. He said, "You can't be getting much pleasure standing in for Jay and I'm fed up working for her. So why don't you come into business with me? Be a sleeping partner *in any way you like*." Then he looked me up and down and had the audacity to wink and tell me to think about it.

'"No thank you," I told him. He's a snake, Jay. I can't believe you never saw through him. I told him to go to hell. Frankly I thought it was a bit of a joke.' Lydia paused, looking a little uncomfortable, then shrugged. 'But I didn't realise what a piece of shit he was. He was furious I wouldn't play his sneaky little game so he tried to threaten me.'

'Why didn't you let me know what was going on before it got to this point?'

'You were incommunicado.' Lydia glowered at Juliet. 'That was supposed to be the whole point – we had the technology to stay in touch. I never realised you were such a technophobe.'

Juliet flushed at the comment. If she were honest, she knew Lydia was right. But it didn't alter the fact that Lydia herself hadn't been quite the businesswoman she'd led Juliet to believe.

'My BlackBerry was stolen and it wasn't always convenient to send emails from the ship,' Juliet began. 'And then I sprained my wrist—' Her string of excuses petered out. That's all they were. Excuses. For not keeping her eye on the ball. A thought struck her. 'What made you come in today?'

'Impulse really.' Lydia leaned back in the chair, totally relaxed, as though they were having a friendly chat. 'I was passing and wondered if there was any news of Neil. Contrary to what you might think, I do feel bad about it all. Jamie was in reception and said you'd come back and that you and Rachel were upstairs. I thought we might as well get everything right out in the open.'

'This is my worst nightmare,' Juliet said. She put her hand to the side of her head which had begun to throb. 'I just don't know what the hell's going on.'

'You need to talk to Bob.'

'I intend to.' Juliet paused for a few moments. 'And Neil, as soon as I can get hold of him.'

'Good luck there.' Lydia pulled a face. 'But talk to Bob first. He'll fill you in on the clients.'

'Whatever's left of them.' Juliet's voice held an edge.

'What do you mean?' Lydia's eyes were wide. 'You don't think Neil's gone off with them?'

'You tell me. I don't know anything except I could stake my life he's not sick.'

'Even if he has,' Lydia argued, 'you've got everything on the computer anyway, haven't you?'

'Of course I have,' Juliet snapped, 'but if he's taken records from the files with the personal notes – important bits of information that jog your memory when you're talking to clients—'

'I didn't bother doing any notes like that,' Lydia interrupted. 'I know the others wrote everything up, but I thought it was a waste of time. I've always had an excellent memory.' She gave one of her triumphant smiles.

Juliet said nothing. She was too angry to tell Lydia that the notes were priceless – the difference between giving a first-class personal service as opposed to the corporates who were notorious for treating their clients as numbers. And that having a good memory wouldn't have helped the rest of the team when Lydia had thrown in the towel.

'Well, there's nothing more I can tell you,' Lydia said, waving a hand dismissively, 'except to say you're well rid of him. And don't worry – I'm not going to send you any bill. We'll put it down to experience.'

What a nerve the woman had.

'A disastrous one for both of us, it seems,' Juliet said through gritted teeth.

'It's a great shame. Brilliant idea that didn't work.' Lydia looked at the wall beyond Juliet's desk. 'But it's no use going over old ground.' She dug into her handbag, pulled out her keys which she jangled in her fingers, and rose to her feet.

'Maybe in time, when things have calmed down, we can have a lunch together.'

She left without a backward glance.

After Lydia shut the door Juliet stayed put at her old desk in its new position and looked around. Nothing was as she had left it. Frowning, she pulled open one of the drawers, the one where she kept her special accounts. The files had gone. It was as though someone had scooped them up and dumped them who knew where. She buzzed downstairs to confront Lydia but Rachel said she'd already left the building.

It was too upsetting to spend anymore time in this depressing space that bore no resemblance to her old office, which had always been welcoming and buzzing. She needed to speak to Bob.

Twenty minutes later he appeared, and beamed when he saw Juliet in reception studying the sales screen with Rachel and sipping her third cup of tea.

'Jay,' he said, giving her a kiss on the cheek, 'I'm so glad to see you back. It's been a bit hairy, as you've heard.'

'I haven't told Jay anything about your phone calls.' Rachel threw him a warning look. 'I thought it better if you tell her yourself.'

'Okay, Rach.' Bob turned to Juliet. 'Why don't you bring your tea into my office and I'll update you.'

She followed him in with a creeping apprehension that this was not going to be a good meeting. She sat on the visitor's chair. Bob took the second one.

'Jay,' he began, 'I'm sure you realise Neil's not on any sick leave, don't you?'

'I had my doubts the first time I rang and he didn't answer. I called him again a couple of hours later and still no reply. And I've heard nothing since. So yes, I suspected as much.' She took a mouthful of tea. 'What do you think he's up to?'

'I think he's poaching your clients.'

'Are you serious? Is that why my clients' files have all disappeared?'

'I've got them nice and safe,' Bob assured her, nodding towards the filing cabinet. 'No way could he have got away with lifting those. That would have been a criminal act. No, it was all the computer files I was worried about.'

'We need to find out if he's tampered with the computers,' Juliet said, recalling Jack's words. She pressed his image firmly to the back of her mind.

'Impossible to tell,' Bob said. 'I had a look – you know I'm not an IT whizz kid but even I know that he could have copied the lot and no one would be any the wiser.'

'We don't know for sure, do we?' Juliet said. 'We can't accuse him until we have some evidence.'

'I'm afraid we *do* know for sure,' Bob said, his grey eyes anxious. 'Kirsty and I have phoned every single client and they've *all* been approached by Neil.'

'And?' Juliet tried desperately to remain calm but inside she was screaming.

'All but three told me they were taking their business elsewhere.'

'What, twenty-two of them?' Her voice rose to a squeak. Bob nodded. 'What about the ones going through?'

'They're safe enough. He can't touch those.'

'But how could the others say they've gone to Neil? They're under contract here. Neil hasn't even got a business.'

'It's not that difficult to set one up.' Bob got up and filled two paper cups with water. He handed her one. 'Especially these days when it can all be done online. You can get a new company up and running in a matter of hours.'

'I can't believe Neil's done this to me. Talk about loyalty. What a bastard.'

'I know it's a shock.' Bob put a hand on her arm. 'And only one of them was brave enough to tell me he'd actually given his business to Neil. That was Mr Turner. He said Reece & Co wouldn't be the same without Jay Reece, and good luck to her if she wanted to spend time in Australia, but he had a business to sell and felt happier going with Neil – he was giving him a chance, he said.'

'But I was only going for a few weeks.'

'Apparently Neil told everyone you were going to be in Australia for an indefinite period and rather than have any break in the service he suggested they go with him in his new business where he can deal with everybody personally. And hinted it was more or less with your blessing!'

'I can't believe it.' She could find no new words for her outrage.

'We said it wasn't true – you were still very much at the helm. So then several asked if they could speak to you personally about their current situation. Of course we were rather stuck as we weren't sure when you'd be back – with the strike and all.'

Juliet's eyes darkened with fury. Neil had destroyed her business. Nine years to build it up and expand it and keep it going.

And when her back was turned for a few weeks this was what she was left with. Three clients. It would be hilarious if it wasn't so shocking.

'There must be something I can do.' She ran a hand through her hair. 'Some law. It must be illegal. I'm going to get a solicitor on to it. They've signed contracts. They can't just break them.'

'I'm no lawyer but I'm not sure there's anything illegal. They may have the right to take their business where they want.'

'Maybe, but that doesn't stop the fact that Neil copied all the files so he was in a position to call everyone – persuade them to leave me. That's what I'll get him on.' She banged her hand on Bob's desk. 'But first I'm going to pay Neil a call.'

36

Juliet fumed as she steered her Mercedes into the last space at the nursing home. There'd been no answer when she'd rung Neil's bell. And his car was not on the drive. She'd have to go back later. She switched off the engine, taking a few deep breaths to calm down before she saw her father. She needed to concentrate on *him* now. How many times had she been to the nursing home? Fifty? It must be but it felt like five hundred. Yet today, even after her break, she felt as depressed as she had the first time.

She sat for a couple of minutes, dreading how she would find him. Then she braced herself, reached for her handbag and opened the car door.

To her surprise her father was sitting on a bench overlooking the gardens. His head was bowed low over his chest. Probably dozing. He was dressed in his usual 'writer's outfit' of old grey flannels and tatty blazer which didn't look warm enough for the fresh autumn day, but then she remembered he never did feel the cold. He would often be at his desk at home, writing his biographies on war heroes, shirt sleeves rolled up even in winter, refusing to switch on the central heating until just before his wife came in from work, no matter that Juliet shivered when she got home from school. He simply ordered her to put an extra jumper on, and even a hat and scarf if it was really penetrating. As though she could do her homework dressed like an Arctic explorer. Funny to think she'd now got his desk. Although there'd been this uneasy relationship for so many years, somehow sitting where he used to sit writing his books gave her a feeling of comfort and continuity. She'd tell him she was using it. He'd be pleased to know the old desk still had some life.

'Hello, Dad,' she said.

'You've come back then,' he answered, raising his head briefly. 'Will said you were on your way.'

'I got in this morning,' she said, kissing his cheek, relieved he still smelt like her father and not any old man, and settled on the bench beside him.

'I'm pleased to see you safely back,' he said, pulling himself straighter and turning a fraction to look at her. His eyes were still a bright pale-blue, though watery with age.

She gave him a smile. 'I'm pleased to see you, too, Dad, and that you're out in the air. I've been worried about you.'

She stole a glance and noticed his once fine profile now sagged in resignation; unexpectedly, it brought a lump to her throat. She couldn't bear to see her father so frail.

'Did they say I'd had another heart attack?'

'Yes.'

'It wasn't that bad. Maybe a bit worse than the others.' He shrugged. 'Well, I'm still here.'

Juliet watched a blackbird peck half-heartedly at some small insect it had spotted. The trees which had shed their glorious leaves and were preparing to fight another winter looked as bereft as she felt. Her father sat silently beside her, his head still bent. She wondered if there'd ever be any real communication between them instead of just these platitudes.

It wasn't as though her father had actually ill-treated her, Juliet recalled, as she glanced again at him; it was simply that he'd had no idea of her needs. She hadn't even had Antonia and Will's support when she was growing up. When they visited, her parents more or less ignored her in the excitement of seeing their two older and more clever offspring. She sighed. Her father turned his head towards her, grey and shrunken, his eyes dull with medication, his face lined with fatigue and strain.

'What was that for?' he asked.

'What?'

'The sigh.'

'I don't know. I suppose nothing works out like you hope it will.' Juliet bit her lip.

Was he giving her an opportunity to be frank? There was so much she wanted to say, her chest felt it would explode. But how could she start such a conversation when it might upset him? She opened her mouth to say something, anything, but quickly shut it. But if he died before they ever spoke of anything important she'd never forgive herself. Purely for something to do she searched in her bag and took out a packet of mints. 'Want one, Dad?'

'No, thanks.' He drummed his fingers on the bench in the space beside her. Another silence. She'd have to be the one to invite him to speak, if only to stop the irritating tapping. Then she remembered she had exactly the same habit. Maybe they were too much alike and that was one of the reasons they hadn't always got along. But she knew it was more than that.

Come on, Juliet. Open it up. She took a deep breath.

'What's the matter, Dad? You seem like you've got something on your mind.'

He hesitated, cleared his throat, and stared at the ground. 'We haven't always seen eye to eye, have we?'

It was as though he'd read her thoughts.

'That wasn't my fault...' Juliet began, then stopped. What was the point when her father was clearly so ill.

'There was a big gap between Antonia and William...and you,' he continued.

'Meaning I was a mistake?'

Her father shook his head, and she noticed his hand, once well

326

shaped with manicured nails, now skeletal and liver-spotted, was trembling on his thigh.

'It always felt like it.' She swallowed hard.

Her father closed his eyes.

'Dad...please answer. You have to tell me. I must understand.'

'Your mother...' He hesitated. 'No...shouldn't be telling you...'

'Telling me what? Dad, please.'

'Your mother...' her father cleared his throat loudly, 'met someone. Before you were born. Well, it was...I put it down to... a bit of a fling.'

Mother had a fling? Her mother? It was almost impossible to believe. She caught his eye and he gave her a weak smile and patted her hand.

'Who was it?' Juliet blurted.

'He owned a shoe shop in Norwich,' he said slowly. 'I used to wonder how she could afford so many new shoes.'

He smiled at her again, his old eyes now creasing with the memory, and she remembered what a lovely sense of humour he'd had when he was in a good mood.

'What happened? Did Mum want a divorce?'

'No, of course not.' Her father sounded impatient that she should think such a thing. 'We had Antonia and William. We made up. But we left Norwich. I was determined about that.'

Incredible that he was telling her something so private. He could have gone to his grave and she'd never have known. She supposed it was because it really didn't matter any more. Her mother was dead. But she knew her father was telling her all this for a reason. She wondered briefly what kind of man her mother had been attracted to. How devastated her father must have been.

'Then you came along. We were delighted.'

Her peppermint stuck in her throat. *They were delighted?* She coughed to dislodge the sweet and tried to take in this new revelation – even checking events in her mind to see if it could possibly be

327

true. Try as she might she could rarely remember a time when she'd felt loved and wanted and special, particularly by her mother. She shook her head, trying to clear the jumble of painful thoughts.

'Then why...?' God, this was painful. As she tried to absorb it all she heard brisk footsteps on the tarmac and a nurse appeared with a blanket.

'Are you warm enough, Mr Bishop?' The nurse draped it around him as though he were a piece of furniture in an unused room. 'There, that's more like it,' she said, satisfied, and glanced at Juliet. 'Is this your daughter?'

'Yes, it's my younger daughter, Juliet,' and Juliet was surprised to find how nice her name sounded from her father.

'I'll leave you with her then. Don't stay out too long – it's getting colder.' Father and daughter watched the nurse's tall bony figure hurry back to the main house.

Her father sat quietly, and then he continued as though they hadn't been interrupted.

'We were delighted,' he repeated. 'We loved you but we were older...didn't always know how to handle you.'

'You make me sound like a tearaway,' Juliet said, wondering what was coming next. 'I suppose I had to stand up for myself as there was no one else.'

'Yes, in that way you were rather like your...like Ruby.'

Should she say something?

Her father began to cough and fumble for his handkerchief somewhere under the blanket. His shoulders heaved but the coughing was almost apologetic, as though he hadn't the strength to let go. Juliet watched him, her heart contracting as she pictured him hunched over his typewriter in his study. A distant father...but anything would be better than this.

Then in a low voice which faded to a whisper, Juliet straining towards him to hear the words, he said, 'Your mother and I should never have made you give up your child.'

37

Jack, Melbourne

'Captain Delaney,' a voice called from behind, 'Richards is waiting for you.'

Jack, immersed in thoughts of Juliet, swung round. A warm breeze caught hold of his hair and impatiently he brushed it out of his eyes. Lucy Renton, one of his best trainees, was running over the tarmac of the small private aerodrome to catch him up.

The more Jack thought about this unknown man that Juliet was apparently still obsessed with, the more dejected he became. He couldn't shake it off. Every time he saw that sad look in those breathtakingly lovely eyes of hers, the catch in her voice when she mentioned the man that must still hold her heart, his stomach heaved. In the old days, before he was married, he'd never been used to any rival, but since the accident and his divorce he'd somehow lost his confidence, though he'd always made a huge effort not to let it show.

Then he'd met Juliet. Almost immediately he'd felt more like his old self. His humour had returned, he'd become interested in others instead of rotting in his own miserable world. It was as though Juliet had begun the healing process. More than that he felt a genuine fondness for her. And a real concern when she was worried or unhappy. And a ridiculous delight when he made her laugh. Or was he simply kidding himself? Was there something else? But now she was gone he felt himself slipping backwards.

Then his brain started working. Women talked to one another. He would bet she'd have told Petra about the man she was still in love with and could never have. Petra would tell him. At least then he'd know what he was up against. He gave a wry smile. Not that he was trying to play the jealous suitor like some hero in a novel – it was simply a mystery he wanted to clear up for his own satisfaction.

Yes, that's what he'd do. He'd phone Petra. First opportunity.

'Be right there, young Lucy,' Jack said with a sudden grin.

'Petra speaking.'

'Petra. It's Jack.'

'Hi, Jack,' Petra sounded delighted. 'How goes it?'

'I'm fine.' He chatted a minute or two and then said, 'Petra, there's something I have to ask you – in the strictest confidence.'

'You sound serious.'

'It is. It's about Juliet.'

'Oh.'

'There's something troubling her, I'm sure of it. She's come close to telling me several times but always changes her mind at the last moment. I think she's unhappy about something which is nothing to do with the business or even the worry of her father. I just wondered if you knew anything. Has she ever confided in you?'

'What do you think the trouble might be?' Petra's tone was guarded.

His instinct had been right.

'Another man,' Jack said. 'Someone she's been in love with for a long time and can't have. He's probably married, or not in love with her, or she knows he's not right for her...I don't know... Could be any of those things or something I haven't even thought of,' he finished lamely.

'And she never mentioned anyone?'

'Well, she sort of hinted once. Said she wanted to go to Sydney to look up family. And when I said I thought her grandparents were in Melbourne she said it was someone else, leading me to believe she meant someone in the family other than the grandparents. But that wasn't the truth. I think I know her quite well now and I'm certain it's not another member of the family she's looking for.'

'I really can't say anything,' Petra said. 'It's for Juliet to tell you, not me.'

'So she *has* talked to you about him?' He tried to stifle the fear of Juliet's feelings for this unknown man, but his stomach twisted.

'Yes. But it was almost by accident. She's kept it bottled up for years.'

'Is it because she hasn't seen him for years?'

'Something like that,' Petra said. 'Look, Jack, I'm sorry I can't say more but I know one thing…she likes you. I mean *really* likes you. She's pretty cut up about having to go back to England.'

'She would be. She's got the mess to sort out in her company. That won't be pleasant. And also her father's seriously ill and I don't think they have the easiest relationship.'

'That's true.'

There was an awkward silence. He could tell he wasn't going to get any more out of Petra.

'Well, thanks for telling me what you could. But it doesn't give me any real answer.'

'Jack, I think you should talk to her in person. She's all mixed up at the moment. Let her get her business sorted first, and her father, then go and see her. You may be surprised with what she tells you.' She paused. 'One other thing, Jack. When I said about her being upset about leaving Oz, I meant she didn't want to say goodbye to *you*.'

His heart leaped. 'It doesn't have to be permanent.'

'Maybe not,' Petra's clear tones came over the receiver, 'but she doesn't know that, does she?'

38

The bench digs into Juliet's bones as her body stiffens. Her face crumples at her father's words. A stabbing pain knifes her chest, almost cutting off her breath. She winces and squeezes her eyes tight, trying to stop the tears which begin to drip down her face. Why now? Dear God, why is he saying this now? She clutches at the arms of the chair, her features distorted. She tries to answer. Impossible. Her head swims.

'They've asked if they can adopt the baby themselves but the woman in the agency said it would be impossible. My father doesn't have a regular job and they're too old, so they wouldn't be suitable.' Mani's voice was thick with tears when he saw Jay a week after she'd broken the news that terrible morning. They were sitting on the sagging sofa in the small square sitting room where Mani lived at home. 'Even though they're the grandparents. She just kept saying they had to do what's best for the baby.' He broke down.

Jay had never seen a boy cry and she was shocked to hear the terrible rasps. It was like some wild animal caught in a trap. She pulled him into her arms, stroking his dark head, and at the same moment an odd quiver ran across her stomach. Instinctively she put her hand over it.

'It's moving,' she said in wonder. 'For the first time. Here, put your hand here.' She guided his slender brown fingers over the place where she'd felt her child stir. 'Can you feel anything?'

Mani shook his head.

'You will when it starts kicking,' she smiled.

Mani gazed at her, his eyes luminous. Then she held him and their tears mingled.

That evening Jay threatened that she and Mani would run away.

'Your father and I have made a decision,' her mother said firmly. 'You'll go to Nannie's this weekend. She's the only person I trust but as far as everyone else knows, you're going to the country for a rest…you're suffering from nerves. And that goes for Antonia and Will. There's no need for them to know either.'

She wasn't even allowed to tell her own brother and sister? Was there nothing she could do? Nothing she could say? Didn't she have any rights at all? It seemed that everything had been taken out of her hands. Mummy and Daddy were wicked. They wouldn't give Mani a chance. Wouldn't even meet him or his parents. She would never, ever forgive them.

Her father was much too sick to tell him how desperately she'd tried to keep her baby.

'Juliet. Are you all right?'

Her father patted her hand. He was silent for a few moments. All she could hear was the pecking of the same blackbird now attacking a worm on the path.

'Maybe it's better to bring it out into the open.'

'No, Dad, I don't…it's too late. I don't want…can't talk about it.' Her eyes brimmed with fresh tears. She found a tissue in her bag and blew her nose.

'You…never…forgave…us.'

Juliet looked at him and saw a sad old man. His eyes were watery as though he, too, wanted to cry. He looked like someone you'd feel sorry for if you passed by his chair in the nursing home and didn't know him. Someone's dad. Only he happened to be hers.

'Can't blame you...your own good,' her father was stuttering now. 'You couldn't know...weren't old enough to understand—'

'What was there to understand?' Juliet wanted to shout, but she spoke as calmly as her trembling voice would allow.

'Too...many...se...secrets.'

'What secrets?' Were there others she didn't know about?

There was a silence. Her father's lips, bloodless now, parted a little, then he pressed them together.

'Come back...tomorrow, Juliet.' His voice had regained some control. 'I want to hear about...Australia.'

Juliet looked at her watch. Almost five. Neil's Audi was back on the drive so he must be home. She pressed the bell for the second time and an impatient voice called, 'Coming.' She heard footsteps pounding along the hall and stood back a little way from the front door. It was flung open and there stood Neil.

'Oh, you're back. Well, you'd better come in.' He held the door wide.

She followed him through to his sitting room which was open plan to the dining room. Piles of papers and brand-new files covered the table, leaving no space for anything such as a dinner plate. Her lips tightened but she said nothing; just sat down on the leather sofa without removing her coat.

There was dead silence. Neil had taken the chair and was staring at her. Well, she wasn't going to be intimidated.

'I think you should start from the beginning, Neil. Tell me what the hell is going on.'

'Lydia's a bitch,' he started.

Juliet put her hand up. 'Cut the abuse, Neil. I want to know the facts, not a load of finger-pointing.'

She was gratified to see Neil flush.

'She had it in for me right at the beginning. I soon realised

I couldn't work with her. She had no methods, no ideas, little common sense...' He broke off and looked at her. 'I suppose you've seen your office?'

'Yes, yes,' she said, 'but get to the point.'

'You hardly contacted us,' Neil went on. Juliet opened her mouth but he continued, 'and I could see the whole business falling to bits. Don't forget, Jay, I was the one who got the business on its feet in those early days. Bringing in some good clients. You can't deny it.'

'I don't,' Juliet said. 'But—'

'So I know how it runs and what work is involved,' he went on, ignoring her. 'But dear Lydia wants all the glory with little input. Then she walked out at ten o'clock one morning. No notice. No explanation.'

'Would your row have had anything to do with her leaving?' She couldn't help the sarcasm.

'You know how Rachel exaggerates.' Neil picked at his fingernail. 'Lydia was annoyed because I told her she wasn't pulling her weight, and she went off in a tantrum.'

'Was that *after* you threatened to blackmail her?'

'Aren't you being rather melodramatic?'

'I'm only repeating what Lydia said.'

'Is that what she told you?' Neil's voice was cool. 'No, Jay, I'd got her number and she knew it.'

'But you walked out the following day,' Juliet flashed. 'Made the excuse you were sick, which clearly wasn't the case.'

'I didn't want to explain to the others before I spoke to you, so it seemed the easiest thing to say.'

'After you copied all the files on the computer.'

Neil looked across at her and sighed.

'You weren't here, Jay. The business was being neglected. We were starting to get complaints. I thought the best thing would be to copy the files and concentrate on them at home where I don't have any distractions.'

'So you admit you copied the files?'

'Yes, I did, and I've told you why.'

'So you didn't think you were doing anything illegal?' Juliet demanded.

'Not at all.' Neil's tone was smooth.

'Well, now I'm home you can come back to the office and carry on with the work.'

'I'm afraid that's not going to happen.'

The air between them crackled. Neil's wall clock ticked by the seconds.

'Why not, exactly?'

'Because the clients want *me* to handle their business. So I decided to set up my own company. It seemed the perfect time. You've never offered me a partnership even though I've worked my balls off for the last eight years.'

'You didn't even discuss it with me.'

'Be honest, Jay. You have no intention. So don't blame me for trying to further my career. You look after number one. So now it's time for me to do the same.'

'By stealing all my clients.'

'If that's what you want to call it. They all said they'd feel more secure with me than staying with Reece & Co when the boss is no longer there.'

'You lied and told them I was away indefinitely.'

'You never gave us a date when you were returning,' Neil smirked.

The bastard. He'd twisted everything. But she knew she must take as much of the blame.

'There's no point in discussing this further.' Juliet stood up, adjusting her coat. 'But I can assure you I won't let it drop. You've stolen my business so you'll be hearing from my solicitor.'

Juliet turned over the yellow pages, running her eyes over the many dozen solicitors advertising themselves, until her head spun. Twice she decided to break down and ask Gerrard if he knew the right person; twice she put the receiver down before he answered. Finally she came across one whose ad sounded different from the others.

We don't take prisoners, it stated. Exactly what she needed.

'Why didn't Ruby come back to England?' Juliet broached the subject as she and her father sat in the conservatory the following afternoon, watching the rain pour through the bare trees. It was so dark inside, one of the nurses had switched on the overhead lights which now shed a sickly glow over her father's face. Thankfully none of the other residents had opted to sit in there.

He frowned, then seemed to make a decision.

'She liked Australia...wanted her independence. Ended up marrying some sheep farmer – worked harder than she'd ever worked. She'd be dead long ago.'

Juliet's thoughts raced. Should she tell her father that his real mother was still alive? And well in her hundreds. That she'd actually seen Ruby – had a conversation with her? That Ruby herself had told her the truth? She glanced at him. His head was bent onto his chest. An idea suddenly occurred to her. She touched his arm.

'Dad,' she began, 'why didn't anyone tell me that Ruby had a child?'

Her father tapped his knee with trembling fingertips. 'What are you talking about?' he mumbled.

'I've worked something out. You see, I found Nannie's diary in the Maritime Museum.' She would pretend she'd read the whole story in Nannie's diary about Ruby being pregnant at the same time, and handing over her baby. More than likely those entries would have been in the missing pages. This way she wouldn't have to tell her father that Ruby was still alive.

Her father's head shot up. 'What diary?'

'One she started on the voyage. You said she'd kept one.'

'If it was in a museum how could you read it?'

'That's another story. But I *have* read it. Nannie sounded like a sad young woman.'

A shadow flitted across her father's face. He twisted his neck to look at her. 'So you know the worst...' he said, slowly. 'You know Ruby is your real grandmother. My *mother*.' He said the last word as though it were beyond contempt. 'And that my *father*...I'll never forgive them.'

'She was young—' Juliet started.

'Don't defend her,' he snapped. 'You never knew her. You don't know what she was capable of.'

It was all she could do to bite back the retort that she *had* met Ruby. That Ruby was an incredible old lady with all her wits about her. And that throughout the visit she was certain Ruby had felt, maybe not regret, but a sadness she'd made the decision to let Harry go. Had more or less broken the contact. But what would be the use? It might tip her father right over the edge, knowing his daughter and Ruby had discussed him. He was already upset at the very mention of Ruby.

She bit her lip. Dare she risk another burning question?

'Dad, in Nannie's diary she mentions a Dr Alexander Townsend. In fact she mentions him several times so he must be important to her.'

Her father closed his eyes. A minute ticked by. She wondered if he'd fallen asleep.

'Dad?'

His eyes flicked open. 'He was her doctor. Delivered Frankie. He was in love with her,' he said slowly, as though it was the first time he'd ever told anyone.

Who wouldn't have fallen in love with Nannie, Juliet thought, remembering the lovely lines of her grandmother's face, and those eyes. Or great-aunt, she corrected herself. Would she ever get used to thinking of Nannie as her great-aunt and not her grandmother?

'Did you ever meet him?'

'I'd be too young.'

It was strange but she didn't think her father was telling the whole truth. She watched him closely but his face was set.

'Frankie was older so she might have remembered him,' Juliet ploughed on. 'What a pity I can't ask her. Did *she* like him, Dad?'

'I really don't know.'

But he didn't look her in the eye. What was he holding back?

'So you don't know what he was like?' Juliet persisted.

'Only that Mum once told me when I was an adult he was the kindest and dearest man she'd ever known.'

This was all quite amazing to Juliet. She'd always thought Pop was the love of Nannie's life, but it seemed she was completely wrong. She couldn't resist the next question.

'Did Nannie love him back?'

'Your Nannie thought the world of him.' Her father closed his eyes again.

'Isn't that because he was such a marvellous doctor on the ship when they went out to Australia – when they had that awful smallpox outbreak? And Nannie helped him so she'd have got to know him a bit, presumably.'

Her father nodded. 'That's partly it. I'll tell you more next time, but if I kick the bucket before that you'll have to speak to Kitty.'

Juliet's eyes widened. 'Who's Kitty?'

'Someone…someone who knows about him…but I don't know where she is. We…lost touch.'

'Do Antonia or Will know where she is?'

'No, no. Neither of them. They're not in the least interested in that sort of thing. No one knows. I don't know. I can't think. I'll try to remember for when you come back. I don't even know if she's alive.'

She'd never heard anyone in the family mention a Kitty. Maybe her father was getting muddled. She was probably one of his old girlfriends. Juliet reached for her bag and got up to leave. Her father opened his eyes.

'Are you off?'

'You're tired, Dad. I'll be back tomorrow when you've rested. I want to hear about Kitty.'

He shook his head as though to say he wished he'd never started this turn of the conversation, and gave a deep yawn.

'Perhaps you're right. I *am* tired.' His watery eyes met hers. He hesitated. 'Have you anything to tell *me*, Jay?'

It was the first time he'd used her diminutive name. Was it on purpose? Was he trying to tell her he'd had plenty of time to think in this place? That some things were just too petty to argue about?

Was he waiting for her to tell him she forgave him to assuage some of the pain of his own guilt? Should she draw a line, or was it too late? Or did he suspect she, too, was withholding something? She'd already decided not to mention Louis. And what was the point now of telling him the truth about Ruby? He hated her.

'Nothing that can't wait until tomorrow, Dad.'

She bent down to kiss him and he put his hand up to her cheek, just for a second or two, before it dropped back onto his knee.

Her brain was too tired to think straight. Neil, Lydia, and now all sorts of family secrets coming to light. Well, she'd put everything on hold until tomorrow.

If she could get a decent night's sleep she might feel up to facing it. She'd go to bed early and not even begin reading her new novel.

But no matter how she tried, how she twisted and turned, how she arranged and rearranged the pillows, she lay for what seemed like hours, her eyes wide open, thoughts whirling, making no sense of her father's last conversation. Her eye caught on the black metal tieback on the nearest curtain. It looked exactly like some revolting beetle, and after a few moments she leapt out of bed to inspect it closer, just to make sure. Feeling foolish she stumbled back into bed again. She forced her eyes to stay closed, aware of every aching bone and muscle in her body as she flexed each arm and leg, trying to bring back the circulation.

The house seemed even quieter than usual. She strained her ears. Not even the pitter-patter of mice which she'd once had in the attic. At least it would have been some sign of life, she thought grimly. Jack's face floated before her. She missed him. What was he doing right at this minute? Was he thinking of her too? Deep breathing. That was the answer. She drew in some long breaths and finally felt herself relaxing and drifting. And there was Jack, murmuring her name, running his hands through her hair, letting it fall between his fingers. Then lifting up her nightdress above her knees and putting his hand between her legs, slowly, lazily caressing the soft damp folds. *Oh, Jack. I love you.* Her head was filled with Jack. His face...his lips...his body...his fingers probing and insistent. The musky smell of him...a sheen of perspiration... his voice calling her name as his finger slipped inside her. 'I want you, darling Juliet. How I want you.' His lips were warm and moist on her parted mouth, his breath coming in quick bursts. Then wave upon wave upon wave – it poured over her scalp in pulsating waves, down her legs, across her belly, down her arms, right to the tips of her fingers in a crescendo of joy and excitement. She shouted his name, tightening her arms around his neck, pulling him closer until finally the flood subsided and her breathing slowed. She was lost. All she could feel was her heart pounding against her ribs. She lay there for several moments, overwhelmed. Then she felt for him, the flat of her hand moving over the other side of the bed, stroking the sheet. It was cold. Empty. She opened her eyes. He wasn't there. Of course he wasn't there, she thought, furious with herself. It had all been a dream. Jack was on the other side of the world and for all she knew, she'd never see him again.

She turned her face into her pillow, tears of frustration slowly rolling down her cheeks.

39

The following morning Juliet stood at the Arrivals gate waiting for Louis. She'd turned it over and over in her mind what she might say when they were on their own, but always came to the same conclusion – that it was best to leave well alone. She dreaded slipping up in some way, blurting out her suspicions. She needed to concentrate on Reece & Co. After all, that was the reason Louis had offered to meet up with her. To be there to talk through all her business problems, not delve into personal stuff which could only embarrass them both.

She'd told him she wouldn't dream of his going to a hotel. She'd welcome his company. Her large guest room and en-suite wasn't used nearly often enough and he could come and go as he pleased.

Every time she thought about Reece & Co she boiled. She had to calm down, clear her head. Glancing up at the Arrivals board she noticed his flight had landed three-quarters of an hour ago. She opened her bag to check her mobile was on in case she'd somehow missed him and he was trying to phone her. Even though she was tall she stood on tiptoe to see above the crowds and watched another plane-load of passengers pour through.

'Hello, Juliet.'

She spun round and there he was, smiling and kissing her on both cheeks. Whoever Louis was, he was wonderful. He offered his free arm and she hooked her hand through it.

'What are the plans?' Louis asked.

'I need to go to the nursing home as soon as I've settled you in. Are you tired? You don't look it,' she added.

He grinned. 'I slept on the plane.' He deftly wheeled his case to avoid a small boy who shot in front of him.

'And I told Gerrard – my ex – I'd see him one evening and bring you to meet him. That is,' she looked up at him, smiling, 'if you can bear it.'

'No worries,' Louis said. 'And I'd like to meet your father before I go back if he's up to it. How's he doing?'

'He's very frail. But we're talking properly...maybe the first time ever.'

Leaving Louis to unpack, Juliet arrived at the nursing home just after lunch. One of the nurses she didn't know told her that her father was very tired and had asked to be put to bed.

'Is he worse?'

'Just tired.' The nurse patted Juliet's arm with a dimpled hand. 'He said he'd had a nice visit with you yesterday and sends his love. Call us later and we'll let you know how he is.'

'So your real grandmother is still alive,' Louis said, as he joined her in the sitting room later that afternoon. 'That's amazing. Did you tell your father?'

'No. I was tempted but I thought it would upset him even more. He hates Ruby with a passion. He says Nannie is his mother in every way and nothing will change that.'

Dad is to Ruby as Louis could be to me.

'I feel sorry for him,' Louis said.

'You men always stick together,' Juliet teased.

Louis smiled. She couldn't help thinking it was Mani's smile. 'Would you like me to go with you?' he said. 'I can't tomorrow, but I could the following day.'

'I'd love you to.'

343

There was a short pause while Louis scrutinised her as though to assess her mood. Then he said, 'Do you want to talk about the business?'

Trying to keep to the facts and not letting her emotions get the better of her, she told him of her meeting with Lydia and Neil. He let her speak without interrupting and when she'd finished he looked at her, his expression full of concern.

'I'm so sorry, Juliet. You must be furious. I think you need some specialist advice. Is it worth asking Gerrard if he can recommend someone?'

'I've got an appointment early tomorrow morning with a solicitor who says he doesn't take prisoners. I'm not letting Neil get away with it.' She stopped, livid that Neil had put her in such a position. In all the years she'd never had any trouble of this sort with any of her employees. 'Anyway,' she went on, 'let's get off the subject. You've got your dentists' conference tomorrow with all those people pontificating about bad teeth and root canals and gum disease.'

'You make it sound quite fun,' Louis said, his brown eyes twinkling.

They both burst out laughing.

'And I think we might as well go and see Gerrard this evening,' Juliet said. 'It'll be good to have you for moral support when he starts droning on at me about leaving my business in Lydia's hands.' She shrugged. 'He did warn me but I took no notice.'

'Think what would have happened if you'd taken notice,' Louis said. 'You would never have gone to Australia. Never met Petra...or Jack.' His face creased in smiles. 'Need I say more?'

Or you, Juliet longed to say. But all she could do was shake her head and return his smile.

'Gerrard doesn't seem a bad sort of guy,' Louis observed next morning as he stacked the dishwasher. 'What happened to you two?'

'We just went in different directions,' Juliet said. 'He'd be easier to live with if he wasn't always right. I haven't told you, but when you went to make your call to Petra he came up with the idea that we should get back together.'

'And?' Louis raised his eyebrows in mock horror.

'No way. Though I do see him from time to time. We have the odd meal together. He cooks for me,' she laughed. 'From never being able to boil an egg, suddenly he produces lovely Italian dishes. But that's as far as it goes.'

'So what did you say to him? Or shouldn't I ask?'

Juliet grinned. 'I told him I couldn't go backwards. We're better as friends. The truth is I don't fancy him so it'd be a disaster, though I probably should have listened to him instead of swanning off to Australia and putting Lydia in charge. He wasted no time in telling me I'd never win a case against Neil. But I don't believe it.'

'Lydia might have been okay if Neil had given her some support.' Louis set the dishwasher to go. 'He sounds the sort who'd want his own business sooner or later but he made a big mistake thinking everyone was as unethical as him.'

'Maybe you're right,' Juliet admitted. 'Well, it's no good dwelling on it. I've just got to do something positive.'

'What time are you seeing your father?'

'About two.'

'I could easily slip the conference…come with you.'

Dad could be his grandfather.

'No, you mustn't. That's why you're here in London. All you dentists talking about cavities…the best way to fill them in. You wouldn't want to miss that.' Louis grinned. 'But come with me tomorrow. This morning it's the solicitor and then I need to go into the office. Work out a plan of action with Bob on the future of Reece & Co.'

The apartment was quiet when Louis left in a cloudburst for the station. Juliet got dressed, pulling on her black wool trousers and cream sweater. She sat at her father's old desk with the daunting pile of post in front of her, sorting it out into separate piles, but after half an hour she grew impatient with all the junk mail and unrequested magazines and dropped them into the recycling basket.

She put the stuff on one side that needed answering and reached in the desk drawer for her packet of paperclips. Though nothing was urgent she'd feel better if her paperwork was neatly pinned together and in the To Do tray. Where was the envelope she kept them in? It must be here somewhere, she thought, her fingers delving into the very back of the drawer. She frowned. The drawer seemed a little deeper than she'd remembered. Her fingers closed over an envelope. She took it out. It wasn't the envelope with the paperclips after all. The envelope was addressed to Harry Bishop, Esq.

The letter had never been opened.

Curious, she turned the envelope over but there was no return address. She squinted at the postmark. Rome? Who did her father know in Rome? And the date. It had been written half a century ago. 1954. Five years before she was born. Why hadn't her father read it after all these years?

Although she longed to rip the envelope open, addressed in flowery writing which was definitely a woman's hand, she knew she wouldn't. She'd give it to him and see whether he was willing to tell her about this unknown female who lived in Rome. Was she a beautiful Italian woman? Had he gone to Italy after the war and met her? He'd never even told her where he'd been posted in the war. Said he didn't want to talk about it. Juliet imagined him looking a little sad when he saw the postmark – someone he'd been in love with before he'd met her mother. A wartime romance. Maybe the relationship had gone sour and one of them had ended it. If the woman had ended it he might have been so heartbroken he couldn't bring himself to rake it all up again. And if *he* had ended it he might have thought the last thing he needed was to hear from her when it was over. But if that was what had happened why hadn't he tossed it in the wastepaper basket? Why keep a letter and not read it? Surely he'd be interested to know what the letter said after all these years.

Juliet couldn't think what to do. If she handed the letter to her father after it had lain in his old desk for nearly a lifetime, would he be angry she'd found it and was asking questions? She tried to imagine him turning the envelope over, and if they were on their own in his room, asking her to read it to him. In her mind's eye she saw him smiling a little as it brought back bittersweet memories. Then she brought herself up sharply. He would never do that. No. He would take the envelope and toss it casually to one side, telling her it was nothing important. And he would make her feel she was prying if she said anything more.

Sighing deeply, she tucked the envelope into her handbag and headed off for the solicitor. She zipped up her black leather ankle boots, and shrugged on her coat. Tying a purple scarf around her neck she glanced in the mirror. She smiled and the woman in the mirror smiled back. Smart and practical. That should please her father when she saw him later, but for the first time in ages there was no rancour in the thought. She looked at her watch, feeling more positive about him than she'd been in years.

As she closed the front door behind her she heard the phone ring. She hesitated. She was already later than she'd intended. Well, whoever it was would have to leave a message.

She dashed out and drove swiftly into town. Kingston-upon-Thames was where she'd been brought up when her parents had moved out of London. She'd always been perfectly happy there. But now it looked different. She parked the car and paid for a ticket, then got out the letter to remind herself of the solicitor's address. She began to walk, noticing things she wouldn't normally. The town had become tacky. Paper cups and disposable food trays had been chucked in shop doorways, someone had heaved their stomach contents into the gutter, and the pavements were covered with chewing gum spots as prolific as measles, made more prominent in the sudden downpour. She pulled a face. Was it because she'd been to Australia that she noticed her own town wasn't quite as she remembered?

She found the road and rang the bell of an ordinary Victorian house with a dull brass plaque fixed to the left-hand side of the entrance bearing the name FOSKETT & PTRS. SOLS. A girl in a too-tight, too-short dress, black tights and bleached hair swept off her face in a long straggly ponytail, opened the door.

Juliet almost changed her mind when she was shown into the waiting room. The only word to describe it was grubby. Two dog-eared magazines had slipped off the piles on the coffee table, cushions remained sunk in by the last visitors, the walls desperately needed a coat of paint, and two mugs of tea stood on the unmanned desk.

After a wait of ten minutes Juliet was about to get up and leave when the blonde girl came back in.

'Mr Foskett will see you now.'

A man's head appeared round the doorway followed by the man himself. He was short and stocky with a head as smooth as a newly laid egg, and check trousers hoisted up by scarlet braces. He broke into a wide smile and ushered her in.

Rupert Bear, Juliet couldn't help thinking as she returned the smile.

'Pleased to meet you,' he said, gripping her hand. 'Name's Foskett. Call me Foss.'

He didn't look like a real solicitor. Her instinct told her to walk away – now. But it was too late. Still beaming, he'd already pulled out a chair and motioned her to sit.

'Now, Ms Reece—' he began.

'Juliet, please,' she said.

'Nice name. All right, Juliet, what can I do for you?'

It only took five minutes for her to explain the events which had led up to her meeting with Neil the evening before. Foss interrupted twice, then nodded for her to continue. He didn't make any notes at all which surprised her – just leaned back in his chair, his pen like a bridge between both sets of stubby fingers, occasionally using it to tap his large nicotine-stained front teeth.

'Right,' he said, when Juliet drew breath. 'I think I get the picture. Your employee, Neil, has done a bunk with your clients' files, saying he was trying to save the business, but that nearly all of them want Neil to continue to look after them in the convenient business that he's just set up? Is that correct?'

'Absolutely.'

'You haven't got a hope in hell.'

'*What?*'

'First, in this particular instance, it's not a criminal offence to copy files and folders, and second, he can probably prove that this Lydia was such a hindrance she stopped the rest of the staff from doing their jobs properly and the business started to slip. You mentioned the rest of the staff weren't at all keen on her. He may have had one or two genuine complaints from people which he would vigorously use in his defence. He'll say he was trying to *save* the business – not destroy it.

'The other point is that no one can stop anyone from earning a living so Neil has every right to set up his own business.' He ignored Juliet's gasp of dismay. 'And even though your clients are under a contract with you it will be almost impossible for you to stop them from going somewhere else, especially if they can prove they weren't being given the service they expected and the boss was away indefinitely.'

'So there's nothing we can do?'

'He's committed a civil offence and you could issue a writ for fraud and damages. That might shake him up a bit. Even bring him back to the company. But would you want him? I don't think so.' He raised his eyebrows waiting for her to concur.

'I certainly wouldn't want him back,' Juliet stuttered with

annoyance. 'I'd never trust him again. Nor would the others. So let's go for the writ.'

'It's my duty to point out to you that you're on shaky ground.' Foss tapped his teeth, 'So I wouldn't even advise you to try. It will cost you a lot of money, the court will be a real test of your nerves, and the judge will be on the employee's side, no doubt about it. I doubt you'll win, Juliet.' He gave her a world-weary smile. 'The best thing you can do is get on with getting your business back on track. It won't be easy, I grant you, but I'm sure you'll pull it round. You've done it once, you'll do it again.'

'I feel I've wasted your time.' Juliet rose to her feet.

'It's never a waste to meet an attractive woman.' Foss saw her out of his office. 'I'm only sorry you haven't got a case. I'd love to have got my teeth into it. To have nailed the bastard.'

Juliet walked back to her car in a daze. How could people get away with such behaviour? Should she try another solicitor? But in her heart she knew it wasn't worth it. Foss would have taken her on if there'd been a snowball's chance. She glanced at her watch. There was just time to call in at the office before she saw her father. Tell Bob about Foss.

'I thought as much,' Bob said. 'It's so difficult to prove these sorts of things.'

'I just don't know what to do,' Juliet's voice wobbled. 'I feel my life's wound up in the business. If I haven't got it then I haven't got a life. Or an identity.'

'That's nonsense. It's only because you've spent the last decade on it.' Bob got up and ambled over to the window. 'Rarely taking a holiday or time off. And not having children it's been your baby. It's understandable that you feel upset.'

Before Juliet could stop herself she placed her arms on her old desk, bowed her head and sobbed.

'Oh, God, Jay, what did I say?' Bob rushed over.

'Nothing.' She looked up, tears streaming down her cheeks, and saw his worried expression. She'd never broken down in front of the staff. Never lost her cool. 'Honestly, nothing. It's me. I'm wound up so tight I feel I'm going to snap.'

'Here, I'll get you a cup of tea.' Bob disappeared.

I can't let this keep happening. I'm going to drive myself and everyone around me bloody mad.

She hadn't stayed long, telling Bob she needed to get to the nursing home. She'd think about all Foss had said later. Make a decision when she'd calmed down.

She mooched round the town going over in her mind, as she had a hundred times already, the last conversation with her father. She could remember it word for word. What had surprised her almost more than her father's revelation that he and her mother shouldn't have made her give up her baby, was that her parents *had* wanted her; had loved her and wanted the best for her. While Antonia and Will had been getting on with their lives she'd had a ball of resentment curled up inside her, festering.

Her father's whispered words echoed again. Why, oh why had he raked it up at this late stage? When had they changed their minds? A spurt of anger erupted as she thought of all the wasted years.

What other secrets was her father talking about? She just hoped he'd be in the mood to open up this afternoon. And she definitely wanted to know more about Kitty.

She needed a coffee before she drove to the nursing home. The last time they'd offered her one it was like hot water with a little milk. She'd had to tip it down her father's sink in his shower room. Yes, a nice strong coffee and a cigarette. Oh, how she longed for a cigarette. On impulse she nipped into the newsagents next door and bought a packet, feeling guilty but determined.

Her favourite coffee house was nearly full and the only vacant seats were in the smoking area. Perfect. Her stomach heaved with the smell of stale tobacco but she wouldn't notice, she told herself, once she'd lit up her own. She ordered her coffee and opened the pack. Strange going through the old ritual. She tapped one out, then remembered she'd thrown her lighter in the bin weeks ago, before the voyage.

Someone here would give her a light. Two teenagers were sitting at the next table puffing at their cigarettes as though their lives depended on it. Probably would one day. She'd be a fool to start up again. Cigarettes were simply props – dangerous ones. She knew that now. Not only that, the smell of the smoke in your hair and on your clothes and breath must be a massive turn-off to anyone close. She'd hate to see Jack recoil when he went to kiss her. If she ever saw him again, that is. With a sigh she put the cigarette back in the packet, swallowed her espresso, and rose to her feet. She left the pack on the table but doubted it would be there long.

Once outside she drew some cold damp air through her nostrils, proud she hadn't succumbed.

That's the last packet of cigarettes I'll ever buy.

Her thoughts were on Ruby as she made her way back to the car. In a strange way she couldn't help liking her. Maybe the young Ruby was selfish and wilful, maybe she'd got herself into trouble, but that was no different to what she herself had done. She was glad she'd met her. Glad Ruby had told her the truth. She would never take Nannie's place in a thousand years but Juliet was sure she couldn't have been all bad. And who was *she* to judge?

It was nearly three o'clock. Concentrate now on Dad, Juliet thought, as she drove towards the nursing home. Don't even think about work either. You can discuss it with Louis this evening. But for now, tell yourself things will fall into place if you just stop agonising. Strange how the roles were reversed when you got older. She remembered when she'd been sick in the night as a child. It was never her mother who came out to her. Always it was Dad, his hand on her forehead as she vomited into the toilet, and just knowing he was there made her feel better. He'd be the one to carry her back to bed, give her a sip of water, read to her until she fell asleep again.

Dad. Even though he'd been strict he hadn't been all bad. She smiled. There was something she wanted to tell him, after all these years. Something she never remembered saying to him. She was going to tell him she loved him. And that she'd forgiven him for that time... Even as she thought the words it was as though a burden had been lifted; the last shreds of bitterness finally drifted away, leaving her calm. At one with herself. At peace.

Her lips curved in a smile as she anticipated her father's reaction. He would smile at her with relief. The image of him was as clear as if he was sitting beside her. For once she didn't dread the visit.

As her apartment was on the way to the nursing home she slipped in, just in case Louis had left a message to find out what time she was going over there. The light was flashing and she pressed the playback button.

'Miss Reece, it's Dr McCaulay here. It's about your father. Would you call The Grange urgently when you get this message? I've left a similar message on your mobile. Time is now 9.35. Thank you.'

She looked at her watch, cursing herself for forgetting to switch on her mobile. It must have been the doctor as she was rushing out this morning. By the time she phoned she could be on her way. What had happened? Had her father taken a turn for the worse?

She grabbed her bag and keys and rushed out.

'I'm so sorry.' One of the nurses sat down with her in the empty visitors' room. 'We called Dr McCaulay straight away but this time the heart attack was fatal. Dr McCaulay sent his apologies that he couldn't stay any longer to tell you in person as he had another emergency. He said to tell you that your father didn't suffer.'

40

Juliet put her key in the door and stumbled into her apartment. She dropped her coat on the nearest chair.

Louis came out of the sitting room.

'Juliet. You've been crying. What's happened?'

She allowed herself to be led to the sofa.

'I didn't get there in time.' Her voice was flat. She looked up at Louis, her eyes wet with tears. 'He had another heart attack and d-d-died before I...before...' she trailed off.

'Oh, God, I'm so sorry,' Louis said, sitting down next to her. 'If only I'd been there with you. I had a feeling about today. About your dad, but I didn't want to ring in case I interrupted anything.' He put his arm round her shoulders. 'It must have been awful. And you shouldn't have been driving.'

'It wouldn't have made any difference. I came home on autopilot but I'm glad I didn't have to come back to an empty flat.' She burst into fresh tears.

His arm tightened around her. 'You've had a traumatic day. Would you prefer to be alone?'

She shook her head.

She went to the bathroom and sat on the edge of the bath for a minute, trying to calm herself, but without warning the most terrible racking sobs burst from her, shaking her to the very core, until she thought she would never stop.

'Juliet?' Louis' voice on the other side of the bathroom door was concerned. 'Can I get you anything?'

'I'm all right. I'll be out in a minute.'

After a few moments she opened the door, still trembling, taking deep jagged breaths. Louis sat her on the sofa, then brought her a glass of water which she gulped down.

'Thanks.' She leaned her head on the back of the sofa, her eyes red raw. 'I'm sorry to act such a fool. I'll be all right. Even though I knew it would happen sooner or later I didn't think I'd feel this bad. God, I'd give anything for a cigarette.' She gave him a guilty smile as she remembered her new resolution.

'Don't you dare,' Louis said. 'My mother smoked and I hated it. The terrible thing was, she was dying of lung cancer. Self-inflicted. That's what was so stupid.'

'How awful.'

'Of course, they weren't my real parents,' Louis continued. 'Did Petra tell you I was adopted when I was a baby?'

I was adopted.

Words Juliet had dreamed of hearing from him but now made her feel sick with fear that if Louis *was* her son, she wouldn't stand the test. She'd given him away to strangers. He wouldn't want anything to do with her. She swallowed hard. What should she say? Dear God, what should she say? Say nothing...say nothing...don't start anything...

'Do you know anything about your real mother?' The words tumbled out. Now it was too late – she couldn't take them back. He'd have to answer. Her heart beat wildly. Her voice must have sounded odd because he threw her a quizzical glance.

'I only know she gave me away. My parents told me when I was about eleven, and I decided there and then I would never forgive her. What had I done that she'd hated me so much she'd handed me over to strangers? As though I was some parcel she hadn't ordered and was sending back. When I was a teenager I used to get even more upset. I imagined her married. Having children and keeping them.

Reading to them. Kissing them goodnight. Forgetting all about me. I used to think, how could she?'

Louis' voice was level and composed – as though he was having to control his pent-up anger.

This was worse, much worse than she'd imagined. Even in her nightmares. She could barely bring herself to glance at this man who she felt certain was her own flesh and blood. Her eyes met his, dulled, she imagined, with painful memories, and she wanted to take him in her arms; explain that she'd been so young, forced into it. Had so desperately wanted to keep him. Instead she sat there, stupefied. A moment later he broke the silence.

'I'm sorry…I'm being tactless, talking about her like that when I should be comforting *you*.'

'No, it's all right. I'm sad for both your mothers. The one you knew and the one you never knew.' She swallowed the lump in her throat. 'I just wish I'd had the chance to tell Dad I loved him…and forgave him…in spite of everything. That's what I was going to do today. Parents are human just like the rest of us…making mistakes, hurting people…probably without meaning to. But it's taken me a long time to realise it.'

'Your father knew you loved him,' Louis said. 'Parents have a way of knowing. It doesn't matter that you weren't able to say the words.'

'Do you really believe that?'

'Yes, I do.'

'Oh, Louis.' She burst into tears again. 'He was waiting for me to tell him, and I didn't. I let him down…even when I knew how ill he was. I thought I needed time to think about everything.' She broke off, sobbing. 'And time was the one thing he didn't have.'

He put his arm round her. 'Just cry it all out. Don't mind me.'

'I'll be all right.' She wiped her eyes again. 'Sorry to be such a wimp. I'm going to start supper.' She gave him a weak smile.

'I'll lay the table.'

In the kitchen she broke down again. But this time it was for Louis. Nothing could ever repair the damage she'd done to him by giving him away. She would never tell him her suspicions. It was better for him to like her as a friend than hate her as a mother. A little calmer for making a decision, she took the plates to the dining room and was touched to find he'd lit candles and had fetched a bottle of Chablis from the cooler.

'How did you get on with the solicitor?' Louis asked, before taking a large forkful of fish pie. 'This is great, by the way.'

'Afraid I can't take the praise. It's the compliments of M&S. No time for cooking at the moment.' She gave a rueful smile. 'Yes, I went to see him. His name's Foss. He's quite a character. I'd love him to represent me. But he said I didn't have much of a chance. Apparently what Neil did wasn't a crime. And you can't stop someone from earning a living.' She looked across at him, her eyes flashing. 'You can't believe it, can you?'

'I can,' Louis said. 'The law is often very unfair. What advice did he give you?'

'To drop it. I could take him to court but it would cost tens of thousands and I'd most likely lose. But I really want to go after him.'

'What's the point?' Louis put down his knife and fork. 'It will take so much of your time and energy, be stressful and costly—'

'That's what he said.'

'If there's a sniff of a case he'd be on to it, believe me. They're in business to make money. He's giving you a definite warning of a negative outcome.'

'I know. I've more or less made up my mind not to pursue it. But it's hard. Neil will get away with it. And he knows it.' Her eyes narrowed with anger. 'What a trusting fool I've been. Supposed to be a successful businesswoman and I've acted like some naïve teenager.'

'We all make mistakes when we're under an emotional strain,' Louis said. 'And as for Neil, let him be. He has to live with himself.

Your health and well-being's much more important. What do you think you're going to do about the business?'

'I'll pretty much have to start off from scratch. My pride says to just get on with it – build it up again and make a success of it, but...' she trailed off.

'But what?'

'Do I really want to pick up the reins again? Have all the aggro?' Absentmindedly, she speared a prawn. 'It's felt like a millstone this last year.'

'Are you sure you're not feeling this way because of Lydia's cock-up?'

'It's probably part of it,' Juliet admitted. 'But I was feeling weighed down with it all *before* I went to Australia. I thought I just needed a break. Recharge the batteries. I've been accused of being a workaholic and I'm beginning to think they're right.' She gave a half smile. 'I've put all my energy into the company at the expense of friends and family, but most of all myself...always trying to prove myself.'

'You know what Aristotle says?'

'No. What does he say?' She leaned forward, genuinely interested.

'He says that work is the objective, which is necessary for us to arrive at the aim, which should be leisure. And we need both for balance.'

'Does he really say that?'

'In so many words. I probably haven't said it quite so succinctly as the great man,' Louis grinned. 'But you get the idea.'

'Well, who am I to argue with Aristotle?' Juliet threw him a smile.

Yet her business was the one thing that defined her. That had made her parents acknowledge she was good at something. That helped to fill the gap of a family. She swallowed. Things were different now. Her parents had wanted her. Had loved her. She thought back to when her mother had died. It must have been eight years ago. A benign brain tumour but it had still killed her in the end. Although she'd felt sorry to see her mother become more and more dependent until in the end she'd had to stay in the cottage hospital, Juliet had never broken down. But thinking about her now she wished she could have talked to her mother and mended the rift. And just when she'd planned to tell her father she loved him it was too late. She felt the tears gather again in her throat.

A few weeks ago she would never have thought his death would have affected her so deeply. Now, she only wished they'd been more honest with one another sooner. Thank God her father had been brave enough to bring some of the things into the open that had played on his mind before it really was too late. And even though she hadn't told him she loved him and forgave him, in her heart she'd made her peace with him. Louis had tried to reassure her that her father knew; that parents have a way of knowing. She desperately wanted to believe him.

She suddenly remembered the letter from the woman in Italy. It wouldn't be prying now, surely, if she read it. Her father was dead. So was the woman, more than likely.

'There's a letter I meant to give Dad. I found it in his desk today. And the weird thing is, it's postmarked Rome, November 1954, yet the envelope's never been opened.'

'Sounds like another family secret coming to light,' Louis grinned.

'I'm not sure whether I can handle any more,' Juliet said, rising up to fetch her bag. She came back with the letter in her hand and carefully slit it open with a knife.

'Shall I read it to you?'

'I'm all ears.'

My dear Harry

I know this letter will come as a surprise after so long, but I wanted you to know I haven't forgotten you. It will probably be no surprise to you that I am living in Rome.

*Can you believe Hedy is twelve? Quite the young lady.
Did I ever tell you I named her after Hedy Lamarr? HL is so
beautiful and so is my darling Hedy.*

*How is Frankie? I am sure you hear from her regularly. You
knew I bumped into her on the ship coming home from Cairo?
She'd been there all along and I'd had no idea. Of course it was
all Top Secret. She was in a bad state of nerves. I do hope she's
completely recovered and is well and happy.*

*Mother keeps in touch and she's coming to see us soon for
a long holiday.*

*Look after yourself, Harry, and think of me sometimes.
All my love,
Kitty Cat*

Juliet swallowed.

'Who's Kitty Cat?' Louis immediately asked.

'Dad mentioned Kitty.' Juliet looked up from the letter. 'It was
about the last thing he said. And that he'd tell me more about her
next time I went.' Her eyes began to sting again. 'She must be an old
girlfriend. I suppose Kitty Cat was his nickname for her. And they
must have had a falling out, else why didn't Dad open her letter?'

'Mmm, not sure,' Louis mused. 'She sounds on very familiar
terms with your family. She certainly knows Frankie.' He paused as
though groping for ideas. 'Maybe she's an old girlfriend but there's
another possibility.' His eyes were alight.

It was no good. Every time she looked at those soft brown
eyes it flashed through her mind – Mani's eyes. His expression. His
hands. She forced herself to listen to what Louis was saying.

'Could she be an actual family member?'

'What do you mean?'

'A cousin, perhaps...'

'I don't see how. I've never heard any mention of her until now.
Surely I would know about her if she was family.'

'Not necessarily. I mean, who is this "mother" she refers to, as if your father should know her. Wouldn't she say "*my* mother" if there wasn't a family connection?'

'That's true.' Juliet frowned.

'Someone does something the family doesn't approve of and the person ends up being ostracised,' Louis said. 'I'm thinking aloud but that could've happened to Kitty. Your father hasn't kept up with her and neither has Frankie, by the sounds of things, although it sounds as though this Kitty expected they would. And if she's just an old girlfriend, why would she get in touch with him out of the blue when she seems to be happily settled?'

'You may be right,' Juliet answered slowly. 'Yes, it does make more sense, somehow.'

'Is Frankie still alive?'

'No. She died ages ago with breast cancer. She was a lovely lady but had a rough time in the war. She was at Heliopolis, the listening station, she once told me, and she had some sort of nervous breakdown after she got home.' Juliet picked up the letter again and skimmed it. 'Whoever Kitty is, or was, she had a daughter called Hedy. So Hedy would more than likely be alive.'

'And probably still living in Rome,' said Louis, 'especially if she'd been brought up Italian.'

She skimmed the letter again. 'Strange she doesn't mention a husband. Maybe Hedy's father was already married. Or she was living with him. They used to call it "living in sin" in those days. And that's probably why the family never mentioned her.' And that sort of thing was just as scandalous well into the seventies, Juliet thought sadly. 'The other thing is,' she added out loud, 'Kitty hasn't signed with any surname, so there's nothing to go on.'

'Unless Kitty is somehow connected to the mysterious Alexander Townsend.'

'Do you mean…?'

'Yes, I do,' Louis said. 'Maybe he's her father.'

361

Juliet sat numb. Could Louis have put his finger on it? Is that who Kitty was? The love-child of Nannie and Dr Alexander Townsend? No, it couldn't be. Nannie was far too respectable for that. But her father had said Dr Townsend had been in love with her. And Nannie had 'thought the world of him' were the words Dad used. But if it were true it threw up a whole load of other questions. Did Pop know about the affair? Did Pop bring Kitty up as his own daughter? If not, where was her grandfather when this was all going on?

'What do you think, Juliet? Is it possible?'

'I can't take it all in,' she said slowly. 'How many more secrets are there?' She briefly held Louis' gaze, then took a large gulp of wine to hide her embarrassment at the unguarded question.

They were both silent for a few moments.

'Maybe it's possible,' she said finally, her brain still reeling. 'But how on earth will I find out for sure?'

'You'll go to Rome, of course.'

'I can't fit that in with everything else that's going on,' Juliet said, her voice rising in panic.

Louis took her hand and pressed it.

'Maybe not now,' he said, 'but you will one day.'

41

Jack, Melbourne

Petra hadn't denied there was another man, Jack thought gloomily, as he poured himself a whisky that same evening. He didn't feel like going out to eat but there was no food in his apartment. Mrs James had cleaned everywhere that morning and it gleamed. He could be living in one of those places they showed in fancy interior magazines. Nothing homely about it in the slightest. Just convenient.

He went over his conversation with Petra again. Juliet liked him. *Really* liked him, Petra had emphasised. But what did that mean? Anyone could like anyone. Didn't mean a bloody thing. He wondered idly what it would feel like to be loved by Juliet. Bloody marvellous, probably. He grinned. Then told himself he was being a silly bugger.

I'll have a look at the weather in London, he thought, logging on to his computer. He peered at the screen. Cold and damp. Juliet would not be happy. She'd revelled in Melbourne's sun. He pictured the two of them strolling along, her hand in the crook of his arm, she wearing a summer dress and sandals, he with shirtsleeves rolled up. If he *did* go to England – and he wasn't at all sure he would – he'd need to take some warm clothes.

And *if* he went, he'd take the newspaper cuttings so she had the whole story. It was especially important that she read the last one, printed two months after the build-up to the court case. That was the one he hoped might help Juliet not to judge him too harshly.

He took the file out of his desk drawer and spread the cuttings on the table. As usual, they made his heart pound just to look at the screaming headlines. He slid the bottom one out and read it for what seemed the hundredth time.

JOURNALIST INSINUATED PILOT UNDER INFLUENCE

Bill Meeks, our head reporter on the incident where pilot Jack Delaney crashed on landing at Canberra Airport last month and which killed all four passengers, has apologised for insinuating that Mr Delaney had traces of alcohol in his blood which might have had a detrimental effect on his ability to fly the plane safely. Dr Edward Penfold has categorically stated there was no trace of alcohol whatsoever in Mr Delaney's blood. The Sydney Morning Herald also apologises for printing the article without thoroughly checking the facts and thereby casting aspersions on Mr Delaney's character. It takes full responsibility for the error. Mr Meeks is no longer employed by this newspaper.

42

'What did you do before Reece & Co?'

Louis' question at supper gave her a start.

'I worked in a similar setup,' she told him. 'It was just a job at first, but then I realised I loved it, and three years on I decided to start my own company.'

She gave a wry smile, trying to put on a brave face; trying not to think this was their last evening. That tomorrow she'd wave him off at the airport. Was it only three days? It seemed she'd known him far longer. And still she didn't know his birthday. Was she such a coward? Or was it really for the best? The two questions fought one another as usual.

She half rose and leaned across the table to refill their glasses.

'And before then?'

'I flitted from one selling job to another. Much to the disappointment of my parents.'

'Why was that?'

'Because Antonia and Will were the brains in the family. They knew exactly what they wanted and went after it. I was the drifter. And whenever the parents were pleased that at last I had a good job, I left.' She took a mouthful of wine and let it drip through her, comfort her. 'Maybe I was being rebellious but anything my parents thought I should do, I did the opposite. I couldn't bear to be like them.' She paused. 'No wonder they found me difficult.'

Louis laughed. 'All parents find their children difficult at times.

It's normal. But I want to know what else you're interested in – besides the small talent of changing people's lives, that is.'

She grinned. 'I'm not sure about that. I love reading when I get the time, and I adore history, classical music…' She paused to think. 'I love ships now, but I didn't know that until I sailed to Australia. But somehow I don't see me as a stew on a ship – too old for a start – though it's probably a great life. I wouldn't even mind another trip on one,' she laughed.

'Do you have any hobbies?'

She hesitated. Her card-making would sound so trite. At least that's how Gerrard had made her feel. *Oh, what the heck.*

'I make cards.'

He leaned towards her. 'What do you mean?'

'Greetings cards. Birthday, Anniversary, Mothering Sunday, Get Well, Bon Voyage, Sorry You're Leaving – you name it.'

'Can you show me some?'

'Okay.' She was surprised. Louis accepted her hobby without any hint of derision. She left the table and came back with a flat box.

'Shall we go into the sitting room if you've finished?' she asked him. 'I'm afraid there isn't any dessert.'

'I don't have a sweet tooth,' Louis laughed. 'I'm a dentist, remember?'

They sat side by side on the sofa, the box of cards between them. Juliet took a few out and handed them over. He looked at each one carefully without making any remark. For some reason Juliet felt nervous. She tapped her fingers on the coffee table without realising she was unconsciously mimicking her father. *Oh, God.* Louis was embarrassed and couldn't even think of anything nice to say. She was about to snatch the cards away and put them in their box when he spoke.

'These are damn good.'

She was so surprised she went pink. 'You're not just saying it?'

'Of course not. You should know me better by now. They're stunning. You're very talented.'

'Thank you. I love making them. All that concentration helps me to relax. That, with a glass or two of wine,' she smiled. 'It's fun making a special card for someone.'

'You know you could develop this.'

'It's just a hobby, Louis. I give them to my family and friends.'

'It's more than that.' He ran his finger down his nose.

That gesture.

'You could make a good business out of it,' Louis went on. 'Teach a few other people who show some talent. Even Petra might be interested. She's quite artistic. You could sell the cards to upmarket department stores. People love handmade stuff. I'll tell you something,' he looked at her with those eyes, 'it would go a bomb in Australia.'

'Really?' The very thought made her head spin.

'Really. Juliet, I think you're on to something. And you'd be doing something you love.' His eyes gleamed. 'You could sell up—'

'The trouble is, I don't have a business anymore to sell. Three clients doth not a business make.' She tried to quip but there was a bitter edge to her voice.

'Well, your apartment is a valuable piece of property, I would think,' Louis said, looking towards the patio doors. 'That river view. It's incredible. That must push the price up.'

'Yes, but there's still a mortgage on it,' Juliet said. 'I had some money as a deposit out of the marital home, but most of my profit from the business has gone straight back in, for extra staff and new computers and stuff. Then I recently took over the top floor for my own office which pushed up the rent. I only bought this apartment when I got divorced less than a year ago, so I wouldn't have made any profit on it yet. To me it was an investment; something I thought I could easily manage, so long as I had an income from the business and had something to sell one day. Goodbye to both those plans.'

Voicing these facts to Louis crystallised Juliet's fears. Financially, she was going to be a lot worse off. She'd definitely have to sell the apartment and get something smaller and it wouldn't be in such a superb location. She'd also have to sell her car; the one other luxury she'd worked hard for. No more of those occasional summer days when she could slide the roof down, the warm breeze in her hair, feeling independent and happy...well, as happy as anyone could be. She still needed to earn a living, and now it would be for longer than she'd anticipated.

'Do you have any savings?' Louis broke into her train of thought.

Juliet nodded. 'Not huge, though. Any savings have always been with the business in mind. In case of a bad year...or worse, a recession.'

'But maybe it's enough to keep you going for a while. And you've got good business skills,' Louis continued, ignoring Juliet wrinkling her nose, 'so you'd eventually make a profit on the cards even if you don't make a fortune. But wouldn't that be the better option? It'd be more fun, anyway.'

'There hasn't been too much fun in my life lately except going off to Australia,' Juliet smiled. 'But as far as the cards go, I doubt I could make any profit from them. People don't want to pay the prices when they can get them for peanuts in the supermarket.'

'I don't think that's true at all,' Louis said. 'They'd be completely different customers.' He picked another one up and examined it. 'They're extremely professional and I don't think you could go wrong.' He looked at her. 'But you need a plan of some sort.'

'If I sold up I'd probably visit Australia again,' Juliet said slowly. 'Get to know more of it. I haven't scraped the tip yet. I want to go up to the Northern Territory and I must go to the Great Barrier Reef, and see Perth—'

'Whoa, Juliet. You're going to need more than a vacation to do all that.'

'I guess.' A smile hovered about her lips.

Louis raised his eyebrows. 'Is this a new idea?'

'It's been churning around for a while…but no more than a dream.'

'We can make dreams come true if we want them badly enough.' Louis sounded unusually serious. He caught her glance and smiled as though to lighten the moment.

'I'm thinking out loud, but maybe if I did sell this,' she gazed around the room as though seeing it through a prospective buyer's eyes, 'and move somewhere cheaper, I could let Bob and Kirsty take what remains of the business; that is, if they wanted it. I'm not sure I really want to put any more of myself into Reece & Co. Maybe all this has happened for good reason – that I change things. Bob and Kirsty are younger than me and they've been loyal and hardworking. It'd be an immediate problem solved if they took me up on it, as it'd relieve me of the rent. That's my biggest financial burden apart from my home. And I think they'd make a success of it, which would be wonderful. A kind of closure.'

'It's a great idea. But I think you should do it on a formal basis and definitely ask for a consideration – in stage payments after a year, say. People always value something more when they pay for it, however modest.'

'And then I'd be free…to live where I please.'

'Maybe even Australia?'

'Maybe, for a few years, if I felt I could do something like the card idea.'

'Well, property prices tend to be lower than the UK, though Sydney and Melbourne aren't cheap.' He looked at her, his face breaking into a grin. 'But isn't there another reason why you *might* have picked Australia as somewhere to *maybe* settle for a few years?' Louis' brown eyes twinkled mischievously as he emphasised the words. 'Don't you and Jack have something going?'

At the sound of his name Juliet felt a flush rise from her neck.

'That was only a shipboard romance.' Louis raised his eyebrows. 'To him, anyway,' she rushed on. 'He doesn't do emotion. And I don't even know my own feelings. Probably no more than infatuation.'

Louis ran his finger down his nose. She shook herself. *People all have little ticks.*

'You know Jack was the pilot, don't you?'

Juliet sucked in her breath. So many times she'd wanted to question Louis about Jack's accident but it had never seemed the right time. Or her business. She could only nod, her eyes glued to his.

'Has he told you what happened?' Louis asked.

'We always have a row whenever it comes up.'

'Jack's a great pilot.' Louis drained his glass. 'One of the best, I'm told. Petra met him when she was modelling out at Ayers Rock. He'd flown her and a couple of other girls to the location and she recommended him as my mother had her sixtieth birthday coming up. In those days Jack was part of a private airline which did events. Unfortunately the day before, his wife told him she'd met someone else, though she wasn't sure whether it was serious enough for her to actually leave him. Nice of her to be so thoughtful, wasn't it?' Juliet had never heard Louis be sarcastic until now. 'No, Juliet, he's not lacking in emotion, believe me. He's just been well and truly kicked.'

She sat very still. Why hadn't Jack explained all this? Didn't he think she was worth confiding in?

'What happened to the wife?' She gulped a mouthful of Chablis, but this time the golden liquid tasted sour.

'Isobella?' Juliet flinched. It was the first time she'd heard the name. 'No idea. She sued for a huge settlement, supposedly for Chiara, the daughter, and refused to see him at all when she found out he had a dodgy leg. She has exceptionally high standards, I'm told. Always perfectly groomed. House immaculate. Everything about her perfect. Apparently, she couldn't stand the idea of a flawed husband. You can imagine the type.' Juliet nodded. 'Apparently things had gone wrong between them a long time before the crash, so Petra said. Not helped by trying to turn Chiara against her father.'

Juliet pictured Jack's fury. She loathed this Isobella even more. 'He did say something about that,' she said, then blurted, 'You don't seem bitter about Jack.'

'I was at first. Why should he live when my parents and the other couple died? Then I heard he'd been badly injured. But worse, it was his mental condition. He was in a state but told Petra he wanted to meet me – if I would agree. Looking at the weather that day maybe he shouldn't have gone up, but we all make errors of judgement. And anyway I encouraged him to go.'

Juliet's mouth fell open. '*You* encouraged him?'

'Yes. He rang me the night before. He was worried about the weather and said if it didn't improve he would have to cancel. I said I hoped it wouldn't come to that as my mother had terminal cancer and it would be her last treat before she went into the hospice. Of course no one knew there was going to be such a violent storm at the other end.'

So Jack had warned Louis.

'The inquest cleared him – it was a case of poor visibility and some technical fault which should have come to light on the final check.'

'What about the traces of alcohol?' She loathed herself for mentioning it. It was disloyal even if it were true. Which it might not be. Newspapers were notorious for exaggeration. That's the way they sold them. And anyway, even if it *was* true, it didn't alter her feelings one jot.

'Who told you that?'

Juliet hesitated. How could she tell Louis she'd checked up on Jack's case through the newspaper archives?

'I-I…maybe I read it somewhere.'

'Forget what you read.' Louis regarded her with his warm brown eyes. 'Jack's completely in the clear regarding any alcohol and any question of his flying skills. Like I said, he's a first-class pilot.'

'Would *you* go up with him now?' Juliet asked.

'In a heartbeat.'

She didn't realise she'd been holding her breath until she released it in a soft sigh. Ever since she'd read those blasted newspaper articles she'd longed to have someone she trusted to tell her Jack hadn't acted irresponsibly, that he hadn't gone up under the influence of drink, that he was still a good pilot. She bit her bottom lip as she remembered how she'd wavered in the newspaper office. Been angry even. That's why it was so good now to hear Louis' opinion. After all, besides Jack, he'd suffered the most from the accident. She only wished Jack could have told her himself. It might have brought them closer. Her heart contracted at the thought of his keeping it all bottled up.

So many misunderstandings and secrets. Jack, Charlie, Nannie, Pop, Ruby, Dr Alexander Townsend, maybe Louis…now Kitty, who she'd never heard of until those last words of her father's, and had no idea where she slotted in.

And so much of it linked to Australia; even the bitterness her father held on to right up until his death, about Ruby, his real mother. Juliet had been the same towards her own parents. Carried the hurt too long. She'd hung on to her secret, just like Ruby. What must that have cost her grandmother? But somehow Juliet felt Ruby was relieved – no, glad – to have told her the truth. Inwardly she shuddered. She hadn't even been as brave as Ruby. Her own father had tried to make amends and she'd practically cut him off. Now it was too late. Tears pricked the back of her eyes as she saw herself in thirty, forty years' time – an old woman, twisted by secrets she'd been too cowardly to face. She mustn't let that happen.

If only she could have won round her parents. They'd assumed Mani had been the one to lead *her* astray and she'd been too frightened to explain. Not that it would have made the slightest difference. They'd been far too paranoid about what the neighbours and the rest of the family would say about a mixed-race grandchild.

What would they have said if she'd introduced the adult Louis as their grandson? This lovely man they'd given up because of people's prejudices. She sighed.

'That was a big sigh.'

'I was thinking how complicated families are. How we don't really know even those closest to us.'

'We have a chance if people are brave enough to come out with the truth.'

She raised her eyes sharply to his. It was uncanny how Louis was voicing her own thoughts. Was he unwittingly giving her an opening to tell him what she suspected? No, it wasn't the right time. Too much was happening and she knew it hadn't yet sunk in that her father was dead. She couldn't take another emotional hit this soon.

'I just wish Jack could have trusted me enough to tell me, that's all,' she said. 'He always said he would – but he kept on putting it off.'

'I expect he tries to push it out of his mind but he doesn't need to beat himself up about it.'

'You're probably right. It seemed like all the two of you had to do was shake hands and it was understood immediately between you both that it was an accident, and that was the end of the matter. No woman would ever be satisfied with that.' She laughed a little self-consciously. 'We'd have to go through it all again, step by step, analysing it...and make a big play of the forgiveness thing. Hugs and kisses and tears, and all that.'

'I'm only grateful Jack didn't give *me* hugs and kisses and tears,' Louis chuckled. 'Let him reserve those for you.'

She smiled, but couldn't help the thought at the back of her mind: would she ever see Jack again?

'Juliet...' Louis said, then seemed to hesitate, 'would it be all right with you if I stayed a day or two longer?'

Her heart overturned. She wouldn't have to say goodbye to him tomorrow. She could put off the dreaded moment. How wonderful.

'Why, of course. I'd love you to. Do you have anything special you want to do?'

'I thought I might go to the Registrar General who I'm told can help me find which agency was involved in my adoption.'

Juliet fought down the rising panic. She hadn't expected this. That Louis wanted to find *her*.

'My parents never gave me any details,' Louis went on. 'I decided when they died that I wanted to find out the truth once and for all about my birth mother. Who she was. Why she did it. They have to give you this kind of information nowadays.'

'Are you sure...after what you said about...' Juliet swallowed hard, her heart beating wildly out of control, 'about never forgiving her?' This was it. This was what she'd dreaded. This was why she'd made a decision not to delve, not to question. Her head swam and she clutched the underneath of her chair so he wouldn't see how nervous she was. Her hands felt clammy but she hung on. She forced herself to look at him and let out a shaky breath.

'Oh, that,' he said, smiling at her. 'I didn't finish what I was saying. I said I'd never forgive her but I was only a kid at the time. Then you grow up and realise there are reasons for things you don't understand when you're young. I guess I feel differently now. I suppose she was one more teenager who got into trouble. I'd just like to know, that's all.' He looked at her. 'Even meet her if she still lives in England.' He gave a rueful smile. 'Mind you, she might not want to meet *me*.'

43

'I think we'll have to look online to see where you need to go,' Juliet said in a voice not her own the following morning. Her stomach turned over every time she thought about Louis' proposed investigation. She clearly heard Ruby's warning in her ears. 'Don't leave it too late,' Ruby had said. 'Be brave. Ask this man the right questions. If you don't, you'll always regret it. Believe me.' But Juliet had made her decision. She was never going to tell him. It was simply too risky. Though now Louis was turning the tables and wanting to find out for himself, and there was nothing she could do or say to stop him. If she did he'd want to know why. But if she just let him go to the Registrar General, wouldn't that be even worse? He'd be sure to find out the information and realise that his birth mother had been in front of his nose all the time. And pretended to be someone she wasn't. He'd hate her and her pretence. The thought made her head reel. Louis would never forgive her any more than she'd ever forgiven herself.

'Do you fancy coming with me? Moral support and all that,' Louis grinned, not seeming to have an inkling of the pain she was going through, but simply showing his beautiful teeth. 'It's bound to be in London.'

How could she tell him she'd rather do anything else than go there, much as she'd love to be with him?

'Are you sure you don't want to go on your own for such a private investigation?'

Louis looked at her. 'Are you okay, Juliet? You're looking very pale. Did you get any sleep at all last night?'

'Some, not much,' she admitted.

'The first few months are the worst,' he said. 'Not something I'd ever forget. But it *does* get better, believe me.'

'I think I'm still in a state of shock with everything.' Her voice sounded thick to her ears. Whatever would he say if she told him he was part of the shock? The reason she hadn't slept a wink, worrying about what he might uncover...and afterwards.

'I know this might not be the best time. But I found something in my parents' desk just before I came over here, and I wanted to show it to you.' He opened a long narrow envelope and pulled out a sheet of paper. It looked to Juliet as though it had been folded and unfolded over many years and become fragile. Louis flattened it on the table with the palm of his hand.

She'd half risen to clear the breakfast things away but her eyes fell on a tiny black and white photograph pinned on one torn corner by a paperclip.

'Me as a baby.' Louis followed her glance. 'The nurse took it and gave it to my parents when they came to collect me.'

'C-can I see it?'

'Sure.' He passed it over.

She didn't need to study it. It was ingrained in her memory. In her heart.

'Louis...' She brought her hand to the base of her throat and coughed hard.

'What's the matter, Juliet? Are you all right?' Louis came over and stood by her, his hand lightly on her shoulder, his face full of concern. He handed her a glass of water but she shook her head.

'Louis,' she gulped, as she looked up at him. 'Please sit down again. I've got something I have to tell you. I've been wanting to say it for a long time...since you've been staying here...but...' She swallowed, trying to clear the lump from the back of her throat.

'You don't need to see the Registrar General.'

'Why don't I?' Louis said, going back to his chair. 'I thought that was the right place to apply first of all, because I don't know the agent. All I have is this letter from the hospital.'

'You don't need to apply to anyone because you're Charlie.'

Louis stared at her for several seconds, then looked down at the cream and red certificate. Juliet's heart thumped hard in her chest as she waited for him to say something. He finally spoke.

'How did you know that's my birth name?'

'Your full birth name is Charlie Bishop, isn't it?'

Louis' eyes widened further.

'Yes. My parents changed it to Louis when they adopted me. But I don't understand—'

'You're *my* Charlie,' she tried again. 'My son. The baby in the photo.'

'But your surname is Reece.'

'My maiden name is Bishop.'

'You're not...are you saying you're my real mother?'

Juliet nodded, tears streaming down her face. 'I was forced to give you up for adoption,' she whispered, 'but I never stopped loving you...from the first moment I saw you and held you. I parted with you because I loved you...not because I didn't. They said you'd have a better life. It broke my heart. And I thought of you every single day.'

Helplessly she watched as Louis went rigid in the chair. She desperately sought his face, trying to read his mind, gauge his reaction, but he was expressionless. A full minute went by. Finally he broke the terrible silence.

'How can this be? It's too much of a coincidence.'

Dear God, he doesn't believe me...his eyes are full of suspicion...no, he believes me all right and he hates me...oh, why did I open my mouth...why did I tell him...I'm going to lose him... at least when he didn't know I had the chance to see him...now he knows...

Her thoughts raced on and on. She felt him watching her as carefully as she'd just been watching him.

'Juliet?'

She had to speak. Say something to make him understand.

'The nurse took a photo of you,' she began in a flat voice. 'She wasn't supposed to and she could've got in trouble, but she slipped it into my pocket. It's the exact copy of yours.'

'Where is it?' His voice was neither warm nor cold, just neutral. She'd almost rather he was angry.

'I kept it in my wallet for thirty years but my bag was stolen in Italy. It broke my heart losing that little photo. I used to look at it every day. Wonder if you were happy. If your parents were loving. If you were married by now with your own family. If I did the right thing. That's what I need to know. If I did the right thing.'

She couldn't look at Louis. She closed her eyes to stop the tears from falling. A warm hand enclosed her own. Her eyes flew open to see Louis smiling at her.

'My mother,' he said softly. 'You're my mother. I've found you after all these years. I wanted to look for you ages before I met Petra but I thought my parents would be upset. They'd think they weren't enough for me. They were such wonderful people I didn't want to hurt them. But when they died I felt they gave me permission and I wouldn't have to feel guilty I was betraying them in any way.' He squeezed her hand. 'I can't believe it. I've found you...' his smile widened, 'or is it you who's found *me?*'

'Oh, Louis.' Juliet's tears fell unchecked. She heard her voice tremble. 'I can't believe this is happening. That you're all right about it. You've no idea how relieved I am. I've been sick with nerves thinking about it. Should I say anything? One day I'd make a decision and tell you what I suspected, the next I'd chicken out. In the end I decided it was for the best to keep Mum.' She gave him a watery smile at her pun.

'I wish you hadn't,' Louis smiled back. 'It would have saved us

378

all a lot of trouble.' His smile broadened.

'But,' she looked directly at him, 'I won't be at all offended if you still want to go to the Registrar's office so you have proof. At the moment you've only got my word.'

'That's all I need,' Louis said firmly as he pressed her hand again. 'This is one of the best days of my life. Just think...' his eyes were sparkling, 'you could've been some old bat and I would have wished to God I hadn't started it. But you're Juliet. I thought you were terrific the first moment Petra introduced me. She'd already told me so much about you that I liked, and—' he broke off. 'Tell me something. Why did you think I was your son? You had no proof.'

'I did a double take when I first set eyes on you at your engagement party,' Juliet said. 'You were quite far away, and talking to Petra, but it just struck me. And then when you were introduced to me it was like looking into Mani's eyes. Your father. Then so many things reminded me of him. Like running your finger down your nose when you're thinking. Your father always did that.'

'Mani,' Louis said. 'Is that his real name?'

'No. It's Subramanian. But everyone called him Mani. He's Indian, from Madras. Of course that was part of the problem. Bad enough I was going to have a baby at sixteen, but with an Indian... my parents couldn't deal with it. They refused to even meet him.' Tears sprang to her eyes as she remembered that dreadful morning. 'But we loved each other and it broke your father's heart that we couldn't keep you. He only had pocket money as an apprentice carpenter and his father didn't have a steady job so his parents weren't allowed to take you, even though they begged for you.'

'Do you know, my parents knew nothing about my real father,' Louis said. 'I did ask them once or twice. They said he must have come from somewhere exotic because of the colour of my skin and black hair but they didn't know anything more. It's wonderful that you can fill in some of the things I've so badly wanted to know.'

'For a start you look just like your father except you're several inches taller. That's probably from my side of the family. But the resemblance is uncanny. When I first set eyes on you it was as though I'd met Mani again after thirty years.'

'It must have been an awful shock,' Louis said.

'It was. But it was the reason I came to Australia in the first place. I told everyone I wanted to follow in my grandparents' footsteps but it was really to be in the same country as you. The same city. I wanted so much to find you but I never dreamed I would.'

'Does Petra know you suspected I was your son?'

'No, I never even hinted. But I did tell Petra I'd had a baby that time my handbag was stolen. Where the photo was. We were in the police station. I actually fainted and when I came to I couldn't stop crying. She knew it had to be something more than a stolen handbag. So I told her about you.' A sudden thought struck Juliet. 'Have you ever told her your birth name was Charlie Bishop?'

'I did once. I think she asked me if Louis was my real name.'

'Can you remember exactly when?'

His eyes narrowed in concentration. 'It was before she went to England on that modelling job. Before you met her. She was talking about my being adopted. And if I'd ever thought about tracing my real parents.'

'That would explain a feeling I had when I told her I had a son that I'd named Charlie. There was something strange in her eyes but I put it down to my imagination.'

'I bet she guessed but couldn't say anything,' Louis said. 'She'd leave it to you to tell me – if you were prepared to. There are so many things I want to know, so many questions…Mother.' He grinned at her.

It was the sweetest word Juliet had ever heard in her whole life.

'Just one thing,' Louis said, getting up from the table and motioning her to get up.

She rose at once.

His arms came round her and she laid her face against his cheek. She breathed in the smell of him. The warmth. She stroked the back of his head as a mother would her child. She only just made out his next words as they were choked with tears.

'I'm so happy to know you're my mother.'

44

'So what's your plan?' Louis asked, after the two of them had laughed and cried and talked for three hours straight about the past. Their past. Louis' life with his adoptive parents in Sydney, which sounded to Juliet idyllic, and Juliet's attempt to put her young life together after they took Charlie away.

'I know it's time to let go,' she said, her head and mind feeling clearer than it had ever been. It was as though a huge cloud had lifted and the sun had shone through. Louis had forgiven her. Had told her she'd done the right thing. For the first time she allowed forgiveness to creep into her heart. She felt ready to make decisions. Do something completely different.

'Being in Australia has made me think again,' she said, 'that I should stop rushing and trying to cram in so much. Especially when it's nearly all to do with work. You only end up a frazzled nutter. And who cares in the end? You haven't impressed anyone. No, I think the Aussies have cracked it.'

'Well, my life's about to change drastically. Not that it hasn't already, big time, finding out you're my mother,' he said, beaming at her. 'But it's about to change again. And Petra's.'

'You've set the date for the wedding?'

'Not yet, but we will.'

'It's a big commitment,' Juliet began. 'Life won't ever be quite the same for either of you—'

'Well, there's something else that's already done that,' Louis interrupted, his eyes shining.

Juliet's heart gave a sudden leap.

'Petra's having a baby?'

'That's it.' His grin practically cut his face in two. 'How did you guess?'

'It was the only thing left.' Juliet laughed as she leapt from her chair to hug him. 'It's wonderful news. If only I had some champagne but we'll have to make do with the last of the red.'

Louis stood up to hug her back and she noticed his eyes gleam with excitement, exactly as Mani's had done when she'd told him all those years ago she was going to have his baby. Her throat tightened. Those precious years would always be missing but she thanked God she had her son now.

'When's it due?'

'In April. You know when she was sick on the ship? She was already pregnant but didn't realise as she had all that trouble with her appendix. I could have lost both of them.' He gave her a rueful smile. 'Thank God all is well. I've been dying to tell you but it's never been quite the right time, with your father and the business and everything. But we want you to visit us. Petra's trying to work out if she can slip a wedding in between now and before the baby's born.'

'How exciting.' Juliet's smile was wide. 'I may not be able to make the wedding but I'll definitely be there for the baby. That should give me time to decide what to do with my business.'

'Well, come as soon as you can. Now I've found you after all this time I want to see as much of you as possible. It's strange...' he looked at her, his eyes studying her every feature, '...but I feel I've known you all my life.'

'Me, too.'

She looked up at Louis' face, so like dear Mani's.

'Petra will write and let you know dates, etcetera. And you can stay with us.'

'That's kind,' Juliet said. 'I don't want to leave it too long now I've found Ruby. She can't last much longer – she's almost a hundred and seven, can you believe? And did I tell you I found my grandmother's diary in Melbourne? It was in a dusty old cabinet in the Maritime Museum. Or rather she's my great-aunt. And it wasn't *me* who retrieved it, it was—'

The phone rang. She looked at her watch. It was getting on for lunchtime, though she was too excited to eat.

'It'll be Antonia in Canada,' she said, getting up and excusing herself to take the call in her bedroom. She'd left messages for her and Will. She steeled herself to give them the sad news.

'Hello, Juliet.' A warm, familiar voice. Making her melt. Jack.

Quivers of excitement like electric shockwaves pulsed through her body, up her arms, over her scalp. She sat heavily on the edge of her bed, hand shaking as she pressed the receiver to her ear. It was too much…after she and Louis…

'Juliet?'

'Yes, it's me.' Her throat filled with tears. She swallowed hard.

'You don't sound like you. Did I disturb you?'

'No, it's all right. Louis and I are just talking.'

'I expect he's a good sounding board,' Jack said. He paused. 'I wanted to know how your father is and if things are better between you.'

'He died.' Juliet gripped the receiver tighter.

'Oh, no. God, that's awful. Are you okay?'

What would he do if I said: No, I'm bloody not? Instead she said flatly, 'Yes, I'm okay.'

'When did it happen?'

'Yesterday.'

'I'm so sorry, Juliet. I wish I was with you but I'm glad Louis is still there. In fact I thought he'd be on his way back by now.'

'He asked if he could stay a couple more days. Said he had something he wanted to do.' She gave a shaky smile. Jack would be amazed when she told him.

'At least you're not on your own.' Jack sounded relieved. 'Give him my best.'

'All right.'

'What about the business?'

'It's complicated,' she said, 'but I'm gradually working things out. At the moment I can't think straight, what with Dad, and...'

No, now was not the time to say anything about Louis. And definitely not over the telephone. It was too momentous. She wanted to hug it to herself for a few days, then she'd gladly declare it to the whole world.

And Mani. He must be told. It wasn't fair if he went through the rest of his life not knowing she'd found their son. That is, if his parents still lived in the same house and would tell her where he was. He'd be married by now with grown-up children, but he must sometimes wonder what had happened to Charlie: whether he was still in Australia...if he was happy. He'd be so proud if he knew his son had made a good life over there, become a dentist, and was engaged to a lovely young woman who was about to make him a grandfather. Juliet smiled. A grandfather. It wasn't possible. To her, Mani would never be more than seventeen...when she'd last seen him.

She and Louis had talked about his father but so far he hadn't suggested finding him. Maybe he was like her, trying to take it all in, and anything more at the moment would be too much. And if Mani was married what would his wife say when she found out her husband had another son? He might not ever have told her. She might be bringing all sorts of trouble to his family. Perhaps it was best to let it be.

She sighed. Life was so complicated.

'What were you going to tell me, Juliet?' Jack broke into her thoughts. 'You know you can tell me anything.'

'Nothing that can't wait,' she answered, wondering not for the first time how he'd sensed she had something important to tell him.

'I thought the call would be Antonia or Will. I left messages for both of them. They don't even know about Dad yet.'

'I won't keep you then.'

'No, it's all right. It's good to hear you.'

Don't hang up, Jack. I need to listen to your voice. Know you care, if only just a little. I want to tell you about Louis. You'll be shocked but it's time I was honest.

There was another long pause.

'Juliet, are you still there?'

To her amazement he sounded frantic.

'Yes, I'm still here.' She choked back the tears.

'I know you've got something else important to tell me. Something that's been on your mind since I first met you. Will you promise to fill me in next time we see each other?'

'Yes,' she managed.

'Promise.'

'I promise.'

'Good.' There was a pause. 'Look, this is bloody difficult trying to have a conversation with you being on the other side of the world. But I just wanted to ask you something.'

She held her breath.

'Do you miss me?' he said.

Irritation suddenly fizzed through her. *There he goes again. Always wanting the attention. Even now, when I need support.* Well, she wouldn't give him the satisfaction. She was just putting together a snippy reply when to her amazement, she heard him say for the first time:

'Because I sure as hell miss you.'

Juliet's navy-blue eyes were luminous as she sat down again at the table.

'It was Jack,' she said simply to Louis' unasked question. 'He's asked if he can come and see my paintings of the *Orsova*...' She

386

broke off as she glanced over her shoulder at the wall where they hung. 'The ship my grandparents sailed on when they went to Melbourne.'

'I've been admiring them,' Louis said, following her gaze. 'And...?' He leaned forward, his eyes twinkling with amusement.

Her heart turned over.

This is my son. And I am his mother.

The realisation that she wasn't dreaming, that it was really true, made her insides go weak. She caught her breath. Louis smiled as though he knew how she was feeling, and nodded for her to go on. She managed to pull herself back to her conversation with Jack.

'I teased him a bit.' Juliet returned his smile. 'I said, "I've told you before – it's a long way to come to see a couple of pictures." He said he was sure I'd make it worth his while.' Her smile broadened. 'Cheeky devil. Anyway, he's coming in December...to spend Christmas.'

'About time Jack did some serious romancing.'

'I don't know about "serious",' she said, amused at Louis' quizzical expression. She'd seen that look once before when she'd held him in her arms so very many years ago.

'How do *you* feel about him?' Louis asked.

His words brought her up with a jolt. She could hardly admit what she felt about Jack to herself, let alone anyone else. But this was her son who she knew would never hurt her.

'I love him,' she said simply.

'And I'd love to know my mother had finally found happiness,' she heard him say as he stretched out his hand to take hers.

A ripple of warmth flowed between them.

'I've already found it,' Juliet answered, her eyes brimming over with joy as she covered Louis' hand with her own.

Epilogue

Sydney

April 2006

The woman with navy-blue eyes sets the table for five on the veranda. She lights candles even though the sun is still warm on her bare arms.

She's moved to the other side of the world and it feels like she's come home.

A car draws up and brakes heavily. The engine cuts. She watches an attractive man cross the open lawn. He has a slight limp but it doesn't slow him down. He sweeps her into his arms. Laughs. Then kisses her, long and deep.

'Missed me?' He has a light accent.

She pretends to deliberate. She hasn't seen him for at least seven hours.

'I might have…a little,' she teases.

This time his lips are passionate and bruising.

'I adore you.'

She jerks her head back in surprise and would have overbalanced if he hadn't tightened his grip. She can't tell who is the most shocked. They burst out laughing.

Another car door slams. They break apart to watch a slim girl with blonde hair caught up in a ponytail jump out and rush to embrace them. She's followed by a heavy-set elderly gentleman, his arms clutching a brown supermarket paper bag to his chest. He manages to release a hand for a few seconds to waggle his fingers at the three of them. Then he shuffles over to the table and places several bottles in the centre. The rear car door opens and a tall dark-haired man with golden skin and warm brown eyes steps out. He's carrying a bundle in his arms as if it's the most precious thing in the world. He kisses the woman's cheek. Everyone starts talking at once.

The brown-eyed man passes the bundle to the woman with the navy-blue eyes.

She remembers more than thirty years ago when she held her own baby for half an hour. She remembers the sweet milky smell of him. The same smell that wafts upwards now from this little dot with skin the colour of a crème caramel, and black hair, shiny as satin. The baby opens its eyes, the deepest blue, and studies her.

'We've named her Charlotte,' says the man with the golden skin, 'but I expect everyone will call her Charlie.' He winks at the woman.

'This calls for a glass of bubbly, if I'm not mistaken,' says the heavy-set man, turning to the others, raking his hand through thinning curls. Everyone smiles at him indulgently as he beams over at the baby.

'I've waited a long time to see you, Charlie,' says the woman, kissing the top of her granddaughter's head, then gazing fondly over at her son. His eyes are full of love and it's as though they've never been apart.

Three generations of a family – together for the first time.

Acknowledgements

As usual, many people contributed to *Juliet's Story*, but here's a list of the ones who deserve a special mention.

Edward Stanton – my husband. I wish I'd had a camera to capture the look of incredulity when I asked him if he would drive me to Tilbury on my birthday to have a look at the docks, as that was where Juliet sailed from (and also Annie and Ferguson in *Annie's Story*). We actually had a fascinating day. As soon as I told the officials I was doing research for my novel they opened doors through which the public would never normally be allowed.

Carole Ann Barnes – my sister and travelling companion when I decided to go to Australia to do some research for both *Annie's Story* and *Juliet's Story*, and at the same time follow the trail of our grandparents. They had planned to emigrate to Australia in 1913, 'to better themselves' but came home seven years later bringing back their two-year-old son who subsequently became our father. Carole and I went the length and almost the breadth of Australia by train, and it wouldn't have been half so much fun without her.

Andy Whitehouse – of Strand Travel. I needed to know exactly what it was like for Juliet to sail to Melbourne by cargo ship, and he patiently answered many of my questions. Against all their rules he persuaded the shipping company to allow me to embark on a cargo ship bound for Hong Kong, and alight in Hamburg. Many of the incidents Juliet encountered actually happened to me, though unfortunately there was no love interest as I was the only passenger! Andy also introduced me to one of his best customers who had travelled the world with Strand – Mary Sketch.

Mary Sketch – She invited me for tea at her quirky flat in Pimlico and we had a wonderful afternoon, with her telling me the most amazing stories. Best of all she showed me the journals she'd kept when on board the cargo ship and asked if I would like to borrow them indefinitely. Would I? I loved reading about her journeys and reread them many times, until I vowed I would make my own voyage as soon as I could take some time off from the business. Mary has now moved to the coast but we occasionally keep in touch. Thank you, Mary, for trusting me with your precious journals and answering my 'ship' questions.

Ever Conquest – the German cargo ship I travelled on. Thank you to the officers and crew, and for the Captain and Chief Engineer who answered my ongoing stream of questions. Apparently this was highly unusual but because they knew I was a writer they seemed happy to co-operate, and even allowed me on to the bridge – a real honour. And a huge thank you to Jesse, the waiter and my steward, for tirelessly looking after me although he worried daily because I didn't eat meat, and what could he possibly give me instead? His triumph (according to him) was a tuna omelette!

Kevin Griffin – Strand Travel has been taken over by The Cruise People. I appealed to Kevin for help in choosing the correct cargo ship for the cover of *Juliet's Story*. He was extremely knowledgeable and the emails with the appropriate image links flew thick and fast.

Lesley Williams – the only woman I ever came across who was the director of her own business selling other people's businesses. I met her in a business networking club, and picked her brains over a superb lunch and excellent wine.

Mike Norrie, Castle Corporate Finance – magnanimously forgiving me when I changed my mind about selling my business with his company due to my getting cold feet, he kindly looked at the extracts in the novel regarding Juliet's business and the legal issues she needed to resolve. He enlightened me as to how a solicitor would advise her and the possible ramifications, but any deviations are my own.

Terri Martin – a fellow writer with an Australian background. She kindly read the manuscript before the final edits and found a few words and phrases the Aussies wouldn't use. But that was nothing compared to her horrified reaction when one of my characters was offered a hot drink of Vegemite. She said Australians would never make a drink of it – it would be too disgusting! I must say from experience, Vegemite doesn't half keep the mossies away. Perhaps that's its main job!

Alison Morton – thriller writer of the Roma Nova series, and the best critique writing partner and friend an author could have. We both enjoy setting to work with our red pens on the other one's first draft, and my novels are all the better for her incredible eye on the tiny detail as well as the big picture. We call it brutal love. Heartfelt thanks once again, Alison.

Romantic Novelists Association – A wonderful bevy of romantic writers in all genres who encouraged me from the first day I joined. I've made so many lovely friends there.